Case Studies in Contempo[rary Criticism]

SERIES EDITOR: Ross C Murfin, *Un*

KATE CHOPIN
The Awakening

Complete, Authoritative Text with Biographical and Historical Contexts, Critical History, and Essays from Five Contemporary Critical Perspectives

EDITED BY

Nancy A. Walker

Vanderbilt University

Bedford Books

BOSTON

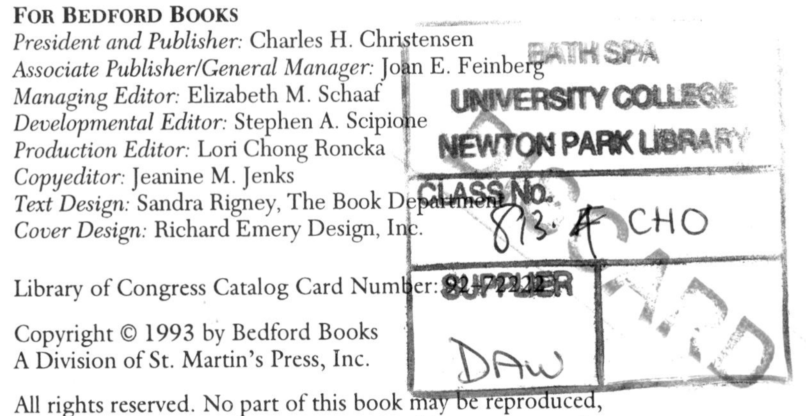

FOR BEDFORD BOOKS
President and Publisher: Charles H. Christensen
Associate Publisher/General Manager: Joan E. Feinberg
Managing Editor: Elizabeth M. Schaaf
Developmental Editor: Stephen A. Scipione
Production Editor: Lori Chong Roncka
Copyeditor: Jeanine M. Jenks
Text Design: Sandra Rigney, The Book Department
Cover Design: Richard Emery Design, Inc.

Library of Congress Catalog Card Number: 92-72222

Copyright © 1993 by Bedford Books
A Division of St. Martin's Press, Inc.

All rights reserved. No part of this book may be reproduced, stored in a retrieval system, or transmitted by any form or by any means, electronic, mechanical, photocopying, recording, or otherwise, except as may be expressly permitted by the applicable copyright statutes or in writing by the Publisher.

Manufactured in the United States of America.

0 9 8 7
k j i h

For information, write: Bedford Books, 75 Arlington Street, Boston, MA 02116 (617-426-7440)

ISBN: 0-312-06235-4 (paperback)
ISBN: 0-312-08984-8 (hardcover)

Published and distributed outside North America by:

MACMILLAN PRESS LTD.
Houndmills, Basingstoke, Hampshire RG21 2XS and London
Companies and representatives throughout the world.

ISBN: 0-333-59491-6

Acknowledgments

"Tradition and the Female Talent: *The Awakening* as a Solitary Book" by Elaine Showalter. From *New Essays on "The Awakening,"* edited by Wendy Martin. © Cambridge University Press 1988. Reprinted with the permission of Cambridge University Press.

Acknowledgments and copyrights are continued at the back of the book on page 343, which constitutes an extension of the copyright page.

About the Series

Case Studies in Contemporary Criticism provide college students with an entrée into the current critical and theoretical ferment in literary studies. Each volume reprints the complete text of a classic literary work and presents critical essays that approach the work from different theoretical perspectives, together with the editors' introductions to both the literary work and the critics' theoretical perspectives.

The volume editor of each *Case Study* has selected and prepared an authoritative text of the classic work, written an introduction to the work's biographical and historical contexts, and surveyed the critical responses to the work since its initial publication. Thus situated biographically, historically, and critically, the work is examined in five critical essays, each representing a theoretical perspective of importance to contemporary literary studies. These essays, prepared especially for undergraduates by exemplary critics, show theory in praxis; whether written by established scholars or exceptional young critics, they demonstrate how current theoretical approaches can generate compelling readings of great literature.

As series editor, I have prepared introductions, with bibliographies, to the theoretical perspectives represented in the five critical essays. Each introduction presents the principal concepts of a particular theory in their historical context and discusses the major figures and key works that have influenced their formulation. It is my hope that these introductions will reveal to students that good criticism is informed by a set of coherent assumptions, and will encourage them to recognize and examine their own assumptions about literature. Finally, I have compiled a glossary of key terms that recur in these volumes and in the discourse of contemporary theory and criticism. We hope that the *Case Studies in Contemporary Criticism* series will reaffirm the richness of its literary works, even as it introduces invigorating new ways to mine their apparently inexhaustible wealth.

Ross C Murfin
Series Editor
University of Miami

About This Volume

The text of *The Awakening* reprinted in Part One is taken from Per Seyersted's standard *The Complete Works of Kate Chopin,* published in two volumes by Louisiana State University Press in 1969. Published seventy years after the novel's original 1899 publication, Seyersted's authoritative text has been reprinted in several paperback editions of the novel issued during the past two decades. In this volume, no alterations have been made to the text itself; however, footnotes have been provided to translate the French words and phrases that appear occasionally in the text.

Part Two includes five critical articles, each of which represents a way of reading *The Awakening* that contemporary scholars have found illuminating. All five essays have been published previously, the earliest in 1973 and the most recent in 1989. Scholarship about Chopin's novel has been rich and voluminous in recent years and has been dominated by a variety of approaches that can be considered feminist in a broad sense. Thus, while Elaine Showalter's essay serves here to represent feminist criticism, Margit Stange's new historicist essay examines certain concepts in feminist thought of the late nineteenth century that may help readers to understand Edna Pontellier's choices and actions. Cynthia Griffin Wolff uses the insights of psychoanalytic theory to achieve such understanding of Chopin's central character. Patricia S. Yaeger and Paula A. Treichler are both concerned with the language of the novel, Yaeger adopting a deconstructionist approach and Treichler a reader-response approach. Taken together, the essays demonstrate the complexity and artistry of Chopin's novel.

Acknowledgments

I wish first to thank the contributors to this volume for their permission to have their essays reprinted, and also for their prompt cooperation at every stage in the process of editing. Caroline Woidat provided valuable assistance in sifting through the scholarship on *The Awakening* and helping to select the essays to be included. I am also grateful to Margaret Meggs, without whose enthusiastic efficiency and computer expertise the volume could not have been edited in a timely fashion. Chantal Philippon-Daniel contributed valuable expertise in her translations of Chopin's French. I am particularly grateful to the students in Professor Corinne Dale's Critical Reading and Writing course at Belmont University in the fall of 1991. As students familiar with the *Case Studies in Contemporary Criticism* series, they made a number of good suggestions about the present volume. At Bedford Books, Charles Christensen, Joan Feinberg, Steve Scipione, Lori Chong, and Elizabeth Schaaf have made the process of contributing to this series a delight. At the University of Miami, Supryia Ray's alert reading and tireless assistance helped keep the book on track. And last but certainly not least, Ross Murfin's enthusiasm, warmth, and editorial skills have immeasurably enhanced this project.

Nancy A. Walker
Vanderbilt University

Contents

PART ONE

The Awakening: The Complete Text

PART TWO

The Awakening: A Case Study in Contemporary Criticism

PART ONE

The Awakening: The Complete Text

Introduction: Biographical and Historical Contexts

St. Louis was in many ways a frontier city when Katherine O'Flaherty—now known to us as Kate Chopin—was born on February 8, 1850. Steamboat traffic up and down the Mississippi River attracted confidence men and drifters, gamblers and prostitutes; wagon trains of settlers heading for the territories to the west stopped there to gather supplies. St. Louis was also a southern city. The O'Flahertys and their neighbors owned slaves and supported the Confederacy when the Civil War divided loyalties in the border state of Missouri. Kate O'Flaherty grew up amid cultural intersections as well as geographical and political ones. Her father, Thomas O'Flaherty, had emigrated from Ireland at the age of eighteen; her mother, Eliza Faris O'Flaherty, was of French descent. Eliza, twenty-three years her husband's junior, was Thomas's second wife; his first wife—also of French heritage—died in childbirth after five years of marriage.

Kate O'Flaherty thus grew up well acquainted with French language and culture—a culture that later influenced her fiction, including *The Awakening*. Her great-grandmother, Madame Victoire Verdon Charleville, undertook Kate's early instruction in the speaking and writing of French and told her stories that emphasized the role of strong women in her maternal ancestry. Thomas O'Flaherty had prospered economically following his move to St. Louis in the 1820s; he was a merchant who sold supplies to settlers going west. But it was successive marriages into two old French St. Louis families that solidified his social position in the city. Such a position, ironically, led to his early death when he and other dignitaries were invited aboard the first railroad train to cross the new Gasconade Bridge west of St. Louis. He and many others were killed when the bridge collapsed. The date was November 1, 1855; Kate was not yet six years old.

Eliza O'Flaherty was left with three children besides Kate: George, the only surviving child of Thomas O'Flaherty's first marriage; Thomas, Jr.; and Kate's younger sister, Jane, who died the following year. The family was by no means a large one for Catholics in the nineteenth century, and Thomas had left them well provided for. Thus, despite the obligatory period of mourning, Kate's life underwent little appreciable change. After being tutored by her great-grandmother, Kate entered the Academy of the Sacred Heart, from which she was graduated in 1868.

During the same years that the popular *New York Ledger* columnist Fanny Fern (pseudonym of Sara Willis Parton) argued for political, economic, and even clothing reforms for women, Kate's education at the hands of the Sacred Heart nuns in St. Louis was designed to inculcate modesty and submissiveness. Although academic standards at the Academy were rigorous, marriage and motherhood were the only futures anyone envisioned for the young women who were students there in the 1850s and 1860s. The O'Flaherty family's identification with the Confederacy during the Civil War (Kate's half-brother George was in the Confederate army, and was killed in the war) would, if anything, have reinforced traditional notions of womanhood.

Writing, however, at least as an avocation, was encouraged in young women of Kate O'Flaherty's social class. Like musical ability (Kate was accomplished on the piano), writing essays and poetry was considered appropriate to womanly grace—perhaps more so in the South than in other parts of the country. An avid reader since childhood, Kate as a teenager began to keep a commonplace book—a journal into which she copied passages of poetry and prose that she found appealing and where she also wrote her own observations, essays, and poetry. She admired the work of the popular poet Longfellow, and in her essay about a classmate who had died she proved that she, too, could be sentimental. Like many young women of her time, Kate read Susan Warner's immensely popular novels *The Wide, Wide World* (1850) and *Queechy* (1852), which, like other popular women's novels of the mid-nineteenth century, underscored women's natural aptitude for the domestic sphere. Although as a teenager she may well have accepted these values uncritically, when she wrote *The Awakening* in the 1890s, Chopin created a heroine who rejected domesticity in favor of her own fulfillment.

Following her graduation from the Academy of the Sacred Heart, however, Kate O'Flaherty followed precisely the path expected of an upper-middle-class young woman: she made her debut into St. Louis society, the purpose of which was to acquaint her with marriageable young men. To her diary she confessed that the endless round of dress fittings, parties, dances, and ritual social calls wearied her and left her little time to read and write, and several times she exercised her considerable wit in describing the artificiality of these social encounters. On one occasion she notes that she has mastered the art of conversation in these circumstances: one need not, she writes, "possess the faculty of speech. . . . All required of you is to have control over the muscles of your face—to look pleased and chagrined, surprised indignant and under *every* circumstance—interested and entertained" (qtd. in Toth 91–92).

Despite her chafing against the requirements of the debutante life, Kate O'Flaherty did meet the man she would marry, Oscar Chopin, as a consequence of the social events of the "season." Oscar Chopin's mother was related to the socially prominent Benoist family, which owned an estate called Oakland in St. Louis—an estate where Kate attended parties during the winter of 1869. The son of a plantation owner in northwest Louisiana, Oscar was six years older than Kate and had studied in France more or less by accident: his father had moved the family there to avoid involvement in the American Civil War. Oscar Chopin had come to St. Louis to study banking in preparation for a career as a cotton factor—an agent for cotton growers and buyers. That he spoke fluent French, was embarked on a promising career, and came from a good family argued in favor of the match, and there is every indication that Kate O'Flaherty felt, as she told her diary, that she was about to be "married to the right man" (Toth 99).

Readers and critics have for years speculated about the extent to which the marriage in *The Awakening* is based on Kate O'Flaherty Chopin's own marriage. In the novel, Edna Pontellier becomes increasingly estranged from her merchant-husband, who regards her, although affectionately, as property. After a period of withdrawal from her duties as a wife and mother, she moves out of her husband's house altogether and goes about the city of New Orleans much as would a single woman. Because *The Awakening* draws upon Chopin's experience of New Orleans Creole culture, readers have been tempted to see the novel as a negative comment upon her own married life in that environment.

Chopin's first surviving short story, written shortly before her marriage, fuels such speculations about the autobiographical nature of *The Awakening*. The story, titled "Emancipation: A Life Fable," concerns an unidentified animal who has lived contentedly in a cage until one day he finds the cage door open and leaves eagerly to explore the adventure of his own life. But there is little evidence to suggest that Kate Chopin viewed marriage as a cage, and every evidence to suggest that her marriage to Oscar Chopin was essentially a happy one. The ecstatic freedom described in "Emancipation"—if indeed it needs autobiographical origins at all—could well have been inspired by Kate O'Flaherty's joy at having escaped her debutante rounds. In addition, the animal in the story is clearly male.

Following their marriage on June 9, 1870, the Chopins left on a three-month honeymoon tour of Europe, ending up in a turbulent Paris soon to be under siege by the Prussian army. Never in physical danger from the revolution that ousted Napoleon, the couple—or so Kate Chopin's diary reports—was excited at witnessing history in the making. The threat of a war in Europe did not keep wealthy Americans from traveling there, and the amenities of luxury hotels and servants provided some distance from international conflict. The Chopins encountered friends and acquaintances in several of the cities they visited. For Americans who could afford it, European travel was a good way to escape a United States still scarred by the Civil War and the assassination of Abraham Lincoln. In a few years a wave would begin of American expatriate writers, including Henry James and Edith Wharton.

But the Chopins' sojourn in Europe was a temporary one, and by the time they took up residence on Magazine Street in New Orleans, domesticity was much on Kate Chopin's mind: she was pregnant with the first of the six children (five sons and a daughter) she would bear during her twelve-year marriage. New Orleans had become culturally divided between the French Creole families, who inhabited the well-known French Quarter, and those they called the "Americans," who lived in the growing neighborhoods on the other side of Canal Street. Despite their French ancestry, the Chopins lived in three different houses in the "American" section during their nine years in New Orleans. Neither had been born in New Orleans, and neither could claim Creole ancestry—that rich mixture of French, Spanish, and African cultural traditions that simmered for decades to form a distinctive and exclusive urban milieu.

Claiming more freedom than would have come naturally to a woman of her social position—and a mother—Kate Chopin took long walks alone and observed the people and activities of the city. Much of what she observed later made its way into her fiction – including *The Awakening* – and gave to her short stories the rich, specific detail that would earn for them the sometimes dismissive label "local color" fiction. Though not wealthy, the Chopins had servants to attend to cooking, cleaning, and child care, so Kate Chopin had some leisure for absorbing her surroundings. Further, like the Pontelliers in *The Awakening,* the Chopins spent the summer months at Grand Isle, a resort in the Gulf of Mexico presumed to be safe from the cholera and yellow fever that were more a threat in sea-level New Orleans. Grand Isle had been established by New Orleans Creoles, and if Kate Chopin did not live among them in the city, she mingled with them during the summer.

Far from losing touch with her St. Louis family and friends, Kate Chopin made several long visits to her mother during the 1870s. In fact, two of her sons were born in St. Louis: Oscar Charles in 1873, and George Francis in 1874. In December 1873, Kate's older brother Tom died after falling from a buggy, and Kate became her mother's only surviving child. Accidental death had claimed first her father and then her brother. And her half-brother George's death in the Civil War was a constant reminder of the violence men could unleash on each other.

The official ending of the Civil War had not, of course, put an end to racial tensions, and while Kate Chopin remained in St. Louis during the summer of 1874, her husband participated in a violent episode that revealed his white supremacist attitudes. The decades following the war were filled with confrontations between southern white Democrats and the officials thrust upon them by the Republican Reconstructionists. Anger at the South's defeat in the war and dismay at having their political affairs run by "Yankees" – some of them black – led to the creation of a number of white supremacist groups, among them the Crescent City White League, which was bent on reestablishing white southern rule even if it required armed rebellion. The immediate target of the Crescent City White League was the Republican governor, William Pitt Kellogg, whose election the league felt had been rigged. Following a brief but bloody battle on Canal Street with the New Orleans police, the league – with Oscar Chopin in one of its militia units – succeeded in briefly removing Kellogg from office.

Oscar Chopin's racial attitudes are thus clear and public; Kate Chopin's are less so. Few women of her time were outspoken on political issues, so what we know of her attitudes can only be gleaned from the fiction she later wrote. Race is seldom the central theme of her fiction, but several stories include sympathetic portraits of black women, and one of her best-known, "Désirée's Baby" (1893), deals with the devastating effect on a young white woman of learning (erroneously) that Negro blood in her background has caused her baby to have Negro characteristics. After her husband's rejection of both her and the infant has led to her suicide, the reader learns that it is her husband's ancestry that has been revealed and not hers. In this, as in other stories, Chopin shows the devastating effects of racial prejudice.

Although in the early 1870s Oscar Chopin's business as a cotton factor had prospered, several crop failures toward the end of the decade, coupled with the yellow-fever epidemic of 1878, prompted the Chopins to leave New Orleans in 1879 and move to Cloutierville, in Natchitoches (pronounced NACK-uh-tosh) Parish, where Oscar owned some land. Cloutierville was a small town surrounded by plantations. Like New Orleans and other Louisiana cities and towns, it had been founded, in 1822, by French settlers, but it lacked the highly developed Creole culture of New Orleans. It was here that Kate Chopin bore her sixth child and only daughter (December 1879); that Oscar Chopin died, three years later; and that, if her most recent biographer, Emily Toth, is correct, Kate Chopin later had an affair that had a profound effect on her life and her fiction.

When the Chopins moved to Cloutierville, Kate was not yet thirty, and her years in New Orleans had given her a sophistication in dress and manner that were uncommon in rural Natchitoches Parish. Although Oscar Chopin was not particularly successful in his new profession as a shopkeeper, the family had servants and participated in the casual social life of the small community in which many residents were related to one another. Local gossip, which Toth records as having been passed from one generation to another, suggests that even before Oscar Chopin died of malaria in December 1882, his wife was known for being flirtatious and independent: she liked to take solitary horseback rides; she smoked cigarettes. The object of her desires was one Albert Sampite, a local landowner known as a womanizer and about the same age as Oscar Chopin. The evidence is maddeningly anecdotal; nevertheless, several factors support Toth's contention. The men in Chopin's fiction who inspire a passionate response from women are darkly handsome like Albert Sampite and are named Alcée, which could represent a shortening of Albert Sampite's name. Further, widows in Chopin's fiction, as Kate Chopin was in 1882, tend to react not with grief but rather with a sense of new possibilities for their lives, which could suggest that Chopin reacted this way as well when she was widowed. And finally, instead of moving with her children to St. Louis after her husband's death, Kate Chopin remained in Cloutierville until 1884, running Oscar's store and struggling to pay off the debts he had accumulated. Only then did she return to her native city and begin her career as a writer.

Within a year of Kate Chopin's return to St. Louis, her mother died at the age of fifty-six. Shortly after that, friends who had read her letters from Louisiana began to encourage her to write for publication. She also bought a house in a different part of St. Louis, as though to signal the beginning of a new stage in her life. Her friends in this new phase were notable more for their intellectual interests and liberal thinking than for their adherence to the rituals of social class and organized religion, and although Chopin herself never became a reformer, her association with this circle undoubtedly had an effect on her fiction, in which her most interesting characters – often women – defy convention. By 1889, when she was thirty-nine, Kate Chopin was a published author: a poem appeared in the Chicago magazine *America,* and short stories were published by the *Philadelphia Musical Journal* and the *St. Louis Post-Dispatch.*

In the same year, Chopin began her first novel, *At Fault.* Set primarily in the Cane River country of Natchitoches Parish, Louisiana, the novel features a young Creole widow who falls in love with a businessman from St. Louis but refuses to marry him because he has been divorced. At her urging, he remarries his alcoholic wife, and only after she drowns in a flood are the two principal characters united. To say that *At Fault* was neither a commercial nor a critical success is an understatement. Failing to find a publisher for the novel, Chopin had it privately printed in 1890. Partly for this reason, *At Fault* received almost no reviews in the national press, and reviewers in Louisiana and St. Louis objected to the portrayal of a drunken woman and to the theme of divorce (despite the precedent of *A Modern Instance,* by the highly respected William Dean Howells). What they did praise was Chopin's ability to render the authentic details of a specific locale – the "local color" they would later identify as the best feature of her short stories. *At Fault* is not the artistic achievement that *The Awakening* is, but it anticipates some of the themes that Chopin's major work deals with far less melodramatically: love between people of radically different backgrounds, the possibility of more than one relationship in a lifetime, and the power of a woman to live by her own principles.

By the early 1890s, Kate Chopin considered herself a professional writer, although she did not earn enough from her writing to support herself and her family. (For that she relied on her inheritance and proceeds from the property in Cloutierville, which she still owned.) Unlike many women writers of the nineteenth century who turned to writing as a means of sustenance, Chopin wrote because she wanted to. Yet she was no dilettante; she quickly learned about the literary market, and her publishing arena moved from regional newspapers to national magazines—including *Vogue* and *The Youth's Companion*. She often wrote about controversial subjects, such as venereal disease, marital infidelity, and miscegenation; yet because she continued to set most of her stories in Louisiana, editors and reviewers responded to the regional flavor and picturesque characters in her work. Thus it is no surprise that her first nationally published book was a collection of stories appropriately titled *Bayou Folk*, published by Houghton Mifflin in the spring of 1894.

Although the reviews of *Bayou Folk* were generally favorable, they disappointed Chopin, and they illustrate the peculiar standards by which reviewers judged the work of women writers in the nineteenth century. Reviewers emphasized the quaint foreignness of her Louisiana characters as though she had described exotic butterflies observed under a microscope, and the word most frequently applied to the stories in the collection was "charming." Ignoring the deeply human themes of her stories, which included wife abuse and the aftermath of slavery, reviewers kept their attention fixed on her style of description, which they found sufficiently decorous to be appropriately feminine.

Women writers, in other words, were expected to adhere in their writing to the same standards of feminine propriety they were to observe in their personal conduct, and if they did not, then what they did was either ignored or their work was castigated as "unladylike." Fanny Fern had discovered this when her 1854 autobiographical novel *Ruth Hall* was roundly condemned because it included satiric portraits of her father and brother; failure to display the proper respect for her male relatives was equated with literary failure. Chopin experienced a similar *ad hominem* critical reaction when *The Awakening* was published because the heroine shunned her domestic duties and enjoyed sensual fulfillment outside of her marriage. *The Awakening* was not the first work in which Chopin had dealt with such issues, but until that point the critics largely failed to see beyond the veneer of local color.

Among the writers whom Kate Chopin admired during the time she was becoming a writer herself were William Dean Howells, Mary E. Wilkins, and Guy de Maupassant. Howells, in his powerful position as editor of *Harper's* and the *Atlantic Monthly* magazines, championed a restrained and genteel form of realism in literature—though some at the time thought him daring. Wilkins, a New Englander, was considered a local color writer for her fiction about the rural northeast, but what Kate Chopin responded to were Wilkins's strong-willed, independent women. With Maupassant, Chopin had a closer intellectual relationship than she had with Howells and Wilkins: she translated a number of his stories from French into English, and in the process was influenced by his studies of solitude and melancholy. For the French naturalist writer Émile Zola she had little use: his journalistic methods caused his work to lack the subtlety she admired in Maupassant.

The failure of *At Fault* and the inspiration of Maupassant were two of the factors that persuaded Chopin to concentrate on writing short fiction (and, occasionally, poetry) during most of the 1890s. She did complete another novel during the decade, *Young Dr. Gosse and Theo,* but following unsuccessful efforts to find a publisher for it, she abandoned the manuscript and eventually destroyed it. For publication of her stories she set her sights on the triumvirate of magazines that had the ability to make a writer's reputation on the national level: the *Atlantic Monthly, Harper's,* and *Century.* Because these periodicals tended to be conservative as well as respectable, the editors considered some of Chopin's themes and plots too daring, and she succeeded in placing her work there only rarely. Even ten years later, Chopin would have found the literary climate more congenial to her work, but in the mid-1890s, Victorian prudery still held sway against fiction that dealt too explicitly with sexuality. Walt Whitman's work (which Chopin greatly admired) was still considered scandalous by much of polite society.

Chopin was fortunate to find the publishing firm of Way & Williams, in Chicago, for her collection of stories, *A Night in Acadie,* published in 1897. Way & Williams, located far from the Boston–New York publishing axis, was consciously testing the limits of propriety, however tentatively, and chose the title of Chopin's collection precisely to suggest a note of sensual pleasure. Barbara Ewell has commented that *A Night in Acadie* conveys a different impression than Chopin's earlier collection: "Chopin's bayou world persists, but its romance and charm seem diminished, its happy endings muted. In fact, there are both fewer love stories and fewer tragic conclusions than before. Melodrama, too, has faded, implying a greater moral ambivalence than in *Bayou Folk*" (94). In short, this is more mature, more daring work, and Emily Toth points out that several of the stories show women undergoing "awakenings" of various kinds (298), pointing to the subject of Chopin's major novel.

While some reviewers chose to focus upon the regional appeal of the stories in *A Night in Acadie* (all of the stories are set in Louisiana), Chopin's artistry—her skill as a writer—seemed now more worthy of note than it had earlier. She was compared to George Washington Cable, a contemporary who also set his fiction in Louisiana, and to Mary E. Wilkins. The comparisons were favorable in each case. Yet Chopin's greater openness about sensuality did not pass unnoticed: *The Critic,* in New York, commented that the story "Athénaïse" suffered from "one or two slight and unnecessary coarsenesses" (Toth 299). While such statements are mild compared to the negative reactions to *The Awakening* that were to follow, they are indicative of the moral vigilance that reviewers of the period felt compelled to maintain.

But with the generally positive reviews of *A Night in Acadie,* Chopin, at the age of forty-seven, seemed to be on a trajectory toward literary prominence. Certainly St. Louis was proud of Chopin's accomplishments, and she was sought after both socially and intellectually. The *St. Louis Post-Dispatch* frequently asked her opinion on issues of the day, and she associated with the arbiters of thought as well as those of taste in the city. It was in this climate that she completed *The Awakening* and a third collection of stories, *A Vocation and a Voice,* both of which were accepted for publication by Way & Williams in 1898. What should have been the pinnacle of her career, however, was destroyed by events she could neither foresee nor control.

Surprisingly, these events did not include the Spanish-American War, even though one of Chopin's sons enlisted. The war was over too quickly for Fred Chopin to become engaged in military action. But the demise of Kate Chopin's Chicago publishing company affected her career in important if indirect ways. By the fall of 1898, both Way & Williams and their rival publishing firm, Stone & Kimball, had decided to cease business, and their assets and contracts were taken over by Herbert S. Stone & Company. Stone issued new contracts for both *The Awakening* and *A Vocation and a Voice,* and published Chopin's novel in the spring of 1899, but the next year Stone notified her that his company had decided not to issue her new collection of stories. Whether the publisher had been stung by the criticism of *The Awakening* or was undergoing financial difficulties is not clear, but the result of his decision was that the last of Chopin's books to be published was her controversial novel *The Awakening,* and the tarnishing of her reputation went unredeemed by what might have been the favorable reception of her stories.

The few prepublication reviews of *The Awakening* were quite positive, although two of them cannot be said to be wholly objective. Lucy

Monroe, who wrote a glowing notice for *Book News*, read manuscripts for Herbert Stone's publishing company and may have had a vested interest in seeing the novel succeed. The sister of Harriet Monroe, who later founded *Poetry* magazine, Lucy Monroe was part of a sophisticated, well-traveled family, and she would have been unlikely to be shocked by a woman who, like Edna Pontellier, seeks something more than the material comfort of her domestic existence. Another positive review appeared in Chopin's hometown press in the *St. Louis Republic*. The reviewer observed with sensitivity that the situation Chopin depicts in the novel is "rare in fiction, but common enough in life" (qtd. in Toth 329).

After the novel was published, however, both it and the author were castigated in the press for the behavior of the novel's heroine. Married to a businessman several years her senior, Edna Pontellier "awakens" to the fact that she is living not for herself but in obedience to the social roles of wife and mother dictated by her era and social class. Inspired by the sensuous atmosphere of the Gulf coast and a mild flirtation with a bachelor named Robert Lebrun, Edna gradually ceases to observe social conventions such as receiving callers on a specified day, and she ultimately moves out of her husband's house into a small house of her own. Edna's extramarital affair occurs not with Robert, who is too cautious and too much of a gentleman to dally with a married woman, but with Alcée Arobin, a far less respectable man. During her period of awakening and searching, Edna has as possible role models two women who represent opposite extremes of female fulfillment: Madame Ratignolle, described by Chopin as a "mother-woman," who seems content with her periodic pregnancies (she gives birth toward the end of the novel), and Mademoiselle Reisz, a pianist who lives alone. Neither life seems, finally, possible for Edna; she has decided that she will not be possessed by her children, and although she is a painter, she is not committed enough to devote herself wholeheartedly to her art.

As Emily Toth points out in her biography of Chopin, it is ironic that reviewers of *The Awakening* virtually ignored a number of potential targets for their disapproval, concentrating instead on Edna's sexual liaison with Alcée Arobin (represented just once in the novel). Conventionally moralistic reviewers might have pointed as well to Chopin's description of a very pregnant Madame Ratignolle, who "looked more beautiful than ever" (75), and even to her labor pains, which Edna witnesses. Pregnant women were not to be seen in public, after all, and in fiction of the period babies tended to materialize out of nowhere. Nor was Chopin particularly reverent about religion; attending mass on

Grand Isle, Edna experiences "a feeling of oppression and drowsiness," and flees the "stifling atmosphere of the church" (54).

Instead of taking Chopin to task for her frankness and irreverence, however, reviewers uniformly focused on Edna Pontellier's growing independence from her socially constructed role, finding her behavior "shocking," "sickening," and "selfish." Even the St. Louis papers did not in this instance stand by a local author; the *Globe-Democrat* reviewer characterized *The Awakening* as "not a healthy book" (qtd. in Toth 341). The *Post-Dispatch* ran both favorable and unfavorable reviews on successive days, the latter containing perhaps the most often-quoted negative line about the novel: "*The Awakening* is too strong drink for moral babes, and should be labeled 'poison.'" Soon the national press joined the chorus, expressing dismay that a writer as "refined" and "poetic" as Chopin had created a novel that one reviewer called "nauseating."

Kate Chopin's only public response to her critics was a flippant one, published in *Book News* in July 1899:

> Having a group of people at my disposal, I thought it might be entertaining (to myself) to throw them together and see what would happen. I never dreamed of Mrs. Pontellier making such a mess of things and working out her own damnation as she did. If I had had the slightest intimation of such a thing I would have excluded her from the company. But when I found out what she was up to, the play was half over and it was too late.

This response is interesting for both what it does and does not say. On the surface, Chopin apologizes for the behavior of her heroine, but her mocking tone tells us that she is not really repentant. Rather, what she conveys is that, given Edna Pontellier's situation, both her awakening and her death were necessary and inevitable. Like the reviewer for the *St. Louis Republic,* Chopin recognized that many women yearned for the kind of freedom that Edna claimed for herself, even if their stories were seldom told, and she also realized that most efforts to act upon such yearnings were doomed to failure.

Although there is no evidence that *The Awakening* was ever banned or removed from library shelves in St. Louis (see Toth 422–25), the overwhelmingly negative reviews effectively removed the novel from wide circulation and influence for fifty years following its publication. The consequence of its essential elimination from literary history is underscored by Elaine Showalter in her essay "Tradition and the Female Talent: *The Awakening* as a Solitary Book." Showalter points out that

Kate Chopin was heir to three successive traditions in women's fiction: the domestic sentimentalists who were popular when she was a young girl; the post–Civil War local color writers, such as Mary E. Wilkins and Sarah Orne Jewett, who considered themselves dedicated to the art form; and the "New Women" writers such as Sarah Grand, who envisioned dramatic new possibilities for women's lives. *The Awakening* draws upon all three traditions, creating a synthesis of their themes and modes of expression. Identification with the maternal and domestic is embodied in Madame Ratignolle and in Edna's love for her own children; the woman as artist is present in Mademoiselle Reisz and Edna's own artistic aspirations; and Edna's vague desire for a life beyond social convention echoes the agenda of late nineteenth-century feminists.

In this sense, *The Awakening* is a pivotal novel, published at the turn of a century that would grant major status to women writers such as Edith Wharton, Willa Cather, and Ellen Glasgow—but it did not have the opportunity to influence these or other writers. Indeed, Willa Cather was one of those who gave the novel a negative review. Although she admired Chopin's talent, Cather found her theme "trite and sordid," and found Edna Pontellier limited by her search for romance (Toth 352). Interestingly, Cather, at the age of twenty-three, was asking for a heroine better able to develop her intellect as well as her emotions, whereas Chopin had depicted a woman whose culture provided neither incentive nor model for women's intellectual achievement—only the passions of maternity, art, or romantic love.

In contrast to Edna Pontellier, Kate Chopin was a highly intellectual woman. Whereas Edna seems to behave instinctively, even in such momentous actions as moving from her husband's house to the "pigeon-house," Chopin was both a capable businesswoman who managed property in Natchitoches Parish and a student of the major intellectual currents of her day. She was particularly drawn to the evolutionary theories of Charles Darwin, and she knew his work well—well enough to argue with it in *The Awakening,* proposes Bert Bender in an article titled "The Teeth of Desire: *The Awakening* and *The Descent of Man.*" Darwin's theory of evolution, with its insistence on the inevitability of the processes of nature, led in the popular imagination of the late nineteenth century to an understanding that all organisms—including human beings—are fated or destined to behave in certain ways or come to certain ends. Authors who allied themselves with this way of viewing life wrote fiction in which people seem unable to exercise free will but instead are propelled toward certain fates by their biological or psychological natures. Such fiction has come to be called "naturalistic," not because it features the natural world but because it deals with the operation of what Darwin termed "natural laws."

Because of the way in which Edna Pontellier seems to drift unthinkingly through *The Awakening,* the novel has sometimes been read as belonging to the naturalistic tradition in fiction. Bender, however, argues that Chopin did not wholeheartedly accept Darwinian theory but instead took issue with parts of what Darwin proposed in *The Descent of Man and Selection in Relation to Sex* (1871)—specifically, his contention that women take a "passive and modest role in sexual relations and the male's physical and mental superiority to the female" (461). Edna, Bender points out, makes her own "sexual selection" in the novel, resisting sexual relations with her husband, Léonce, being attracted to Robert Lebrun, and consummating her passion with Alcée Arobin. Further, whereas Darwin, a product of the Victorian era, believed that women's passivity and modesty contributed to the development of civilized life, Chopin found that his theories denied the possibility of enduring human love. If, in other words, science can prove that both women and men make selections of partners on the basis of sexual need, the result—as is the case with Edna—could well be loneliness, or to use Chopin's word, "solitude."

In fact, the working title of *The Awakening* was *A Solitary Soul,* and the change in title is an interesting one. To call Edna Pontellier a "solitary soul" is to set her apart from a culture that places a high value on belonging and connection. It is in some ways, then, a negative characterization, while at the same time it suggests that the author feels pity—or at least sympathy—for her central character. Calling the novel *The Awakening,* however, is a different matter. We associate "awakening" with new beginnings, new understandings, and hope for the future, all of which are positive. Moreover, we should note that Chopin did not title her novel *Edna's Awakening* or *One Woman's Awakening* but rather *The Awakening,* which suggests that Chopin saw something universal in Edna's experience, and further, that she intended the novel as a general critique of a culture that severely restricted women's opportunities for emotional fulfillment and self-expression.

Meanwhile, Kate Chopin was far from being a "solitary soul." If publicly *The Awakening* was being roundly condemned as beneath her dignity and talents, many of her friends sent Chopin letters of lavish praise for her novel. Although dismayed by the public censure of her book, she kept up an active social life in St. Louis, associating with people who generally admired and respected her. With her children grown or nearly so, Chopin had more time for her own pursuits. During the fall of 1899, she spent several weeks in the Wisconsin lake country, returning just in time to prepare for her daughter Lelia's debut in St. Louis society. Even though critics had nearly uniformly found *The Awakening* an "improper" novel, Chopin's fellow citizens did not turn their backs on her, and the *St. Louis Post-Dispatch* devoted a long article to her in late November of that year, championing her as a significant author whom residents of the city should be proud to have in their midst.

Such sentiments are at odds with the story, which circulated for years, that *The Awakening* was removed from the shelves of St. Louis bookstores and libraries in the wake of the unfavorable reviews. The story seems to have originated in conversations that Chopin's early biographers, Daniel Rankin and Per Seyersted, had with her acquaintances and family members, especially her son Felix, many years after the publication of the novel. So persistent has this story been, finding its way into scholarly articles as well as biographies, that Emily Toth devotes several pages of her biography of Chopin to establishing that it lacks a basis in fact. Both the Mercantile Library and the St. Louis Public Library had several copies of *The Awakening* on their shelves, and Toth finds no evidence that either library was hesitant to lend it to patrons. Ironically, however, as she points out, the story of its banning may ultimately have increased the number of the novel's readers because many of us are eager to read what others seek to prohibit us from reading.

Another rumor that gained currency is that Chopin was so devastated by the negative reaction to *The Awakening* that she quit writing altogether at this point. While it is true that she did not publish another novel or collection of stories, that fact has more to do with her premature death in 1904 than with her reaction to the critics of her second novel. In 1900, *The Youth's Companion* accepted several of Chopin's stories for children, and *Vogue* published "The White Eagle" in July of that year. Her opinions were still sought by the local newspapers as well. Yet her literary production after the turn of the century never matched that of the 1890s, and by 1902 poor health required her to curtail her social activities.

Kate Chopin died, apparently of a brain hemorrhage, in August 1904, while residents of St. Louis were welcoming visitors to the World's Fair that had opened in the western part of the city. For forty of her fifty-four years, she had lived in St. Louis, but her reputation as a writer rested on her depictions of the people and culture of Louisiana.

At the time of her death she was regarded primarily as the creator of charming sketches of Creole and Cajun life; it would be many years before *The Awakening* was acknowledged as her masterpiece.

Each reader of *The Awakening* must decide whether to view Edna Pontellier's experience as positive or negative—or both. Of what does her "awakening" consist? How does one interpret the ending? Is Edna doomed or freed? In the text that follows, Kate Chopin has provided a complex story that admits of no easy answers but is sure to raise some questions.

Nancy A. Walker

WORKS CITED

Bender, Bert. "The Teeth of Desire: *The Awakening* and *The Descent of Man*." *American Literature* 63 (1991): 459–73.

Ewell, Barbara C. *Kate Chopin*. New York: Ungar, 1986.

Toth, Emily. *Kate Chopin*. New York: Morrow, 1990.

The Awakening

I

A green and yellow parrot, which hung in a cage outside the door, kept repeating over and over:

"*Allez vous-en! Allez vous-en! Sapristi!*° That's all right!"

He could speak a little Spanish, and also a language which nobody understood, unless it was the mocking-bird that hung on the other side of the door, whistling his fluty notes out upon the breeze with maddening persistence.

Mr. Pontellier, unable to read his newspaper with any degree of comfort, arose with an expression and an exclamation of disgust. He walked down the gallery and across the narrow "bridges" which connected the Lebrun cottages one with the other. He had been seated before the door of the main house. The parrot and the mocking-bird were the property of Madame Lebrun, and they had the right to make all the noise they wished. Mr. Pontellier had the privilege of quitting their society when they ceased to be entertaining.

He stopped before the door of his own cottage, which was the fourth one from the main building and next to the last. Seating himself in a wicker rocker which was there, he once more applied himself to

Allez . . . Sapristi!: Go away! Go away! For God's sake! [All notes are the volume editor's.]

the task of reading the newspaper. The day was Sunday; the paper was a day old. The Sunday papers had not yet reached Grand Isle. He was already acquainted with the market reports, and he glanced restlessly over the editorials and bits of news which he had not had time to read before quitting New Orleans the day before.

Mr. Pontellier wore eye-glasses. He was a man of forty, of medium height and rather slender build; he stooped a little. His hair was brown and straight, parted on one side. His beard was neatly and closely trimmed.

Once in a while he withdrew his glance from the newspaper and looked about him. There was more noise than ever over at the house. The main building was called "the house," to distinguish it from the cottages. The chattering and whistling birds were still at it. Two young girls, the Farival twins, were playing a duet from "Zampa" upon the piano. Madame Lebrun was bustling in and out, giving orders in a high key to a yard-boy whenever she got inside the house, and directions in an equally high voice to a dining-room servant whenever she got outside. She was a fresh, pretty woman, clad always in white with elbow sleeves. Her starched skirts crinkled as she came and went. Farther down, before one of the cottages, a lady in black was walking demurely up and down, telling her beads. A good many persons of the *pension*° had gone over to the *Chênière Caminada* in Beaudelet's lugger to hear mass. Some young people were out under the water-oaks playing croquet. Mr. Pontellier's two children were there—sturdy little fellows of four and five. A quadroon nurse followed them about with a far-away, meditative air.

Mr. Pontellier finally lit a cigar and began to smoke, letting the paper drag idly from his hand. He fixed his gaze upon a white sunshade that was advancing at snail's pace from the beach. He could see it plainly between the gaunt trunks of the water-oaks and across the stretch of yellow camomile. The gulf looked far away, melting hazily into the blue of the horizon. The sunshade continued to approach slowly. Beneath its pink-lined shelter were his wife, Mrs. Pontellier, and young Robert Lebrun. When they reached the cottage, the two seated themselves with some appearance of fatigue upon the upper step of the porch, facing each other, each leaning against a supporting post.

"What folly! to bathe at such an hour in such heat!" exclaimed Mr.

pension: Boardinghouse.

Pontellier. He himself had taken a plunge at daylight. That was why the morning seemed long to him.

"You are burnt beyond recognition," he added, looking at his wife as one looks at a valuable piece of personal property which has suffered some damage. She held up her hands, strong, shapely hands, and surveyed them critically, drawing up her lawn sleeves above the wrists. Looking at them reminded her of her rings, which she had given to her husband before leaving for the beach. She silently reached out to him, and he, understanding, took the rings from his vest pocket and dropped them into her open palm. She slipped them upon her fingers; then clasping her knees, she looked across at Robert and began to laugh. The rings sparkled upon her fingers. He sent back an answering smile.

"What is it?" asked Pontellier, looking lazily and amused from one to the other. It was some utter nonsense; some adventure out there in the water, and they both tried to relate it at once. It did not seem half so amusing when told. They realized this, and so did Mr. Pontellier. He yawned and stretched himself. Then he got up, saying he had half a mind to go over to Klein's hotel and play a game of billiards.

"Come go along, Lebrun," he proposed to Robert. But Robert admitted quite frankly that he preferred to stay where he was and talk to Mrs. Pontellier.

"Well, send him about his business when he bores you, Edna," instructed her husband as he prepared to leave.

"Here, take the umbrella," she exclaimed, holding it out to him. He accepted the sunshade, and lifting it over his head descended the steps and walked away.

"Coming back to dinner?" his wife called after him. He halted a moment and shrugged his shoulders. He felt in his vest pocket; there was a ten-dollar bill there. He did not know; perhaps he would return for the early dinner and perhaps he would not. It all depended upon the company which he found over at Klein's and the size of "the game." He did not say this, but she understood it, and laughed, nodding good-by to him.

Both children wanted to follow their father when they saw him starting out. He kissed them and promised to bring them back bonbons and peanuts.

II

Mrs. Pontellier's eyes were quick and bright; they were a yellowish brown, about the color of her hair. She had a way of turning them swiftly upon an object and holding them there as if lost in some inward maze of contemplation or thought.

Her eyebrows were a shade darker than her hair. They were thick and almost horizontal, emphasizing the depth of her eyes. She was rather handsome than beautiful. Her face was captivating by reason of a certain frankness of expression and a contradictory subtle play of features. Her manner was engaging.

Robert rolled a cigarette. He smoked cigarettes because he could not afford cigars, he said. He had a cigar in his pocket which Mr. Pontellier had presented him with, and he was saving it for his after-dinner smoke.

This seemed quite proper and natural on his part. In coloring he was not unlike his companion. A clean-shaved face made the resemblance more pronounced than it would otherwise have been. There rested no shadow of care upon his open countenance. His eyes gathered in and reflected the light and languor of the summer day.

Mrs. Pontellier reached over for a palm-leaf fan that lay on the porch and began to fan herself, while Robert sent between his lips light puffs from his cigarette. They chatted incessantly: about the things around them; their amusing adventure out in the water—it had again assumed its entertaining aspect; about the wind, the trees, the people who had gone to the *Chênière;* about the children playing croquet under the oaks, and the Farival twins, who were now performing the overture to "The Poet and the Peasant." Robert talked a good deal about himself. He was very young, and did not know any better. Mrs. Pontellier talked a little about herself for the same reason. Each was interested in what the other said. Robert spoke of his intention to go to Mexico in the autumn, where fortune awaited him. He was always intending to go to Mexico, but some way never got there. Meanwhile he held on to his modest position in a mercantile house in New Orleans, where an equal familiarity with English, French and Spanish gave him no small value as a clerk and correspondent.

He was spending his summer vacation, as he always did, with his mother at Grand Isle. In former times, before Robert could remember, "the house" had been a summer luxury of the Lebruns. Now, flanked by its dozen or more cottages, which were always filled with exclusive visitors from the "*Quartier Français*,"° it enabled Madame Lebrun to maintain the easy and comfortable existence which appeared to be her birthright.

Quartier Français: French Quarter.

Mrs. Pontellier talked about her father's Mississippi plantation and her girlhood home in the old Kentucky blue-grass country. She was an American woman, with a small infusion of French which seemed to have been lost in dilution. She read a letter from her sister, who was away in the East, and who had engaged herself to be married. Robert was interested, and wanted to know what manner of girls the sisters were, what the father was like, and how long the mother had been dead.

When Mrs. Pontellier folded the letter it was time for her to dress for the early dinner.

"I see Léonce isn't coming back," she said, with a glance in the direction whence her husband had disappeared. Robert supposed he was not, as there were a good many New Orleans club men over at Klein's.

When Mrs. Pontellier left him to enter her room, the young man descended the steps and strolled over toward the croquet players, where, during the half-hour before dinner, he amused himself with the little Pontellier children, who were very fond of him.

III

It was eleven o'clock that night when Mr. Pontellier returned from Klein's hotel. He was in an excellent humor, in high spirits, and very talkative. His entrance awoke his wife, who was in bed and fast asleep when he came in. He talked to her while he undressed, telling her anecdotes and bits of news and gossip that he had gathered during the day. From his trousers pockets he took a fistful of crumpled bank notes and a good deal of silver coin, which he piled on the bureau indiscriminately with keys, knife, handkerchief, and whatever else happened to be in his pockets. She was overcome with sleep, and answered him with little half utterances.

He thought it very discouraging that his wife, who was the sole object of his existence, evinced so little interest in things which concerned him, and valued so little his conversation.

Mr. Pontellier had forgotten the bonbons and peanuts for the boys. Notwithstanding he loved them very much, and went into the adjoining room where they slept to take a look at them and make sure that they were resting comfortably. The result of his investigation was far from satisfactory. He turned and shifted the youngsters about in bed. One of them began to kick and talk about a basket full of crabs.

Mr. Pontellier returned to his wife with the information that Raoul had a high fever and needed looking after. Then he lit a cigar and went and sat near the open door to smoke it.

Mrs. Pontellier was quite sure Raoul had no fever. He had gone to bed perfectly well, she said, and nothing had ailed him all day. Mr. Pontellier was too well acquainted with fever symptoms to be mistaken. He assured her the child was consuming at that moment in the next room.

He reproached his wife with her inattention, her habitual neglect of the children. If it was not a mother's place to look after children, whose on earth was it? He himself had his hands full with his brokerage business. He could not be in two places at once; making a living for his family on the street, and staying at home to see that no harm befell them. He talked in a monotonous, insistent way.

Mrs. Pontellier sprang out of bed and went into the next room. She soon came back and sat on the edge of the bed, leaning her head down on the pillow. She said nothing, and refused to answer her husband when he questioned her. When his cigar was smoked out he went to bed, and in half a minute he was fast asleep.

Mrs. Pontellier was by that time thoroughly awake. She began to cry a little, and wiped her eyes on the sleeve of her *peignoir.*° Blowing out the candle, which her husband had left burning, she slipped her bare feet into a pair of satin *mules*° at the foot of the bed and went out on the porch, where she sat down in the wicker chair and began to rock gently to and fro.

It was then past midnight. The cottages were all dark. A single faint light gleamed out from the hallway of the house. There was no sound abroad except the hooting of an old owl in the top of a water-oak, and the everlasting voice of the sea, that was not uplifted at that soft hour. It broke like a mournful lullaby upon the night.

The tears came so fast to Mrs. Pontellier's eyes that the damp sleeve of her *peignoir* no longer served to dry them. She was holding the back of her chair with one hand; her loose sleeve had slipped almost to the shoulder of her uplifted arm. Turning, she thrust her face, steaming and wet, into the bend of her arm, and she went on crying there, not caring any longer to dry her face, her eyes, her arms. She could not have told why she was crying. Such experiences as the foregoing were not uncommon in her married life. They seemed never before to have weighed

peignoir: Dressing gown. ***mules:*** Slippers.

much against the abundance of her husband's kindness and a uniform devotion which had come to be tacit and self-understood.

An indescribable oppression, which seemed to generate in some unfamiliar part of her consciousness, filled her whole being with a vague anguish. It was like a shadow, like a mist passing across her soul's summer day. It was strange and unfamiliar; it was a mood. She did not sit there inwardly upbraiding her husband, lamenting at Fate, which had directed her footsteps to the path which they had taken. She was just having a good cry all to herself. The mosquitoes made merry over her, biting her firm, round arms and nipping at her bare insteps.

The little stinging, buzzing imps succeeded in dispelling a mood which might have held her there in the darkness half a night longer.

The following morning Mr. Pontellier was up in good time to take the rockaway which was to convey him to the steamer at the wharf. He was returning to the city to his business, and they would not see him again at the Island till the coming Saturday. He had regained his composure, which seemed to have been somewhat impaired the night before. He was eager to be gone, as he looked forward to a lively week in Carondelet Street.

Mr. Pontellier gave his wife half of the money which he had brought away from Klein's hotel the evening before. She liked money as well as most women, and accepted it with no little satisfaction.

"It will buy a handsome wedding present for Sister Janet!" she exclaimed, smoothing out the bills as she counted them one by one.

"Oh! we'll treat Sister Janet better than that, my dear," he laughed, as he prepared to kiss her good-by.

The boys were tumbling about, clinging to his legs, imploring that numerous things be brought back to them. Mr. Pontellier was a great favorite, and ladies, men, children, even nurses, were always on hand to say good-by to him. His wife stood smiling and waving, the boys shouting, as he disappeared in the old rockaway down the sandy road.

A few days later a box arrived for Mrs. Pontellier from New Orleans. It was from her husband. It was filled with *friandises,*° with luscious and toothsome bits—the finest of fruits, *patés,*° a rare bottle or two, delicious syrups, and bonbons in abundance.

Mrs. Pontellier was always very generous with the contents of such a box; she was quite used to receiving them when away from home. The *patés* and fruit were brought to the dining-room; the bonbons were passed around. And the ladies, selecting with dainty and discriminating

friandises: Delicacies. ***patés:*** Pies.

fingers and a little greedily, all declared that Mr. Pontellier was the best husband in the world. Mrs. Pontellier was forced to admit that she knew of none better.

IV

It would have been a difficult matter for Mr. Pontellier to define to his own satisfaction or any one else's wherein his wife failed in her duty toward their children. It was something which he felt rather than perceived, and he never voiced the feeling without subsequent regret and ample atonement.

If one of the little Pontellier boys took a tumble whilst at play, he was not apt to rush crying to his mother's arms for comfort; he would more likely pick himself up, wipe the water out of his eyes and the sand out of his mouth, and go on playing. Tots as they were, they pulled together and stood their ground in childish battles with doubled fists and uplifted voices, which usually prevailed against the other mother-tots. The quadroon nurse was looked upon as a huge encumbrance, only good to button up waists and panties and to brush and part hair; since it seemed to be a law of society that hair must be parted and brushed.

In short, Mrs. Pontellier was not a mother-woman. The mother-women seemed to prevail that summer at Grand Isle. It was easy to know them, fluttering about with extended, protecting wings when any harm, real or imaginary, threatened their precious brood. They were women who idolized their children, worshiped their husbands, and esteemed it a holy privilege to efface themselves as individuals and grow wings as ministering angels.

Many of them were delicious in the rôle; one of them was the embodiment of every womanly grace and charm. If her husband did not adore her, he was a brute, deserving of death by slow torture. Her name was Adèle Ratignolle. There are no words to describe her save the old ones that have served so often to picture the bygone heroine of romance and the fair lady of our dreams. There was nothing subtle or hidden about her charms; her beauty was all there, flaming and apparent: the spun-gold hair that comb nor confining pin could restrain; the blue eyes that were like nothing but sapphires; two lips that pouted, that were so red one could only think of cherries or some other delicious crimson fruit in looking at them. She was growing a little stout, but it did not seem to detract an iota from the grace of every step, pose, gesture. One would not have wanted her white neck a mite less full or her beautiful arms more slender. Never were hands more exquisite than hers, and it was a joy to look at them when she threaded her needle or adjusted her gold thimble to her taper middle finger as she sewed away on the little night-drawers or fashioned a bodice or a bib.

Madame Ratignolle was very fond of Mrs. Pontellier, and often she took her sewing and went over to sit with her in the afternoons. She was sitting there the afternoon of the day the box arrived from New Orleans. She had possession of the rocker, and she was busily engaged in sewing upon a diminutive pair of night-drawers.

She had brought the pattern of the drawers for Mrs. Pontellier to cut out—a marvel of construction, fashioned to enclose a baby's body so effectually that only two small eyes might look out from the garment, like an Eskimo's. They were designed for winter wear, when treacherous drafts came down chimneys and insidious currents of deadly cold found their way through key-holes.

Mrs. Pontellier's mind was quite at rest concerning the present material needs of her children, and she could not see the use of anticipating and making winter night garments the subject of her summer meditations. But she did not want to appear unamiable and uninterested, so she had brought forth newspapers, which she spread upon the floor of the gallery, and under Madame Ratignolle's directions she had cut a pattern of the impervious garment.

Robert was there, seated as he had been the Sunday before, and Mrs. Pontellier also occupied her former position on the upper step, leaning listlessly against the post. Beside her was a box of bonbons, which she held out at intervals to Madame Ratignolle.

That lady seemed at a loss to make a selection, but finally settled upon a stick of nougat, wondering if it were not too rich; whether it could possibly hurt her. Madame Ratignolle had been married seven years. About every two years she had a baby. At that time she had three babies, and was beginning to think of a fourth one. She was always talking about her "condition." Her "condition" was in no way apparent, and no one would have known a thing about it but for her persistence in making it the subject of conversation.

Robert started to reassure her, asserting that he had known a lady who had subsisted upon nougat during the entire—but seeing the color mount into Mrs. Pontellier's face he checked himself and changed the subject.

Mrs. Pontellier, though she had married a Creole,° was not thor-

Creole: A descendant of French and Spanish settlers of the New Orleans area. Beginning in the early eighteenth century, the Creoles developed a highly sophisticated urban culture.

oughly at home in the society of Creoles; never before had she been thrown so intimately among them. There were only Creoles that summer at Lebrun's. They all knew each other, and felt like one large family, among whom existed the most amicable relations. A characteristic which distinguished them and which impressed Mrs. Pontellier most forcibly was their entire absence of prudery. Their freedom of expression was at first incomprehensible to her, though she had no difficulty in reconciling it with a lofty chastity which in the Creole woman seems to be inborn and unmistakable.

Never would Edna Pontellier forget the shock with which she heard Madame Ratignolle relating to old Monsieur Farival the harrowing story of one of her *accouchements*,° withholding no intimate detail. She was growing accustomed to like shocks, but she could not keep the mounting color back from her cheeks. Oftener than once her coming had interrupted the droll story with which Robert was entertaining some amused group of married women.

A book had gone the rounds of the *pension*. When it came her turn to read it, she did so with profound astonishment. She felt moved to read the book in secret and solitude, though none of the others had done so—to hide it from view at the sound of approaching footsteps. It was openly criticised and freely discussed at table. Mrs. Pontellier gave over being astonished, and concluded that wonders would never cease.

V

They formed a congenial group sitting there that summer afternoon—Madame Ratignolle sewing away, often stopping to relate a story or incident with much expressive gesture of her perfect hands; Robert and Mrs. Pontellier sitting idle, exchanging occasional words, glances or smiles which indicated a certain advanced stage of intimacy and *camaraderie*.°

He had lived in her shadow during the past month. No one thought anything of it. Many had predicted that Robert would devote himself to Mrs. Pontellier when he arrived. Since the age of fifteen, which was eleven years before, Robert each summer at Grand Isle had constituted himself the devoted attendant of some fair dame or damsel.

accouchements: Confinements; that is, childbirth. ***camaraderie:*** Good fellowship.

Sometimes it was a young girl, again a widow; but as often as not it was some interesting married woman.

For two consecutive seasons he lived in the sunlight of Mademoiselle Duvigné's presence. But she died between summers; then Robert posed as an inconsolable, prostrating himself at the feet of Madame Ratignolle for whatever crumbs of sympathy and comfort she might be pleased to vouchsafe.

Mrs. Pontellier liked to sit and gaze at her fair companion as she might look upon a faultless Madonna.

"Could any one fathom the cruelty beneath that fair exterior?" murmured Robert. "She knew that I adored her once, and she let me adore her. It was 'Robert, come; go; stand up; sit down; do this; do that; see if the baby sleeps; my thimble, please, that I left God knows where. Come and read Daudet to me while I sew.'"

"Par example!° I never had to ask. You were always there under my feet, like a troublesome cat."

"You mean like an adoring dog. And just as soon as Ratignolle appeared on the scene, then it *was* like a dog. '*Passez! Adieu! Allez vous-en!*'"°

"Perhaps I feared to make Alphonse jealous," she interjoined, with excessive naïveté. That made them all laugh. The right hand jealous of the left! The heart jealous of the soul! But for that matter, the Creole husband is never jealous; with him the gangrene passion is one which has become dwarfed by disuse.

Meanwhile Robert, addressing Mrs. Pontellier, continued to tell of his one time hopeless passion for Madame Ratignolle; of sleepless nights, of consuming flames till the very sea sizzled when he took his daily plunge. While the lady at the needle kept up a little running, contemptuous comment:

"*Blagueur—farceur—gros bête va!*"°

He never assumed this serio-comic tone when alone with Mrs. Pontellier. She never knew precisely what to make of it; at that moment it was impossible for her to guess how much of it was jest and what proportion was earnest. It was understood that he had often spoken words of love to Madame Ratignolle, without any thought of being taken seriously. Mrs. Pontellier was glad he had not assumed a similar rôle toward herself. It would have been unacceptable and annoying.

Mrs. Pontellier had brought her sketching materials, which she

Par example!: Oh really! ***Passez . . . vous-en!:*** Go! Good-bye! Go away! ***Blagueur . . . va!:*** Jester—joker—silly you go!

sometimes dabbled with in an unprofessional way. She liked the dabbling. She felt in it satisfaction of a kind which no other employment afforded her.

She had long wished to try herself on Madame Ratignolle. Never had that lady seemed a more tempting subject than at that moment, seated there like some sensuous Madonna, with the gleam of the fading day enriching her splendid color.

Robert crossed over and seated himself upon the step below Mrs. Pontellier, that he might watch her work. She handled her brushes with a certain ease and freedom which came, not from long and close acquaintance with them, but from a natural aptitude. Robert followed her work with close attention, giving forth little ejaculatory expressions of appreciation in French, which he addressed to Madame Ratignolle.

"*Mais ce n'est pas mal! Elle s'y connait, elle a de la force, oui.*"°

During his oblivious attention he once quietly rested his head against Mrs. Pontellier's arm. As gently she repulsed him. Once again he repeated the offense. She could not but believe it to be thoughtlessness on his part; yet that was no reason she should submit to it. She did not remonstrate, except again to repulse him quietly but firmly. He offered no apology.

The picture completed bore no resemblance to Madame Ratignolle. She was greatly disappointed to find that it did not look like her. But it was a fair enough piece of work, and in many respects satisfying.

Mrs. Pontellier evidently did not think so. After surveying the sketch critically she drew a broad smudge of paint across its surface, and crumpled the paper between her hands.

The youngsters came tumbling up the steps, the quadroon following at the respectful distance which they required her to observe. Mrs. Pontellier made them carry her paints and things into the house. She sought to detain them for a little talk and some pleasantry. But they were greatly in earnest. They had only come to investigate the contents of the bonbon box. They accepted without murmuring what she chose to give them, each holding out two chubby hands scoop-like, in the vain hope that they might be filled; and then away they went.

The sun was low in the west, and the breeze soft and languorous that came up from the south, charged with the seductive odor of the sea. Children, freshly befurbelowed, were gathering for their games under the oaks. Their voices were high and penetrating.

Madame Ratignolle folded her sewing, placing thimble, scissors and

Mais . . . oui: But it is not bad! She knows what she is doing, doesn't she.

thread all neatly together in the roll, which she pinned securely. She complained of faintness. Mrs. Pontellier flew for the cologne water and a fan. She bathed Madame Ratignolle's face with cologne, while Robert plied the fan with unnecessary vigor.

The spell was soon over, and Mrs. Pontellier could not help wondering if there were not a little imagination responsible for its origin, for the rose tint had never faded from her friend's face.

She stood watching the fair woman walk down the long line of galleries with the grace and majesty which queens are sometimes supposed to possess. Her little ones ran to meet her. Two of them clung about her white skirts, the third she took from its nurse and with a thousand endearments bore it along in her own fond, encircling arms. Though, as everybody well knew, the doctor had forbidden her to lift so much as a pin!

"Are you going bathing?" asked Robert of Mrs. Pontellier. It was not so much a question as a reminder.

"Oh, no," she answered, with a tone of indecision. "I'm tired; I think not." Her glance wandered from his face away toward the Gulf, whose sonorous murmur reached her like a loving but imperative entreaty.

"Oh, come!" he insisted. "You mustn't miss your bath. Come on. The water must be delicious; it will not hurt you. Come."

He reached up for her big, rough straw hat that hung on a peg outside the door, and put it on her head. They descended the steps, and walked away together toward the beach. The sun was low in the west and the breeze was soft and warm.

VI

Edna Pontellier could not have told why, wishing to go to the beach with Robert, she should in the first place have declined, and in the second place have followed in obedience to one of the two contradictory impulses which impelled her.

A certain light was beginning to dawn dimly within her,—the light which, showing the way, forbids it.

At the early period it served but to bewilder her. It moved her to dreams, to thoughtfulness, to the shadowy anguish which had overcome her the midnight when she had abandoned herself to tears.

In short, Mrs. Pontellier was beginning to realize her position in the universe as a human being, and to recognize her relations as an individual to the world within and about her. This may seem like a ponderous weight of wisdom to descend upon the soul of a young woman of twenty-eight—perhaps more wisdom than the Holy Ghost is usually pleased to vouchsafe to any woman.

But the beginning of things, of a world especially, is necessarily vague, tangled, chaotic, and exceedingly disturbing. How few of us ever emerge from such beginning! How many souls perish in its tumult!

The voice of the sea is seductive; never ceasing, whispering, clamoring, murmuring, inviting the soul to wander for a spell in abysses of solitude; to lose itself in mazes of inward contemplation.

The voice of the sea speaks to the soul. The touch of the sea is sensuous, enfolding the body in its soft, close embrace.

VII

Mrs. Pontellier was not a woman given to confidences, a characteristic hitherto contrary to her nature. Even as a child she had lived her own small life all within herself. At a very early period she had apprehended instinctively the dual life—that outward existence which conforms, the inward life which questions.

That summer at Grand Isle she began to loosen a little the mantle of reserve that had always enveloped her. There may have been—there must have been—influences, both subtle and apparent, working in their several ways to induce her to do this; but the most obvious was the influence of Adèle Ratignolle. The excessive physical charm of the Creole had first attracted her, for Edna had a sensuous susceptibility to beauty. Then the candor of the woman's whole existence, which every one might read, and which formed so striking a contrast to her own habitual reserve—this might have furnished a link. Who can tell what metals the gods use in forging the subtle bond which we call sympathy, which we might as well call love.

The two women went away one morning to the beach together, arm in arm, under the huge white sunshade. Edna had prevailed upon Madame Ratignolle to leave the children behind, though she could not induce her to relinquish a diminutive roll of needle-work, which Adèle begged to be allowed to slip into the depths of her pocket. In some unaccountable way they had escaped from Robert.

The walk to the beach was no inconsiderable one, consisting as it did of a long, sandy path, upon which a sporadic and tangled growth that bordered it on either side made frequent and unexpected inroads.

There were acres of yellow camomile reaching out on either hand. Further away still, vegetable gardens abounded, with frequent small plantations of orange or lemon trees intervening. The dark green clusters glistened from afar in the sun.

The women were both of goodly height, Madame Ratignolle possessing the more feminine and matronly figure. The charm of Edna Pontellier's physique stole insensibly upon you. The lines of her body were long, clean and symmetrical; it was a body which occasionally fell into splendid poses; there was no suggestion of the trim, stereotyped fashion-plate about it. A casual and indiscriminating observer, in passing, might not cast a second glance upon the figure. But with more feeling and discernment he would have recognized the noble beauty of its modeling, and the graceful severity of poise and movement, which made Edna Pontellier different from the crowd.

She wore a cool muslin that morning—white, with a waving vertical line of brown running through it; also a white linen collar and the big straw hat which she had taken from the peg outside the door. The hat rested any way on her yellow-brown hair, that waved a little, was heavy, and clung close to her head.

Madame Ratignolle, more careful of her complexion, had twined a gauze veil about her head. She wore dogskin gloves, with gauntlets that protected her wrists. She was dressed in pure white, with a fluffiness of ruffles that became her. The draperies and fluttering things which she wore suited her rich, luxuriant beauty as a greater severity of line could not have done.

There were a number of bath-houses along the beach, of rough but solid construction, built with small, protecting galleries facing the water. Each house consisted of two compartments, and each family at Lebrun's possessed a compartment for itself, fitted out with all the essential paraphernalia of the bath and whatever other conveniences the owners might desire. The two women had no intention of bathing; they had just strolled down to the beach for a walk and to be alone and near the water. The Pontellier and Ratignolle compartments adjoined one another under the same roof.

Mrs. Pontellier had brought down her key through force of habit. Unlocking the door of her bath-room she went inside, and soon emerged, bringing a rug, which she spread upon the floor of the gallery, and two huge hair pillows covered with crash, which she placed against the front of the building.

The two seated themselves there in the shade of the porch, side by side, with their backs against the pillows and their feet extended.

Madame Ratignolle removed her veil, wiped her face with a rather delicate handkerchief, and fanned herself with the fan which she always carried suspended somewhere about her person by a long, narrow ribbon. Edna removed her collar and opened her dress at the throat. She took the fan from Madame Ratignolle and began to fan both herself and her companion. It was very warm, and for a while they did nothing but exchange remarks about the heat, the sun, the glare. But there was a breeze blowing, a choppy, stiff wind that whipped the water into froth. It fluttered the skirts of the two women and kept them for a while engaged in adjusting, readjusting, tucking in, securing hair-pins and hat-pins. A few persons were sporting some distance away in the water. The beach was very still of human sound at that hour. The lady in black was reading her morning devotions on the porch of a neighboring bath-house. Two young lovers were exchanging their hearts' yearnings beneath the children's tent, which they had found unoccupied.

Edna Pontellier, casting her eyes about, had finally kept them at rest upon the sea. The day was clear and carried the gaze out as far as the blue sky went; there were a few white clouds suspended idly over the horizon. A lateen sail was visible in the direction of Cat Island, and others to the south seemed almost motionless in the far distance.

"Of whom—of what are you thinking?" asked Adèle of her companion, whose countenance she had been watching with a little amused attention, arrested by the absorbed expression which seemed to have seized and fixed every feature into statuesque repose.

"Nothing," returned Mrs. Pontellier, with a start, adding at once: "How stupid! But it seems to me it is the reply we make instinctively to such a question. Let me see," she went on, throwing back her head and narrowing her fine eyes till they shone like two vivid points of light. "Let me see. I was really not conscious of thinking of anything; but perhaps I can retrace my thoughts."

"Oh! never mind!" laughed Madame Ratignolle. "I am not quite so exacting. I will let you off this time. It is really too hot to think, especially to think about thinking."

"But for the fun of it," persisted Edna. "First of all, the sight of the water stretching so far away, those motionless sails against the blue sky, made a delicious picture that I just wanted to sit and look at. The hot wind beating in my face made me think—without any connection that I can trace—of a summer day in Kentucky, of a meadow that seemed as big as the ocean to the very little girl walking through the grass, which was higher than her waist. She threw out her arms as if swimming when she walked, beating the tall grass as one strikes out in the water. Oh, I see the connection now!"

"Where were you going that day in Kentucky, walking through the grass?"

"I don't remember now. I was just walking diagonally across a big field. My sun-bonnet obstructed the view. I could see only the stretch of green before me, and I felt as if I must walk on forever, without coming to the end of it. I don't remember whether I was frightened or pleased. I must have been entertained.

"Likely as not it was Sunday," she laughed; "and I was running away from prayers, from the Presbyterian service, read in a spirit of gloom by my father that chills me yet to think of."

"And have you been running away from prayers ever since, *ma chère?*"° asked Madame Ratignolle, amused.

"No! oh, no!" Edna hastened to say. "I was a little unthinking child in those days, just following a misleading impulse without question. On the contrary, during one period of my life religion took a firm hold upon me; after I was twelve and until—until—why, I suppose until now, though I never thought much about it—just driven along by habit. But do you know," she broke off, turning her quick eyes upon Madame Ratignolle and leaning forward a little so as to bring her face quite close to that of her companion, "sometimes I feel this summer as if I were walking through the green meadow again; idly, aimlessly, unthinking and unguided."

Madame Ratignolle laid her hand over that of Mrs. Pontellier, which was near her. Seeing that the hand was not withdrawn, she clasped it firmly and warmly. She even stroked it a little, fondly, with the other hand, murmuring in an undertone, "*Pauvre chérie.*"°

The action was at first a little confusing to Edna, but she soon lent herself readily to the Creole's gentle caress. She was not accustomed to an outward and spoken expression of affection, either in herself or in others. She and her younger sister, Janet, had quarreled a good deal through force of unfortunate habit. Her older sister, Margaret, was matronly and dignified, probably from having assumed matronly and housewifely responsibilities too early in life, their mother having died when they were quite young. Margaret was not effusive; she was practical. Edna had had an occasional girl friend, but whether accidentally or not, they seemed to have been all of one type—the self-contained.

ma chère: My dear. ***Pauvre chérie:*** Poor darling.

She never realized that the reserve of her own character had much, perhaps everything, to do with this. Her most intimate friend at school had been one of rather exceptional intellectual gifts, who wrote fine-sounding essays, which Edna admired and strove to imitate; and with her she talked and glowed over the English classics, and sometimes held religious and political controversies.

Edna often wondered at one propensity which sometimes had inwardly disturbed her without causing any outward show or manifestation on her part. At a very early age—perhaps it was when she traversed the ocean of waving grass—she remembered that she had been passionately enamored of a dignified and sad-eyed cavalry officer who visited her father in Kentucky. She could not leave his presence when he was there, nor remove her eyes from his face, which was something like Napoleon's, with a lock of black hair falling across the forehead. But the cavalry officer melted imperceptibly out of her existence.

At another time her affections were deeply engaged by a young gentleman who visited a lady on a neighboring plantation. It was after they went to Mississippi to live. The young man was engaged to be married to the young lady, and they sometimes called upon Margaret, driving over of afternoons in a buggy. Edna was a little miss, just merging into her teens; and the realization that she herself was nothing, nothing, nothing to the engaged young man was a bitter affliction to her. But he, too, went the way of dreams.

She was a grown young woman when she was overtaken by what she supposed to be the climax of her fate. It was when the face and figure of a great tragedian began to haunt her imagination and stir her senses. The persistence of the infatuation lent it an aspect of genuineness. The hopelessness of it colored it with the lofty tones of a great passion.

The picture of the tragedian stood enframed upon her desk. Any one may possess the portrait of a tragedian without exciting suspicion or comment. (This was a sinister reflection which she cherished.) In the presence of others she expressed admiration for his exalted gifts, as she handed the photograph around and dwelt upon the fidelity of the likeness. When alone she sometimes picked it up and kissed the cold glass passionately.

Her marriage to Léonce Pontellier was purely an accident, in this respect resembling many other marriages which masquerade as the decrees of Fate. It was in the midst of her secret great passion that she met him. He fell in love, as men are in the habit of doing, and pressed his suit with an earnestness and an ardor which left nothing to be desired. He pleased her; his absolute devotion flattered her. She fancied there was a sympathy of thought and taste between them, in which fancy she was mistaken. Add to this the violent opposition of her father and her sister Margaret to her marriage with a Catholic, and we need seek no further for the motives which led her to accept Monsieur Pontellier for her husband.

The acme of bliss, which would have been a marriage with the tragedian, was not for her in this world. As the devoted wife of a man who worshiped her, she felt she would take her place with a certain dignity in the world of reality, closing the portals forever behind her upon the realm of romance and dreams.

But it was not long before the tragedian had gone to join the cavalry officer and the engaged young man and a few others; and Edna found herself face to face with the realities. She grew fond of her husband, realizing with some unaccountable satisfaction that no trace of passion or excessive and fictitious warmth colored her affection, thereby threatening its dissolution.

She was fond of her children in an uneven, impulsive way. She would sometimes gather them passionately to her heart; she would sometimes forget them. The year before they had spent part of the summer with their grandmother Pontellier in Iberville. Feeling secure regarding their happiness and welfare, she did not miss them except with an occasional intense longing. Their absence was a sort of relief, though she did not admit this, even to herself. It seemed to free her of a responsibility which she had blindly assumed and for which Fate had not fitted her.

Edna did not reveal so much as all this to Madame Ratignolle that summer day when they sat with faces turned to the sea. But a good part of it escaped her. She had put her head down on Madame Ratignolle's shoulder. She was flushed and felt intoxicated with the sound of her own voice and the unaccustomed taste of candor. It muddled her like wine, or like a first breath of freedom.

There was the sound of approaching voices. It was Robert, surrounded by a troop of children, searching for them. The two little Pontelliers were with him, and he carried Madame Ratignolle's little girl in his arms. There were other children beside, and two nurse-maids followed, looking disagreeable and resigned.

The women at once rose and began to shake out their draperies and relax their muscles. Mrs. Pontellier threw the cushions and rug into the bath-house. The children all scampered off to the awning, and they stood there in a line, gazing upon the intruding lovers, still exchanging vows and sighs. The lovers got up, with only a silent protest, and walked slowly away somewhere else.

The children possessed themselves of the tent, and Mrs. Pontellier went over to join them.

Madame Ratignolle begged Robert to accompany her to the house; she complained of cramp in her limbs and stiffness of the joints. She leaned draggingly upon his arm as they walked.

VIII

"Do me a favor, Robert," spoke the pretty woman at his side, almost as soon as she and Robert had started on their slow, homeward way. She looked up in his face, leaning on his arm beneath the encircling shadow of the umbrella which he had lifted.

"Granted; as many as you like," he returned, glancing down into her eyes that were full of thoughtfulness and some speculation.

"I only ask for one; let Mrs. Pontellier alone."

"*Tiens!*" he exclaimed, with a sudden, boyish laugh. "*Voilà que Madame Ratignolle est jalouse!*"°

"Nonsense! I'm in earnest; I mean what I say. Let Mrs. Pontellier alone."

"Why?" he asked; himself growing serious at his companion's solicitation.

"She is not one of us; she is not like us. She might make the unfortunate blunder of taking you seriously."

His face flushed with annoyance, and taking off his soft hat he began to beat it impatiently against his leg as he walked. "Why shouldn't she take me seriously?" he demanded sharply. "Am I a comedian, a clown, a jack-in-the-box? Why shouldn't she? You Creoles! I have no patience with you! Am I always to be regarded as a feature of an amusing programme? I hope Mrs. Pontellier does take me seriously. I hope she has discernment enough to find in me something besides the *blagueur.*° If I thought there was any doubt—"

"Oh, enough, Robert!" she broke into his heated outburst. "You are not thinking of what you are saying. You speak with about as little reflection as we might expect from one of those children down there playing in the sand. If your attentions to any married women here were

Tiens! . . . jalouse!: Ah! Madame Ratignolle is jealous perhaps! ***blagueur:*** Joker.

ever offered with any intention of being convincing, you would not be the gentleman we all know you to be, and you would be unfit to associate with the wives and daughters of the people who trust you."

Madame Ratignolle had spoken what she believed to be the law and the gospel. The young man shrugged his shoulders impatiently.

"Oh! well! That isn't it," slamming his hat down vehemently upon his head. "You ought to feel that such things are not flattering to say to a fellow."

"Should our whole intercourse consist of an exchange of compliments? *Ma foi!*"°

"It isn't pleasant to have a woman tell you—" he went on, unheedingly, but breaking off suddenly: "Now if I were like Arobin—you remember Alcée Arobin and that story of the consul's wife at Biloxi?" And he related the story of Alcée Arobin and the consul's wife; and another about the tenor of the French Opera, who received letters which should never have been written; and still other stories, grave and gay, till Mrs. Pontellier and her possible propensity for taking young men seriously was apparently forgotten.

Madame Ratignolle, when they had regained her cottage, went in to take the hour's rest which she considered helpful. Before leaving her, Robert begged her pardon for the impatience—he called it rudeness—with which he had received her well-meant caution.

"You made one mistake, Adèle," he said, with a light smile; "there is no earthly possibility of Mrs. Pontellier ever taking me seriously. You should have warned me against taking myself seriously. Your advice might then have carried some weight and given me subject for some reflection. *Au revoir.*° But you look tired," he added, solicitously. "Would you like a cup of bouillon? Shall I stir you a toddy? Let me mix you a toddy with a drop of Angostura."

She acceded to the suggestion of bouillon, which was grateful and acceptable. He went himself to the kitchen, which was a building apart from the cottages and lying to the rear of the house. And he himself brought her the golden-brown bouillion, in a dainty Sèvres cup, with a flaky cracker or two on the saucer.

She thrust a bare, white arm from the curtain which shielded her open door, and received the cup from his hands. She told him he was a *bon garçon,*° and she meant it. Robert thanked her and turned away toward "the house."

The lovers were just entering the grounds of the *pension*. They were

Ma foi!: Indeed! *Au revoir:* Good-bye. *bon garçon:* Nice fellow.

leaning toward each other as the water-oaks bent from the sea. There was not a particle of earth beneath their feet. Their heads might have been turned upside-down, so absolutely did they tread upon blue ether. The lady in black, creeping behind them, looked a trifle paler and more jaded than usual. There was no sign of Mrs. Pontellier and the children. Robert scanned the distance for any such apparition. They would doubtless remain away till the dinner hour. The young man ascended to his mother's room. It was situated at the top of the house, made up of odd angles and a queer, sloping ceiling. Two broad dormer windows looked out toward the Gulf, and as far across it as a man's eye might reach. The furnishings of the room were light, cool, and practical.

Madam Lebrun was busily engaged at the sewing-machine. A little black girl sat on the floor, and with her hands worked the treadle of the machine. The Creole woman does not take any chances which may be avoided of imperiling her health.

Robert went over and seated himself on the broad sill of one of the dormer windows. He took a book from his pocket and began energetically to read it, judging by the precision and frequency with which he turned the leaves. The sewing-machine made a resounding clatter in the room; it was of a ponderous, by-gone make. In the lulls, Robert and his mother exchanged bits of desultory conversation.

"Where is Mrs. Pontellier?"

"Down at the beach with the children."

"I promised to lend her the Goncourt. Don't forget to take it down when you go; it's there on the bookshelf over the small table." Clatter, clatter, clatter, bang! for the next five or eight minutes.

"Where is Victor going with the rockaway?"

"The rockaway? Victor?"

"Yes; down there in front. He seems to be getting ready to drive away somewhere."

"Call him." Clatter, clatter!

Robert uttered a shrill, piercing whistle which might have been heard back at the wharf.

"He won't look up."

Madame Lebrun flew to the window. She called "Victor!" She waved a handkerchief and called again. The young fellow below got into the vehicle and started the horse off at a gallop.

Madam Lebrun went back to the machine, crimson with annoyance. Victor was the younger son and brother—a *tête montée,*° with a temper which invited violence and a will which no ax could break.

tête montée: Hothead.

"Whenever you say the word I'm ready to thrash any amount of reason into him that he's able to hold."

"If your father had only lived!" Clatter, clatter, clatter, clatter, bang! It was a fixed belief with Madame Lebrun that the conduct of the universe and all things pertaining thereto would have been manifestly of a more intelligent and higher order had not Monsieur Lebrun been removed to other spheres during the early years of their married life.

"What do you hear from Montel?" Montel was a middle-aged gentleman whose vain ambition and desire for the past twenty years had been to fill the void which Monsieur Lebrun's taking off had left in the Lebrun household. Clatter, clatter, bang, clatter!

"I have a letter somewhere," looking in the machine drawer and finding the letter in the bottom of the work-basket. "He says to tell you he will be in Vera Cruz the beginning of next month"—clatter, clatter!—"and if you still have the intention of joining him"—bang! clatter, clatter, bang!

"Why didn't you tell me so before, mother? You know I wanted—" Clatter, clatter, clatter!

"Do you see Mrs. Pontellier starting back with the children? She will be in late to luncheon again. She never starts to get ready for luncheon till the last minute." Clatter, clatter! "Where are you going?"

"Where did you say the Goncourt was?"

IX

Every light in the hall was ablaze; every lamp turned as high as it could be without smoking the chimney or threatening explosion. The lamps were fixed at intervals against the wall, encircling the whole room. Some one had gathered orange and lemon branches, and with these fashioned graceful festoons between. The dark green of the branches stood out and glistened against the white muslin curtains which draped the windows, and which puffed, floated, and flapped at the capricious will of a stiff breeze that swept up from the Gulf.

It was Saturday night a few weeks after the intimate conversation held between Robert and Madame Ratignolle on their way from the beach. An unusual number of husbands, fathers, and friends had come down to stay over Sunday; and they were being suitably entertained by their families, with the material help of Madame Lebrun. The dining tables had all been removed to one end of the hall, and the chairs ranged about in rows and in clusters. Each little family group had had its say and exchanged its domestic gossip earlier in the evening. There was now an apparent disposition to relax; to widen the circle of confidences and give a more general tone to the conversation.

Many of the children had been permitted to sit up beyond their usual bedtime. A small band of them were lying on their stomachs on the floor looking at the colored sheets of the comic papers which Mr. Pontellier had brought down. The little Pontellier boys were permitting them to do so, and making their authority felt.

Music, dancing, and a recitation or two were the entertainments furnished, or rather, offered. But there was nothing systematic about the programme, no appearance of prearrangement nor even premeditation.

At an early hour in the evening the Farival twins were prevailed upon to play the piano. They were girls of fourteen, always clad in the Virgin's colors, blue and white, having been dedicated to the Blessed Virgin at their baptism. They played a duet from "Zampa," and at the earnest solicitation of every one present followed it with the overture to "The Poet and the Peasant."

"*Allez vous-en! Sapristi!*"° shrieked the parrot outside the door. He was the only being present who possessed sufficient candor to admit that he was not listening to these gracious performances for the first time that summer. Old Monsieur Farival, grandfather of the twins, grew indignant over the interruption and insisted upon having the bird removed and consigned to regions of darkness. Victor Lebrun objected; and his decrees were as immutable as those of Fate. The parrot fortunately offered no further interruption to the entertainment, the whole venom of his nature apparently having been cherished up and hurled against the twins in that one impetuous outburst.

Later a young brother and sister gave recitations, which every one present had heard many times at winter evening entertainments in the city.

A little girl performed a skirt dance in the center of the floor. The mother played her accompaniments and at the same time watched her daughter with greedy admiration and nervous apprehension. She need have had no apprehension. The child was mistress of the situation. She had been properly dressed for the occasion in black tulle and black silk tights. Her little neck and arms were bare, and her hair, artificially crimped, stood out like fluffy black plumes over her head. Her poses were full of grace, and her little black-shod toes twinkled as they shot

Allez . . . Sapristi!: Go away! For God's sake!

out and upward with a rapidity and suddenness which were bewildering.

But there was no reason why every one should not dance. Madame Ratignolle could not, so it was she who gaily consented to play for the others. She played very well, keeping excellent waltz time and infusing an expression into the strains which was indeed inspiring. She was keeping up her music on account of the children, she said; because she and her husband both considered it a means of brightening the home and making it attractive.

Almost every one danced but the twins, who could not be induced to separate during the brief period when one or the other should be whirling around the room in the arms of a man. They might have danced together, but they did not think of it.

The children were sent to bed. Some went submissively; others with shrieks and protests as they were dragged away. They had been permitted to sit up till after the ice-cream, which naturally marked the limit of human indulgence.

The ice-cream was passed around with cake—gold and silver cake arranged on platters in alternate slices; it had been made and frozen during the afternoon back of the kitchen by two black women, under the supervision of Victor. It was pronounced a great success—excellent if it had only contained a little less vanilla or a little more sugar, if it had been frozen a degree harder, and if the salt might have been kept out of portions of it. Victor was proud of his achievement, and went about recommending it and urging every one to partake of it to excess.

After Mrs. Pontellier had danced twice with her husband, once with Robert, and once with Monsieur Ratignolle, who was thin and tall and swayed like a reed in the wind when he danced, she went out on the gallery and seated herself on the low window-sill, where she commanded a view of all that went on in the hall and could look out toward the Gulf. There was a soft effulgence in the east. The moon was coming up, and its mystic shimmer was casting a million lights across the distant, restless water.

"Would you like to hear Mademoiselle Reisz play?" asked Robert, coming out on the porch where she was. Of course Edna would like to hear Mademoiselle Reisz play; but she feared it would be useless to entreat her.

"I'll ask her," he said. "I'll tell her that you want to hear her. She likes you. She will come." He turned and hurried away to one of the far cottages, where Mademoiselle Reisz was shuffling away. She was dragging a chair in and out of her room, and at intervals objecting to the crying of a baby, which a nurse in the adjoining cottage was endeavoring to put to sleep. She was a disagreeable little woman, no longer young, who had quarreled with almost every one, owing to a temper which was self-assertive and a disposition to trample upon the rights of others. Robert prevailed upon her without any too great difficulty.

She entered the hall with him during a lull in the dance. She made an awkward, imperious little bow as she went in. She was a homely woman, with a small weazened face and body and eyes that glowed. She had absolutely no taste in dress, and wore a batch of rusty black lace with a bunch of artificial violets pinned to the side of her hair.

"Ask Mrs. Pontellier what she would like to hear me play," she requested of Robert. She sat perfectly still before the piano, not touching the keys, while Robert carried her message to Edna at the window. A general air of surprise and genuine satisfaction fell upon every one as they saw the pianist enter. There was a settling down, and a prevailing air of expectancy everywhere. Edna was a trifle embarrassed at being thus singled out for the imperious little woman's favor. She would not dare to choose, and begged that Mademoiselle Reisz would please herself in her selections.

Edna was what she herself called very fond of music. Musical strains, well rendered, had a way of evoking pictures in her mind. She sometimes liked to sit in the room of mornings when Madame Ratignolle played or practiced. One piece which that lady played Edna had entitled "Solitude." It was a short, plaintive, minor strain. The name of the piece was something else, but she called it "Solitude." When she heard it there came before her imagination the figure of a man standing beside a desolate rock on the seashore. He was naked. His attitude was one of hopeless resignation as he looked toward a distant bird winging its flight away from him.

Another piece called to her mind a dainty young woman clad in an Empire gown, taking mincing dancing steps as she came down a long avenue between tall hedges. Again, another reminded her of children at play, and still another of nothing on earth but a demure lady stroking a cat.

The very first chords which Mademoiselle Reisz struck upon the piano sent a keen tremor down Mrs. Pontellier's spinal column. It was not the first time she had heard an artist at the piano. Perhaps it was the first time she was ready, perhaps the first time her being was tempered to take an impress of the abiding truth.

She waited for the material pictures which she thought would gather and blaze before her imagination. She waited in vain. She saw no pictures of solitude, of hope, of longing, or of despair. But the very passions themselves were aroused within her soul, swaying it, lashing it, as the waves daily beat upon her splendid body. She trembled, she was choking, and the tears blinded her.

Mademoiselle had finished. She arose, and bowing her stiff, lofty bow, she went away, stopping for neither thanks nor applause. As she passed along the gallery she patted Edna upon the shoulder.

"Well, how did you like my music?" she asked. The young woman was unable to answer; she pressed the hand of the pianist convulsively. Mademoiselle Reisz perceived her agitation and even her tears. She patted her again upon the shoulder as she said:

"You are the only one worth playing for. Those others? Bah!" and she went shuffling and sidling on down the gallery toward her room.

But she was mistaken about "those others." Her playing had aroused a fever of enthusiasm. "What passion!" "What an artist!" "I have always said no one could play Chopin like Mademoiselle Reisz!" "That last prelude! Bon Dieu!° It shakes a man!"

It was growing late, and there was a general disposition to disband. But some one, perhaps it was Robert, thought of a bath at that mystic hour and under that mystic moon.

X

At all events Robert proposed it, and there was not a dissenting voice. There was not one but was ready to follow when he led the way. He did not lead the way, however, he directed the way; and he himself loitered behind with the lovers, who had betrayed a disposition to linger and hold themselves apart. He walked between them, whether with malicious or mischievous intent was not wholly clear, even to himself.

The Pontelliers and Ratignolles walked ahead; the women leaning upon the arms of their husbands. Edna could hear Robert's voice behind them, and could sometimes hear what he said. She wondered why he did not join them. It was unlike him not to. Of late he had sometimes held away from her for an entire day, redoubling his devotion upon the next and the next, as though to make up for hours that had been lost. She missed him the days when some pretext served to take

Bon Dieu!: Good God!

him away from her, just as one misses the sun on a cloudy day without having thought much about the sun when it was shining.

The people walked in little groups toward the beach. They talked and laughed; some of them sang. There was a band playing down at Klein's hotel, and the strains reached them faintly, tempered by the distance. There were strange, rare odors abroad—a tangle of the sea smell and of weeds and damp, new-plowed earth, mingled with the heavy perfume of a field of white blossoms somewhere near. But the night sat lightly upon the sea and the land. There was no weight of darkness; there were no shadows. The white light of the moon had fallen upon the world like the mystery and the softness of sleep.

Most of them walked into the water as though into a native element. The sea was quiet now, and swelled lazily in broad billows that melted into one another and did not break except upon the beach in little foamy crests that coiled back like slow, white serpents.

Edna had attempted all summer to learn to swim. She had received instructions from both the men and women; in some instances from the children. Robert had pursued a system of lessons almost daily; and he was nearly at the point of discouragement in realizing the futility of his efforts. A certain ungovernable dread hung about her when in the water, unless there was a hand near by that might reach out and reassure her.

But that night she was like the little tottering, stumbling, clutching child, who of a sudden realizes its powers, and walks for the first time alone, boldly and with over-confidence. She could have shouted for joy. She did shout for joy, as with a sweeping stroke or two she lifted her body to the surface of the water.

A feeling of exultation overtook her, as if some power of significant import had been given her to control the working of her body and her soul. She grew daring and reckless, overestimating her strength. She wanted to swim far out, where no woman had swum before.

Her unlooked-for achievement was the subject of wonder, applause, and admiration. Each one congratulated himself that his special teachings had accomplished this desired end.

"How easy it is!" she thought. "It is nothing," she said aloud; "why did I not discover before that it was nothing. Think of the time I have lost splashing about like a baby!" She would not join the groups in their sports and bouts, but intoxicated with her newly conquered power, she swam out alone.

She turned her face seaward to gather in an impression of space and solitude, which the vast expanse of water, meeting and melting with the moonlit sky, conveyed to her excited fancy. As she swam she seemed to be reaching out for the unlimited in which to lose herself.

Once she turned and looked toward the shore, toward the people she had left there. She had not gone any great distance—that is, what would have been a great distance for an experienced swimmer. But to her unaccustomed vision the stretch of water behind her assumed the aspect of a barrier which her unaided strength would never be able to overcome.

A quick vision of death smote her soul, and for a second of time appalled and enfeebled her senses. But by an effort she rallied her staggering faculties and managed to regain the land.

She made no mention of her encounter with death and her flash of terror, except to say to her husband, "I thought I should have perished out there alone."

"You were not so very far, my dear; I was watching you," he told her.

Edna went at once to the bath-house, and she had put on her dry clothes and was ready to return home before the others had left the water. She started to walk away alone. They all called to her and shouted to her. She waved a dissenting hand, and went on, paying no further heed to their renewed cries which sought to detain her.

"Sometimes I am tempted to think that Mrs. Pontellier is capricious," said Madame Lebrun, who was amusing herself immensely and feared that Edna's abrupt departure might put an end to the pleasure.

"I know she is," assented Mr. Pontellier; "sometimes, not often."

Edna had not traversed a quarter of the distance on her way home before she was overtaken by Robert.

"Did you think I was afraid?" she asked him, without a shade of annoyance.

"No; I knew you weren't afraid."

"Then why did you come? Why didn't you stay out there with the others?"

"I never thought of it."

"Thought of what?"

"Of anything. What difference does it make?"

"I'm very tired," she uttered, complainingly.

"I know you are."

"You don't know anything about it. Why should you know? I never was so exhausted in my life. But it isn't unpleasant. A thousand emotions have swept through me to-night. I don't comprehend half of them. Don't mind what I'm saying; I am just thinking aloud. I wonder if I shall ever be stirred again as Mademoiselle Reisz's playing moved me to-night. I wonder if any night on earth will ever again be like this one.

It is like a night in a dream. The people about me are like some uncanny, half-human beings. There must be spirits abroad to-night."

"There are," whispered Robert. "Didn't you know this was the twenty-eighth of August?"

"The twenty-eighth of August?"

"Yes. On the twenty-eighth of August, at the hour of midnight, and if the moon is shining—the moon must be shining—a spirit that has haunted these shores for ages rises up from the Gulf. With its own penetrating vision the spirit seeks some one mortal worthy to hold him company, worthy of being exalted for a few hours into realms of the semi-celestials. His search has always hitherto been fruitless, and he has sunk back, disheartened, into the sea. But to-night he found Mrs. Pontellier. Perhaps he will never wholly release her from the spell. Perhaps she will never again suffer a poor, unworthy earthling to walk in the shadow of her divine presence."

"Don't banter me," she said, wounded at what appeared to be his flippancy. He did not mind the entreaty, but the tone with its delicate note of pathos was like a reproach. He could not explain; he could not tell her that he had penetrated her mood and understood. He said nothing except to offer her his arm, for, by her own admission, she was exhausted. She had been walking alone with her arms hanging limp, letting her white skirts trail along the dewy path. She took his arm, but did not lean upon it. She let her hand lie listlessly, as though her thoughts were elsewhere—somewhere in advance of her body, and she was striving to overtake them.

Robert assisted her into the hammock which swung from the post before her door out to the trunk of a tree.

"Will you stay out here and wait for Mr. Pontellier?" he asked.

"I'll stay out here. Good-night."

"Shall I get you a pillow?"

"There's one here," she said, feeling about, for they were in the shadow.

"It must be soiled; the children have been tumbling it about."

"No matter." And having discovered the pillow, she adjusted it beneath her head. She extended herself in the hammock with a deep breath of relief. She was not a supercilious or an over-dainty woman. She was not much given to reclining in the hammock, and when she did so it was with no cat-like suggestion of voluptuous ease, but with a beneficent repose which seemed to invade her whole body.

"Shall I stay with you till Mr. Pontellier comes?" asked Robert, seating himself on the outer edge of one of the steps and taking hold of the hammock rope which was fastened to the post.

"If you wish. Don't swing the hammock. Will you get my white shawl which I left on the window-sill over at the house?"

"Are you chilly?"

"No; but I shall be presently."

"Presently?" he laughed. "Do you know what time it is? How long are you going to stay out here?"

"I don't know. Will you get the shawl?"

"Of course I will," he said, rising. He went over to the house, walking along the grass. She watched his figure pass in and out of the strips of moonlight. It was past midnight. It was very quiet.

When he returned with the shawl she took it and kept it in her hand. She did not put it around her.

"Did you say I should stay till Mr. Pontellier came back?"

"I said you might if you wished to."

He seated himself again and rolled a cigarette, which he smoked in silence. Neither did Mrs. Pontellier speak. No multitude of words could have been more significant than those moments of silence, or more pregnant with the first-felt throbbings of desire.

When the voices of the bathers were heard approaching, Robert said good-night. She did not answer him. He thought she was asleep. Again she watched his figure pass in and out of the strips of moonlight as he walked away.

XI

"What are you doing out here, Edna? I thought I should find you in bed," said her husband, when he discovered her lying there. He had walked up with Madame Lebrun and left her at the house. His wife did not reply.

"Are you asleep?" he asked, bending down close to look at her.

"No." Her eyes gleamed bright and intense, with no sleepy shadows, as they looked into his.

"Do you know it is past one o'clock? Come on," and he mounted the steps and went into their room.

"Edna!" called Mr. Pontellier from within, after a few moments had gone by.

"Don't wait for me," she answered. He thrust his head through the door.

"You will take cold out there," he said, irritably. "What folly is this? Why don't you come in?"

"It isn't cold; I have my shawl."

"The mosquitoes will devour you."

"There are no mosquitoes."

She heard him moving about the room; every sound indicating impatience and irritation. Another time she would have gone in at his request. She would, through habit, have yielded to his desire; not with any sense of submission or obedience to his compelling wishes, but unthinkingly, as we walk, move, sit, stand, go through the daily treadmill of the life which has been portioned out to us.

"Edna, dear, are you not coming in soon?" he asked again, this time fondly, with a note of entreaty.

"No; I am going to stay out here."

"This is more than folly," he blurted out. "I can't permit you to stay out there all night. You must come in the house instantly."

With a writhing motion she settled herself more securely in the hammock. She perceived that her will had blazed up, stubborn and resistant. She could not at that moment have done other than denied and resisted. She wondered if her husband had ever spoken to her like that before, and if she had submitted to his command. Of course she had; she remembered that she had. But she could not realize why or how she should have yielded, feeling as she then did.

"Léonce, go to bed," she said. "I mean to stay out here. I don't wish to go in, and I don't intend to. Don't speak to me like that again; I shall not answer you."

Mr. Pontellier had prepared for bed, but he slipped on an extra garment. He opened a bottle of wine, of which he kept a small and select supply in a buffet of his own. He drank a glass of the wine and went out on the gallery and offered a glass to his wife. She did not wish any. He drew up the rocker, hoisted his slippered feet on the rail, and proceeded to smoke a cigar. He smoked two cigars; then he went inside and drank another glass of wine. Mrs. Pontellier again declined to accept a glass when it was offered to her. Mr. Pontellier once more seated himself with elevated feet, and after a reasonable interval of time smoked some more cigars.

Edna began to feel like one who awakens gradually out of a dream, a delicious, grotesque, impossible dream, to feel again the realities pressing into her soul. The physical need for sleep began to overtake her; the exuberance which had sustained and exalted her spirit left her helpless and yielding to the conditions which crowded her in.

The stillest hour of the night had come, the hour before dawn, when the world seems to hold its breath. The moon hung low, and had turned from silver to copper in the sleeping sky. The old owl no longer hooted, and the water-oaks had ceased to moan as they bent their heads.

Edna arose, cramped from lying so long and still in the hammock. She tottered up the steps, clutching feebly at the post before passing into the house.

"Are you coming in, Léonce?" she asked, turning her face toward her husband.

"Yes, dear," he answered, with a glance following a misty puff of smoke. "Just as soon as I have finished my cigar."

XII

She slept but a few hours. They were troubled and feverish hours, disturbed with dreams that were intangible, that eluded her, leaving only an impression upon her half-awakened senses of something unattainable. She was up and dressed in the cool of the early morning. The air was invigorating and steadied somewhat her faculties. However, she was not seeking refreshment or help from any source, either external or from within. She was blindly following whatever impulse moved her, as if she had placed herself in alien hands for direction, and freed her soul of responsibility.

Most of the people at this early hour were still in bed and asleep. A few, who intended to go over to the *Chênière* for mass, were moving about. The lovers, who had laid their plans the night before, were already strolling toward the wharf. The lady in black, with her Sunday prayer-book, velvet and gold-clasped, and her Sunday silver beads, was following them at no great distance. Old Monsieur Farival was up, and was more than half inclined to do anything that suggested itself. He put on his big straw hat, and taking his umbrella from the stand in the hall, followed the lady in black, never overtaking her.

The little negro girl who worked Madame Lebrun's sewing-machine was sweeping the galleries with long, absent-minded strokes of the broom. Edna sent her up into the house to awaken Robert.

"Tell him I am going to the *Chênière*. The boat is ready; tell him to hurry."

He had soon joined her. She had never sent for him before. She had never asked for him. She had never seemed to want him before.

She did not appear conscious that she had done anything unusual in commanding his presence. He was apparently equally unconscious of anything extraordinary in the situation. But his face was suffused with a quiet glow when he met her.

They went together back to the kitchen to drink coffee. There was no time to wait for any nicety of service. They stood outside the window and the cook passed them their coffee and a roll, which they drank and ate from the window-sill. Edna said it tasted good. She had not thought of coffee nor of anything. He told her he had often noticed that she lacked forethought.

"Wasn't it enough to think of going to the *Chênière* and waking you up?" she laughed. "Do I have to think of everything?—as Léonce says when he's in a bad humor. I don't blame him; he'd never be in a bad humor if it weren't for me." They took a short cut across the sands. At a distance they could see the curious procession moving toward the wharf—the lovers, shoulder to shoulder, creeping; the lady in black, gaining steadily upon them; old Monsieur Farival, losing ground inch by inch, and a young barefooted Spanish girl, with a red kerchief on her head and a basket on her arm, bringing up the rear.

Robert knew the girl, and he talked to her a little in the boat. No one present understood what they said. Her name was Mariequita. She had a round, sly, piquant face and pretty black eyes. Her hands were small, and she kept them folded over the handle of her basket. Her feet were broad and coarse. She did not strive to hide them. Edna looked at her feet, and noticed the sand and slime between her brown toes.

Beaudelet grumbled because Mariequita was there, taking up so much room. In reality he was annoyed at having old Monsieur Farival, who considered himself the better sailor of the two. But he would not quarrel with so old a man as Monsieur Farival, so he quarreled with Mariequita. The girl was deprecatory at one moment, appealing to Robert. She was saucy the next, moving her head up and down, making "eyes" at Robert and making "mouths" at Beaudelet.

The lovers were all alone. They saw nothing, they heard nothing. The lady in black was counting her beads for the third time. Old Monsieur Farival talked incessantly of what he knew about handling a boat, and of what Beaudelet did not know on the same subject.

Edna liked it all. She looked Mariequita up and down, from her ugly brown toes to her pretty black eyes, and back again.

"Why does she look at me like that?" inquired the girl of Robert.

"Maybe she thinks you are pretty. Shall I ask her?"

"No. Is she your sweetheart?"

"She's a married lady, and has two children."

"Oh! well! Francisco ran away with Sylvano's wife, who had four children. They took all his money and one of the children and stole his boat."

"Shut up!"

"Does she understand?"

"Oh, hush!"

"Are those two married over there—leaning on each other?"

"Of course not," laughed Robert.

"Of course not," echoed Mariequita, with a serious, confirmatory bob of the head.

The sun was high up and beginning to bite. The swift breeze seemed to Edna to bury the sting of it into the pores of her face and hands. Robert held his umbrella over her.

As they went cutting sidewise through the water, the sails bellied taut, with the wind filling and overflowing them. Old Monsieur Farival laughed sardonically at something as he looked at the sails, and Beaudelet swore at the old man under his breath.

Sailing across the bay to the *Chênière Caminada,* Edna felt as if she were being borne away from some anchorage which had held her fast, whose chains had been loosening—had snapped the night before when the mystic spirit was abroad, leaving her free to drift whithersoever she chose to set her sails. Robert spoke to her incessantly; he no longer noticed Mariequita. The girl had shrimps in her bamboo basket. They were covered with Spanish moss. She beat the moss down impatiently, and muttered to herself sullenly.

"Let us go to Grande Terre to-morrow?" said Robert in a low voice.

"What shall we do there?"

"Climb up the hill to the old fort and look at the little wriggling gold snakes, and watch the lizards sun themselves."

She gazed away toward Grande Terre and thought she would like to be alone there with Robert, in the sun, listening to the ocean's roar and watching the slimy lizards writhe in and out among the ruins of the old fort.

"And the next day or the next we can sail to the Bayou Brulow," he went on.

"What shall we do there?"

"Anything—cast bait for fish."

"No; we'll go back to Grande Terre. Let the fish alone."

"We'll go wherever you like," he said, "I'll have Tonie come over and help me patch and trim my boat. We shall not need Beaudelet nor any one. Are you afraid of the pirogue?"

"Oh, no."

"Then I'll take you some night in the pirogue when the moon shines. Maybe your Gulf spirit will whisper to you in which of these islands the treasures are hidden—direct you to the very spot, perhaps."

"And in a day we should be rich!" she laughed. "I'd give it all to you, the pirate gold and every bit of treasure we could dig up. I think you would know how to spend it. Pirate gold isn't a thing to be hoarded or utilized. It is something to squander and throw to the four winds, for the fun of seeing the golden specks fly."

"We'd share it, and scatter it together," he said. His face flushed.

They all went together up to the quaint little Gothic church of Our Lady of Lourdes, gleaming all brown and yellow with paint in the sun's glare.

Only Beaudelet remained behind, tinkering at his boat, and Mariequita walked away with her basket of shrimps, casting a look of childish ill-humor and reproach at Robert from the corner of her eye.

XIII

A feeling of oppression and drowsiness overcame Edna during the service. Her head began to ache, and the lights on the altar swayed before her eyes. Another time she might have made an effort to regain her composure; but her one thought was to quit the stifling atmosphere of the church and reach the open air. She arose, climbing over Robert's feet with a muttered apology. Old Monsieur Farival, flurried, curious, stood up, but upon seeing that Robert had followed Mrs. Pontellier, he sank back into his seat. He whispered an anxious inquiry of the lady in black, who did not notice him or reply, but kept her eyes fastened upon the pages of her velvet prayer-book.

"I felt giddy and almost overcome," Edna said, lifting her hands instinctively to her head and pushing her straw hat up from her forehead. "I couldn't have stayed through the service." They were outside in the shadow of the church. Robert was full of solicitude.

"It was folly to have thought of going in the first place, let alone staying. Come over to Madame Antoine's; you can rest there." He took her arm and led her away, looking anxiously and continuously down into her face.

How still it was, with only the voice of the sea whispering through the reeds that grew in the salt-water pools! The long line of little gray, weather-beaten houses nestled peacefully among the orange trees. It must always have been God's day on that low, drowsy island, Edna thought. They stopped, leaning over a jagged fence made of sea-drift, to ask for water. A youth, a mild-faced Acadian,° was drawing water from the cistern, which was nothing more than a rusty buoy, with an opening on one side, sunk in the ground. The water which the youth handed to them in a tin pail was not cold to taste, but it was cool to her heated face, and it greatly revived and refreshed her.

Madam Antoine's cot was at the far end of the village. She welcomed them with all the native hospitality, as she would have opened her door to let the sunlight in. She was fat, and walked heavily and clumsily across the floor. She could speak no English, but when Robert made her understand that the lady who accompanied him was ill and desired to rest, she was all eagerness to make Edna feel at home and to dispose of her comfortably.

The whole place was immaculately clean, and the big, four-posted bed, snow-white, invited one to repose. It stood in a small side room which looked out across a narrow grass plot toward the shed, where there was a disabled boat lying keel upward.

Madame Antoine had not gone to mass. Her son Tonie had, but she supposed he would soon be back, and she invited Robert to be seated and wait for him. But he went and sat outside the door and smoked. Madame Antoine busied herself in the large front room preparing dinner. She was boiling mullets over a few red coals in the huge fireplace.

Edna, left alone in the little side room, loosened her clothes, removing the greater part of them. She bathed her face, her neck and arms in the basin that stood between the windows. She took off her shoes and stockings and stretched herself in the very center of the high, white bed. How luxurious it felt to rest thus in a strange, quaint bed, with its sweet country odor of laurel lingering about the sheets and mattress! She stretched her strong limbs that ached a little. She ran her fingers through her loosened hair for a while. She looked at her round arms as she held them straight up and rubbed them one after the other, observing closely, as if it were something she saw for the first time, the fine,

Acadian: A descendant of French Canadians expelled by the British in 1755 from Acadia (Nova Scotia). Acadians (also called "Cajuns") settled along the rivers and bayous of southern Louisiana.

firm quality and texture of her flesh. She clasped her hands easily above her head, and it was thus she fell asleep.

She slept lightly at first, half awake and drowsily attentive to the things about her. She could hear Madame Antoine's heavy, scraping tread as she walked back and forth on the sanded floor. Some chickens were clucking outside the windows, scratching for bits of gravel in the grass. Later she half heard the voices of Robert and Tonie talking under the shed. She did not stir. Even her eyelids rested numb and heavily over her sleepy eyes. The voices went on—Tonie's slow, Acadian drawl, Robert's quick, soft, smooth French. She understood French imperfectly unless directly addressed, and the voices were only part of the other drowsy, muffled sounds lulling her senses.

When Edna awoke it was with the conviction that she had slept long and soundly. The voices were hushed under the shed. Madame Antoine's step was no longer to be heard in the adjoining room. Even the chickens had gone elsewhere to scratch and cluck. The mosquito bar was drawn over her; the old woman had come in while she slept and let down the bar. Edna arose quietly from the bed, and looking between the curtains of the window, she saw by the slanting rays of the sun that the afternoon was far advanced. Robert was out there under the shed, reclining in the shade against the sloping keel of the overturned boat. He was reading from a book. Tonie was no longer with him. She wondered what had become of the rest of the party. She peeped out at him two or three times as she stood washing herself in the little basin between the windows.

Madame Antoine had laid some coarse, clean towels upon a chair, and had placed a box of *poudre de riz*° within easy reach. Edna dabbed the powder upon her nose and cheeks as she looked at herself closely in the little distorted mirror which hung on the wall above the basin. Her eyes were bright and wide awake and her face glowed.

When she had completed her toilet she walked into the adjoining room. She was very hungry. No one was there. But there was a cloth spread upon the table that stood against the wall, and a cover was laid for one, with a crusty brown loaf and a bottle of wine beside the plate. Edna bit a piece from the brown loaf, tearing it with her strong, white teeth. She poured some of the wine into the glass and drank it down. Then she went softly out of doors, and plucking an orange from the

poudre de riz: Face powder.

low-hanging bough of a tree, threw it at Robert, who did not know she was awake and up.

An illumination broke over his whole face when he saw her and joined her under the orange tree.

"How many years have I slept?" she inquired. "The whole island seems changed. A new race of beings must have sprung up, leaving only you and me as past relics. How many ages ago did Madame Antoine and Tonie die? and when did our people from Grand Isle disappear from the earth?"

He familiarly adjusted a ruffle upon her shoulder.

"You have slept precisely one hundred years. I was left here to guard your slumbers; and for one hundred years I have been out under the shed reading a book. The only evil I couldn't prevent was to keep a broiled fowl from drying up."

"If it has turned to stone, still will I eat it," said Edna, moving with him into the house. "But really, what has become of Monsieur Farival and the others?"

"Gone hours ago. When they found that you were sleeping they thought it best not to awake you. Any way, I wouldn't have let them. What was I here for?"

"I wonder if Léonce will be uneasy!" she speculated, as she seated herself at table.

"Of course not; he knows you are with me," Robert replied, as he busied himself among sundry pans and covered dishes which had been left standing on the hearth.

"Where are Madame Antoine and her son?" asked Edna.

"Gone to Vespers, and to visit some friends, I believe. I am to take you back in Tonie's boat whenever you are ready to go."

He stirred the smoldering ashes till the broiled fowl began to sizzle afresh. He served her with no mean repast, dripping the coffee anew and sharing it with her. Madame Antoine had cooked little else than the mullets, but while Edna slept Robert had foraged the island. He was childishly gratified to discover her appetite, and to see the relish with which she ate the food which he had procured for her.

"Shall we go right away?" she asked, after draining her glass and brushing together the crumbs of the crusty loaf.

"The sun isn't as low as it will be in two hours," he answered.

"The sun will be gone in two hours."

"Well, let it go; who cares!"

They waited a good while under the orange trees, till Madame Antoine came back, panting, waddling, with a thousand apologies to explain her absence. Tonie did not dare to return. He was shy, and would not willingly face any woman except his mother.

It was very pleasant to stay there under the orange trees, while the sun dipped lower and lower, turning the western sky to flaming copper and gold. The shadows lengthened and crept out like stealthy, grotesque monsters across the grass.

Edna and Robert both sat upon the ground—that is, he lay upon the ground beside her, occasionally picking at the hem of her muslin gown.

Madame Antoine seated her fat body, broad and squat, upon a bench beside the door. She had been talking all the afternoon, and had wound herself up to the story-telling pitch.

And what stories she told them! But twice in her life she had left the *Chênière Caminada,* and then for the briefest span. All her years she had squatted and waddled there upon the island, gathering legends of the Baratarians and the sea. The night came on, with the moon to lighten it. Edna could hear the whispering voices of dead men and the click of muffled gold.

When she and Robert stepped into Tonie's boat, with the red lateen sail, misty spirit forms were prowling in the shadows and among the reeds, and upon the water were phantom ships, speeding to cover.

XIV

The youngest boy, Etienne, had been very naughty, Madame Ratignolle said, as she delivered him into the hands of his mother. He had been unwilling to go to bed and had made a scene; whereupon she had taken charge of him and pacified him as well as she could. Raoul had been in bed and asleep for two hours.

The youngster was in his long white nightgown, that kept tripping him up as Madame Ratignolle led him along by the hand. With the other chubby fist he rubbed his eyes, which were heavy with sleep and ill humor. Edna took him in her arms, and seating herself in the rocker, began to coddle and caress him, calling him all manner of tender names, soothing him to sleep.

It was not more than nine o'clock. No one had yet gone to bed but the children.

Léonce had been very uneasy at first, Madame Ratignolle said, and had wanted to start at once for the *Chênière*. But Monsieur Farival had assured him that his wife was only overcome with sleep and fatigue, that Tonie would bring her safely back later in the day; and he had thus been dissuaded from crossing the bay. He had gone over to Klein's, looking up some cotton broker whom he wished to see in regard to securities, exchanges, stocks, bonds, or something of the sort, Madame Ratignolle did not remember what. He said he would not remain away late. She herself was suffering from heat and oppression, she said. She carried a bottle of salts and a large fan. She would not consent to remain with Edna, for Monsieur Ratignolle was alone, and he detested above all things to be left alone.

When Etienne had fallen asleep Edna bore him into the back room, and Robert went and lifted the mosquito bar that she might lay the child comfortably in his bed. The quadroon had vanished. When they emerged from the cottage Robert bade Edna good-night.

"Do you know we have been together the whole livelong day, Robert—since early this morning?" she said at parting.

"All but the hundred years when you were sleeping. Good-night."

He pressed her hand and went away in the direction of the beach. He did not join any of the others, but walked alone toward the Gulf.

Edna stayed outside, awaiting her husband's return. She had no desire to sleep or to retire; nor did she feel like going over to sit with the Ratignolles, or to join Madame Lebrun and a group whose animated voices reached her as they sat in conversation before the house. She let her mind wander back over her stay at Grand Isle; and she tried to discover wherein this summer had been different from any and every other summer of her life. She could only realize that she herself—her present self—was in some way different from the other self. That she was seeing with different eyes and making the acquaintance of new conditions in herself that colored and changed her environment, she did not yet suspect.

She wondered why Robert had gone away and left her. It did not occur to her to think he might have grown tired of being with her the livelong day. She was not tired, and she felt that he was not. She regretted that he had gone. It was so much more natural to have him stay when he was not absolutely required to leave her.

As Edna waited for her husband she sang low a little song that Robert had sung as they crossed the bay. It began with "Ah! *Si tu savais,*" and every verse ended with "*si tu savais.*"°

si tu savais: If you knew.

Robert's voice was not pretentious. It was musical and true. The voice, the notes, the whole refrain haunted her memory.

XV

When Edna entered the dining-room one evening a little late, as was her habit, an unusually animated conversation seemed to be going on. Several persons were talking at once, and Victor's voice was predominating, even over that of his mother. Edna had returned late from her bath, had dressed in some haste, and her face was flushed. Her head, set off by her dainty white gown, suggested a rich, rare blossom. She took her seat at table between old Monsieur Farival and Madame Ratignolle.

As she seated herself and was about to begin to eat her soup, which had been served when she entered the room, several persons informed her simultaneously that Robert was going to Mexico. She laid her spoon down and looked about her bewildered. He had been with her, reading to her all the morning, and had never even mentioned such a place as Mexico. She had not seen him during the afternoon; she had heard some one say he was at the house, upstairs with his mother. This she had thought nothing of, though she was surprised when he did not join her later in the afternoon, when she went down to the beach.

She looked across at him, where he sat beside Madame Lebrun, who presided. Edna's face was a blank picture of bewilderment, which she never thought of disguising. He lifted his eyebrows with the pretext of a smile as he returned her glance. He looked embarrassed and uneasy.

"When is he going?" she asked of everybody in general, as if Robert were not there to answer for himself.

"To-night!" "This very evening!" "Did you ever!" "What possesses him!" were some of the replies she gathered, uttered simultaneously in French and English.

"Impossible!" she exclaimed. "How can a person start off from Grand Isle to Mexico at a moment's notice, as if he were going over to Klein's or to the wharf or down to the beach?"

"I said all along I was going to Mexico; I've been saying so for years!" cried Robert, in an excited and irritable tone, with the air of a man defending himself against a swarm of stinging insects.

Madame Lebrun knocked on the table with her knife handle.

"Please let Robert explain why he is going, and why he is going to-night," she called out. "Really, this table is getting to be more and more like Bedlam every day, with everybody talking at once. Sometimes—I hope God will forgive me—but positively, sometimes I wish Victor would lose the power of speech."

Victor laughed sardonically as he thanked his mother for her holy wish, of which he failed to see the benefit to anybody, except that it might afford her a more ample opportunity and license to talk herself.

Monsieur Farival thought that Victor should have been taken out in mid-ocean in his earliest youth and drowned. Victor thought there would be more logic in thus disposing of old people with an established claim for making themselves universally obnoxious. Madame Lebrun grew a trifle hysterical; Robert called his brother some sharp, hard names.

"There's nothing much to explain, mother," he said; though he explained, nevertheless—looking chiefly at Edna—that he could only meet the gentleman whom he intended to join at Vera Cruz by taking such and such a steamer, which left New Orleans on such a day; that Beaudelet was going out with his lugger-load of vegetables that night, which gave him an opportunity of reaching the city and making his vessel in time.

"But when did you make up your mind to all this?" demanded Monsieur Farival.

"This afternoon," returned Robert, with a shade of annoyance.

"At what time this afternoon?" persisted the old gentleman, with nagging determination, as if he were cross-questioning a criminal in a court of justice.

"At four o'clock this afternoon, Monsieur Farival," Robert replied, in a high voice and with a lofty air, which reminded Edna of some gentleman on the stage.

She had forced herself to eat most of her soup, and now she was picking the flaky bits of a *court bouillon*° with her fork.

The lovers were profiting by the general conversation on Mexico to speak in whispers of matters which they rightly considered were interesting to no one but themselves. The lady in black had once received a pair of prayer-beads of curious workmanship from Mexico, with very special indulgence attached to them, but she had never been able to ascertain whether the indulgence extended outside the Mexican border. Father Fochel of the Cathedral had attempted to explain it; but he had not done so to her satisfaction. And she begged that Robert would interest himself, and discover, if possible, whether she was entitled to

court bouillon: Fish poached in broth.

the indulgence accompanying the remarkably curious Mexican prayer-beads.

Madame Ratignolle hoped that Robert would exercise extreme caution in dealing with the Mexicans, who, she considered, were a treacherous people, unscrupulous and revengeful. She trusted she did them no injustice in thus condemning them as a race. She had known personally but one Mexican, who made and sold excellent tamales, and whom she would have trusted implicitly, so soft-spoken was he. One day he was arrested for stabbing his wife. She never knew whether he had been hanged or not.

Victor had grown hilarious, and was attempting to tell an anecdote about a Mexican girl who served chocolate one winter in a restaurant in Dauphine Street. No one would listen to him but old Monsieur Farival, who went into convulsions over the droll story.

Edna wondered if they had all gone mad, to be talking and clamoring at that rate. She herself could think of nothing to say about Mexico or the Mexicans.

"At what time do you leave?" she asked Robert.

"At ten," he told her. "Beaudelet wants to wait for the moon."

"Are you all ready to go?"

"Quite ready. I shall only take a hand-bag, and shall pack my trunk in the city."

He turned to answer some question put to him by his mother, and Edna, having finished her black coffee, left the table.

She went directly to her room. The little cottage was close and stuffy after leaving the outer air. But she did not mind; there appeared to be a hundred different things demanding her attention indoors. She began to set the toilet-stand to rights, grumbling at the negligence of the quadroon, who was in the adjoining room putting the children to bed. She gathered together stray garments that were hanging on the backs of chairs, and put each where it belonged in closet or bureau drawer. She changed her gown for a more comfortable and commodious wrapper. She rearranged her hair, combing and brushing it with unusual energy. Then she went in and assisted the quadroon in getting the boys to bed.

They were very playful and inclined to talk—to do anything but lie quiet and go to sleep. Edna sent the quadroon away to her supper and told her she need not return. Then she sat and told the children a story. Instead of soothing it excited them, and added to their wakefulness. She left them in heated argument, speculating about the conclusion of the tale which their mother promised to finish the following night.

The little black girl came in to say that Madame Lebrun would like to have Mrs. Pontellier go and sit with them over at the house till Mr. Robert went away. Edna returned answer that she had already undressed, that she did not feel quite well, but perhaps she would go over to the house later. She started to dress again, and got as far advanced as to remove her *peignoir*. But changing her mind once more she resumed the *peignoir*, and went outside and sat down before her door. She was overheated and irritable, and fanned herself energetically for a while. Madame Ratignolle came down to discover what was the matter.

"All that noise and confusion at the table must have upset me," replied Edna, "and moreover, I hate shocks and surprises. The idea of Robert starting off in such a ridiculously sudden and dramatic way! As if it were a matter of life and death! Never saying a word about it all morning when he was with me."

"Yes," agreed Madame Ratignolle. "I think it was showing us all—you especially—very little consideration. It wouldn't have surprised me in any of the others; those Lebruns are all given to heroics. But I must say I should never have expected such a thing from Robert. Are you not coming down? Come on, dear; it doesn't look friendly."

"No," said Edna, a little sullenly. "I can't go to the trouble of dressing again; I don't feel like it."

"You needn't dress; you look all right; fasten a belt around your waist. Just look at me!"

"No," persisted Edna; "but you go on. Madame Lebrun might be offended if we both stayed away."

Madame Ratignolle kissed Edna good-night, and went away, being in truth rather desirous of joining in the general and animated conversation which was still in progress concerning Mexico and the Mexicans.

Somewhat later Robert came up, carrying his hand-bag.

"Aren't you feeling well?" he asked.

"Oh, well enough. Are you going right away?"

He lit a match and looked at his watch. "In twenty minutes," he said. The sudden and brief flare of the match emphasized the darkness for a while. He sat down upon a stool which the children had left out on the porch.

"Get a chair," said Edna.

"This will do," he replied. He put on his soft hat and nervously took it off again, and wiping his face with his handkerchief, complained of the heat.

"Take the fan," said Edna, offering it to him.

"Oh, no! Thank you. It does no good; you have to stop fanning some time, and feel all the more uncomfortable afterward."

"That's one of the ridiculous things which men always say. I have never known one to speak otherwise of fanning. How long will you be gone?"

"Forever, perhaps. I don't know. It depends upon a good many things."

"Well, in case it shouldn't be forever, how long will it be?"

"I don't know."

"This seems to me perfectly preposterous and uncalled for. I don't like it. I don't understand your motive for silence and mystery, never saying a word to me about it this morning." He remained silent, not offering to defend himself. He only said, after a moment:

"Don't part from me in an ill-humor. I never knew you to be out of patience with me before."

"I don't want to part in any ill-humor," she said. "But can't you understand? I've grown used to seeing you, to having you with me all the time, and your action seems unfriendly, even unkind. You don't even offer an excuse for it. Why, I was planning to be together, thinking of how pleasant it would be to see you in the city next winter."

"So was I," he blurted. "Perhaps that's the—" He stood up suddenly and held out his hand. "Good-by, my dear Mrs. Pontellier; good-by. You won't—I hope you won't completely forget me." She clung to his hand, striving to detain him.

"Write to me when you get there, won't you, Robert?" she entreated.

"I will, thank you. Good-by."

How unlike Robert! The merest acquaintance would have said something more emphatic than "I will, thank you; good-by," to such a request.

He had evidently already taken leave of the people over at the house, for he descended the steps and went to join Beaudelet, who was out there with an oar across his shoulder waiting for Robert. They walked away in the darkness. She could only hear Beaudelet's voice; Robert had apparently not even spoken a word of greeting to his companion.

Edna bit her handkerchief convulsively, striving to hold back and to hide, even from herself as she would have hidden from another, the emotion which was troubling—tearing—her. Her eyes were brimming with tears.

For the first time she recognized anew the symptoms of infatuation which she had felt incipiently as a child, as a girl in her earliest teens, and later as a young woman. The recognition did not lessen the reality, the poignancy of the revelation by any suggestion or promise of instability. The past was nothing to her; offered no lesson which she was willing to heed. The future was a mystery which she never attempted to penetrate. The present alone was significant; was hers, to torture her as it was doing then with the biting conviction that she had lost that which she had held, that she had been denied that which her impassioned, newly awakened being demanded.

XVI

"Do you miss your friend greatly?" asked Mademoiselle Reisz one morning as she came creeping up behind Edna, who had just left her cottage on her way to the beach. She spent much of her time in the water since she had acquired finally the art of swimming. As their stay at Grand Isle drew near its close, she felt that she could not give too much time to a diversion which afforded her the only real pleasurable moments that she knew. When Mademoiselle Reisz came and touched her upon the shoulder and spoke to her, the woman seemed to echo the thought which was ever in Edna's mind; or, better, the feeling which constantly possessed her.

Robert's going had some way taken the brightness, the color, the meaning out of everything. The conditions of her life were in no way changed, but her whole existence was dulled, like a faded garment which seems to be no longer worth wearing. She sought him everywhere—in others whom she induced to talk about him. She went up in the mornings to Madame Lebrun's room, braving the clatter of the old sewing-machine. She sat there and chatted at intervals as Robert had done. She gazed around the room at the pictures and photographs hanging upon the wall, and discovered in some corner an old family album, which she examined with the keenest interest, appealing to Madame Lebrun for enlightenment concerning the many figures and faces which she discovered between its pages.

There was a picture of Madame Lebrun with Robert as a baby, seated in her lap, a round-faced infant with a fist in his mouth. The eyes alone in the baby suggested the man. And that was he also in kilts, at the age of five, wearing long curls and holding a whip in his hand. It made Edna laugh, and she laughed, too, at the portrait in his first long trousers; while another interested her, taken when he left for college, looking thin, long-faced, with eyes full of fire, ambition and great intentions. But there was no recent picture, none which suggested the

Robert who had gone away five days ago, leaving a void and wilderness behind him.

"Oh, Robert stopped having his pictures taken when he had to pay for them himself! He found wiser use for his money, he says," explained Madame Lebrun. She had a letter from him, written before he left New Orleans. Edna wished to see the letter, and Madam Lebrun told her to look for it either on the table or the dresser, or perhaps it was on the mantelpiece.

The letter was on the bookshelf. It possessed the greatest interest and attraction for Edna; the envelope, its size and shape, the post-mark, the handwriting. She examined every detail of the outside before opening it. There were only a few lines, setting forth that he would leave the city that afternoon, that he had packed his trunk in good shape, that he was well, and sent her his love and begged to be affectionately remembered to all. There was no special message to Edna except a postscript saying that if Mrs. Pontellier desired to finish the book which he had been reading to her, his mother would find it in his room, among other books there on the table. Edna experienced a pang of jealousy because he had written to his mother rather than to her.

Every one seemed to take for granted that she missed him. Even her husband, when he came down the Saturday following Robert's departure, expressed regret that he had gone.

"How do you get on without him, Edna?" he asked.

"It's very dull without him," she admitted. Mr. Pontellier had seen Robert in the city, and Edna asked him a dozen questions or more. Where had they met? On Carondelet Street, in the morning. They had gone "in" and had a drink and a cigar together. What had they talked about? Chiefly about his prospects in Mexico, which Mr. Pontellier thought were promising. How did he look? How did he seem—grave, or gay, or how? Quite cheerful, and wholly taken up with the idea of his trip, which Mr. Pontellier found altogether natural in a young fellow about to seek fortune and adventure in a strange, queer country.

Edna tapped her foot impatiently, and wondered why the children persisted in playing in the sun when they might be under the trees. She went down and led them out of the sun, scolding the quadroon for not being more attentive.

It did not strike her as in the least grotesque that she should be making of Robert the object of conversation and leading her husband to speak of him. The sentiment which she entertained for Robert in no way resembled that which she felt for her husband, or had ever felt, or ever expected to feel. She had all her life long been accustomed to harbor thoughts and emotions which never voiced themselves. They had never taken the form of struggles. They belonged to her and were her own, and she entertained the conviction that she had a right to them and that they concerned no one but herself. Edna had once told Madame Ratignolle that she would never sacrifice herself for her children, or for any one. Then had followed a rather heated argument; the two women did not appear to understand each other or to be talking the same language. Edna tried to appease her friend, to explain.

"I would give up the unessential; I would give my money, I would give my life for my children; but I wouldn't give myself. I can't make it more clear; it's only something which I am beginning to comprehend, which is revealing itself to me."

"I don't know what you would call the essential, or what you mean by the unessential," said Madame Ratignolle, cheerfully; "but a woman who would give her life for her children could do no more than that—your Bible tells you so. I'm sure I couldn't do more than that."

"Oh, yes you could!" laughed Edna.

She was not surprised at Mademoiselle Reisz's question the morning that lady, following her to the beach, tapped her on the shoulder and asked if she did not greatly miss her young friend.

"Oh, good morning, Mademoiselle; is it you? Why, of course I miss Robert. Are you going down to bathe?"

"Why should I go down to bathe at the very end of the season when I haven't been in the surf all summer," replied the woman, disagreeably.

"I beg your pardon," offered Edna, in some embarrassment, for she should have remembered that Mademoiselle Reisz's avoidance of the water had furnished a theme for much pleasantry. Some among them thought it was on account of her false hair, or the dread of getting the violets wet, while others attributed it to the natural aversion for water sometimes believed to accompany the artistic temperament. Mademoiselle offered Edna some chocolates in a paper bag, which she took from her pocket, by way of showing that she bore no ill feeling. She habitually ate chocolates for their sustaining quality; they contained much nutriment in small compass, she said. They saved her from starvation, as Madame Lebrun's table was utterly impossible; and no one save so impertinent a woman as Madame Lebrun could think of offering such food to people and requiring them to pay for it.

"She must feel very lonely without her son," said Edna, desiring to change the subject. "Her favorite son, too. It must have been quite hard to let him go."

Mademoiselle laughed maliciously.

"Her favorite son! Oh, dear! Who could have been imposing such a tale upon you? Aline Lebrun lives for Victor, and for Victor alone. She has spoiled him into the worthless creature he is. She worships him and the ground he walks on. Robert is very well in a way, to give up all the money he can earn to the family, and keep the barest pittance for himself. Favorite son, indeed! I miss the poor fellow myself, my dear. I liked to see him and to hear him about the place—the only Lebrun who is worth a pinch of salt. He comes to see me often in the city. I like to play to him. That Victor! hanging would be too good for him. It's a wonder Robert hasn't beaten him to death long ago."

"I thought he had great patience with his brother," offered Edna, glad to be talking about Robert, no matter what was said.

"Oh! he thrashed him well enough a year or two ago," said Mademoiselle. "It was about a Spanish girl, whom Victor considered that he had some sort of claim upon. He met Robert one day talking to the girl, or walking with her, or bathing with her, or carrying her basket—I don't remember what;—and he became so insulting and abusive that Robert gave him a thrashing on the spot that has kept him comparatively in order for a good while. It's about time he was getting another."

"Was her name Mariequita?" asked Edna.

"Mariequita—yes, that was it; Mariequita. I had forgotten. Oh, she's a sly one, and a bad one, that Mariequita!"

Edna looked down at Mademoiselle Reisz and wondered how she could have listened to her venom so long. For some reason she felt depressed, almost unhappy. She had not intended to go into the water; but she donned her bathing suit, and left Mademoiselle alone, seated under the shade of the children's tent. The water was growing cooler as the season advanced. Edna plunged and swam about with an abandon that thrilled and invigorated her. She remained a long time in the water, half hoping that Mademoiselle Reisz would not wait for her.

But Mademoiselle waited. She was very amiable during the walk back, and raved much over Edna's appearance in her bathing suit. She talked about music. She hoped that Edna would go to see her in the city, and wrote her address with the stub of a pencil on a piece of card which she found in her pocket.

"When do you leave?" asked Edna.

"Next Monday; and you?"

"The following week," answered Edna, adding, "It has been a pleasant summer, hasn't it, Mademoiselle?"

"Well," agreed Mademoiselle Reisz, with a shrug, "rather pleasant, if it hadn't been for the mosquitoes and the Farival twins."

XVII

The Pontelliers possessed a very charming home on Esplanade Street in New Orleans. It was a large, double cottage, with a broad front veranda, whose round, fluted colunns supported the sloping roof. The house was painted a dazzling white; the outside shutters, or jalousies, were green. In the yard, which was kept scrupulously neat, were flowers and plants of every description which flourishes in South Louisiana. Within doors the appointments were perfect after the conventional type. The softest carpets and rugs covered the floors; rich and tasteful draperies hung at doors and windows. There were paintings, selected with judgment and discrimination, upon the walls. The cut glass, the silver, the heavy damask which daily appeared upon the table were the envy of many women whose husbands were less generous than Mr. Pontellier.

Mr. Pontellier was very fond of walking about his house examining its various appointments and details, to see that nothing was amiss. He greatly valued his possessions, chiefly because they were his, and derived genuine pleasure from contemplating a painting, a statuette, a rare lace curtain—no matter what—after he had bought it and placed it among his household gods.

On Tuesday afternoons—Tuesday being Mrs. Pontellier's reception day—there was a constant stream of callers—women who came in carriages or in the street cars, or walked when the air was soft and distance permitted. A light-colored mulatto boy, in dress coat and bearing a diminutive silver tray for the reception of cards, admitted them. A maid, in white fluted cap, offered the callers liqueur, coffee, or chocolate, as they might desire. Mrs. Pontellier, attired in a handsome reception gown, remained in the drawing-room the entire afternoon receiving her visitors. Men sometimes called in the evening with their wives.

This had been the programme which Mrs. Pontellier had religiously followed since her marriage, six years before. Certain evenings during the week she and her husband attended the opera or sometimes the play.

Mr. Pontellier left his home in the mornings between nine and ten o'clock, and rarely returned before half-past six or seven in the evening—dinner being served at half-past seven.

He and his wife seated themselves at table one Tuesday evening, a few weeks after their return from Grand Isle. They were alone together. The boys were being put to bed; the patter of their bare, escaping feet could be heard occasionally, as well as the pursuing voice of the quadroon, lifted in mild protest and entreaty. Mrs. Pontellier did not wear her usual Tuesday reception gown; she was in ordinary house dress. Mr. Pontellier, who was observant about such things, noticed it, as he served the soup and handed it to the boy in waiting.

"Tired out, Edna? Whom did you have? Many callers?" he asked. He tasted his soup and began to season it with pepper, salt, vinegar, mustard—everything within reach.

"There were a good many," replied Edna, who was eating her soup with evident satisfaction. "I found their cards when I got home; I was out."

"Out!" exclaimed her husband, with something like genuine consternation in his voice as he laid down the vinegar cruet and looked at her through his glasses. "Why, what could have taken you out on Tuesday? What did you have to do?"

"Nothing. I simply felt like going out, and I went out."

"Well, I hope you left some suitable excuse," said her husband, somewhat appeased, as he added a dash of cayenne pepper to the soup.

"No, I left no excuse. I told Joe to say I was out, that was all."

"Why, my dear, I should think you'd understand by this time that people don't do such things; we've got to observe *les convenances*° if we ever expect to get on and keep up with the procession. If you felt that you had to leave home this afternoon, you should have left some suitable explanation for your absence.

"This soup is really impossible; it's strange that woman hasn't learned yet to make a decent soup. Any free-lunch stand in town serves a better one. Was Mrs. Belthrop here?"

"Bring the tray with the cards, Joe. I don't remember who was here.

The boy retired and returned after a moment, bringing the tiny silver tray, which was covered with ladies' visiting cards. He handed it to Mrs. Pontellier.

"Give it to Mr. Pontellier," she said.

Joe offered the tray to Mr. Pontellier, and removed the soup.

Mr. Pontellier scanned the names of his wife's callers, reading some of them aloud, with comments as he read.

les convenances: Proprieties; social conventions.

"'The Misses Delasidas.' I worked a big deal in futures for their father this morning; nice girls; it's time they were getting married. 'Mrs. Belthrop.' I tell you what it is, Edna; you can't afford to snub Mrs. Belthrop. Why, Belthrop could buy and sell us ten times over. His business is worth a good, round sum to me. You'd better write her a note. 'Mrs. James Highcamp.' Hugh! the less you have to do with Mrs. Highcamp, the better. 'Madame Laforcé.' Came all the way from Carrolton, too, poor old soul. 'Miss Wiggs,' 'Mrs. Eleanor Boltons.'" He pushed the cards aside.

"Mercy!" exclaimed Edna, who had been fuming. "Why are you taking the thing so seriously and making such a fuss over it?"

"I'm not making any fuss over it. But it's just such seeming trifles that we've got to take seriously; such things count."

The fish was scorched. Mr. Pontellier would not touch it. Edna said she did not mind a little scorched taste. The roast was in some way not to his fancy, and he did not like the manner in which the vegetables were served.

"It seems to me," he said, "we spend money enough in this house to procure at least one meal a day which a man could eat and retain his self-respect."

"You used to think the cook was a treasure," returned Edna, indifferently.

"Perhaps she was when she first came; but cooks are only human. They need looking after, like any other class of persons that you employ. Suppose I didn't look after the clerks in my office, just let them run things their own way; they'd soon make a nice mess of me and my business."

"Where are you going?" asked Edna, seeing that her husband arose from table without having eaten a morsel except a taste of the highly-seasoned soup.

"I'm going to get my dinner at the club. Good night." He went into the hall, took his hat and stick from the stand, and left the house.

She was somewhat familiar with such scenes. They had often made her very unhappy. On a few previous occasions she had been completely deprived of any desire to finish her dinner. Sometimes she had gone into the kitchen to administer a tardy rebuke to the cook. Once she went to her room and studied the cookbook during an entire evening, finally writing out a menu for the week, which left her harassed with a feeling that, after all, she had accomplished no good that was worth the name.

But that evening Edna finished her dinner alone, with forced deliberation. Her face was flushed and her eyes flamed with some inward fire that lighted them. After finishing her dinner she went to her room, having instructed the boy to tell any other callers that she was indisposed.

It was a large, beautiful room, rich and picturesque in the soft, dim light which the maid had turned low. She went and stood at an open window and looked out upon the deep tangle of the garden below. All the mystery and witchery of the night seemed to have gathered there amid the perfumes and the dusky and tortuous outlines of flowers and foliage. She was seeking herself and finding herself in just such sweet, half-darkness which met her moods. But the voices were not soothing that came to her from the darkness and the sky above and the stars. They jeered and sounded mournful notes without promise, devoid even of hope. She turned back into the room and began to walk to and fro down its whole length, without stopping, without resting. She carried in her hands a thin handkerchief, which she tore into ribbons, rolled into a ball, and flung from her. Once she stopped, and taking off her wedding ring, flung it upon the carpet. When she saw it lying there, she stamped her heel upon it, striving to crush it. But her small boot heel did not make an indenture, not a mark upon the little glittering circlet.

In a sweeping passion she seized a glass vase from the table and flung it upon the tiles of the hearth. She wanted to destroy something. The crash and clatter were what she wanted to hear.

A maid, alarmed at the din of breaking glass, entered the room to discover what was the matter.

"A vase fell upon the hearth," said Edna. "Never mind; leave it till morning."

"Oh! you might get some of the glass in your feet, ma'am," insisted the young woman, picking up bits of the broken vase that were scattered upon the carpet. "And here's your ring, ma'am, under the chair."

Edna held out her hand, and taking the ring, slipped it upon her finger.

XVIII

The following morning Mr. Pontellier, upon leaving for his office, asked Edna if she would not meet him in town in order to look at some new fixtures for the library.

"I hardly think we need new fixtures, Léonce. Don't let us get anything new; you are too extravagant. I don't believe you ever think of saving or putting by."

"The way to become rich is to make money, my dear Edna, not to save it," he said. He regretted that she did not feel inclined to go with him and select new fixtures. He kissed her good-by, and told her she was not looking well and must take care of herself. She was unusually pale and very quiet.

She stood on the front veranda as he quitted the house, and absently picked a few sprays of jessamine that grew upon a trellis near by. She inhaled the odor of the blossoms and thrust them into the bosom of her white morning gown. The boys were dragging along the banquette a small "express wagon," which they had filled with blocks and sticks. The quadroon was following them with little quick steps, having assumed a fictitious animation and alacrity for the occasion. A fruit vender was crying his wares in the street.

Edna looked straight before her with a self-absorbed expression upon her face. She felt no interest in anything about her. The street, the children, the fruit vender, the flowers growing there under her eyes, were all part and parcel of an alien world which had suddenly become antagonistic.

She went back into the house. She had thought of speaking to the cook concerning her blunders of the previous night; but Mr. Pontellier had saved her that disagreeable mission, for which she was so poorly fitted. Mr. Pontellier's arguments were usually convincing with those whom he employed. He left home feeling quite sure that he and Edna would sit down that evening, and possibly a few subsequent evenings, to a dinner deserving of the name.

Edna spent an hour or two in looking over some of her old sketches. She could see their shortcomings and defects, which were glaring in her eyes. She tried to work a little but found she was not in the humor. Finally she gathered together a few of the sketches—those which she considered the least discreditable; and she carried them with her when, a little later, she dressed and left the house. She looked handsome and distinguished in her street gown. The tan of the seashore had left her face, and her forehead was smooth, white, and polished beneath her heavy yellow-brown hair. There were a few freckles on her face, and a small, dark mole near the under lip and one on the temple, half-hidden in her hair.

As Edna walked along the street she was thinking of Robert. She was still under the spell of her infatuation. She had tried to forget him, realizing the inutility of remembering. But the thought of him was like an obsession, ever pressing itself upon her. It was not that she dwelt upon details of their acquaintance, or recalled in any special or peculiar way his personality; it was his being, his existence, which dominated her thought, fading sometimes as if it would melt into the mist of the forgotten, reviving again with an intensity which filled her with an incomprehensible longing.

Edna was on her way to Madame Ratignolle's. Their intimacy, begun at Grand Isle, had not declined, and they had seen each other with some frequency since their return to the city. The Ratignolles lived at no great distance from Edna's home, on the corner of a side street, where Monsieur Ratignolle owned and conducted a drug store which enjoyed a steady and prosperous trade. His father had been in the business before him, and Monsieur Ratignolle stood well in the community and bore an enviable reputation for integrity and clear-headedness. His family lived in commodious apartments over the store, having an entrance on the side within the *porte cochère.*° There was something which Edna thought very French, very foreign, about their whole manner of living. In the large and pleasant salon which extended across the width of the house, the Ratignolles entertained their friends once a fortnight with a *soirée musicale,*° sometimes diversified by card-playing. There was a friend who played upon the 'cello. One brought his flute and another his violin, while there were some who sang and a number who performed upon the piano with various degrees of taste and agility. The Ratignolles' *soirées musicales* were widely known, and it was considered a privilege to be invited to them.

Edna found her friend engaged in assorting the clothes which had returned that morning from the laundry. She at once abandoned her occupation upon seeing Edna, who had been ushered without ceremony into her presence.

"'Cité can do it as well as I; it is really her business," she explained to Edna, who apologized for interrupting her. And she summoned a young black woman, whom she instructed, in French, to be very careful in checking off the list which she handed her. She told her to notice particularly if a fine linen handkerchief of Monsieur Ratignolle's, which was missing last week, had been returned; and to be sure to set to one side such pieces as required mending and darning.

Then placing an arm around Edna's waist, she led her to the front

porte cochère: Carriage entrance. ***soirée musicale:*** Evening of musical entertainment.

of the house, to the salon, where it was cool and sweet with the odor of great roses that stood upon the hearth in jars.

Madame Ratignolle looked more beautiful than ever there at home, in a negligé which left her arms almost wholly bare and exposed the rich, melting curves of her white throat.

"Perhaps I shall be able to paint your picture some day," said Edna with a smile when they were seated. She produced the roll of sketches and started to unfold them. "I believe I ought to work again. I feel as if I wanted to be doing something. What do you think of them? Do you think it worth while to take it up again and study some more? I might study for a while with Laidpore."

She knew that Madame Ratignolle's opinion in such a matter would be next to valueless, that she herself had not alone decided, but determined; but she sought the words of praise and encouragement that would help her to put heart into her venture.

"Your talent is immense, dear!"

"Nonsense!" protested Edna, well pleased.

"Immense, I tell you," persisted Madame Ratignolle, surveying the sketches one by one, at close range, then holding them at arm's length, narrowing her eyes, and dropping her head on one side. "Surely, this Bavarian peasant is worthy of framing; and this basket of apples! never have I seen anything more lifelike. One might almost be tempted to reach out a hand and take one."

Edna could not control a feeling which bordered upon complacency at her friend's praise, even realizing, as she did, its true worth. She retained a few of the sketches, and gave all the rest to Madame Ratignolle, who appreciated the gift far beyond its value and proudly exhibited the pictures to her husband when he came up from the store a little later for his midday dinner.

Mr. Ratignolle was one of those men who are called the salt of the earth. His cheerfulness was unbounded, and it was matched by his goodness of heart, his broad charity, and common sense. He and his wife spoke English with an accent which was only discernible through its un-English emphasis and a certain carefulness and deliberation. Edna's husband spoke English with no accent whatever. The Ratignolles understood each other perfectly. If ever the fusion of two human beings into one has been accomplished on this sphere it was surely in their union.

As Edna seated herself at table with them she thought, "Better a dinner of herbs," though it did not take her long to discover that it was no dinner of herbs, but a delicious repast, simple, choice, and in every way satisfying.

Monsieur Ratignolle was delighted to see her, though he found her looking not so well as at Grand Isle, and he advised a tonic. He talked a good deal on various topics, a little politics, some city news and neighborhood gossip. He spoke with an animation and earnestness that gave an exaggerated importance to every syllable he uttered. His wife was keenly interested in everything he said, laying down her fork the better to listen, chiming in, taking the words out of his mouth.

Edna felt depressed rather than soothed after leaving them. The little glimpse of domestic harmony which had been offered her, gave her no regret, no longing. It was not a condition of life which fitted her, and she could see in it but an appalling and hopeless ennui. She was moved by a kind of commiseration for Madame Ratignolle,—a pity for that colorless existence which never uplifted its possessor beyond the region of blind contentment, in which no moment of anguish ever visited her soul, in which she would never have the taste of life's delirium. Edna vaguely wondered what she meant by "life's delirium." It had crossed her thought like some unsought, extraneous impression.

XIX

Edna could not help but think that it was very foolish, very childish, to have stamped upon her wedding ring and smashed the crystal vase upon the tiles. She was visited by no more outbursts, moving her to such futile expedients. She began to do as she liked and to feel as she liked. She completely abandoned her Tuesdays at home, and did not return the visits of those who had called upon her. She made no ineffectual efforts to conduct her household *en bonne ménagère,*° going and coming as it suited her fancy, and, so far as she was able, lending herself to any passing caprice.

Mr. Pontellier had been a rather courteous husband so long as he met a certain tacit submissiveness in his wife. But her new and unexpected line of conduct completely bewildered him. It shocked him. Then her absolute disregard for her duties as a wife angered him. When Mr. Pontellier became rude, Edna grew insolent. She had resolved never to take another step backward.

"It seems to me the utmost folly for a woman at the head of a

en bonne ménagère: As a good housewife.

household, and the mother of children, to spend in an atelier days which would be better employed contriving for the comfort of her family."

"I feel like painting," answered Edna. "Perhaps I shan't always feel like it."

"Then in God's name paint! but don't let the family go to the devil. There's Madame Ratignolle; because she keeps up her music, she doesn't let everything else go to chaos. And she's more of a musician than you are a painter."

"She isn't a musician, and I'm not a painter. It isn't on account of painting that I let things go."

"On account of what, then?"

"Oh! I don't know. Let me alone; you bother me."

It sometimes entered Mr. Pontellier's mind to wonder if his wife were not growing a little unbalanced mentally. He could see plainly that she was not herself. That is, he could not see that she was becoming herself and daily casting aside that fictitious self which we assume like a garment with which to appear before the world.

Her husband let her alone as she requested, and went away to his office. Edna went up to her atelier—a bright room in the top of the house. She was working with great energy and interest, without accomplishing anything, however, which satisfied her even in the smallest degree. For a time she had the whole household enrolled in the service of art. The boys posed for her. They thought it amusing at first, but the occupation soon lost its attractiveness when they discovered that it was not a game arranged especially for their entertainment. The quadroon sat for hours before Edna's palette, patient as a savage, while the house-maid took charge of the children, and the drawing-room went undusted. But the house-maid, too, served her term as model when Edna perceived that the young woman's back and shoulders were molded on classic lines, and that her hair, loosened from its confining cap, became an inspiration. While Edna worked she sometimes sang low the little air, "*Ah! si tu savais!*"

It moved her with recollections. She could hear again the ripple of the water, the flapping sail. She could see the glint of the moon upon the bay, and could feel the soft, gusty beating of the hot south wind. A subtle current of desire passed through her body, weakening her hold upon the brushes and making her eyes burn.

There were days when she was very happy without knowing why. She was happy to be alive and breathing, when her whole being seemed to be one with the sunlight, the color, the odors, the luxuriant warmth of some perfect Southern day. She liked then to wander alone into strange and unfamiliar places. She discovered many a sunny, sleepy corner, fashioned to dream in. And she found it good to dream and to be alone and unmolested.

There were days when she was unhappy, she did not know why,—when it did not seem worth while to be glad or sorry, to be alive or dead; when life appeared to her like a grotesque pandemonium and humanity like worms struggling blindly toward inevitable annihilation. She could not work on such a day, nor weave fancies to stir her pulses and warm her blood.

XX

It was during such a mood that Edna hunted up Mademoiselle Reisz. She had not forgotten the rather disagreeable impression left upon her by their last interview; but she nevertheless felt a desire to see her—above all, to listen while she played upon the piano. Quite early in the afternoon she started upon her quest for the pianist. Unfortunately, she had mislaid or lost Mademoiselle Reisz's card, and looking up her address in the city directory, she found that the woman lived on Bienville Street, some distance away. The directory which fell into her hands was a year or more old, however, and upon reaching the number indicated, Edna discovered that the house was occupied by a respectable family of mulattoes who had *chambres garnies*° to let. They had been living there for six months, and knew absolutely nothing of a Mademoiselle Reisz. In fact, they knew nothing of any of their neighbors; their lodgers were all people of the highest distinction, they assured Edna. She did not linger to discuss class distinctions with Madame Pouponne, but hastened to a neighboring grocery store, feeling sure that Mademoiselle would have left her address with the proprietor.

He knew Mademoiselle Reisz a good deal better than he wanted to know her, he informed his questioner. In truth, he did not want to know her at all, or anything concerning her—the most disagreeable and unpopular woman who ever lived in Bienville Street. He thanked heaven she had left the neighborhood, and was equally thankful that he did not know where she had gone.

Edna's desire to see Mademoiselle Reisz had increased tenfold since these unlooked-for obstacles had arisen to thwart it. She was wondering

chambres garnies: Furnished rooms.

who could give her the information she sought, when it suddenly occurred to her that Madame Lebrun would be the one most likely to do so. She knew it was useless to ask Madame Ratignolle, who was on the most distant terms with the musician, and preferred to know nothing concerning her. She had once been almost as emphatic in expressing herself upon the subject as the corner grocer.

Edna knew that Madame Lebrun had returned to the city, for it was the middle of November. And she also knew where the Lebruns lived, on Chartres Street.

Their home from the outside looked like a prison, with iron bars before the door and lower windows. The iron bars were a relic of the old *régime,*° and no one had ever thought of dislodging them. At the side was a high fence enclosing the garden. A gate or door opening upon the street was locked. Edna rang the bell at this side garden gate, and stood upon the banquette, waiting to be admitted.

It was Victor who opened the gate for her. A black woman, wiping her hands upon her apron, was close at his heels. Before she saw them Edna could hear them in altercation, the woman—plainly an anomaly—claiming the right to be allowed to perform her duties, one of which was to answer the bell.

Victor was surprised and delighted to see Mrs. Pontellier, and he made no attempt to conceal either his astonishment or his delight. He was a dark-browed, good-looking youngster of nineteen, greatly resembling his mother, but with ten times her impetuosity. He instructed the black woman to go at once and inform Madame Lebrun that Mrs. Pontellier desired to see her. The woman grumbled a refusal to do part of her duty when she had not been permitted to do it all, and started back to her interrupted task of weeding the garden. Whereupon Victor administered a rebuke in the form of a volley of abuse, which, owing to its rapidity and incoherence, was all but incomprehensible to Edna. Whatever it was, the rebuke was convincing, for the woman dropped her hoe and went mumbling into the house.

Edna did not wish to enter. It was very pleasant there on the side porch, where there were chairs, a wicker lounge, and a small table. She seated herself, for she was tired from her long tramp; and she began to rock gently and smooth out the folds of her silk parasol. Victor drew up his chair beside her. He at once explained that the black woman's offensive conduct was all due to imperfect training, as he was not there to take her in hand. He had only come up from the island the morning

régime: The Spanish rule of 1766–1803.

before, and expected to return next day. He stayed all winter at the island; he lived there, and kept the place in order and got things ready for the summer visitors.

But a man needed occasional relaxation, he informed Mrs. Pontellier, and every now and again he drummed up a pretext to bring him to the city. My! but he had had a time of it the evening before! He wouldn't want his mother to know, and he began to talk in a whisper. He was scintillant with recollections. Of course, he couldn't think of telling Mrs. Pontellier all about it, she being a woman and not comprehending such things. But it all began with a girl peeping and smiling at him through the shutters as he passed by. Oh! but she was a beauty! Certainly he smiled back, and went up and talked to her. Mrs. Pontellier did not know him if she supposed he was one to let an opportunity like that escape him. Despite herself, the youngster amused her. She must have betrayed in her look some degree of interest or entertainment. The boy grew more daring, and Mrs. Pontellier might have found herself, in a little while, listening to a highly colored story but for the timely appearance of Madame Lebrun.

That lady was still clad in white, according to her custom of the summer. Her eyes beamed an effusive welcome. Would not Mrs. Pontellier go inside? Would she partake of some refreshment? Why had she not been there before? How was that dear Mr. Pontellier and how were those sweet children? Had Mrs. Pontellier ever known such a warm November?

Victor went and reclined on the wicker lounge behind his mother's chair, where he commanded a view of Edna's face. He had taken her parasol from her hands while he spoke to her, and he now lifted it and twirled it above him as he lay on his back. When Madame Lebrun complained that it was *so* dull coming back to the city; that she saw *so* few people now; that even Victor, when he came up from the island for a day or two, had *so* much to occupy him and engage his time; then it was that the youth went into contortions on the lounge and winked mischievously at Edna. She somehow felt like a confederate in crime, and tried to look severe and disapproving.

There had been but two letters from Robert, with little in them, they told her. Victor said it was really not worth while to go inside for the letters, when his mother entreated him to go in search of them. He remembered the contents, which in truth he rattled off very glibly when put to the test.

One letter was written from Vera Cruz and the other from the City of Mexico. He had met Montel, who was doing everything toward his advancement. So far, the financial situation was no improvement over the one he had left in New Orleans, but of course the prospects were vastly better. He wrote of the City of Mexico, the buildings, the people and their habits, the conditions of life which he found there. He sent his love to the family. He inclosed a check to his mother, and hoped she would affectionately remember him to all his friends. That was about the substance of the two letters. Edna felt that if there had been a message for her, she would have received it. The despondent frame of mind in which she had left home began again to overtake her, and she remembered that she wished to find Mademoiselle Reisz.

Madame Lebrun knew where Mademoiselle Reisz lived. She gave Edna the address, regretting that she would not consent to stay and spend the remainder of the afternoon, and pay a visit to Mademoiselle Reisz some other day. The afternoon was already well advanced.

Victor escorted her out upon the banquette, lifted her parasol, and held it over her while he walked to the car with her. He entreated her to bear in mind that the disclosures of the afternoon were strictly confidential. She laughed and bantered him a little, remembering too late that she should have been dignified and reserved.

"How handsome Mrs. Pontellier looked!" said Madame Lebrun to her son.

"Ravishing!" he admitted. "The city atmosphere has improved her. Some way she doesn't seem like the same woman."

XXI

Some people contended that the reason Mademoiselle Reisz always chose apartments up under the roof was to discourage the approach of beggars, peddlars and callers. There were plenty of windows in her little front room. They were for the most part dingy, but as they were nearly always open it did not make so much difference. They often admitted into the room a good deal of smoke and soot; but at the same time all the light and air that there was came through them. From her windows could be seen the crescent of the river, the masts of ships and the big chimneys of the Mississippi steamers. A magnificent piano crowded the apartment. In the next room she slept, and in the third and last she harbored a gasoline stove on which she cooked her meals when disinclined to descend to the neighboring restaurant. It was there also that she ate, keeping her belongings in a rare old buffet, dingy and battered from a hundred years of use.

When Edna knocked at Mademoiselle Reisz's front room door and entered, she discovered that person standing beside the window, engaged in mending or patching an old prunella gaiter. The little musician laughed all over when she saw Edna. Her laugh consisted of a contortion of the face and all the muscles of the body. She seemed strikingly homely, standing there in the afternoon light. She still wore the shabby lace and the artificial bunch of violets on the side of her head.

"So you remembered me at last," said Mademoiselle. "I had said to myself, 'Ah, bah! she will never come.'"

"Did you want me to come?" asked Edna with a smile.

"I had not thought much about it," answered Mademoiselle. The two had seated themselves on a little bumpy sofa which stood against the wall. "I am glad, however, that you came. I have the water boiling back there, and was just about to make some coffee. You will drink a cup with me. And how is *la belle dame?*° Always handsome! always healthy! always contented!" She took Edna's hand between her strong wiry fingers, holding it loosely without warmth, and executing a sort of double theme upon the back and palm.

"Yes," she went on; "I sometimes thought: 'She will never come. She promised as those women in society always do, without meaning it. She will not come.' For I really don't believe you like me, Mrs. Pontellier."

"I don't know whether I like you or not," replied Edna, gazing down at the little woman with a quizzical look.

The candor of Mrs. Pontellier's admission greatly pleased Mademoiselle Reisz. She expressed her gratification by repairing forthwith to the region of the gasoline stove and rewarding her guest with the promised cup of coffee. The coffee and the biscuit accompanying it proved very acceptable to Edna, who had declined refreshment at Madame Lebrun's and was now beginning to feel hungry. Mademoiselle set the tray which she brought in upon a small table near at hand, and seated herself once again on the lumpy sofa.

"I have had a letter from your friend," she remarked, as she poured a little cream into Edna's cup and handed it to her.

"My friend?"

"Yes, your friend Robert. He wrote to me from the City of Mexico."

"Wrote to *you?*" repeated Edna in amazement, stirring her coffee absently.

la belle dame: The pretty lady.

"Yes, to me. Why not? Don't stir all the warmth out of your coffee; drink it. Though the letter might as well have been sent to you; it was nothing but Mrs. Pontellier from beginning to end."

"Let me see it," requested the young woman, entreatingly.

"No; a letter concerns no one but the person who writes it and the one to whom it is written."

"Haven't you just said it concerned me from beginning to end?"

"It was written about you, not to you. 'Have you seen Mrs. Pontellier? How is she looking?' he asks. 'As Mrs. Pontellier says,' or 'as Mrs. Pontellier once said.' 'If Mrs. Pontellier should call upon you, play for her that Impromptu of Chopin's, my favorite. I heard it here a day or two ago, but not as you play it. I should like to know how it affects her,' and so on, as if he supposed we were constantly in each other's society."

"Let me see the letter."

"Oh, no."

"Have you answered it?"

"No."

"Let me see the letter."

"No, and again, no."

"Then play the Impromptu for me."

"It is growing late; what time do you have to be home?"

"Time doesn't concern me. Your question seems a little rude. Play the Impromptu."

"But you have told me nothing of yourself. What are you doing?"

"Painting!" laughed Edna. "I am becoming an artist. Think of it!"

"Ah! an artist! You have pretensions, Madame."

"Why pretensions? Do you think I could not become an artist?"

"I do not know you well enough to say. I do not know your talent or your temperament. To be an artist includes much; one must possess many gifts—absolute gifts—which have not been acquired by one's own effort. And, moreover, to succeed, the artist must possess the courageous soul."

"What do you mean by the courageous soul?"

"Courageous, *ma foi!*° The brave soul. The soul that dares and defies."

"Show me the letter and play for me the Impromptu. You see that I have persistence. Does that quality count for anything in art?"

ma foi!: Indeed!

"It counts with a foolish old woman whom you have captivated," replied Mademoiselle, with her wriggling laugh.

The letter was right there at hand in the drawer of the little table upon which Edna had just placed her coffee cup. Mademoiselle opened the drawer and drew forth the letter, the topmost one. She placed it in Edna's hands, and without further comment arose and went to the piano.

Mademoiselle played a soft interlude. It was an improvisation. She sat low at the instrument, and the lines of her body settled into ungraceful curves and angles that gave it an appearance of deformity. Gradually and imperceptibly the interlude melted into the soft opening minor chords of the Chopin Impromptu.

Edna did not know when the Impromptu began or ended. She sat in the sofa corner reading Robert's letter by the fading light. Mademoiselle had glided from the Chopin into the quivering love-notes of Isolde's song, and back again to the Impromptu with its soulful and poignant longing.

The shadows deepened in the little room. The music grew strange and fantastic—turbulent, insistent, plaintive and soft with entreaty. The shadows grew deeper. The music filled the room. It floated out upon the night, over the housetops, the crescent of the river, losing itself in the silence of the upper air.

Edna was sobbing, just as she had wept one midnight at Grand Isle when strange, new voices awoke in her. She arose in some agitation to take her departure. "May I come again, Mademoiselle?" she asked at the threshold.

"Come whenever you feel like it. Be careful; the stairs and landings are dark; don't stumble."

Mademoiselle reëntered and lit a candle. Robert's letter was on the floor. She stooped and picked it up. It was crumpled and damp with tears. Mademoiselle smoothed the letter out, restored it to the envelope, and replaced it in the table drawer.

XXII

One morning on his way into town Mr. Pontellier stopped at the house of his old friend and family physician, Doctor Mandelet. The Doctor was a semi-retired physician, resting, as the saying is, upon his laurels. He bore a reputation for wisdom rather than skill—leaving the active practice of medicine to his assistants and younger contemporaries—and was much sought for in matters of consultation. A few families, united to him by bonds of friendship, he still attended when they required the services of a physician. The Pontelliers were among these.

Mr. Pontellier found the Doctor reading at the open window of his study. His house stood rather far back from the street, in the center of a delightful garden, so that it was quiet and peaceful at the old gentleman's study window. He was a great reader. He stared up disapprovingly over his eye-glasses as Mr. Pontellier entered, wondering who had the temerity to disturb him at that hour of the morning.

"Ah, Pontellier! Not sick, I hope. Come and have a seat. What news do you bring this morning?" He was quite portly, with a profusion of gray hair, and small blue eyes.which age had robbed of much of their brightness but none of their penetration.

"Oh! I'm never sick, Doctor. You know that I come of tough fiber—of that old Creole race of Pontelliers that dry up and finally blow away. I came to consult—no, not precisely to consult—to talk to you about Edna. I don't know what ails her."

"Madame Pontellier not well?" marveled the Doctor. "Why, I saw her—I think it was a week ago—walking along Canal Street, the picture of health, it seemed to me."

"Yes, yes; she seems quite well," said Mr. Pontellier, leaning forward and whirling his stick between his two hands; "but she doesn't act well. She's odd, she's not like herself. I can't make her out, and I thought perhaps you'd help me."

"How does she act?" inquired the doctor.

"Well, it isn't easy to explain," said Mr. Pontellier, throwing himself back in his chair. "She lets the housekeeping go to the dickens."

"Well, well; women are not all alike, my dear Pontellier. We've got to consider—"

"I know that; I told you I couldn't explain. Her whole attitude—toward me and everybody and everything—has changed. You know I have a quick temper, but I don't want to quarrel or be rude to a woman, especially my wife; yet I'm driven to it, and feel like ten thousand devils after I've made a fool of myself. She's making it devilishly uncomfortable for me," he went on nervously. "She's got some sort of notion in her head concerning the eternal rights of women; and—you understand—we meet in the morning at the breakfast table."

The old gentleman lifted his shaggy eyebrows, protruded his thick nether lip, and tapped the arms of his chair with his cushioned fingertips.

"What have you been doing to her, Pontellier?"

"Doing! *Parbleu!*"°

"Has she," asked the Doctor, with a smile, "has she been associating of late with a circle of pseudo-intellectual women—super-spiritual superior beings? My wife has been telling me about them."

"That's the trouble," broke in Mr. Pontellier, "she hasn't been associating with any one. She has abandoned her Tuesdays at home, has thrown over all her acquaintances, and goes tramping about by herself, moping in the street-cars, getting in after dark. I tell you she's peculiar. I don't like it; I feel a little worried over it."

This was a new aspect for the Doctor. "Nothing hereditary?" he asked, seriously. "Nothing peculiar about her family antecedents, is there?"

"On, no, indeed! She comes of sound old Presbyterian Kentucky stock. The old gentleman, her father, I have heard, used to atone for his week-day sins with his Sunday devotions. I know for a fact, that his race horses literally ran away with the prettiest bit of Kentucky farming land I ever laid eyes upon. Margaret—you know Margaret—she has all the Presbyterianism undiluted. And the youngest is something of a vixen. By the way, she gets married in a couple of weeks from now."

"Send your wife up to the wedding," exclaimed the Doctor, foreseeing a happy solution. "Let her stay among her own people for a while; it will do her good."

"That's what I want her to do. She won't go to the marriage. She says a wedding is one of the most lamentable spectacles on earth. Nice thing for a woman to say to her husband!" exclaimed Mr. Pontellier, fuming anew at the recollection.

"Pontellier," said the Doctor, after a moment's reflection, "let your wife alone for a while. Don't bother her, and don't let her bother you. Woman, my dear friend, is a very peculiar and delicate organism—a sensitive and highly organized woman, such as I know Mrs. Pontellier to be, is especially peculiar. It would require an inspired psychologist to deal successfully with them. And when ordinary fellows like you and me attempt to cope with their idiosyncrasies the result is bungling. Most women are moody and whimsical. This is some passing whim of your wife, due to some cause or causes which you and I needn't try to fathom. But it will pass happily over, especially if you let her alone. Send her around to see me."

"Oh! I couldn't do that; there'd be no reason for it," objected Mr. Pontellier.

Parbleu!: Of course!

"Then I'll go around and see her," said the Doctor. "I'll drop in to dinner some evening *en bon ami*."°

"Do! by all means," urged Mr. Pontellier. "What evening will you come? Say Thursday. Will you come Thursday?" he asked, rising to take his leave.

"Very well; Thursday. My wife may possibly have some engagement for me Thursday. In case she has, I shall let you know. Otherwise, you may expect me."

Mr. Pontellier turned before leaving to say:

"I am going to New York on business very soon. I have a big scheme on hand, and want to be on the field proper to pull the ropes and handle the ribbons. We'll let you in on the inside if you say so, Doctor," he laughed.

"No, I thank you, my dear sir," returned the Doctor. "I leave such ventures to you younger men with the fever of life still in your blood."

"What I wanted to say," continued Mr. Pontellier, with his hand on the knob; "I may have to be absent a good while. Would you advise me to take Edna along?"

"By all means, if she wishes to go. If not, leave her here. Don't contradict her. The mood will pass, I assure you. It may take a month, two, three months—possibly longer, but it will pass; have patience."

"Well, good-by, *à jeudi*,"° said Mr. Pontellier, as he let himself out.

The Doctor would have liked during the course of conversation to ask, "Is there any man in the case?" but he knew his Creole too well to make such a blunder as that.

He did not resume his book immediately, but sat for a while meditatively looking out into the garden.

XXIII

Edna's father was in the city, and had been with them several days. She was not very warmly or deeply attached to him, but they had certain tastes in common, and when together they were companionable. His coming was in the nature of a welcome disturbance; it seemed to furnish a new direction for her emotions.

He had come to purchase a wedding gift for his daughter, Janet, and an outfit for himself in which he might make a creditable appearance at her marriage. Mr. Pontellier had selected the bridal gift, as every one

en bon ami: As a good friend. ***à jeudi:*** Until Thursday.

immediately connected with him always deferred to his taste in such matters. And his suggestions on the question of dress—which too often assumes the nature of a problem—were of inestimable value to his father-in-law. But for the past few days the old gentleman had been upon Edna's hands, and in his society she was becoming acquainted with a new set of sensations. He had been a colonel in the Confederate army, and still maintained, with the title, the military bearing which had always accompanied it. His hair and mustache were white and silky, emphasizing the rugged bronze of his face. He was tall and thin, and wore his coats padded, which gave a fictitious breadth and depth to his shoulders and chest. Edna and her father looked very distinguished together, and excited a good deal of notice during their perambulations. Upon his arrival she began by introducing him to her atelier and making a sketch of him. He took the whole matter very seriously. If her talent had been ten-fold greater than it was, it would not have surprised him, convinced as he was that he had bequeathed to all of his daughters the germs of a masterful capability, which only depended upon their own efforts to be directed toward successful achievement.

Before her pencil he sat rigid and unflinching, as he had faced the cannon's mouth in days gone by. He resented the intrusion of the children, who gaped with wondering eyes at him, sitting so stiff up there in their mother's bright atelier. When they drew near he motioned them away with an expressive action of the foot, loath to disturb the fixed lines of his countenance, his arms, or his rigid shoulders.

Edna, anxious to entertain him, invited Mademoiselle Reisz to meet him, having promised him a treat in her piano playing; but Mademoiselle declined the invitation. So together they attended a *soirée musicale* at the Ratignolles'. Monsieur and Madame Ratignolle made much of the Colonel, installing him as the guest of honor and engaging him at once to dine with them the following Sunday, or any day which he might select. Madame coquetted with him in the most captivating and naïve manner, with eyes, gestures, and a profusion of compliments, till the Colonel's old head felt thirty years younger on his padded shoulders. Edna marveled, not comprehending. She herself was almost devoid of coquetry.

There were one or two men whom she observed at the *soirée musicale;* but she would never have felt moved to any kittenish display to attract their notice—to any feline or feminine wiles to express herself toward them. Their personality attracted her in an agreeable way. Her fancy selected them, and she was glad when a lull in the music gave them an opportunity to meet her and talk with her. Often on the street the glance of strange eyes had lingered in her memory, and sometimes had disturbed her.

Mr. Pontellier did not attend these *soirées musicales*. He considered them *bourgeois*,° and found more diversion at the club. To Madame Ratignolle he said the music dispensed at her *soirées* was too "heavy," too far beyond his untrained comprehension. His excuse flattered her. But she disapproved of Mr. Pontellier's club, and she was frank enough to tell Edna so.

"It's a pity Mr. Pontellier doesn't stay home more in the evenings. I think you would be more—well, if you don't mind my saying it—more united, if he did."

"Oh! dear no!" said Edna, with a blank look in her eyes. "What should I do if he stayed home? We wouldn't have anything to say to each other."

She had not much of anything to say to her father, for that matter; but he did not antagonize her. She discovered that he interested her, though she realized that he might not interest her long; and for the first time in her life she felt as if she were thoroughly acquainted with him. He kept her busy serving him and ministering to his wants. It amused her to do so. She would not permit a servant or one of the children to do anything for him which she might do herself. Her husband noticed, and thought it was the expression of a deep filial attachment which he had never suspected.

The Colonel drank numerous "toddies" during the course of the day, which left him, however, imperturbed. He was an expert at concocting strong drinks. He had even invented some, to which he had given fantastic names, and for whose manufacture he required diverse ingredients that it devolved upon Edna to procure for him.

When Doctor Mandelet dined with the Pontelliers on Thursday he could discern in Mrs. Pontellier no trace of that morbid condition which her husband had reported to him. She was excited and in a manner radiant. She and her father had been to the race course, and their thoughts when they seated themselves at table were still occupied with the events of the afternoon, and their talk was still of the track. The Doctor had not kept pace with turf affairs. He had certain recollections of racing in what he called "the good old times" when the Lecompte stables flourished, and he drew upon this fund of memories so that he might not be left out and seem wholly devoid of the modern spirit. But he failed to impose upon the Colonel, and was even far from impressing

bourgeois: Middle-class.

him with this trumped-up knowledge of bygone days. Edna had staked her father on his last venture, with the most gratifying results to both of them. Besides, they had met some very charming people, according to the Colonel's impressions. Mrs. Mortimer Merriman and Mrs. James Highcamp, who were there with Alcée Arobin, had joined them and had enlivened the hours in a fashion that warmed him to think of.

Mr. Pontellier himself had no particular leaning toward horse-racing, and was even rather inclined to discourage it as a pastime, especially when he considered the fate of that blue-grass farm in Kentucky. He endeavored, in a general way, to express a particular disapproval, and only succeeded in arousing the ire and opposition of his father-in-law. A pretty dispute followed, in which Edna warmly espoused her father's cause and the Doctor remained neutral.

He observed his hostess attentively from under his shaggy brows, and noted a subtle change which had transformed her from the listless woman he had known into a being who, for the moment, seemed palpitant with the forces of life. Her speech was warm and energetic. There was no repression in her glance or gesture. She reminded him of some beautiful, sleek animal waking up in the sun.

The dinner was excellent. The claret was warm and the champagne was cold, and under their beneficent influence the threatened unpleasantness melted and vanished with the fumes of the wine.

Mr. Pontellier warmed up and grew reminiscent. He told some amusing plantation experiences, recollections of old Iberville and his youth, when he hunted 'possum in company with some friendly darky; thrashed the pecan tress, shot the grosbec, and roamed the woods and fields in mischievous idleness.

The Colonel, with little sense of humor and of the fitness of things, related a somber episode of those dark and bitter days, in which he had acted a conspicuous part and always formed a central figure. Nor was the Doctor happier in his selection, when he told the old, ever new and curious story of the waning of a woman's love, seeking strange, new channels, only to return to its legitimate source after days of fierce unrest. It was one of the many little human documents which had been unfolded to him during his long career as a physician. The story did not seem especially to impress Edna. She had one of her own to tell, of a woman who paddled away with her lover one night in a pirogue and never came back. They were lost amid the Baratarian Islands, and no one ever heard of them or found trace of them from that day to this. It was a pure invention. She said that Madame Antoine had related it to her. That, also, was an invention. Perhaps it was a dream she had

had. But every glowing word seemed real to those who listened. They could feel the hot breath of the Southern night; they could hear the long sweep of the pirogue through the glistening moonlit water, the beating of birds' wings, rising startled from among the reeds in the salt-water pools; they could see the faces of the lovers, pale, close together, rapt in oblivious forgetfulness, drifting into the unknown.

The champagne was cold, and its subtle fumes played fantastic tricks with Edna's memory that night.

Outside, away from the glow of the fire and the soft lamplight, the night was chill and murky. The Doctor doubled his old-fashioned cloak across his breast as he strode home through the darkness. He knew his fellow-creatures better than most men; knew that inner life which so seldom unfolds itself to unanointed eyes. He was sorry he had accepted Pontellier's invitation. He was growing old, and beginning to need rest and an imperturbed spirit. He did not want the secrets of other lives thrust upon him.

"I hope it isn't Arobin," he muttered to himself as he walked. "I hope to heaven it isn't Alcée Arobin."

XXIV

Edna and her father had a warm, and almost violent dispute upon the subject of her refusal to attend her sister's wedding. Mr. Pontellier declined to interfere, to interpose either his influence or his authority. He was following Doctor Mandelet's advice, and letting her do as she liked. The Colonel reproached his daughter for her lack of filial kindness and respect, her want of sisterly affection and womanly consideration. His arguments were labored and unconvincing. He doubted if Janet would accept any excuse—forgetting that Edna had offered none. He doubted if Janet would ever speak to her again, and he was sure Margaret would not.

Edna was glad to be rid of her father when he finally took himself off with his wedding garments and his bridal gifts, with his padded shoulders, his Bible reading, his "toddies" and ponderous oaths.

Mr. Pontellier followed him closely. He meant to stop at the wedding on his way to New York and endeavor by every means which money and love could devise to atone somewhat for Edna's incomprehensible action.

"You are too lenient, too lenient by far, Léonce," asserted the Colonel. "Authority, coercion are what is needed. Put your foot down good and hard; the only way to manage a wife. Take my word for it."

e Colonel was perhaps unaware that he had coerced his own wife ier grave. Mr. Pontellier had a vague suspicion of it which he t... ght it needless to mention at that late day.

Edna was not so consciously gratified at her husband's leaving home as she had been over the departure of her father. As the day approached when he was to leave her for a comparatively long stay, she grew melting and affectionate, remembering his many acts of consideration and his repeated expressions of an ardent attachment. She was solicitous about his health and his welfare. She bustled around, looking after his clothing, thinking about heavy underwear, quite as Madame Ratignolle would have done under similar circumstances. She cried when he went away, calling him her dear, good friend, and she was quite certain she would grow lonely before very long and go to join him in New York.

But after all, a radiant peace settled upon her when she at last found herself alone. Even the children were gone. Old Madame Pontellier had come herself and carried them off to Iberville with their quadroon. The old madame did not venture to say she was afraid they would be neglected during Léonce's absence; she hardly ventured to think so. She was hungry for them—even a little fierce in her attachment. She did not want them to be wholly "children of the pavement," she always said when begging to have them for a space. She wished them to know the country, with its streams, its fields, its woods, its freedom, so delicious to the young. She wished them to taste something of the life their father had lived and known and loved when he, too, was a little child.

When Edna was at last alone, she breathed a big, genuine sigh of relief. A feeling that was unfamiliar but very delicious came over her. She walked all through the house, from one room to another, as if inspecting it for the first time. She tried the various chairs and lounges, as if she had never sat and reclined upon them before. And she perambulated around the outside of the house, investigating, looking to see if windows and shutters were secure and in order. The flowers were like new acquaintances; she approached them in a familiar spirit, and made herself at home among them. The garden walks were damp, and Edna called to the maid to bring out her rubber sandals. And there she stayed, and stooped, digging around the plants, trimming, picking dead, dry leaves. The children's little dog came out, interfering, getting in her way. She scolded him, laughed at him, played with him. The garden smelled so good and looked so pretty in the afternoon sunlight. Edna plucked all the bright flowers she could find, and went into the house with them, she and the little dog.

Even the kitchen assumed a sudden interesting character which she had never before perceived. She went in to give directions to the cook, to say that the butcher would have to bring much less meat, that they would require only half their usual quantity of bread, of milk and groceries. She told the cook that she herself would be greatly occupied during Mr. Pontellier's absence, and she begged her to take all thought and responsibility of the larder upon her own shoulders.

That night Edna dined alone. The candelabra, with a few candles in the center of the table, gave all the light she needed. Outside the circle of light in which she sat, the large dining-room looked solemn and shadowy. The cook, placed upon her mettle, served a delicious repast—a luscious tenderloin broiled *à point.*° The wine tasted good; the *marron glacé*° seemed to be just what she wanted. It was so pleasant, too, to dine in a comfortable *peignoir.*

She thought a little sentimentally about Léonce and the children, and wondered what they were doing. As she gave a dainty scrap or two to the doggie, she talked intimately to him about Etienne and Raoul. He was beside himself with astonishment and delight over these companionable advances, and showed his appreciation by his little quick, snappy barks and a lively agitation.

Then Edna sat in the library after dinner and read Emerson until she grew sleepy. She realized that she had neglected her reading, and determined to start anew upon a course of improving studies, now that her time was completely her own to do with as she liked.

After a refreshing bath, Edna went to bed. And as she snuggled comfortably beneath the eiderdown a sense of restfulness invaded her, such as she had not known before.

XXV

When the weather was dark and cloudy, Edna could not work. She needed the sun to mellow and temper her mood to the sticking point. She had reached a stage when she seemed to be no longer feeling her way, working, when in the humor, with sureness and ease. And being devoid of ambition, and striving not toward accomplishment, she drew satisfaction from the work in itself.

On rainy or melancholy days Edna went out and sought the society of the friends she had made at Grand Isle. Or else she stayed indoors

à point: Just right. ***marron glacé:*** Glazed chestnuts.

and nursed a mood with which she was becoming too familiar for her own comfort and peace of mind. It was not despair; but it seemed to her as if life were passing by, leaving its promise broken and unfulfilled. Yet there were other days when she listened, was led on and deceived by fresh promises which her youth held out to her.

She went again to the races, and again. Alcée Arobin and Mrs. Highcamp called for her one bright afternoon in Arobin's drag. Mrs. Highcamp was a worldly but unaffected, intelligent, slim, tall blonde woman in the forties, with an indifferent manner and blue eyes that stared. She had a daughter who served her as a pretext for cultivating the society of young men of fashion. Alcée Arobin was one of them. He was a familiar figure at the race course, the opera, the fashionable clubs. There was a perpetual smile in his eyes, which seldom failed to awaken a corresponding cheerfulness in any one who looked into them and listened to his good-humored voice. His manner was quiet, and at times a little insolent. He possessed a good figure, a pleasing face, not overburdened with depth of thought or feeling; and his dress was that of the conventional man of fashion.

He admired Edna extravagantly, after meeting her at the races with her father. He had met her before on other occasions, but she had seemed to him unapproachable until that day. It was at his instigation that Mrs. Highcamp called to ask her to go with them to the Jockey Club to witness the turf event of the season.

There were possibly a few track men out there who knew the race horse as well as Edna, but there was certainly none who knew it better. She sat between her two companions as one having authority to speak. She laughed at Arobin's pretensions, and deplored Mrs. Highcamp's ignorance. The race horse was a friend and intimate associate of her childhood. The atmosphere of the stables and the breath of the blue grass paddock revived in her memory and lingered in her nostrils. She did not perceive that she was talking like her father as the sleek geldings ambled in review before them. She played for very high stakes, and fortune favored her. The fever of the game flamed in her cheeks and eyes, and it got into her blood and into her brain like an intoxicant. People turned their heads to look at her, and more than one lent an attentive ear to her utterances, hoping thereby to secure the elusive but ever-desired "tip." Arobin caught the contagion of excitement which drew him to Edna like a magnet. Mrs. Highcamp remained, as usual, unmoved, with her indifferent stare and uplifted eyebrows.

Edna stayed and dined with Mrs. Highcamp upon being urged to do so. Arobin also remained and sent away his drag.

The dinner was quiet and uninteresting, save for the cheerful efforts of Arobin to enliven things. Mrs. Highcamp deplored the absence of her daughter from the races, and tried to convey to her what she had missed by going to the "Dante reading" instead of joining them. The girl held a geranium leaf up to her nose and said nothing, but looked knowing and noncommittal. Mr. Highcamp was a plain, bald-headed man, who only talked under compulsion. He was unresponsive. Mrs. Highcamp was full of delicate courtesy and consideration toward her husband. She addressed most of her conversation to him at table. They sat in the library after dinner and read the evening papers together under the droplight; while the younger people went into the drawing-room near by and talked.

Miss Highcamp played some selections from Grieg upon the piano. She seemed to have apprehended all of the composer's coldness and none of his poetry. While Edna listened she could not help wondering if she had lost her taste for music.

When the time came for her to go home, Mr. Highcamp grunted a lame offer to escort her, looking down at his slippered feet with tactless concern. It was Arobin who took her home. The car ride was long, and it was late when they reached Esplanade Street. Arobin asked permission to enter for a second to light his cigarette—his match safe was empty. He filled his match safe, but did not light his cigarette until he left her, after she had expressed her willingness to go to the races with him again.

Edna was neither tired nor sleepy. She was hungry again, for the Highcamp dinner, though of excellent quality, had lacked abundance. She rummaged in the larder and brought forth a slice of Gruyère and some crackers. She opened a bottle of beer which she found in the ice-box. Edna felt extremely restless and excited. She vacantly hummed a fantastic tune as she poked at the wood embers on the hearth and munched a cracker.

She wanted something to happen—something, anything; she did not know what. She regretted that she had not made Arobin stay a half hour to talk over the horses with her. She counted the money she had won. But there was nothing else to do, so she went to bed, and tossed there for hours in a sort of monotonous agitation.

In the middle of the night she remembered that she had forgotten to write her regular letter to her husband; and she decided to do so next day and tell him about her afternoon at the Jockey Club. She lay wide awake composing a letter which was nothing like the one which she wrote next day. When the maid awoke her in the morning Edna was dreaming of Mr. Highcamp playing the piano at the entrance of a music store on Canal Street, while his wife was saying to Alcée Arobin, as they boarded an Esplanade Street car:

"What a pity that so much talent has been neglected! but I must go."

When, a few days later, Alcée Arobin again called for Edna in his drag, Mrs. Highcamp was not with him. He said they would pick her up. But as that lady had not been apprised of his intention of picking her up, she was not at home. The daughter was just leaving the house to attend the meeting of a branch Folk Lore Society, and regretted that she could not accompany them. Arobin appeared nonplused, and asked Edna if there were any one else she cared to ask.

She did not deem it worth while to go in search of any of the fashionable acquaintances from whom she had withdrawn herself. She thought of Madame Ratignolle, but knew that her fair friend did not leave the house, except to take a languid walk around the block with her husband after nightfall. Mademoiselle Reisz would have laughed at such a request from Edna. Madame Lebrun might have enjoyed the outing, but for some reason Edna did not want her. So they went alone, she and Arobin.

The afternoon was intensely interesting to her. The excitement came back upon her like a remittent fever. Her talk grew familiar and confidential. It was no labor to become intimate with Arobin. His manner invited easy confidence. The preliminary stage of becoming acquainted was one which he always endeavored to ignore when a pretty and engaging woman was concerned.

He stayed and dined with Edna. He stayed and sat beside the wood fire. They laughed and talked; and before it was time to go he was telling her how different life might have been if he had known her years before. With ingenuous frankness he spoke of what a wicked, ill-disciplined boy he had been, and impulsively drew up his cuff to exhibit upon his wrist the scar from a saber cut which he had received in a duel outside of Paris when he was nineteen. She touched his hand as she scanned the red cicatrice on the inside of his white wrist. A quick impulse that was somewhat spasmodic impelled her fingers to close in a sort of clutch upon his hand. He felt the pressure of her pointed nails in the flesh of his palm.

She arose hastily and walked toward the mantel.

"The sight of a wound or scar always agitates and sickens me," she said. "I shouldn't have looked at it."

"I beg your pardon," he entreated, following her; "it never occurred to me that it might be repulsive."

He stood close to her, and the effrontery in his eyes repelled the old, vanishing self in her, yet drew all her awakening sensuousness. He saw enough in her face to impel him to take her hand and hold it while he said his lingering good night.

"Will you go to the races again?" he asked.

"No," she said. "I've had enough of the races. I don't want to lose all the money I've won, and I've got to work when the weather is bright, instead of—"

"Yes; work; to be sure. You promised to show me your work. What morning may I come up to your atelier? To-morrow?"

"No!"

"Day after?"

"No, no."

"Oh, please don't refuse me! I know something of such things. I might help you with a stray suggestion or two."

"No. Good night. Why don't you go after you have said good night? I don't like you," she went on in a high, excited pitch, attempting to draw away her hand. She felt that her words lacked dignity and sincerity, and she knew that he felt it.

"I'm sorry you don't like me. I'm sorry I offended you. How have I offended you? What have I done? Can't you forgive me?" And he bent and pressed his lips upon her hand as if he wished never more to withdraw them.

"Mr. Arobin," she complained, "I'm greatly upset by the excitement of the afternoon; I'm not myself. My manner must have misled you in some way. I wish you to go, please." She spoke in a monotonous, dull tone. He took his hat from the table, and stood with eyes turned from her, looking into the dying fire. For a moment or two he kept an impressive silence.

"Your manner has not misled me, Mrs. Pontellier," he said finally. "My own emotions have done that. I couldn't help it. When I'm near you, how could I help it? Don't think anything of it, don't bother, please. You see, I go when you command me. If you wish me to stay away, I shall do so. If you let me come back, I—oh! you will let me come back?"

He cast one appealing glance at her, to which she made no response. Alcée Arobin's manner was so genuine that it often deceived even himself.

Edna did not care or think whether it were genuine or not. When she was alone she looked mechanically at the back of her hand which he had kissed so warmly. Then she leaned her head down on the mantelpiece. She felt somewhat like a woman who in a moment of passion is betrayed into an act of infidelity, and realizes the significance of the act without being wholly awakened from its glamour. The thought was passing vaguely through her mind, "What would he think?"

She did not mean her husband; she was thinking of Robert Lebrun. Her husband seemed to her now like a person whom she had married without love as an excuse.

She lit a candle and went up to her room. Alcée Arobin was absolutely nothing to her. Yet his presence, his manners, the warmth of his glances, and above all the touch of his lips upon her hand had acted like a narcotic upon her.

She slept a languorous sleep, interwoven with vanishing dreams.

XXVI

Alcée Arobin wrote Edna an elaborate note of apology, palpitant with sincerity. It embarrassed her; for in a cooler, quieter moment it appeared to her absurd that she should have taken his action so seriously, so dramatically. She felt sure that the significance of the whole occurrence had lain in her own self-consciousness. If she ignored his note it would give undue importance to a trivial affair. If she replied to it in a serious spirit it would still leave in his mind the impression that she had in a susceptible moment yielded to his influence. After all, it was no great matter to have one's hand kissed. She was provoked at his having written the apology. She answered in as light and bantering a spirit as she fancied it deserved, and said she would be glad to have him look in upon her at work whenever he felt the inclination and his business gave him the opportunity.

He responded at once by presenting himself at her home with all his disarming naïveté. And then there was scarcely a day which followed that she did not see him or was not reminded of him. He was prolific in pretexts. His attitude became one of good-humored subservience and tacit adoration. He was ready at all times to submit to her moods, which were as often kind as they were cold. She grew accustomed to him. They became intimate and friendly by imperceptible degrees, and then by leaps. He sometimes talked in a way that astonished her at first and brought the crimson into her face; in a way that pleased her at last, appealing to the animalism that stirred impatiently within her.

There was nothing which so quieted the turmoil of Edna's senses as a visit to Mademoiselle Reisz. It was then, in the presence of that personality which was offensive to her, that the woman, by her divine art, seemed to reach Edna's spirit and set it free.

It was misty, with heavy, lowering atmosphere, one afternoon, when Edna climbed the stairs to the pianist's apartments under the roof. Her clothes were dripping with moisture. She felt chilled and pinched as she entered the room. Mademoiselle was poking at a rusty stove that smoked a little and warmed the room indifferently. She was endeavoring to heat a pot of chocolate on the stove. The room looked cheerless and dingy to Edna as she entered. A bust of Beethoven, covered with a hood of dust, scowled at her from the mantelpiece.

"Ah! here comes the sunlight!" exclaimed Mademoiselle, rising from her knees before the stove. "Now it will be warm and bright enough; I can let the fire alone."

She closed the stove door with a bang, and approaching, assisted in removing Edna's dripping mackintosh.

"You are cold; you look miserable. The chocolate will soon be hot. But would you rather have a taste of brandy? I have scarcely touched the bottle which you brought me for my cold." A piece of red flannel was wrapped around Mademoiselle's throat; a stiff neck compelled her to hold her head on one side.

"I will take some brandy," said Edna, shivering as she removed her gloves and overshoes. She drank the liquor from the glass as a man would have done. Then flinging herself upon the uncomfortable sofa she said, "Mademoiselle, I am going to move away from my house on Esplanade Street."

"Ah!" ejaculated the musician, neither surprised nor especially interested. Nothing ever seemed to astonish her very much. She was endeavoring to adjust the bunch of violets which had become loose from its fastening in her hair. Edna drew her down upon the sofa, and taking a pin from her own hair, secured the shabby artificial flowers in their accustomed place.

"Aren't you astonished?"

"Passably. Where are you going? to New York? to Iberville? to your father in Mississippi? where?"

"Just two steps away," laughed Edna, "in a little four-room house around the corner. It looks so cozy, so inviting and restful, whenever I pass by; and it's for rent. I'm tired looking after that big house. It never seemed like mine, anyway—like home. It's too much trouble. I have to keep too many servants. I am tired bothering with them."

"That is not your true reason, *ma belle.*° There is no use in telling me lies. I don't know your reason, but you have not told me the truth." Edna did not protest or endeavor to justify herself.

"The house, the money that provides for it, are not mine. Isn't that enough reason?"

"They are your husband's," returned Mademoiselle, with a shrug and a malicious elevation of the eyebrows.

"Oh! I see there is no deceiving you. Then let me tell you: It is a caprice. I have a little money of my own from my mother's estate, which my father sends me by driblets. I won a large sum this winter on the races, and I am beginning to sell my sketches. Laidpore is more and more pleased with my work; he says it grows in force and individuality. I cannot judge of that myself, but I feel that I have gained in ease and confidence. However, as I said, I have sold a good many through Laidpore. I can live in the tiny house for little or nothing, with one servant. Old Celestine, who works occasionally for me, says she will come stay with me and do my work. I know I shall like it, like the feeling of freedom and independence."

"What does your husband say?"

"I have not told him yet. I only thought of it this morning. He will think I am demented, no doubt. Perhaps you think so."

Mademoiselle shook her head slowly. "Your reason is not yet clear to me," she said.

Neither was it quite clear to Edna herself; but it unfolded itself as she sat for a while in silence. Instinct had prompted her to put away her husband's bounty in casting off her allegiance. She did not know how it would be when he returned. There would have to be an understanding, an explanation. Conditions would some way adjust themselves, she felt; but whatever came, she had resolved never again to belong to another than herself.

"I shall give a grand dinner before I leave the old house!" Edna exclaimed. "You will have to come to it, Mademoiselle. I will give you everything that you like to eat and to drink. We shall sing and laugh and be merry for once." And she uttered a sigh that came from the very depths of her being.

ma belle: My dear.

If Mademoiselle happened to have received a letter from Robert during the interval of Edna's visits, she would give her the letter unsolicited. And she would seat herself at the piano and play as her humor prompted her while the young woman read the letter.

The little stove was roaring; it was red-hot, and the chocolate in the tin sizzled and sputtered. Edna went forward and opened the stove door, and Mademoiselle rising, took a letter from under the bust of Beethoven and handed it to Edna.

"Another! so soon!" she exclaimed, her eyes filled with delight. "Tell me, Mademoiselle, does he know that I see his letters?"

"Never in the world! He would be angry and would never write to me again if he thought so. Does he write to you? Never a line. Does he send you a message? Never a word. It is because he loves you, poor fool, and is trying to forget you, since you are not free to listen to him or to belong to him."

"Why do you show me his letters, then?"

"Haven't you begged for them? Can I refuse you anything? Oh! you cannot deceive me," and Mademoiselle approached her beloved instrument and began to play. Edna did not at once read the letter. She sat holding it in her hand, while the music penetrated her whole being like an effulgence, warming and brightening the dark places of her soul. It prepared her for joy and exultation.

"Oh!" she exclaimed, letting the letter fall to the floor. "Why did you not tell me?" She went and grasped Mademoiselle's hands up from the keys. "Oh! unkind! malicious! Why did you not tell me?"

"That he was coming back? No great news, *ma foi*. I wonder he did not come long ago."

"But when, when?" cried Edna, impatiently. "He does not say when."

"He says 'very soon.' You know as much about it as I do; it is all in the letter."

"But why? Why is he coming? Oh, if I thought—" and she snatched the letter from the floor and turned the pages this way and that way, looking for the reason, which was left untold.

"If I were young and in love with a man," said Mademoiselle, turning on the stool and pressing her wiry hands between her knees as she looked down at Edna, who sat on the floor holding the letter, "it seems to me he would have to be some *grand esprit;*° a man with lofty aims and ability to reach them; one who stood high enough to attract the

grand esprit: Great mind.

notice of his fellow-men. It seems to me if I were young and in love I should never deem a man of ordinary caliber worthy of my devotion."

"Now it is you who are telling lies and seeking to deceive me, Mademoiselle; or else you have never been in love, and know nothing about it. Why," went on Edna, clasping her knees and looking up into Mademoiselle's twisted face, "do you suppose a woman knows why she loves? Does she select? Does she say to herself: 'Go to! Here is a distinguished statesman with presidential possibilities; I shall proceed to fall in love with him.' Or, 'I shall set my heart upon this musician, whose fame is on every tongue?' Or, 'This financier, who controls the world's money markets?'"

"You are purposely misunderstanding me, *ma reine.*° Are you in love with Robert?"

"Yes," said Edna. It was the first time she had admitted it, and a glow overspread her face, blotching it with red spots.

"Why?" asked her companion. "Why do you love him when you ought not to?"

Edna, with a motion or two, dragged herself on her knees before Mademoiselle Reisz, who took the glowing face between her two hands.

"Why? Because his hair is brown and grows away from his temples; because he opens and shuts his eyes, and his nose is a little out of drawing; because he has two lips and a square chin, and a little finger which he can't straighten from having played baseball too energetically in his youth. Because—"

"Because you do, in short," laughed Mademoiselle. "What will you do when he comes back?" she asked.

"Do? Nothing, except feel glad and happy to be alive."

She was already glad and happy to be alive at the mere thought of his return. The murky, lowering sky, which had depressed her a few hours before, seemed bracing and invigorating as she splashed through the streets on her way home.

She stopped at a confectioner's and ordered a huge box of bonbons for the children in Iberville. She slipped a card in the box, on which she scribbled a tender message and sent an abundance of kisses.

Before dinner in the evening Edna wrote a charming letter to her husband, telling him of her intention to move for a while into the little house around the block, and to give a farewell dinner before leaving, regretting that he was not there to share it, to help her out with the

ma reine: My queen.

menu and assist her in entertaining the guests. Her letter was brilliant and brimming with cheerfulness.

XXVII

"What is the matter with you?" asked Arobin that evening. "I never found you in such a happy mood." Edna was tired by that time, and was reclining on the lounge before the fire.

"Don't you know the weather prophet has told us we shall see the sun pretty soon?"

"Well, that ought to be reason enough," he acquiesced. "You wouldn't give me another if I sat here all night imploring you." He sat close to her on a low tabouret, and as he spoke his fingers lightly touched the hair that fell a little over her forehead. She liked the touch of his fingers through her hair, and closed her eyes sensitively.

"One of these days," she said, "I'm going to pull myself together for a while and think—try to determine what character of a woman I am; for, candidly, I don't know. By all the codes which I am acquainted with, I am a devilishly wicked specimen of the sex. But some way I can't convince myself that I am. I must think about it."

"Don't. What's the use? Why should you bother thinking about it when I can tell you what manner of woman you are." His fingers strayed occasionally down to her warm, smooth cheeks and firm chin, which was growing a little full and double.

"Oh, yes! You will tell me that I am adorable; everything that is captivating. Spare yourself the effort."

"No; I shan't tell you anything of the sort, though I shouldn't be lying if I did."

"Do you know Mademoiselle Reisz?" she asked irrelevantly.

"The pianist? I know her by sight. I've heard her play."

"She says queer things sometimes in a bantering way that you don't notice at the time and you find yourself thinking about afterward."

"For instance?"

"Well, for instance, when I left her to-day, she put her arms around me and felt my shoulder blades, to see if my wings were strong, she said. 'The bird that would soar above the level plain of tradition and prejudice must have strong wings. It is a sad spectacle to see the weaklings bruised, exhausted, fluttering back to earth.'"

"Whither would you soar?"

"I'm not thinking of any extraordinary flights. I only half comprehend her."

"I've heard she's partially demented," said Arobin.

"She seems to me wonderfully sane," Edna replied.

"I'm told she's extremely disagreeable and unpleasant. Why have you introduced her at a moment when I desired to talk of you?"

"Oh! talk of me if you like," cried Edna, clasping her hands beneath her head; "but let me think of something else while you do."

"I'm jealous of your thoughts to-night. They're making you a little kinder than usual; but some way I feel as if they were wandering, as if they were not here with me." She only looked at him and smiled. His eyes were very near. He leaned upon the lounge with an arm extended across her, while the other hand still rested upon her hair. They continued silently to look into each other's eyes. When he leaned forward and kissed her, she clasped his head, holding his lips to hers.

It was the first kiss of her life to which her nature had really responded. It was a flaming torch that kindled desire.

XXVIII

Edna cried a little that night after Arobin left her. It was only one phase of the multitudinous emotions which had assailed her. There was with her an overwhelming feeling of irresponsibility. There was the shock of the unexpected and the unaccustomed. There was her husband's reproach looking at her from the external things around her which he had provided for her external existence. There was Robert's reproach making itself felt by a quicker, fiercer, more overpowering love, which had awakened within her toward him. Above all, there was understanding. She felt as if a mist had been lifted from her eyes, enabling her to look upon and comprehend the significance of life, that monster made up of beauty and brutality. But among the conflicting sensations which assailed her, there was neither shame nor remorse. There was a dull pang of regret because it was not the kiss of love which had inflamed her, because it was not love which had held this cup of life to her lips.

XXIX

Without even waiting for an answer from her husband regarding his opinion or wishes in the matter, Edna hastened her preparations for quitting her home on Esplanade Street and moving into the little house around the block. A feverish anxiety attended her every action in that direction. There was no moment of deliberation, no interval of repose between the thought and its fulfillment. Early upon the morning following those hours passed in Arobin's society, Edna set about securing her new abode and hurrying her arrangements for occupying it. Within the precincts of her home she felt like one who has entered and lingered within the portals of some forbidden temple in which a thousand muffled voices bade her begone.

Whatever was her own in the house, everything which she had acquired aside from her husband's bounty, she caused to be transported to the other house, supplying simple and meager deficiencies from her own resources.

Arobin found her with rolled sleeves, working in company with the house-maid when he looked in during the afternoon. She was splendid and robust, and had never appeared handsomer than in the old blue gown, with a red silk handkerchief knotted at random around her head to protect her hair from the dust. She was mounted upon a high stepladder, unhooking a picture from the wall when he entered. He had found the front door open, and had followed his ring by walking in unceremoniously.

"Come down!" he said. "Do you want to kill yourself?" She greeted him with affected carelessness, and appeared absorbed in her occupation.

If he had expected to find her languishing, reproachful, or indulging in sentimental tears, he must have been greatly surprised.

He was no doubt prepared for any emergency, ready for any one of the foregoing attitudes, just as he bent himself easily and naturally to the situation which confronted him.

"Please come down," he insisted, holding the ladder and looking up at her.

"No," she answered; "Ellen is afraid to mount the ladder. Joe is working over at the 'pigeon house'—that's the name Ellen gives it, because it's so small and looks like a pigeon house—and some one has to do this."

Arobin pulled off his coat, and expressed himself ready and willing to tempt fate in her place. Ellen brought him one of her dust-caps, and went into contortions of mirth, which she found it impossible to control, when she saw him put it on before the mirror as grotesquely as he could. Edna herself could not refrain from smiling when she fastened it at his request. So it was he who in turn mounted the ladder, unhooking pictures and curtains, and dislodging ornaments as Edna directed.

When he had finished he took off his dust-cap and went out to wash his hands.

Edna was sitting on the tabouret, idly brushing the tips of a feather duster along the carpet when he came in again.

"Is there anything more you will let me do?" he asked.

"That is all," she answered. "Ellen can manage the rest." She kept the young woman occupied in the drawing-room, unwilling to be left alone with Arobin.

"What about the dinner?" he asked; "the grand event, the *coup d'état?*"°

"It will be day after to-morrow. Why do you call it the '*coup d'état?*' Oh! it will be very fine; all my best of everything—crystal, silver and gold, Sèvres, flowers, music, and champagne to swim in. I'll let Léonce pay the bills. I wonder what he'll say when he sees the bills."

"And you ask me why I call it a *coup d'état?*" Arobin had put on his coat, and he stood before her and asked if his cravat was plumb. She told him it was, looking no higher than the tip of his collar.

"When do you go to the 'pigeon house?'—with all due acknowledgment to Ellen."

"Day after to-morrow, after the dinner. I shall sleep there."

"Ellen, will you very kindly get me a glass of water?" asked Arobin. "The dust in the curtains, if you will pardon me for hinting such a thing, has parched my throat to a crisp."

"While Ellen gets the water," said Edna, rising, "I will say good-by and let you go. I must get rid of this grime, and I have a million things to do and think of."

"When shall I see you?" asked Arobin, seeking to detain her, the maid having left the room.

"At the dinner, of course. You are invited."

"Not before?—not to-night or to-morrow morning or to-morrow noon or night? or the day after morning or noon? Can't you see yourself, without my telling you, what an eternity it is?"

He had followed her into the hall and to the foot of the stairway, looking up at her as she mounted with her face half turned to him.

"Not an instant sooner," she said. But she laughed and looked at him with eyes that at once gave him courage to wait and made it torture to wait.

coup d'état: A sudden and decisive act.

XXX

Though Edna had spoken of the dinner as a very grand affair, it was in truth a very small affair and very select, in so much as the guests invited were few and were selected with discrimination. She had counted upon an even dozen seating themselves at her round mahogany board, forgetting for the moment that Madame Ratignolle was to the last degree *souffrante*° and unpresentable, and not foreseeing that Madame Lebrun would send a thousand regrets at the last moment. So there were only ten, after all, which made a cozy, comfortable number.

There were Mr. and Mrs. Merriman, a pretty, vivacious little woman in the thirties; her husband, a jovial fellow, something of a shallow-pate, who laughed a good deal at other people's witticisms, and had thereby made himself extremely popular. Mrs. Highcamp had accompanied them. Of course, there was Alcée Arobin; and Mademoiselle Reisz had consented to come. Edna had sent her a fresh bunch of violets with black lace trimmings for her hair. Monsieur Ratignolle brought himself and his wife's excuses. Victor Lebrun, who happened to be in the city, bent upon relaxation, had accepted with alacrity. There was a Miss Mayblunt, no longer in her teens, who looked at the world through lorgnettes and with the keenest interest. It was thought and said that she was intellectual; it was suspected of her that she wrote under a *nom de guerre*.° She had come with a gentleman by the name of Gouvernail, connected with one of the daily papers, of whom nothing special could be said, except that he was observant and seemed quiet and inoffensive. Edna herself made the tenth, and at half-past eight they seated themselves at table, Arobin and Monsieur Ratignolle on either side of their hostess.

Mrs. Highcamp sat between Arobin and Victor Lebrun. Then came Mrs. Merriman, Mr. Gouvernail, Miss Mayblunt, Mr. Merriman, and Mademoiselle Reisz next to Monsieur Ratignolle.

There was something extremely gorgeous about the appearance of the table, an effect of splendor conveyed by a cover of pale yellow satin under strips of lace-work. There were wax candles in massive brass candelabra, burning softly under yellow silk shades; full, fragrant roses, yellow and red, abounded. There were silver and gold, as she had said there would be, and crystal which glittered like the gems which the women wore.

The ordinary stiff dining chairs had been discarded for the occasion

souffrante: Unwell. ***nom de guerre:*** Fictitious name.

and replaced by the most commodious and luxurious which could be collected throughout the house. Mademoiselle Reisz, being exceedingly diminutive, was elevated upon cushions, as small children are sometimes hoisted at table upon bulky volumes.

"Something new, Edna?" exclaimed Miss Mayblunt, with lorgnette directed toward a magnificent cluster of diamonds that sparkled, that almost sputtered, in Edna's hair, just over the center of her forehead.

"Quite new; 'brand' new, in fact; a present from my husband. It arrived this morning from New York. I may as well admit that this is my birthday, and that I am twenty-nine. In good time I expect you to drink my health. Meanwhile, I shall ask you to begin with this cocktail, composed—would you say 'composed?'" with an appeal to Miss Mayblunt—"composed by my father in honor of Sister Janet's wedding."

Before each guest stood a tiny glass that looked and sparkled like a garnet gem.

"Then, all things considered," spoke Arobin, "it might not be amiss to start out by drinking the Colonel's health in the cocktail which he composed, on the birthday of the most charming of women—the daughter whom he invented."

Mr. Merriman's laugh at this sally was such a genuine outburst and so contagious that it started the dinner with an agreeable swing that never slackened.

Miss Mayblunt begged to be allowed to keep her cocktail untouched before her, just to look at. The color was marvelous! She could compare it to nothing she had ever seen, and the garnet lights which it emitted were unspeakably rare. She pronounced the Colonel an artist, and stuck to it.

Monsieur Ratignolle was prepared to take things seriously: the *mets,*° the *entre-mets,*° the service, the decorations, even the people. He looked up from his pompono and inquired of Arobin if he were related to the gentleman of that name who formed one of the firm of Laitner and Arobin, lawyers. The young man admitted that Laitner was a warm personal friend, who permitted Arobin's name to decorate the firm's letterheads and to appear upon a shingle that graced Perdido Street.

"There are so many inquisitive people and institutions abounding," said Arobin, "that one is really forced as a matter of convenience these days to assume the virtue of an occupation if he has it not."

Monsieur Ratignolle stared a little, and turned to ask Mademoiselle

mets: Dishes. ***entre-mets:*** Side dishes.

Reisz if she considered the symphony concerts up to the standard which had been set the previous winter. Mademoiselle Reisz answered Monsieur Ratignolle in French, which Edna thought a little rude, under the circumstances, but characteristic. Mademoiselle had only disagreeable things to say of the symphony concerts, and insulting remarks to make of all the musicians of New Orleans, singly and collectively. All her interest seemed to be centered upon the delicacies placed before her.

Mr. Merriman said that Mr. Arobin's remark about inquisitive people reminded him of a man from Waco the other day at the St. Charles Hotel—but as Mr. Merriman's stories were always lame and lacking point, his wife seldom permitted him to complete them. She interrupted him to ask if he remembered the name of the author whose book she had bought the week before to send to a friend in Geneva. She was talking "books" with Mr. Gouvernail and trying to draw from him his opinion upon current literary topics. Her husband told the story of the Waco man privately to Miss Mayblunt, who pretended to be greatly amused and to think it extremely clever.

Mrs. Highcamp hung with languid but unaffected interest upon the warm and impetuous volubility of her left-hand neighbor, Victor Lebrun. Her attention was never for a moment withdrawn from him after seating herself at table; and when he turned to Mrs. Merriman, who was prettier and more vivacious than Mrs. Highcamp, she waited with easy indifference for an opportunity to reclaim his attention. There was the occasional sound of music, of mandolins, sufficiently removed to be an agreeable accompaniment rather than an interruption to the conversation. Outside the soft, monotonous splash of a fountain could be heard; the sound penetrated into the room with the heavy odor of jessamine that came through the open windows.

The golden shimmer of Edna's satin gown spread in rich folds on either side of her. There was a soft fall of lace encircling her shoulders. It was the color of her skin, without the glow, the myriad living tints that one may sometimes discover in vibrant flesh. There was something in her attitude, in her whole appearance when she leaned her head against the high-backed chair and spread her arms, which suggested the regal woman, the one who rules, who looks on, who stands alone.

But as she sat there amid her guests, she felt the old ennui overtaking her; the hopelessness which so often assailed her, which came upon her like an obsession, like something extraneous, independent of volition. It was something which announced itself; a chill breath that seemed to issue from some vast cavern wherein discords wailed. There came over her the acute longing which always summoned into her spiritual vision the presence of the beloved one, overpowering her at once with a sense of the unattainable.

The moments glided on, while a feeling of good fellowship passed around the circle like a mystic cord, holding and binding these people together with jest and laughter. Monsieur Ratignolle was the first to break the pleasant charm. At ten o'clock he excused himself. Madame Ratignolle was waiting for him at home. She was *bien souffrante,* and she was filled with vague dread, which only her husband's presence could allay.

Mademoiselle Reisz arose with Monsieur Ratignolle, who offered to escort her to the car. She had eaten well; she had tasted the good, rich wines, and they must have turned her head, for she bowed pleasantly to all as she withdrew from table. She kissed Edna upon the shoulder, and whispered: "*Bonne nuit, ma reine; soyez sage.*"° She had been a little bewildered upon rising, or rather, descending from her cushions, and Monsieur Ratignolle gallantly took her arm and led her away.

Mrs. Highcamp was weaving a garland of roses, yellow and red. When she had finished the garland, she laid it lightly upon Victor's black curls. He was reclining far back in the luxurious chair, holding a glass of champagne to the light.

As if a magician's wand had touched him, the garland of roses transformed him into a vision of Oriental beauty. His cheeks were the color of crushed grapes, and his dusky eyes glowed with a languishing fire.

"*Sapristi!*" exclaimed Arobin.

But Mrs. Highcamp had one more touch to add to the picture. She took from the back of her chair a white silken scarf, with which she had covered her shoulders in the early part of the evening. She draped it across the boy in graceful folds, and in a way to conceal his black, conventional evening dress. He did not seem to mind what she did to him, only smiled, showing a faint gleam of white teeth, while he continued to gaze with narrowing eyes at the light through his glass of champagne.

"Oh! to be able to paint in color rather than in words!" exclaimed Miss Mayblunt, losing herself in a rhapsodic dream as she looked at him.

"'There was a graven image of Desire
Painted with red blood on a ground of gold.'"

murmured Gouvernail, under his breath.

The effect of the wine upon Victor was to change his accustomed

Bonne . . . sage: Good night, my queen; be good.

volubility into silence. He seemed to have abandoned himself to a reverie, and to be seeing pleasing visions in the amber bead.

"Sing," entreated Mrs. Highcamp. "Won't you sing to us?"

"Let him alone," said Arobin.

"He's posing," offered Mr. Merriman; "let him have it out."

"I believe he's paralyzed," laughed Mrs. Merriman. And leaning over the youth's chair, she took the glass from his hand and held it to his lips. He sipped the wine slowly, and when he had drained the glass she laid it upon the table and wiped his lips with her little filmy handkerchief.

"Yes, I'll sing for you," he said, turning in his chair toward Mrs. Highcamp. He clasped his hands behind his head, and looking up at the ceiling began to hum a little, trying his voice like a musician tuning an instrument. Then, looking at Edna, he began to sing:

"Ah! si tu savais!"

"Stop!" she cried, "don't sing that. I don't want you to sing it," and she laid her glass so impetuously and blindly upon the table as to shatter it against a caraffe. The wine spilled over Arobin's legs and some of it trickled down upon Mrs. Highcamp's black gauze gown. Victor had lost all idea of courtesy, or else he thought his hostess was not in earnest, for he laughed and went on:

"Ah! si tu savais
Ce que tes yeux me disent"—°

"Oh! you mustn't! you mustn't," exclaimed Edna, and pushing back her chair she got up, and going behind him placed her hand over his mouth. He kissed the soft palm that pressed upon his lips.

"No, no, I won't, Mrs. Pontellier. I didn't know you meant it," looking up at her with caressing eyes. The touch of his lips was like a pleasing sting to her hand. She lifted the garland of roses from his head and flung it across the room.

"Come, Victor; you've posed long enough. Give Mrs. Highcamp her scarf."

Mrs. Highcamp undraped the scarf from about him with her own hands. Miss Mayblunt and Mr. Gouvernail suddenly conceived the notion that it was time to say good night. And Mr. and Mrs. Merriman wondered how it could be so late.

Before parting from Victor, Mrs. Highcamp invited him to call

Ah! . . . disent: Ah! if you knew / What your eyes are telling me.

upon her daughter, who she knew would be charmed to meet him and talk French and sing French songs with him. Victor expressed his desire and intention to call upon Miss Highcamp at the first opportunity which presented itself. He asked if Arobin were going his way. Arobin was not.

The mandolin players had long since stolen away. A profound stillness had fallen upon the broad, beautiful street. The voices of Edna's disbanding guests jarred like a discordant note upon the quiet harmony of the night.

XXXI

"Well?" questioned Arobin, who had remained with Edna after the others had departed.

"Well," she reiterated, and stood up, stretching her arms, and feeling the need to relax her muscles after having been so long seated.

"What next?" he asked.

"The servants are all gone. They left when the musicians did. I have dismissed them. The house has to be closed and locked, and I shall trot around to the pigeon house, and shall send Celestine over in the morning to straighten things up."

He looked around, and began to turn out some of the lights.

"What about upstairs?" he inquired.

"I think it is all right; but there may be a window or two unlatched. We had better look; you might take a candle and see. And bring me my wrap and hat on the foot of the bed in the middle room."

He went up with the light, and Edna began closing doors and windows. She hated to shut in the smoke and the fumes of the wine. Arobin found her cape and hat, which he brought down and helped her to put on.

When everything was secured and the lights put out, they left through the front door, Arobin locking it and taking the key, which he carried for Edna. He helped her down the steps.

"Will you have a spray of jessamine?" he asked, breaking off a few blossoms as he passed.

"No; I don't want anything."

She seemed disheartened, and had nothing to say. She took his arm, which he offered her, holding up the weight of her satin train with the other hand. She looked down, noticing the black line of his leg moving in and out so close to her against the yellow shimmer of her gown.

There was the whistle of a railway train somewhere in the distance, and the midnight bells were ringing. They met no one in their short walk.

The "pigeon-house" stood behind a locked gate, and a shallow *parterre*° that had been somewhat neglected. There was a small front porch, upon which a long window and the front door opened. The door opened directly into the parlor; there was no side entry. Back in the yard was a room for servants, in which old Celestine had been ensconced.

Edna had left a lamp burning low upon the table. She had succeeded in making the room look habitable and homelike. There were some books on the table and a lounge near at hand. On the floor was a fresh matting, covered with a rug or two; and on the walls hung a few tasteful pictures. But the room was filled with flowers. These were a surprise to her. Arobin had sent them, and had had Celestine distribute them during Edna's absence. Her bedroom was adjoining, and across a small passage were the dining-room and kitchen.

Edna seated herself with every appearance of discomfort.

"Are you tired?" he asked.

"Yes, and chilled, and miserable. I feel as if I had been wound up to a certain pitch—too tight—and something inside of me had snapped." She rested her head against the table upon her bare arm.

"You want to rest," he said, "and to be quiet. I'll go; I'll leave you and let you rest."

"Yes," she replied.

He stood up beside her and smoothed her hair with his soft, magnetic hand. His touch conveyed to her a certain physical comfort. She could have fallen quietly asleep there if he had continued to pass his hand over her hair. He brushed the hair upward from the nape of her neck.

"I hope you will feel better and happier in the morning," he said. "You have tried to do too much in the past few days. The dinner was the last straw; you might have dispensed with it."

"Yes," she admitted; "it was stupid."

"No, it was delightful; but it has worn you out." His hand had strayed to her beautiful shoulders, and he could feel the response of her flesh to his touch. He seated himself beside her and kissed her lightly upon the shoulder.

"I thought you were going away," she said, in an uneven voice.

"I am, after I have said good night."

parterre: Flowerbed.

"Good night," she murmured.

He did not answer, except to continue to caress her. He did not say good night until she had become supple to his gentle, seductive entreaties.

XXXII

When Mr. Pontellier learned of his wife's intention to abandon her home and take up her residence elsewhere, he immediately wrote her a letter of unqualified disapproval and remonstrance. She had given reasons which he was unwilling to acknowledge as adequate. He hoped she had not acted upon her rash impulse; and he begged her to consider first, foremost, and above all else, what people would say. He was not dreaming of scandal when he uttered this warning; that was a thing which would never had entered into his mind to consider in connection with his wife's name or his own. He was simply thinking of his financial integrity. It might get noised about that the Pontelliers had met with reverses, and were forced to conduct their *ménage*° on a humbler scale than heretofore. It might do incalculable mischief to his business prospects.

But remembering Edna's whimsical turn of mind of late, and foreseeing that she had immediately acted upon her impetuous determination, he grasped the situation with his usual promptness and handled it with his well-known business tact and cleverness.

The same mail which brought to Edna his letter of disapproval carried instructions—the most minute instructions—to a well-known architect concerning the remodeling of his home, changes which he had long contemplated, and which he desired carried forward during his temporary absence.

Expert and reliable packers and movers were engaged to convey the furniture, carpets, pictures—everything movable, in short—to places of security. And in an incredibly short time the Pontellier house was turned over to the artisans. There was to be an addition—a small snuggery; there was to be frescoing, and hardwood flooring was to be put into such rooms as had not yet been subjected to this improvement.

Furthermore, in one of the daily papers appeared a brief notice to the effect that Mr. and Mrs. Pontellier were contemplating a summer

ménage: Household.

sojourn abroad, and that their handsome residence on Esplanade Street was undergoing sumptuous alterations, and would not be ready for occupancy until their return. Mr. Pontellier had saved appearances!

Edna admired the skill of his maneuver, and avoided any occasion to balk his intentions. When the situation as set forth by Mr. Pontellier was accepted and taken for granted, she was apparently satisfied that it should be so.

The pigeon-house pleased her. It at once assumed the intimate character of a home, while she herself invested it with a charm which it reflected like a warm glow. There was with her a feeling of having descended in the social scale, with a corresponding sense of having risen in the spiritual. Every step which she took toward relieving herself from obligations added to her strength and expansion as an individual. She began to look with her own eyes; to see and to apprehend the deeper undercurrents of life. No longer was she content to "feed upon opinion" when her own soul had invited her.

After a little while, a few days, in fact, Edna went up and spent a week with her children in Iberville. They were delicious February days, with all the summer's promise hovering in the air.

How glad she was to see the children! She wept for very pleasure when she felt their little arms clasping her; their hard, ruddy cheeks pressed against her own glowing cheeks. She looked into their faces with hungry eyes that could not be satisfied with looking. And what stories they had to tell their mother! About the pigs, the cows, the mules! About riding to the mill behind Gluglu; fishing back in the lake with their Uncle Jasper; picking pecans with Lidie's little black brood, and hauling chips in their express wagon. It was a thousand times more fun to haul real chips for old lame Susie's real fire than to drag painted blocks along the banquette on Esplanade Street!

She went with them herself to see the pigs and the cows, to look at the darkies laying the cane, to thrash the pecan trees, and catch fish in the back lake. She lived with them a whole week long, giving them all of herself, and gathering and filling herself with their young existence. They listened, breathless, when she told them the house in Esplanade Street was crowded with workmen, hammering, nailing, sawing, and filling the place with clatter. They wanted to know where their bed was; what had been done with their rocking-horse; and where did Joe sleep, and where had Ellen gone, and the cook? But, above all, they were fired with a desire to see the little house around the block. Was there any place to play? Were there any boys next door? Raoul, with pessimistic foreboding, was convinced that there were only girls next door. Where would they sleep, and where would papa sleep? She told them the fairies would fix it all right.

The old Madame was charmed with Edna's visit, and showered all manner of delicate attentions upon her. She was delighted to know that the Esplanade Street house was in a dismantled condition. It gave her the promise and pretext to keep the children indefinitely.

It was with a wrench and a pang that Edna left her children. She carried away with her the sound of their voices and the touch of their cheeks. All along the journey homeward their presence lingered with her like the memory of a delicious song. But by the time she had regained the city the song no longer echoed in her soul. She was again alone.

XXXIII

It happened sometimes when Edna went to see Mademoiselle Reisz that the little musician was absent, giving a lesson or making some small necessary household purchase. The key was always left in a secret hiding-place in the entry, which Edna knew. If Mademoiselle happened to be away, Edna would usually enter and wait for her return.

When she knocked at Mademoiselle Reisz's door one afternoon there was no response; so unlocking the door, as usual, she entered and found the apartment deserted, as she had expected. Her day had been quite filled up, and it was for a rest, for a refuge, and to talk about Robert, that she sought out her friend.

She had worked at her canvas—a young Italian character study—all the morning, completing the work without the model; but there had been many interruptions, some incident to her modest housekeeping, and others of a social nature.

Madame Ratignolle had dragged herself over, avoiding the too public thoroughfares, she said. She complained that Edna had neglected her much of late. Besides, she was consumed with curiosity to see the little house and the manner in which it was conducted. She wanted to hear all about the dinner party; Monsieur Ratignolle had left *so* early. What had happened after he left? The champagne and grapes which Edna sent over were *too* delicious. She had so little appetite; they had refreshed and toned her stomach. Where on earth was she going to put Mr. Pontellier in that little house, and the boys? And then she made Edna promise to go to her when her hour of trial overtook her.

"At any time—any time of the day or night, dear," Edna assured her.

Before leaving Madame Ratignolle said:

"In some way you seem to me like a child, Edna. You seem to act without a certain amount of reflection which is necessary in this life. That is the reason I want to say you mustn't mind if I advise you to be a little careful while you are living here alone. Why don't you have some one come and stay with you? Wouldn't Mademoiselle Reisz come?"

"No; she wouldn't wish to come, and I shouldn't want her always with me."

"Well, the reason—you know how evil-minded the world is—some one was talking of Alcée Arobin visiting you. Of course, it wouldn't matter if Mr. Arobin had not such a dreadful reputation. Monsieur Ratignolle was telling me that his attentions alone are considered enough to ruin a woman's name."

"Does he boast of his successes?" asked Edna, indifferently, squinting at her picture.

"No, I think not. I believe he is a decent fellow as far as that goes. But his character is so well known among the men. I shan't be able to come back and see you; it was very, very imprudent to-day."

"Mind the step!" cried Edna.

"Don't neglect me," entreated Madame Ratignolle; "and don't mind what I said about Arobin, or having some one to stay with you."

"Of course not," Edna laughed. "You may say anything you like to me." They kissed each other good-by. Madame Ratignolle had not far to go, and Edna stood on the porch a while watching her walk down the street.

Then in the afternoon Mrs. Merriman and Mrs. Highcamp had made their "party call." Edna felt that they might have dispensed with the formality. They had also come to invite her to play *vingt-et-un*° one evening at Mrs. Merriman's. She was asked to go early, to dinner, and Mr. Merriman or Mr. Arobin would take her home. Edna accepted in a half-hearted way. She sometimes felt very tired of Mrs. Highcamp and Mrs. Merriman.

Late in the afternoon she sought refuge with Mademoiselle Reisz, and stayed there alone, waiting for her, feeling a kind of repose invade her with the very atmosphere of the shabby, unpretentious little room.

Edna sat at the window, which looked out over the house-tops and across the river. The window frame was filled with pots of flowers, and

vingt-et-un: Twenty-one, a card game.

she sat and picked the dry leaves from a rose geranium. The day was warm, and the breeze which blew from the river was very pleasant. She removed her hat and laid it on the piano. She went on picking the leaves and digging around the plants with her hat pin. Once she thought she heard Mademoiselle Reisz approaching. But it was a young black girl, who came in, bringing a small bundle of laundry, which she deposited in the adjoining room, and went away.

Edna seated herself at the piano, and softly picked out with one hand the bars of a piece of music which lay open before her. A half-hour went by. There was the occasional sound of people going and coming in the lower hall. She was growing interested in her occupation of picking out the aria, when there was a second rap at the door. She vaguely wondered what these people did when they found Mademoiselle's door locked.

"Come in," she called, turning her face toward the door. And this time it was Robert Lebrun who presented himself. She attempted to rise; she could not have done so without betraying the agitation which mastered her at sight of him, so she fell back upon the stool, only exclaiming, "Why, Robert!"

He came and clasped her hand, seemingly without knowing what he was saying or doing.

"Mrs. Pontellier! How do you happen—oh! how well you look! Is Mademoiselle Reisz not here? I never expected to see you."

"When did you come back?" asked Edna in an unsteady voice, wiping her face with her handkerchief. She seemed ill at ease on the piano stool, and he begged her to take the chair by the window. She did so, mechanically, while he seated himself on the stool.

"I returned day before yesterday," he answered, while he leaned his arm on the keys, bringing forth a crash of discordant sound.

"Day before yesterday!" she repeated, aloud; and went on thinking to herself, "day before yesterday," in a sort of an uncomprehending way. She had pictured him seeing her at the very first hour, and he had lived under the same sky since day before yesterday; while only by accident had he stumbled upon her. Mademoiselle must have lied when she said, "Poor fool, he loves you."

"Day before yesterday," she repeated, breaking off a spray of Mademoiselle's geranium; "then if you had not met me here to-day you wouldn't—when—that is, didn't you mean to come and see me?"

"Of course, I should have gone to see you. There have been so many things— " he turned the leaves of Mademoiselle's music nervously. "I started in at once yesterday with the old firm. After all there is as much chance for me here as there was there—that is, I might find it profitable some day. The Mexicans were not very congenial."

So he had come back because the Mexicans were not congenial; because business was as profitable here as there; because of any reason, and not because he cared to be near her. She remembered the day she sat on the floor, turning the pages of his letter, seeking the reason which was left untold.

She had not noticed how he looked—only feeling his presence; but she turned deliberately and observed him. After all, he had been absent but a few months, and was not changed. His hair—the color of hers—waved back from his temples in the same way as before. His skin was not more burned than it had been at Grand Isle. She found in his eyes, when he looked at her for one silent moment, the same tender caress, with an added warmth and entreaty which had not been there before—the same glance which had penetrated to the sleeping places of her soul and awakened them.

A hundred times Edna had pictured Robert's return, and imagined their first meeting. It was usually at her home, whither he had sought her out at once. She always fancied him expressing or betraying in some way his love for her. And here, the reality was that they sat ten feet apart, she at the window, crushing geranium leaves in her hand and smelling them, he twirling around on the piano stool, saying:

"I was very much surprised to hear of Mr. Pontellier's absence; it's a wonder Mademoiselle Reisz did not tell me; and your moving—mother told me yesterday. I should think you would have gone to New York with him, or to Iberville with the children, rather than be bothered here with housekeeping. And you are going abroad, too, I hear. We shan't have you at Grand Isle next summer; it won't seem—do you see much of Mademoiselle Reisz? She often spoke of you in the few letters she wrote."

"Do you remember that you promised to write to me when you went away?" A flush overspread his whole face.

"I couldn't believe that my letters would be of any interest to you."

"That is an excuse; it isn't the truth." Edna reached for her hat on the piano. She adjusted it, sticking the hat pin through the heavy coil of hair with some deliberation.

"Are you not going to wait for Mademoiselle Reisz?" asked Robert.

"No; I have found when she is absent this long, she is liable not to come back till late." She drew on her gloves, and Robert picked up his hat.

"Won't you wait for her?" asked Edna.

"Not if you think she will not be back till late," adding, as if suddenly aware of some discourtesy in his speech, "and I should miss the pleasure of walking home with you." Edna locked the door and put the key back in its hiding-place.

They went together, picking their way across muddy streets and sidewalks encumbered with the cheap display of small tradesmen. Part of the distance they rode in the car, and after disembarking, passed the Pontellier mansion, which looked broken and half torn asunder. Robert had never known the house, and looked at it with interest.

"I never knew you in your home," he remarked.

"I am glad you did not."

"Why?" She did not answer. They went on around the corner, and it seemed as if her dreams were coming true after all, when he followed her into the little house.

"You must stay and dine with me, Robert. You see I am all alone, and it is so long since I have seen you. There is so much I want to ask you."

She took off her hat and gloves. He stood irresolute, making some excuse about his mother who expected him; he even muttered something about an engagement. She struck a match and lit the lamp on the table; it was growing dusk. When he saw her face in the lamp-light, looking pained, with all the soft lines gone out of it, he threw his hat aside and seated himself.

"Oh! you know I want to stay if you will let me!" he exclaimed. All the softness came back. She laughed, and went and put her hand on his shoulder.

"This is the first moment you have seemed like the old Robert. I'll go tell Celestine." She hurried away to tell Celestine to set an extra place. She even sent her off in search of some added delicacy which she had not thought of for herself. And she recommended great care in dripping the coffee and having the omelet done to a proper turn.

When she reëntered, Robert was turning over magazines, sketches, and things that lay upon the table in great disorder. He picked up a photograph, and exclaimed:

"Alcée Arobin! What on earth is his picture doing here?"

"I tried to make a sketch of his head one day," answered Edna, "and he thought the photograph might help me. It was at the other house. I thought it had been left there. I must have packed it up with my drawing materials."

"I should think you would give it back to him if you have finished with it."

"Oh! I have a great many such photographs. I never think of returning them. They don't amount to anything." Robert kept on looking at the picture.

"It seems to me—do you think his head worth drawing? Is he a friend of Mr. Pontellier's? You never said you knew him."

"He isn't a friend of Mr. Pontellier's; he's a friend of mine. I always knew him—that is, it is only of late that I know him pretty well. But I'd rather talk about you, and know what you have been seeing and doing and feeling out there in Mexico." Robert threw aside the picture.

"I've been seeing the waves and the white beach of Grand Isle; the quiet, grassy street of the *Chênière;* the old fort at Grande Terre. I've been working like a machine, and feeling like a lost soul. There was nothing interesting."

She leaned her head upon her hand to shade her eyes from the light.

"And what have you been seeing and doing and feeling all these days?" he asked.

"I've been seeing the waves and the white beach of Grand Isle; the quiet, grassy street of the *Chênière Caminada;* the old sunny fort at Grande Terre. I've been working with a little more comprehension than a machine and still feeling like a lost soul. There was nothing interesting."

"Mrs. Pontellier, you are cruel," he said, with feeling, closing his eyes and resting his head back in his chair. They remained in silence till old Celestine announced dinner.

XXXIV

The dining-room was very small. Edna's round mahogany would have almost filled it. As it was there was but a step or two from the little table to the kitchen, to the mantel, the small buffet, and the side door that opened out on the narrow brick-paved yard.

A certain degree of ceremony settled upon them with the announcement of dinner. There was no return to personalities. Robert related incidents of his sojourn in Mexico, and Edna talked of events likely to interest him, which had occurred during his absence. The dinner was of ordinary quality, except for the few delicacies which she had sent out to purchase. Old Celestine, with a bandana *tignon*° twisted about her head, hobbled in and out, taking a personal interest in every-

tignon: Variation of *chignon*, a knot of hair worn at the nape of the neck.

thing; and she lingered occasionally to talk patois with Robert, whom she had known as a boy.

He went out to a neighboring cigar stand to purchase cigarette papers, and when he came back he found that Celestine had served the black coffee in the parlor.

"Perhaps I shouldn't have come back," he said. "When you are tired of me, tell me to go."

"You never tire me. You must have forgotten the hours and hours at Grand Isle in which we grew accustomed to each other and used to being together."

"I have forgotten nothing at Grand Isle," he said, not looking at her, but rolling a cigarette. His tobacco pouch, which he laid upon the table, was a fantastic embroidered silk affair, evidently the handiwork of a woman.

"You used to carry your tobacco in a rubber pouch," said Edna, picking up the pouch and examining the needlework.

"Yes; it was lost."

"Where did you buy this one? In Mexico?"

"It was given to me by a Vera Cruz girl; they are very generous," he replied, striking a match and lighting his cigarette.

"They are very handsome, I suppose, those Mexican women; very picturesque, with their black eyes and their lace scarfs."

"Some are; others are hideous. Just as you find women everywhere."

"What was she like—the one who gave you the pouch? You must have known her very well."

"She was very ordinary. She wasn't of the slightest importance. I knew her well enough."

"Did you visit at her house? Was it interesting? I should like to know and hear about the people you met, and the impressions they made on you."

"There are some people who leave impressions not so lasting as the imprint of an oar upon the water."

"Was she such a one?"

"It would be ungenerous for me to admit that she was of that order and kind." He thrust the pouch back in his pocket, as if to put away the subject with the trifle which had brought it up.

Arobin dropped in with a message from Mrs. Merriman, to say that the card party was postponed on account of the illness of one of her children.

"How do you do, Arobin?" said Robert, rising from the obscurity.

"Oh! Lebrun. To be sure! I heard yesterday you were back. How did they treat you down in Mexique?"

"Fairly well."

"But not well enough to keep you there. Stunning girls, though, in Mexico. I thought I should never get away from Vera Cruz when I was down there a couple of years ago."

"Did they embroider slippers and tobacco pouches and hatbands and things for you?" asked Edna.

"Oh! my! no! I didn't get so deep in their regard. I fear they made more impression on me than I made on them."

"You were less fortunate than Robert, then."

"I am always less fortunate than Robert. Has he been imparting tender confidences?"

"I've been imposing myself long enough," said Robert, rising, and shaking hands with Edna. "Please convey my regards to Mr. Pontellier when you write."

He shook hands with Arobin and went away.

"Fine fellow, that Lebrun," said Arobin when Robert had gone. "I never heard you speak of him."

"I knew him last summer at Grand Isle," she replied. "Here is that photograph of yours. Don't you want it?"

"What do I want with it? Throw it away." She threw it back on the table.

"I'm not going to Mrs. Merriman's," she said. "If you see her, tell her so. But perhaps I had better write. I think I shall write now, and say that I am sorry her child is sick, and tell her not to count on me."

"It would be a good scheme," acquiesced Arobin. "I don't blame you; stupid lot!"

Edna opened the blotter, and having procured paper and pen, began to write the note. Arobin lit a cigar and read the evening paper, which he had in his pocket.

"What is the date?" she asked. He told her.

"Will you mail this for me when you go out?"

"Certainly." He read to her little bits out of the newspaper, while she straightened things on the table.

"What do you want to do?" he asked, throwing aside the paper. "Do you want to go out for a walk or a drive or anything? It would be a fine night to drive."

"No; I don't want to do anything but just be quiet. You go away and amuse yourself. Don't stay."

"I'll go away if I must; but I shan't amuse myself. You know that I only live when I am near you."

He stood up to bid her good night.

"Is that one of the things you always say to women?"

"I have said it before, but I don't think I ever came so near meaning it," he answered with a smile. There were no warm lights in her eyes; only a dreamy, absent look.

"Good night. I adore you. Sleep well," he said, and he kissed her hand and went away.

She stayed alone in a kind of reverie—a sort of stupor. Step by step she lived over every instant of the time she had been with Robert after he had entered Mademoiselle Reisz's door. She recalled his words, his looks. How few and meager they had been for her hungry heart! A vision—a transcendently seductive vision of a Mexican girl arose before her. She writhed with a jealous pang. She wondered when he would come back. He had not said he would come back. She had been with him, had heard his voice and touched his hand. But some way he had seemed nearer to her off there in Mexico.

XXXV

The morning was full of sunlight and hope. Edna could see before her no denial—only the promise of excessive joy. She lay in bed awake, with bright eyes full of speculation. "He loves you, poor fool." If she could but get that conviction firmly fixed in her mind, what mattered about the rest? She felt she had been childish and unwise the night before in giving herself over to despondency. She recapitulated the motives which no doubt explained Robert's reserve. They were not insurmountable; they would not hold if he really loved her; they could not hold against her own passion, which he must come to realize in time. She pictured him going to his business that morning. She even saw how he was dressed; how he walked down one street, and turned the corner of another; saw him bending over his desk, talking to people who entered the office, going to his lunch, and perhaps watching for her on the street. He would come to her in the afternoon or evening, sit and roll his cigarette, talk a little, and go away as he had done the night before. But how delicious it would be to have him there with her! She would have no regrets, nor seek to penetrate his reserve if he still chose to wear it.

Edna ate her breakfast only half dressed. The maid brought her a delicious printed scrawl from Raoul, expressing his love, asking her to send him some bonbons, and telling her they had found that morning ten tiny white pigs all lying in a row beside Lidie's big white pig.

A letter also came from her husband, saying he hoped to be back early in March, and then they would get ready for that journey abroad which he had promised her so long, which he felt now fully able to afford; he felt able to travel as people should, without any thought of small economies—thanks to his recent speculations in Wall Street.

Much to her surprise she received a note from Arobin, written at midnight from the club. It was to say good morning to her, to hope she had slept well, to assure her of his devotion, which he trusted she in some faintest manner returned.

All these letters were pleasing to her. She answered the children in a cheerful frame of mind, promising them bonbons, and congratulating them upon their happy find of the little pigs.

She answered her husband with friendly evasiveness—not with any fixed design to mislead him, only because all sense of reality had gone out of her life; she had abandoned herself to Fate, and awaited the consequences with indifference.

To Arobin's note she made no reply. She put it under Celestine's stove-lid.

Edna worked several hours with much spirit. She saw no one but a picture dealer, who asked her if it were true that she was going abroad to study in Paris.

She said possibly she might, and he negotiated with her for some Parisian studies to reach him in time for the holiday trade in December.

Robert did not come that day. She was keenly disappointed. He did not come the following day, nor the next. Each morning she awoke with hope, and each night she was a prey to despondency. She was tempted to seek him out. But far from yielding to the impulse, she avoided any occasion which might throw her in his way. She did not go to Mademoiselle Reisz's nor pass by Madame Lebrun's as she might have done if he had still been in Mexico.

When Arobin, one night, urged her to drive with him, she went—out to the lake, on the Shell Road. His horses were full of mettle, and even a little unmanageable. She liked the rapid gait at which they spun along, and the quick, sharp sound of the horses' hoofs on the hard road. They did not stop anywhere to eat or to drink. Arobin was not needlessly imprudent. But they ate and they drank when they regained Edna's little dining-room—which was comparatively early in the evening.

It was late when he left her. It was getting to be more than a passing whim with Arobin to see her and be with her. He had detected the latent sensuality, which unfolded under his delicate sense of her nature's requirements like a torpid, torrid, sensitive blossom.

There was no despondency when she fell asleep that night; nor was there hope when she awoke in the morning.

XXXVI

There was a garden out in the suburbs; a small, leafy corner, with a few green tables under the orange trees. An old cat slept all day on the stone step in the sun, and an old *mulatresse*° slept her idle hours away in her chair at the open window, till some one happened to knock on one of the green tables. She had milk and cream cheese to sell, and bread and butter. There was no one who could make such excellent coffee or fry a chicken so golden brown as she.

The place was too modest to attract the attention of people of fashion, and so quiet as to have escaped the notice of those in search of pleasure and dissipation. Edna had discovered it accidentally one day when the high-board gate stood ajar. She caught sight of a little green table, blotched with the checkered sunlight that filtered through the quivering leaves overhead. Within she had found the slumbering *mulatresse,* the drowsy cat, and a glass of milk which reminded her of the milk she had tasted in Iberville.

She often stopped there during her perambulations; sometimes taking a book with her, and sitting an hour or two under the trees when she found the place deserted. Once or twice she took a quiet dinner there alone, having instructed Celestine beforehand to prepare no dinner at home. It was the last place in the city where she would have expected to meet any one she knew.

Still she was not astonished when, as she was partaking of a modest dinner late in the afternoon, looking into an open book, stroking the cat, which had made friends with her—she was not greatly astonished to see Robert come in at the tall garden gate.

"I am destined to see you only by accident," she said, shoving the cat off the chair beside her. He was surprised, ill at ease, almost embarrassed at meeting her thus so unexpectedly.

"Do you come here often?" he asked.

mulatresse: Mulatto woman.

"I almost live here," she said.

"I used to drop in very often for a cup of Catiche's good coffee. This is the first time since I came back."

"She'll bring you a plate, and you will share my dinner. There's always enough for two—even three." Edna had intended to be indifferent and as reserved as he when she met him; she had reached the determination by a laborious train of reasoning, incident to one of her despondent moods. But her resolve melted when she saw him before her, seated there beside her in the little garden, as if a designing Providence had led him into her path.

"Why have you kept away from me, Robert?" she asked, closing the book that lay open on the table.

"Why are you so personal, Mrs. Pontellier? Why do you force me to idiotic subterfuges?" he exclaimed with sudden warmth. "I suppose there's no use telling you I've been very busy, or that I've been sick, or that I've been to see you and not found you at home. Please let me off with any one of these excuses."

"You are the embodiment of selfishness," she said. "You save yourself something—I don't know what—but there is some selfish motive, and in sparing yourself you never consider for a moment what I think, or how I feel your neglect and indifference. I suppose this is what you would call unwomanly; but I have got into a habit of expressing myself. It doesn't matter to me, and you may think me unwomanly if you like."

"No; I only think you cruel, as I said the other day. Maybe not intentionally cruel; but you seem to be forcing me into disclosures which can result in nothing; as if you would have me bare a wound for the pleasure of looking at it, without the intention or power of healing it."

"I'm spoiling your dinner, Robert; never mind what I say. You haven't eaten a morsel."

"I only came in for a cup of coffee." His sensitive face was all disfigured with excitement.

"Isn't this a delightful place?" she remarked. "I am so glad it has never actually been discovered. It is so quiet, so sweet, here. Do you notice there is scarcely a sound to be heard? It's so out of the way; and a good walk from the car. However, I don't mind walking. I always feel so sorry for women who don't like to walk; they miss so much—so many rare little glimpses of life; and we women learn so little of life on the whole.

"Catiche's coffee is always hot. I don't know how she manages it, here in the open air. Celestine's coffee gets cold bringing it from the kitchen to the dining-room. Three lumps! How can you drink it so sweet? Take some of the cress with your chop; it's so biting and crisp. Then there's the advantage of being able to smoke with your coffee out here. Now, in the city—aren't you going to smoke?"

"After a while," he said, laying a cigar on the table.

"Who gave it to you?" she laughed.

"I bought it. I suppose I'm getting reckless; I bought a whole box." She was determined not to be personal again and make him uncomfortable.

The cat made friends with him, and climbed into his lap when he smoked his cigar. He stroked her silky fur, and talked a little about her. He looked at Edna's book, which he had read; and he told her the end, to save her the trouble of wading through it, he said.

Again he accompanied her back to her home; and it was after dusk when they reached the little "pigeon-house." She did not ask him to remain, which he was grateful for, as it permitted him to stay without the discomfort of blundering through an excuse which he had no intention of considering. He helped her to light the lamp; then she went into her room to take off her hat and to bathe her face and hands.

When she came back Robert was not examining the pictures and magazines as before; he sat off in the shadow, leaning his head back on the chair as if in a reverie. Edna lingered a moment beside the table, arranging the books there. Then she went across the room to where he sat. She bent over the arm of his chair and called his name.

"Robert," she said, "are you asleep?"

"No," he answered, looking up at her.

She leaned over and kissed him—a soft, cool, delicate kiss, whose voluptuous sting penetrated his whole being—then she moved away from him. He followed, and took her in his arms, just holding her close to him. She put her hand up to his face and pressed his cheek against her own. The action was full of love and tenderness. He sought her lips again. Then he drew her down upon the sofa beside him and held her hand in both of his.

"Now you know," he said, "now you know what I have been fighting against since last summer at Grand Isle; what drove me away and drove me back again."

"Why have you been fighting against it?" she asked. Her face glowed with soft lights.

"Why? Because you were not free; you were Léonce Pontellier's wife. I couldn't help loving you if you were ten times his wife; but so long as I went away from you and kept away I could help telling you so." She put her free hand up to his shoulder, and then against his cheek, rubbing it softly. He kissed her again. His face was warm and flushed.

"There in Mexico I was thinking of you all the time, and longing for you."

"But not writing to me," she interrupted.

"Something put into my head that you cared for me; and I lost my senses. I forgot everything but a wild dream of your some way becoming my wife."

"Your wife!"

"Religion, loyalty, everything would give way if only you cared."

"Then you must have forgotten that I was Léonce Pontellier's wife."

"Oh! I was demented, dreaming of wild, impossible things, recalling men who had set their wives free, we have heard of such things."

"Yes, we have heard of such things."

"I came back full of vague, mad intentions. And when I got here—"

"When you got here you never came near me!" She was still caressing his cheek.

"I realized what a cur I was to dream of such a thing, even if you had been willing."

She took his face between her hands and looked into it as if she would never withdraw her eyes more. She kissed him on the forehead, the eyes, the cheeks, and the lips.

"You have been a very, very foolish boy, wasting your time dreaming of impossible things when you speak of Mr. Pontellier setting me free! I am no longer one of Mr. Pontellier's possessions to dispose of or not. I give myself where I choose. If he were to say, 'Here, Robert, take her and be happy; she is yours,' I should laugh at you both."

His face grew a little white, "What do you mean?" he asked.

There was a knock at the door. Old Celestine came in to say that Madame Ratignolle's servant had come around the back way with a message that Madame had been taken sick and begged Mrs. Pontellier to go to her immediately.

"Yes, yes," said Edna, rising; "I promised. Tell her yes—to wait for me. I'll go back with her."

"Let me walk over with you," offered Robert.

"No," she said; "I will go with the servant." She went into her room to put on her hat, and when she came in again she sat once more upon the sofa beside him. He had not stirred. She put her arms about his neck.

"Good-by, my sweet Robert. Tell me good-by." He kissed her with a degree of passion which had not before entered into his caress, and strained her to him.

"I love you," she whispered, "only you; no one but you. It was you who awoke me last summer out of a life-long, stupid dream. Oh! you have made me so unhappy with your indifference. Oh! I have suffered, suffered! Now you are here we shall love each other, my Robert. We shall be everything to each other. Nothing else in the world is of any consequence. I must go to my friend; but you will wait for me? No matter how late; you will wait for me, Robert?"

"Don't go; don't go! Oh! Edna, stay with me," he pleaded. "Why should you go? Stay with me, stay with me."

"I shall come back as soon as I can; I shall find you here." She buried her face in his neck, and said good-by again. Her seductive voice, together with his great love for her, had enthralled his senses, had deprived him of every impulse but the longing to hold her and keep her.

XXXVII

Edna looked in at the drug store. Monsieur Ratignolle was putting up a mixture himself, very carefully, dropping a red liquid into a tiny glass. He was grateful to Edna for having come; her presence would be a comfort to his wife. Madame Ratignolle's sister, who had always been with her at such trying times, had not been able to come up from the plantation, and Adèle had been inconsolable until Mrs. Pontellier so kindly promised to come to her. The nurse had been with them at night for the past week, as she lived a great distance away. And Dr. Mandelet had been coming and going all the afternoon. They were then looking for him any moment.

Edna hastened upstairs by a private stairway that led from the rear of the store to the apartments above. The children were all sleeping in a back room. Madame Ratignolle was in the salon, whither she had strayed in her suffering impatience. She sat on the sofa, clad in an ample white *peignoir*, holding a handkerchief tight in her hand with a nervous clutch. Her face was drawn and pinched, her sweet blue eyes haggard and unnatural. All her beautiful hair had been drawn back and plaited. It lay in a long braid on the sofa pillow, coiled like a golden serpent.

The nurse, a comfortable looking *Griffe*° woman in white apron and cap, was urging her to return to her bedroom.

"There is no use, there is no use," she said at once to Edna. "We must get rid of Mandelet; he is getting too old and careless. He said he would be here at half-past seven; now it must be eight. See what time it is, Joséphine."

The woman was possessed of a cheerful nature, and refused to take any situation too seriously, especially a situation with which she was so familiar. She urged Madame to have courage and patience. But Madame only set her teeth hard into her under lip, and Edna saw the sweat gather in beads on her white forehead. After a moment or two she uttered a profound sigh and wiped her face with the handkerchief rolled in a ball. She appeared exhausted. The nurse gave her a fresh handkerchief, sprinkled with cologne water.

"This is too much!" she cried. "Mandelet ought to be killed! Where is Alphonse? Is it possible I am to be abandoned like this—neglected by every one?"

"Neglected, indeed!" exclaimed the nurse. Wasn't she there? And here was Mrs. Pontellier leaving, no doubt, a pleasant evening at home to devote to her? And wasn't Monsieur Ratignolle coming that very instant through the hall? And Joséphine was quite sure she had heard Doctor Mandelet's coupé. Yes, there it was, down at the door.

Adèle consented to go back to her room. She sat on the edge of a little low couch next to her bed.

Doctor Mandelet paid no attention to Madame Ratignolle's upbraidings. He was accustomed to them at such times, and was too well convinced of her loyalty to doubt it.

He was glad to see Edna, and wanted her to go with him into the salon and entertain him. But Madame Ratignolle would not consent that Edna should leave her for an instant. Between agonizing moments, she chatted a little, and said it took her mind off her sufferings.

Edna began to feel uneasy. She was seized with a vague dread. Her own like experiences seemed far away, unreal, and only half remembered. She recalled faintly an ecstasy of pain, the heavy odor of chloroform, a stupor which had deadened sensation, and an awakening to find a little new life to which she had given being, added to the great unnumbered multitude of souls that come and go.

She began to wish she had not come; her presence was not necessary. She might have invented a pretext for staying away; she might even

Griffe: The offspring of a mulatto and a Negro.

invent a pretext now for going. But Edna did not go. With an inward agony, with a flaming, outspoken revolt against the ways of Nature, she witnessed the scene of torture.

She was still stunned and speechless with emotion when later she leaned over her friend to kiss her and softly say good-by. Adèle, pressing her cheek, whispered in an exhausted voice: "Think of the children, Edna. Oh think of the children! Remember them!"

XXXVIII

Edna still felt dazed when she got outside in the open air. The Doctor's coupé had returned for him and stood before the *porte cochère*. She did not wish to enter the coupé, and told Doctor Mandelet she would walk; she was not afraid, and would go alone. He directed his carriage to meet him at Mrs. Pontellier's, and he started to walk home with her.

Up—away up, over the narrow street between the tall houses, the stars were blazing. The air was mild and caressing, but cool with the breath of spring and the night. They walked slowly, the Doctor with a heavy, measured tread and his hands behind him; Edna, in an absent-minded way, as she had walked one night at Grand Isle, as if her thoughts had gone ahead of her and she was striving to overtake them.

"You shouldn't have been there, Mrs. Pontellier," he said. "That was no place for you. Adèle is full of whims at such times. There were a dozen women she might have had with her, unimpressionable women. I felt that it was cruel, cruel. You shouldn't have gone."

"Oh, well!" she answered, indifferently. "I don't know that it matters after all. One has to think of the children some time or other; the sooner the better."

"When is Léonce coming back?"

"Quite soon. Some time in March."

"And you are going abroad?"

"Perhaps—no, I am not going. I'm not going to be forced into doing things. I don't want to go abroad. I want to be let alone. Nobody has any right—except the children, perhaps—and even then, it seems to me—or it did seem—" She felt that her speech was voicing the incoherency of her thoughts, and stopped abruptly.

"The trouble is," sighed the Doctor, grasping her meaning intuitively, "that youth is given up to illusions. It seems to be a provision of Nature; a decoy to secure mothers for the race. And Nature takes no account of moral consequences, of arbitrary conditions which we create, and which we feel obliged to maintain at any cost."

"Yes," she said. "The years that are gone seem like dreams—if one might go on sleeping and dreaming—but to wake up and find—oh! well! perhaps it is better to wake up after all, even to suffer, rather than to remain a dupe to illusions all one's life."

"It seems to me, my dear child," said the Doctor at parting, holding her hand, "you seem to me to be in trouble. I am not going to ask for your confidence. I will only say that if ever you feel moved to give it to me, perhaps I might help you. I know I would understand, and I tell you there are not many who would—not many, my dear."

"Some way I don't feel moved to speak of things that trouble me. Don't think I am ungrateful or that I don't appreciate your sympathy. There are periods of despondency and suffering which take possession of me. But I don't want anything but my own way. That is wanting a good deal, of course, when you have to trample upon the lives, the hearts, the prejudices of others—but no matter—still, I shouldn't want to trample upon the little lives. Oh! I don't know what I'm saying, Doctor. Good night. Don't blame me for anything."

"Yes, I will blame you if you don't come and see me soon. We will talk of things you never have dreamt of talking about before. It will do us both good. I don't want you to blame yourself, whatever comes. Good night, my child."

She let herself in at the gate, but instead of entering she sat upon the step of the porch. The night was quiet and soothing. All the tearing emotion of the last few hours seemed to fall away from her like a somber, uncomfortable garment, which she had but to loosen to be rid of. She went back to that hour before Adèle had sent for her; and her senses kindled afresh in thinking of Robert's words, the pressure of his arms, and the feeling of his lips upon her own. She could picture at that moment no greater bliss on earth than possession of the beloved one. His expression of love had already given him to her in part. When she thought that he was there at hand, waiting for her, she grew numb with the intoxication of expectancy. It was so late; he would be asleep perhaps. She would awaken him with a kiss. She hoped he would be asleep that she might arouse him with her caresses.

Still, she remembered Adèle's voice whispering, "Think of the children; think of them." She meant to think of them; that determination had driven into her soul like a death wound—but not to-night. To-morrow would be time to think of everything.

Robert was not waiting for her in the little parlor. He was nowhere at hand. The house was empty. But he had scrawled on a piece of paper that lay in the lamplight:

"I love you. Good-by—because I love you."

Edna grew faint when she read the words. She went and sat on the sofa. Then she stretched herself out there, never uttering a sound. She did not sleep. She did not go to bed. The lamp sputtered and went out. She was still awake in the morning, when Celestine unlocked the kitchen door and came in to light the fire.

XXXIX

Victor, with hammer and nails and scraps of scantling, was patching a corner of one of the galleries. Mariequita sat near by, dangling her legs, watching him work, and handing him nails from the tool-box. The sun was beating down upon them. The girl had covered her head with her apron folded into a square pad. They had been talking for an hour or more. She was never tired of hearing Victor describe the dinner at Mrs. Pontellier's. He exaggerated every detail, making it appear a veritable Lucullean feast. The flowers were in tubs, he said. The champagne was quaffed from huge golden goblets. Venus rising from the foam could have presented no more entrancing a spectacle than Mrs. Pontellier, blazing with beauty and diamonds at the head of the board, while the other women were all of them youthful houris, possessed of incomparable charms.

She got it into her head that Victor was in love with Mrs. Pontellier, and he gave her evasive answers, framed so as to confirm her belief. She grew sullen and cried a little, threatening to go off and leave him to his fine ladies. There were a dozen men crazy about her at the *Chênière;* and since it was the fashion to be in love with married people, why, she could run away any time she liked to New Orleans with Célina's husband.

Célina's husband was a fool, a coward, and a pig, and to prove it to her, Victor intended to hammer his head into a jelly the next time he encountered him. This assurance was very consoling to Mariequita. She dried her eyes, and grew cheerful at the prospect.

They were still talking of the dinner and the allurements of city life when Mrs. Pontellier herself slipped around the corner of the house. The two youngsters stayed dumb with amazement before what they considered to be an apparition. But it was really she in flesh and blood, looking tired and a little travel-stained.

"I walked up from the wharf," she said, "and heard the hammering. I supposed it was you, mending the porch. It's a good thing. I was always tripping over those loose planks last summer. How dreary and deserted everything looks!"

It took Victor some little time to comprehend that she had come in Beaudelet's lugger, that she had come alone, and for no purpose but to rest.

"There's nothing fixed up yet, you see. I'll give you my room; it's the only place."

"Any corner will do," she assured him.

"And if you can stand Philomel's cooking," he went on, "though I might try to get her mother while you are here. Do you think she would come?" turning to Mariequita.

Mariequita thought that perhaps Philomel's mother might come for a few days, and money enough.

Beholding Mrs. Pontellier make her appearance, the girl had at once suspected a lovers' rendezvous. But Victor's astonishment was so genuine, and Mrs. Pontellier's indifference so apparent, that the disturbing notion did not lodge long in her brain. She contemplated with the greatest interest this woman who gave the most sumptuous dinners in America, and who had all the men in New Orleans at her feet.

"What time will you have dinner?" asked Edna. "I'm very hungry; but don't get anything extra."

"I'll have it ready in little or no time," he said, bustling and packing away his tools. "You may go to my room to brush up and rest yourself. Mariequita will show you."

"Thank you," said Edna. "But, do you know, I have a notion to go down to the beach and take a good wash and even a little swim, before dinner?"

"The water is too cold!" they both exclaimed. "Don't think of it."

"Well, I might go down and try—dip my toes in. Why, it seems to me the sun is hot enough to have warmed the very depths of the ocean. Could you get me a couple of towels? I'd better go right away, so as to be back in time. It would be a little too chilly if I waited till this afternoon."

Mariequita ran over to Victor's room, and returned with some towels, which she gave to Edna.

"I hope you have fish for dinner," said Edna, as she started to walk away; "but don't do anything extra if you haven't."

"Run and find Philomel's mother," Victor instructed the girl. "I'll go to the kitchen and see what I can do. By Gimminy! Women have no consideration! She might have sent me word."

Edna walked on down to the beach rather mechanically, not noticing anything special except that the sun was hot. She was not dwelling upon any particular train of thought. She had done all the thinking which was necessary after Robert went away, when she lay awake upon the sofa till morning.

She had said over and over to herself: "To-day it is Arobin; to-morrow it will be some one else. It makes no difference to me, it doesn't matter about Léonce Pontellier—but Raoul and Etienne!" She understood now clearly what she had meant long ago when she said to Adèle Ratignolle that she would give up the unessential, but she would never sacrifice herself for her children.

Despondency had come upon her there in the wakeful night, and had never lifted. There was no one thing in the world that she desired. There was no human being whom she wanted near her except Robert; and she even realized that the day would come when he, too, and the thought of him would melt out of her existence, leaving her alone. The children appeared before her like antagonists who had overcome her; who had overpowered and sought to drag her into the soul's slavery for the rest of her days. But she knew a way to elude them. She was not thinking of these things when she walked down to the beach.

The water of the Gulf stretched out before her, gleaming with the million lights of the sun. The voice of the sea is seductive, never ceasing, whispering, clamoring, murmuring, inviting the soul to wander in abysses of solitude. All along the white beach, up and down, there was no living thing in sight. A bird with a broken wing was beating the air above, reeling, fluttering, circling disabled down, down to the water.

Edna had found her old bathing suit still hanging, faded, upon its accustomed peg.

She put it on, leaving her clothing in the bath-house. But when she was there beside the sea, absolutely alone, she cast the unpleasant, pricking garments from her, and for the first time in her life she stood naked in the open air, at the mercy of the sun, the breeze that beat upon her, and the waves that invited her.

How strange and awful it seemed to stand naked under the sky! how delicious! She felt like some new-born creature, opening its eyes in a familiar world that it had never known.

The foamy wavelets curled up to her white feet, and coiled like serpents about her ankles. She walked out. The water was chill, but she walked on. The water was deep, but she lifted her white body and reached out with a long, sweeping stroke. The touch of the sea is sensuous, enfolding the body in its soft, close embrace.

She went on and on. She remembered the night she swam far out, and recalled the terror that seized her at the fear of being unable to regain the shore. She did not look back now, but went on and on, thinking of the blue-grass meadow that she had traversed when a little child, believing that it had no beginning and no end.

Her arms and legs were growing tired.

She thought of Léonce and the children. They were a part of her life. But they need not have thought that they could possess her, body and soul. How Mademoiselle Reisz would have laughed, perhaps sneered, if she knew! "And you call yourself an artist! What pretensions, Madame! The artist must possess the courageous soul that dares and defies."

Exhaustion was pressing upon and overpowering her.

"Good-by—because I love you." He did not know; he did not understand. He would never understand. Perhaps Doctor Mandelet would have understood if she had seen him—but it was too late; the shore was far behind her, and her strength was gone.

She looked into the distance, and the old terror flamed up for an instant, then sank again. Edna heard her father's voice and her sister Margaret's. She heard the barking of an old dog that was chained to the sycamore tree. The spurs of the cavalry officer clanged as he walked across the porch. There was the hum of bees, and the musky odor of pinks filled the air.

PART TWO

The Awakening: A Case Study in Contemporary Criticism

A Critical History of *The Awakening*

In 1956, Kenneth Eble praised *The Awakening* but called it "a forgotten novel." Twenty years later, *The Awakening* became part of the Critical Editions series published by W. W. Norton, which suggested that it was frequently assigned in college literature classes. In 1988 it was the subject of the sixteenth volume in the Approaches to Teaching World Literature series published by the Modern Language Association, taking its place alongside such acknowledged classics as Chaucer's *The Canterbury Tales,* Milton's *Paradise Lost,* and Melville's *Moby-Dick.* Indeed, it was the first work by a female author to be included in this series. A survey conducted in the 1980s by Paul Lauter of the Feminist Press revealed that Chopin was the thirty-seventh most frequently taught American writer in colleges and universities. In one sense, it took a long time for Chopin's novel, published in 1899, to be recognized as the fine novel that it is, but on the other hand, given the fifty years of critical neglect that followed its publication, the novel's rise to prominence following its rediscovery was meteoric.

The fifty-year interval between the publication of *The Awakening* and Eble's enthusiastic essay in the *Western Humanities Review* was a period of enormous change in literary criticism and in the moral climate of America. In 1899, vestiges of Victorian prudery still influenced the critical response to literature; a novel was as likely to be judged on its moral message as on its artistic merits. Thus a reviewer for the *Chicago*

Times-Herald chastised Kate Chopin for entering "the overworked field of sex fiction" (qtd. in Culley 149). In 1956, in a society that had become far more secular and open, and in which professional critics had been schooled in a formalist theory that left aside moral judgment, Kenneth Eble could write with admiration, "Quite frankly, the book is about sex" (263). Yet it is not the book's subject matter that primarily interested Eble but rather the skill with which Chopin had written it: "The claim of the book upon the reader's attention is simple. It is a first-rate novel. The justification for urging its importance is that we have few enough novels of its stature" (262).

By the early 1970s, it was the insights of feminist literary critics that revealed the complexity of both art and message in *The Awakening*. If it had been a formalist (also called New Critical) approach that allowed Kenneth Eble to appreciate the novel on its own artistic terms, fifteen years later feminist critics began to use psychoanalytic theory, linguistics, classical mythology, and new perceptions of the cultural position of women in the late nineteenth century to reveal the novel's richness. Instead of being a selfish, immoral woman, Edna could be seen as a person occupying a particular historical moment and having personality traits that influenced the course she took in (fictional) life and finally in death. And Kate Chopin was, in the process, elevated from the status of minor local color writer to that of author of a major American novel.

The history of critical response to *The Awakening* is particularly instructive in assessing changes in the status of women as writers, as critics and scholars, and as heroines of novels from the late nineteenth century to the present day. As a female author, Kate Chopin was especially susceptible to charges that she had written an immoral and potentially dangerous novel. The nineteenth-century "cult of gentility" gave women particular responsibility for safeguarding the moral and spiritual tenor of the family and, by extension, the nation. For a woman writer, then, to portray sympathetically a woman who abdicates her domestic responsibilities in favor of her own needs was to undermine the very fabric of civilized society; if Edna Pontellier was guilty of domestic desertion as well as sexual indiscretion, then Kate Chopin was, as her creator, equally guilty.

Kate Chopin's proposal, in her mock-apology for *The Awakening* in 1899, that Edna Pontellier was a character with a mind of her own ("I never dreamed of Mrs. Pontellier making such a mess of things") seems not accidental but rather a direct response to the tone of early reviews of the novel. The reviewers themselves seemed unable to regard Edna as a fictional creation; instead they saw her as a woman who deserved to be lectured to for behaving badly. "At the very outset of the story," wrote a reviewer for the *St. Louis Globe-Democrat,* "one feels that the heroine should pray for deliverance from temptation" (qtd. in Culley 146), and the *New Orleans Times-Democrat* chided her for not being sufficiently maternal: Edna "fails to perceive that the relation of a mother to her children is far more important than the gratification of a passion which experience has taught her is, by its very nature, evanescent" (qtd. in Culley 150). Edna's death at the end of the novel seemed to many reviewers to be exactly the punishment she deserved. The reviewer for *Public Opinion,* for example, announced that he or she was "well satisfied when Mrs. Pontellier deliberately swims out to her death in the waters of the gulf" (qtd. in Culley 151).

Such chastising had its effect. In 1906, the rights were transferred to the firm of Duffield & Company and *The Awakening* was republished; but by then it had sunk like a rock from public view. Indeed, between 1899 and 1901 Chopin earned just a little more than $150 in royalties from sales of the novel. Writing about *The Awakening* in 1909, ten years after its publication, Percival Pollard dismissed it as lacking credibility: "'The Awakening' asks us to believe that a young woman who had been several years married, and had borne children, had never, in all that time, been properly 'awake.' It would be an arresting question for students of sleep-walking, but one must not venture down that path now" (qtd. in Culley 160). The only major work on Chopin published before the 1960s was Daniel Rankin's *Kate Chopin and Her Creole Stories* (1932). As the title suggests, Rankin, who was Chopin's first biographer, regarded her primarily as a regional writer—an assessment that was to hold sway for years—and he had little respect for *The Awakening.* Rankin proposed that the novel had its origins in the stories Chopin had been told when she was an "impressionable youth" and that she was influenced by "[Aubrey] Beardsley's hideous and haunting pictures, with their disfiguring leer of sensuality" (174). The novel, Rankin continues, owes much to the "erotic morbidity" of European novels of the late nineteenth century (175); he describes it as "exotic in setting, morbid in theme, erotic in motivation" (175).

Despite the popularity of her short stories, many of them collected in *Bayou Folk* (1894) and *A Night in Acadie* (1897), Chopin was not included in many of the literary histories and other reference works during the first half of the century. Fred Lewis Pattee's *Cambridge History of American Literature,* published in 1918, omits her, although Pattee did praise her short stories in *The Development of the American Short Story* (1923). When her work is mentioned at all in these early histories, she is classified, along with George Washington Cable, as an author of southern local color stories. Such is the case, for example, in the 1948 *Literary History of the United States*, as well as in subsequent editions in 1953 and 1963. As late as 1962, *The Reader's Encyclopedia of American Literature* also emphasized her short fiction, noting that when she "turned to novel writing," it was "not with great success." *The Reader's Encyclopedia* characterizes *The Awakening* as dealing with "themes of extramarital love and miscegenation" (176), the latter of which is a factual error, for Chopin's novel never touches upon miscegenation.

Isolated voices, however, gave the novel its due even before the 1960s. Writing about Chopin for the 1930 edition of the *Dictionary of American Biography*, Dorothy Anne Dondore gives special praise to her story "Désirée's Baby" and to *The Awakening*, observing that "one of the tragedies of recent American literature" is that "Mrs. Chopin should have written this book two decades in advance of its time" (91). And in 1952, in *The Confident Years, 1885–1915*, Van Wyck Brooks wrote, "But there was one novel of the nineties in the South that should have been remembered, one small perfect book that mattered more than the whole life-work of many a prolific writer" (341).

Perhaps not surprisingly, scholars outside the United States played a major role in the midcentury revival of *The Awakening*. When the novel was first published, reviewers were alarmed by the possibility that Chopin had been influenced by what they considered decadent European literature, but in 1953 the French critic Cyrille Arnavon turned what had been for these reviewers a negative assessment into a positive view by comparing *The Awakening* to Gustave Flaubert's 1856 novel, *Madame Bovary*, and then translating *The Awakening* into French. Emma Bovary, in Flaubert's novel, shares with Edna Pontellier a desire for a kind of passion she does not find in her marriage; following an extramarital affair, she commits suicide by taking poison. Parallels between the novels are not precise, and it is especially significant that whereas Flaubert takes an external view of Emma Bovary, presenting her rather like a case study, Chopin allows the reader to view events from Edna's consciousness. As Susan J. Rosowski puts it, "The ironic distance of *Madame Bovary* is replaced by a high degree of narrative sympathy" (46).

Nevertheless, the plot lines of the two novels are sufficiently similar to invite comparison, and Arnavon was not the first reader of *The Awakening* to liken it to *Madame Bovary*. Such comparison is the opening statement of Willa Cather's 1899 review of Chopin's novel for the *Pittsburgh Leader:* "A Creole *Bovary* is this little novel of Miss Chopin's."

Unlike Arnavon more than fifty years later, however, Cather did not find the similarity to Flaubert's novel a cause for celebrating:

> There was, indeed, no need that a second *Madame Bovary* should be written, but an author's choice of themes is frequently as inexplicable as his choice of a wife. It is governed by some innate temperamental bias that cannot be diagrammed. This is particularly so in women who write, and I shall not attempt to say why Miss Chopin has devoted so exquisite and sensitive, well-governed a style to so trite and sordid a theme. (qtd. in Culley 153)

Following Arnavon, a number of critics have pursued the comparison of *The Awakening* to *Madame Bovary* and to other novels as well. Most recently, Susan J. Rosowski has explored the subgenre of the "novel of awakening," in which she includes, in addition to Flaubert's novel, Willa Cather's *My Mortal Enemy* (1926), Agnes Smedley's *Daughter of Earth* (1929), and George Eliot's *Middlemarch* (1871–72).

Comparing one novel to another, even if the purpose is to show how one author has influenced another, can be a limited form of criticism. On the other hand, readers may be influenced in how they think about novels by the company they are placed in by scholars, and perhaps the greatest contribution that Cyrille Arnavon made to Kate Chopin's reputation as an author was to place her in the company not only of Flaubert but also of American realist writers such as Theodore Dreiser and Frank Norris rather than classing her with local colorists such as George Washington Cable and Sarah Orne Jewett. The treatment of sex and marriage in *The Awakening,* Arnavon proposed, had a realism that transcended geographical region. In 1962, the highly regarded Edmund Wilson echoed Arnavon when he declared that Chopin's depiction of infidelity had anticipated that of the English novelist D. H. Lawrence. By the middle of the twentieth century, then, frank discussion of sexuality and infidelity was cause for praise rather than censure.

The single person most responsible for bringing Kate Chopin's work to wide public attention was, like Arnavon, not an American scholar. Per Seyersted, a Norwegian, was influenced by Arnavon's enthusiasm for her work in the late 1950s, and in 1969 he published the first comprehensive critical biography of Chopin. Even more important, in the same year he published the two-volume set *The Complete Works of Kate Chopin,* which includes ninety-six stories, twenty poems, and the texts of both *At Fault* and *The Awakening* as well as more than a dozen of her essays. Serious Chopin scholarship can thus be said to date from the publication of Seyersted's volumes; the majority of her published work was finally available in libraries across the country. Edmund Wilson wrote the foreword to *The Complete Works of Kate Chopin*. He expressed his gratitude to the Norwegian Seyersted for "reconstructing . . . both the work and the personality of this daring and accomplished woman" (15).

In his critical biography of Chopin, Seyersted reveals the zeal of one who has made an important literary "find" in some of his chapter titles: "A Daring Writer Banned," "The Long-Neglected Pioneer." His chapter on *The Awakening*, however, is judiciously appreciative. Like his mentor, Cyrille Arnavon, he explores the parallels between Chopin's novel and *Madame Bovary*, but his major contribution is to place Chopin squarely in the tradition of turn-of-the-century realism as well as indicating the ways in which she was a "pioneer." Seyersted emphasizes that *The Awakening* merits consideration alongside works by Stephen Crane, Hamlin Garland, Frank Norris, and Theodore Dreiser—"the American pioneer writers of the 1890s" (190). But to a greater extent than these writers, Seyersted finds Chopin to be an author ahead of her time:

> Kate Chopin is a rare, transitional figure in modern literature. In her illustrations of the female condition she forms a link between George Sand and Simone de Beauvoir. In her descriptions of the power of sexuality she reflects the ideas of such a work as *Hippolytus* and foreshadows the forceful 20th-century treatments of Eros. (194)

Precisely because of her "daring" creation of Edna Pontellier, however, Seyersted predicted that negative criticism of *The Awakening* would persist: "Mrs. Pontellier will for a long time to come be faced with male condescension and prejudice," while "most female readers . . . are likely to take to their hearts this deeply moving portrait of a woman's growth into self-awareness" (199).

In addition to being erroneous, Seyersted's prediction seems curious in light of the fact that almost all of *The Awakening*'s earlier champions had been men. What Seyersted could not have foreseen was the dramatic increase in the number of female literary scholars in the 1970s and 1980s, and the concomitant development of several varieties of feminist literary theory, all of which have found *The Awakening* a congenial text.

As Margaret Culley points out in the Norton Critical Edition of *The Awakening*, the critics of the novel in the 1960s, including Seyersted, were first concerned with establishing the literary traditions of which

Chopin's work is a part, after which they turned their attention to the novel as a work of art, examining patterns of imagery and style. By the 1970s, the focus of critical inquiry shifted to the ambiguity of the ending, the characterization of Edna Pontellier, and the various influences which may have played a role in the shaping of the novel (143). So swiftly did critical responses to the novel accumulate that by the mid-1970s Marlene Springer compiled an annotated bibliography of commentary on Chopin's work from 1890 to 1973. Some of the reviews and articles listed in Springer's bibliography deal with Chopin's short fiction, of course, but one can already see the burgeoning interest in *The Awakening*.

Even as late as 1970, some critics were still insisting upon Chopin's significance as a regional writer. John R. May, in "Local Color in *The Awakening*," stressed Chopin's use of specific details regarding Creole culture and the New Orleans and Grand Isle settings in order to propose that "Edna [has] been awakened by the alien Creole environment" rather than by "a growing awareness of her sexual needs" (1037). May thus resists universalizing the novel's theme. He distinguishes between the "local color novel," in which "the identity of the setting is integral to the very unfolding of the theme," and the novel in which the locale is "incidental to a theme that could as well be set anywhere," declaring that "*The Awakening* is clearly of the former type" (1040). In the same year, George M. Spangler, in "Kate Chopin's *The Awakening:* A Partial Dissent," took issue with the ending of the novel, arguing that if one were to believe in Edna's "strength of will, her ruthless determination to go her own way" until this point, it is out of character for her to commit suicide. Such an ending, Spangler insists, is the "conclusion for an ordinary sentimental novel" (254) rather than for the novel Chopin had written. This flaw reduced the novel in Spangler's view from the status of "extraordinary masterpiece" to that of "very good, very interesting novel" (255).

During the 1970s, three separate editions of *The Awakening* were issued, each volume including a selection of Chopin's short stories as well. *The Awakening* had clearly become the centerpiece of her work, but the stories retained their own interest, increasingly so as they were seen to prefigure or echo the themes and characterizations of the novel. In 1970, Lewis Leary edited such a collection, and the following year he published a collection of essays on southern literature, two of which concern Chopin. Like other critics of the period, Leary concentrates on the patterns of imagery in the novel, stressing the extent to which Chopin echoed Walt Whitman, particularly in her use of the sea as a dominant force in Edna's experience. In contrast to Spangler, Leary sees *The Awakening* as a unified whole and Edna as a "valiant woman, worthy of place beside other fictional heroines who have tested emancipation and failed—Nathaniel Hawthorne's Hester Prynne, Gustave Flaubert's Emma Bovary, or Henry James's Isabel Archer" (174). In 1974, Per Seyersted edited for the Feminist Press *"The Storm" and Other Stories with "The Awakening,"* and two years later Barbara Solomon edited as a Signet Classic a third collection including *The Awakening*.

By the end of the 1970s, Kate Chopin's readers had available more primary sources for study: Per Seyersted and Emily Toth collaborated on the production of *A Kate Chopin Miscellany* (published, appropriately enough, by the Northwestern State University Press in Natchitoches [pronounced NACK-uh-tosh], Louisiana), a volume that includes the texts of several of Chopin's stories, two of her diaries, and an assortment of letters, essays, and poems. The collaboration of Seyersted and Toth is one representation of an unusual aspect of Chopin scholarship: the way in which the central scholars of her work have passed the torch to one another. Seyersted had the cooperation of Daniel Rankin in preparing his 1969 critical biography, and Seyersted later shared his sources and materials with Emily Toth as she embarked on her own biography of Chopin, which was published in 1990. The work of each successive scholar expanded on and clarified the previous work.

The most recent addition to the source books assisting Kate Chopin scholarship is Thomas Bonner's 1988 *The Kate Chopin Companion*. For Bonner, as for Seyersted and Toth, the study of Chopin has been a consuming life's work. The *Companion* consists of four elements. Occupying the most space is a glossary of the names of places and characters in Chopin's work and life as well as terms used in her work (for example, such French words as *banquette*) and brief synopses of the short stories. Also included in the volume are Chopin's translations of French fiction (primarily by Maupassant), period maps of the geographical settings of Chopin's life and her fiction, and a detailed bibliographical essay.

The development of critical studies of *The Awakening* since 1969 has been affected by both the process of establishing the novel in the canon of American literature and the proliferation of critical approaches to literature during the same time. It is perhaps fortunate that in the 1950s and 1960s when Chopin's novel was being rediscovered, the formalist approach of the New Critical school of literary theory was still dominant in critical circles, because the close attention to the forms, patterns, and structure of literary works favored by the formalists established *The Awakening* as a work of art rather than as the document of flawed morality that its early reviewers had reacted to. Thus, the assessments of Eble, Brooks, and Leary were important steps in the process of separating the book from its author and rescuing it from oblivion.

One strand in criticism of *The Awakening* during the past two decades is what has come to be termed the "New Historicist" approach—that is, seeing the novel in terms of its own historical moment, as a product of and response to the ideas, values, beliefs, and events of a particular time. A number of critics have analyzed such issues as the Creole culture in which the novel is largely set, the conflict between the ideals of the Victorian woman and the "new woman" of the late nineteenth century, and attitudes toward motherhood and sexuality that women such as Edna Pontellier might have shared. While such an approach to the "then" of the novel might seem to have a great deal in common with the "local color" school, the two critical movements are actually quite different. Those who see works of fiction as examples of local color are concerned primarily with the surface details. How do people speak? How do they dress? What local or regional customs or geographical features are evident in the work? New historicists, on the other hand, go beyond these surface representations to explore fundamental realities informing the novel. Whereas someone looking for elements of local color, for example, might note how the author describes the clothing that children wear, the new historicist critic would investigate the theories of childrearing that were in wide currency when the author was writing. Further, to classify a work as contributing to local color is often to emphasize those elements of it that are quaint or picturesque or nostalgic—and which can easily become stereotypical—whereas the new historicist attempts to peel away nostalgia for the past and view a place and time as it might have been experienced by the author's characters.

In "Revolt Against Nature: The Problematic Modernism of *The Awakening*" (1988), Michael T. Gilmore examines the meanings that the word and concept of "nature" would have had for Americans of the 1890s. Having traditionally believed that "the nation's historic source of strength" was "its special tie to the physical environment" (60), Americans were disturbed by such phenomena as Frederick Jackson Turner's 1893 pronouncement of the closing of the frontier, rapid industrialization, and challenges to conventional ideas of the family. Such symptoms of movement away from what was considered "natural," Gilmore suggests, created deep anxieties about national and individual identity. In her rebellion against the "natural" role of wife and mother, Edna seems initially to exemplify this drift toward modernist uncertainty, but Gilmore proposes that Chopin demonstrates in several ways that Edna remains bound by notions of the "natural": her painting is representational, the music to which she responds replicates the sounds of the natural world, and, most importantly, she believes in a fixed, inviolable "self" rather than "the decentered, internally conflicted self made familiar in the twentieth century by Freud" (83). Gilmore thus sees the novel as paradoxical, and Edna's suicide at the end is in his view not the result of an "awakening" but instead caused by her failure to resist a nineteenth-century understanding of the "natural."

Another way of interpreting *The Awakening* through historical context is to examine the values of the Creole culture that Chopin depicts and to explore the effect they could have had on a young Presbyterian woman from Kentucky. Such an approach raises several questions: Does the open sensuality of characters such as Robert Lebrun and Adèle Ratignolle cause Edna to experience a sexual awakening? Does her inability to reconcile her strict upbringing with the openness of Creole society lead to her death? In "An American Dilemma: Cultural Conflict in Kate Chopin's *The Awakening*" (1983), Priscilla Leder argues that while in some ways Edna's immersion in the sensual world of the Creoles is liberating for her, the very fact that within it she is able to have her biological needs fulfilled reminds her that woman's traditional fate is to be reduced to and defined by her biological function. Leder notes that the theme of cultural conflict was a common one in nineteenth-century American literature, and she compares Edna's situation with that of James Fenimore Cooper's Natty Bumppo among the Indians and Herman Melville's Tommo among the Polynesians. Because Cooper's and Melville's male protagonists have a freedom that Edna lacks—they can escape to forest or sea—they are not as threatened by a loss of identity.

A very different way of using history as a key to understanding a literary work is to examine its parallels with well-known myths or legends. Critics who take such an approach do not necessarily argue that authors consciously borrow classical stories to shape their own plots; they suggest, instead, that the stories told in mythology endure because of the essential human experiences they describe. Several essays about *The Awakening* published in the mid-1980s see the novel as having parallels to Greek myths, and two of them provide an interesting contrast: Sandra M. Gilbert, in "The Second Coming of Aphrodite" (1987), sees

Edna as the Greek goddess of love, reunified at the end with her natural element, water, whereas Rosemary F. Franklin, in "*The Awakening* and the Failure of Psyche" (1984), places Edna in a related myth, as Psyche committing suicide instead of being reunited with the god Eros. To view Edna Pontellier as Aphrodite, as Gilbert does, is to see her as powerful and autonomous, a goddess born in the sea (as in some sense Edna is when she learns to swim at Grand Isle) who is free to exercise her own sexuality. One of the key scenes in the novel for Gilbert's reading is the dinner party that Edna gives just before she moves out of her husband's house, at which Chopin describes Edna as "the regal woman, the one who rules, who looks on, who stands alone" (109). By this point, Gilbert asserts, Edna has become a character in a "feminist fantasy" (92) that "propose[s] a feminist and matriarchal myth of Aphrodite/Venus as an alternative to the masculinist and patriarchal myth of Jesus" (91). Through the "colony of women" at Grand Isle, Gilbert proposes that Edna has entered a "pagan fictive world" that is "absolutely incompatible with the fictions of gentility and Christianity by which her 'real' world lives" (101). Seen in this context, Edna's final swim is "not into death but back into her own life, back into her own vision, back into the imaginative openness of her childhood" (104).

Instead of as Aphrodite, Rosemary Franklin sees Edna as Psyche, a mortal woman whose beauty made the goddess Aphrodite jealous in Greek mythology. Her punishment of Psyche was thwarted by Aphrodite's son Eros, whom Psyche was permitted to love on condition that she not see him. When she broke her promise, Aphrodite punished Psyche with a series of tasks so difficult that she considered suicide, but Eros once again intervened and the mortal woman was allowed to live among the gods. Many scholars, including Franklin, view the story of Psyche as a paradigm of female development, with the continual temptation to passivity represented by the impulse toward suicide. Franklin sees Creole culture as the "immortals" to whom Edna is the "mortal" outsider whose several quests for mature identity form the plot of the novel. Yet unlike Psyche in the myth, Edna has neither the strength nor the intervention of the god Eros to assist her in surmounting the obstacles before her. Like Gilbert, Franklin sees the dinner-party scene as a pivotal one, but she points out that soon after Edna is described as "the regal woman," a feeling of despair overcomes her: "she felt the old ennui overtaking her; the hopelessness which so often assailed her, which came upon her like an obsession" (109). The passivity of suicide that Psyche was able to resist is too strong for Edna, and when she finally swims into the Gulf, Franklin says, "she goes down to darkness, absorbed in a regressive illusion—that she is wading into the bluegrass meadow of her childhood" (526).

The Greek word *psyche* originally meant "breath" and quickly came to represent the spirit or soul. When the science of psychology developed in the late nineteenth century, its name suggested that it was devoted to the study of that part of us that is not visible but that is nonetheless very powerful: our motivations, thought processes, dreams, and desires. One approach to literary study is to apply the theories of psychologists to characters—to attempt to determine the inner conflicts and struggles that can explain characters' attitudes and actions. Given the sometimes enigmatic nature of Edna Pontellier's behavior in *The Awakening,* and the emphasis that Chopin places on dreaming, awakening, and fantasy, the novel lends itself to psychoanalytic investigation, and early in the past two decades of close attention to *The Awakening,* Cynthia Griffin Wolff began this line of inquiry in her essay "Thanatos and Eros: Kate Chopin's *The Awakening,*" which is reprinted in this volume.

Whereas Wolff sees Edna as having characteristics of the schizoid personality—one who feels split between two "selves"—Wayne Batten, in his 1985 article "Illusion and Archetype: The Curious Story of Edna Pontellier," uses the theories of psychologist Carl Jung to try to understand why Edna's story is so "curious." Jung's concept of what he called the "collective unconscious"—a kind of submerged memory shared by all human beings—included certain images, or "archetypes." One of these archetypes is the "demon lover," the seductive but dangerous lover who possesses and destroys a woman. Batten argues that Edna finds nothing in the world around her to help her do battle with the power of this phantom lover, so that at the end of the novel, as she swims into the Gulf, she is returning to "her first demon lover," the cavalry officer with whom she had been infatuated as a young girl (88).

As should be clear by now, the single aspect of *The Awakening* that has interested critics the most is its ending. In part this fascination stems from the fact that the ending is ambiguous: Edna gives no conscious thought to killing herself as she takes off her clothes and begins what will be her final swim, nor does she appear to be in a particularly despairing mood. Indeed, she seems simply to have misjudged her own stamina: "the shore was far behind her, and her strength was gone" (137). Another reason for the frequent emphasis on the conclusion of the novel, however, especially during the past two decades, is the desire on the part of many critics—especially those who would call their approaches feminist—to see *The Awakening* as a departure from the tradition in which heroines who transgressed the rules of society had to be punished by death. Such is the fate of Flaubert's Emma Bovary, and Lily Bart in Edith Wharton's *The House of Mirth* (1905). Chopin's sympathetic presentation of Edna Pontellier's struggle to free herself from being a possession has caused a number of readers to see the ending either as proof of the negative power of society against a rebellious woman or as a transcendent experience in which Edna reaches a reconciliation.

A few critics, however, including Gina M. Burchard, regard Edna's death at the end of *The Awakening* as evidence of Chopin's own essential conservatism regarding a woman's role. In her 1984 essay "Kate Chopin's Problematical Womanliness: The Frontier of American Feminism," Burchard argues that Chopin was deeply ambivalent about the feminist impulses of her own day, and that she seems to have been quite content with the traditional roles of wife and mother that her heroine finds confining. Burchard further proposes that Chopin "internalized the prevailing notion that intellectual women were 'unfeminine'" (36), so that even in her attitude toward her own writing she displayed "a fear of too much seriousness" (37). For Burchard, Edna's suicide seems too dramatic an action to be a legitimate response to her experience; the ending "neutralizes" her protest, and might have been Chopin's way of satisfying her Victorian readers and "stav[ing] off criticism of [Edna's] unconventional behavior" (47).

Whether or not Chopin was ambivalent in her portrayal of Edna, the novel is filled with ambiguities other than its conclusion, making it possible for critics to "deconstruct" it—that is, to see in the novel meanings and messages that are in opposition to those that seem most obvious. On the surface, for example, in her confusion about how to conduct her life Edna seems poised between two women who appear contented and fulfilled in the roles they have chosen: the "mother-woman," Adèle Ratignolle, and the independent artist, Mademoiselle Reisz. Yet as Peggy Skaggs has suggested, an attentive reading of the novel reveals numerous clues that neither of these women is as enviable as we might at first suppose. Adèle Ratignolle, Skaggs points out, is consumed by her role as a mother: "her entire sense of who she is depends upon her maternal capacity" (92). Further, although she talks constantly about pregnancy and childbirth, Skaggs points to evidence that even though giving birth is supposed to be "her moment of glory to be savored to the fullest," she actually dreads the experience. The pianist, Mademoiselle Reisz, has attained a freedom from conventional expectations for women to which Edna might aspire, but Skaggs argues that it has cost her dearly. Chopin describes her as "disagreeable," and notes that she laughs "maliciously"; as an indication of her isolated state, no one in the novel ever calls her by her first name (95).

Peggy Skaggs's *Kate Chopin,* part of the Twayne United States Authors Series, was one of two book-length studies of Kate Chopin's work published in the mid-1980s. In 1986, Barbara Ewell contributed her *Kate Chopin* to the Ungar Publishing Company's Literature and Life series. At the conclusion of her discussion of *The Awakening,* Ewell writes of the novel's power to engage the reader:

> The novel quickly implicates us in its probing of such moral questions as the nature of sexuality, selfhood, and freedom, the meaning of adultery and suicide, and the relationship between biological destiny and personal choice. It is a novel that moves and disturbs us by its confrontation with the sheer obstinacy of our collective and individual humanity. (158)

By emphasizing the extent to which the novel causes readers to examine their own responses to the issues it raises, Ewell suggests a central tenet of what has come to be called "reader-response" criticism: that as readers we bring to a work of literature our individual experiences, prejudices, and expectations, which the text then rewards, challenges, or modifies. The act of reading, then, is a process of negotiation for meaning between reader and text. For examples of this we need only return to a consideration of the early reviewers of *The Awakening,* whose experience with both literature and cultural prescriptions of propriety caused so many of them to see the novel as indecent or even dangerous. A reader in the 1990s, in contrast, comes to the novel with a different set of expectations of what both novels and women will and should do.

In an essay in the 1988 *Approaches to Teaching Kate Chopin's "The Awakening,"* Elizabeth Rankin discusses the process of making students aware of themselves as readers of Chopin's novel. By asking students to stop reading halfway through the novel and predict the outcome of the plot, Rankin focuses their attention on both the clues to the ending that Chopin has provided and their own expectations about how people in certain circumstances will behave, both in literature and in life. One reason, Rankin suggests, that *The Awakening* lends itself so well to considerations of reader response is that the reading of books and the construction of stories are central elements of the novel itself. Both Edna Pontellier and Robert Lebrun are readers of novels, and Edna's primary dilemma is to construct a story for her own life. In Rankin's words,

Edna "must find a place to stand in [her] world, a place that is both within her culture and outside it, just as the reader must stand both within and outside the text" (151).

The five essays that follow take different approaches to *The Awakening*'s meaning and its place in the literary history of America, but all of them can be said to be feminist in orientation, in the sense that each critic sees Chopin's central character as a woman struggling—with more or less success—to attain autonomy and selfhood in a culture that presents serious obstacles to such attainment. Both Elaine Showalter's "Tradition and the Female Talent: *The Awakening* as a Solitary Book" and Margit Stange's "Personal Property: Exchange Value and the Female Self in *The Awakening*" seek to provide a contemporary context for the novel, although they do so in quite different ways. Showalter regards *The Awakening* as a "revolutionary" book, which drew upon a tradition of women's literature but marked a departure from that tradition that could have had a significant impact on the direction that fiction would take in the early twentieth century had it not been effectively removed from wide circulation and influenced by negative reviews. Stange takes a new historicist approach, investigating the concept of "self-ownership" in the late nineteenth century in order to illuminate Edna's preoccupation with her body as either the property of others or belonging to herself.

The remaining three essays address in various ways the ambiguities of the novel that have fascinated readers for decades. In "Thanatos and Eros: Kate Chopin's *The Awakening*," Cynthia Griffin Wolff looks at clues to Edna's psychological state, concluding that her inability to find fulfillment as an adult woman is caused by the force of a "self" that remains fixed, in Freudian terms, at an infantile stage that seeks sensual gratification. Patricia S. Yaeger, in "'A Language Nobody Understood': Emancipatory Strategies in *The Awakening*," deconstructs the novel to propose that rather than psychological inadequacy, Edna's problem is linguistic inadequacy: unable to articulate her own story, she is a victim of the scripts that others have written for her. Yaeger argues that the real subversive force of the novel is not Edna's act of adultery, but the utopian yearnings that would, if truly expressed, violate the social code in which she is trapped. Paula A. Treichler's "The Construction of Ambiguity in *The Awakening:* A Linguistic Analysis" also investigates the role of language in the novel, but Treichler is concerned with the way in which Chopin's use of language forces us to read the novel as ambiguous. Treichler argues that the language of the novel repeatedly contradicts or undercuts what it purports to describe, leaving the reader with a sense of confusion that mirrors Edna's own.

Nancy A. Walker

WORKS CITED

Batten, Wayne. "Illusion and Archetype: The Curious Story of Edna Pontellier." *The Southern Literary Journal* 18 (Fall 1985): 73–88.

Brooks, Van Wyck. *The Confident Years, 1885–1915.* New York: Dutton, 1952.

Burchard, Gina M. "Kate Chopin's Problematical Womanliness: The Frontier of American Feminism." *Journal of the American Studies Association of Texas* 15 (1984): 35–45.

Culley, Margaret, ed. *The Awakening.* New York: Norton, 1976.

Dondore, Dorothy Anne. "Kate O'Flaherty Chopin." *Dictionary of American Biography,* Vol. IV. New York: Scribner's, 1930. 90–91.

Eble, Kenneth. "A Forgotten Novel: Kate Chopin's *The Awakening.*" *Western Humanities Review* X (Summer 1956): 261–69.

Ewell, Barbara. *Kate Chopin.* New York: Ungar, 1986.

Franklin, Rosemary F. "*The Awakening* and the Failure of Psyche." *American Literature* 56 (December 1984): 510–26.

Gilbert, Sandra M. "The Second Coming of Aphrodite." *Kate Chopin.* Ed. Harold Bloom. New York: Chelsea, 1987. 89–113.

Gilmore, Michael T. "Revolt Against Nature: The Problematic Modernism of *The Awakening.*" *New Essays on "The Awakening."* Ed. Wendy Martin. New York: Cambridge UP, 1988. 59–87.

Herzberg, Max J., ed. *The Reader's Encyclopedia of American Literature.* New York: Crowell, 1962.

Leder, Priscilla. "An American Dilemma: Cultural Conflict in Kate Chopin's *The Awakening.*" *Southern Studies* 22 (Spring 1983): 97–104.

Rankin, Daniel S. *Kate Chopin and Her Creole Stories.* Philadelphia: U of Pennsylvania P, 1932.

Rankin, Elizabeth. "A Reader-Response Approach." *Approaches to Teaching Chopin's "The Awakening."* Ed. Bernard Koloski. New York: MLA, 1988. 150–55.

Rosowski, Susan J. "The Novel of Awakening." *Kate Chopin*. Ed. Harold Bloom. New York: Chelsea, 1987. 43–59.

Seyersted, Per, ed. *The Complete Works of Kate Chopin*. 2 vols. Baton Rouge: Louisiana State UP, 1969.

———. *Kate Chopin: A Critical Biography*. Baton Rouge: Louisiana State UP, 1969.

Skaggs, Peggy. *Kate Chopin*. Boston: Twayne, 1985.

Feminist Criticism and *The Awakening*

WHAT IS FEMINIST CRITICISM?

Feminist criticism comes in many forms, and feminist critics have a variety of goals. Some are interested in rediscovering the works of women writers overlooked by a masculine-dominated culture. Others have revisited books by male authors and reviewed them from a woman's point of view to understand how they both reflect and shape the attitudes that have held women back.

Since the early 1970s three strains of feminist criticism have emerged, strains that can be categorized as French, American, and British. These categories should not be allowed to obscure either the global implications of the women's movement or the fact that interests and ideas have been shared by feminists from France, Great Britain, and the United States. British and American feminists have examined similar problems while writing about many of the same writers and works, and American feminists have recently become more receptive to French theories about femininity and writing. Historically speaking, however, French, American, and British feminists have examined similar problems from somewhat different perspectives.

French feminists have tended to focus their attention on language, analyzing the ways in which meaning is produced. They have concluded that language as we commonly think of it is a decidedly male realm. Drawing on the ideas of the psychoanalytic philosopher Jacques Lacan, French feminists remind us that language is a realm of public discourse. A child enters the linguistic realm just as it comes to grasp its separateness from its mother, just about the time that boys identify with their father, the family representative of culture. The language learned reflects a binary logic that opposes such terms as active / passive, masculine / feminine, sun / moon, father / mother, head / heart, son / daughter, intelligent / sensitive, brother / sister, form / matter, phallus / vagina, reason / emotion. Because this logic tends to group with masculinity such qualities as light, thought, and activity, French feminists have said that the structure of language is phallocentric: it privileges the phallus and, more generally, masculinity by associating them with things and values more appreciated by the (masculine-dominated) culture. Moreover, French feminists believe, "masculine desire dominates speech and posits woman as an idealized fantasy-fulfillment for the incurable emotional lack caused by separation from the mother" (Jones 83).

In the view of French feminists, language is associated with separation from the mother. Its distinctions represent the world from the male point of view, and it systematically forces women to choose: either they can imagine and represent themselves as men imagine and represent them (in which case they may speak, but will speak as men) or they can choose "silence," becoming in the process "the invisible and unheard sex" (Jones 83).

But some influential French feminists have argued that language only *seems* to give women such a narrow range of choices. There is another possibility, namely that women can develop a *feminine* language. In various ways, early French feminists such as Annie Leclerc, Xavière Gauthier, and Marguerite Duras have suggested that there is something that may be called *l'écriture féminine:* women's writing. Recently, Julia Kristeva has said that feminine language is "semiotic," not "symbolic." Rather than rigidly opposing and ranking elements of reality, rather than symbolizing one thing but not another in terms of a third, feminine language is rhythmic and unifying. If from the male perspective it seems fluid to the point of being chaotic, that is a fault of the male perspective.

According to Kristeva, feminine language is derived from the preoedipal period of fusion between mother and child. Associated with the maternal, feminine language is not only threatening to culture, which is patriarchal, but also a medium through which women may be creative in new ways. But Kristeva has paired her central, liberating claim—that truly feminist innovation in all fields requires an understanding of the relation between maternity and feminine creation—with a warning. A feminist language that refuses to participate in "masculine" discourse, that places its future entirely in a feminine, semiotic discourse, risks being politically marginalized by men. That is to say, it risks being relegated to the outskirts (pun intended) of what is considered socially and politically significant.

Kristeva, who associates feminine writing with the female body, is joined in her views by other leading French feminists. Hélène Cixous, for instance, also posits an essential connection between the woman's body, whose sexual pleasure has been repressed and denied expression, and women's writing. "Write your self. Your body must be heard," Cixous urges; once they learn to write their bodies, women will not only realize their sexuality but enter history and move toward a future based on a "feminine" economy of giving rather than the "masculine" economy of hoarding (Cixous 250). For Luce Irigaray, women's sexual pleasure (*jouissance*) cannot be expressed by the dominant, ordered, "logical," masculine language. She explores the connection between women's sexuality and women's language through the following analogy: as women's *jouissance* is more multiple than men's unitary, phallic pleasure ("woman has sex organs just about everywhere"), so "feminine" language is more diffusive than its "masculine" counterpart. ("That is undoubtedly the reason . . . her language . . . goes off in all directions and . . . he is unable to discern the coherence," Irigaray writes [101–03].)

Cixous's and Irigaray's emphasis on feminine writing as an expression of the female body has drawn criticism from other French feminists. Many argue that an emphasis on the body either reduces "the feminine" to a biological essence or elevates it in a way that shifts the valuation of masculine and feminine but retains the binary categories. For Christine Fauré, Irigaray's celebration of women's difference fails to address the issue of masculine dominance, and a Marxist-feminist, Catherine Clément, has warned that "poetic" descriptions of what constitutes the feminine will not challenge that dominance in the realm of production. The boys will still make the toys, and decide who gets to use them. In her effort to redefine women as political rather than as sexual beings, Monique Wittig has called for the abolition of sexual categories that Cixous and Irigaray retain and revalue as they celebrate women's writing.

American feminist critics have shared with French critics both an interest in and a cautious distrust of the concept of feminine writing. Annette Kolodny, for instance, has worried that the "richness and variety of women's writing" will be missed if we see in it only its "feminine mode" or "style" ("Some Notes" 78). And yet Kolodny herself proceeds, in the same essay, to point out that women *have* had their own style, which includes reflexive constructions ("she found herself crying") and particular, recurring themes (clothing and self-fashioning are two that Kolodny mentions; other American feminists have focused on madness, disease, and the demonic).

Interested as they have become in the "French" subject of feminine style, American feminist critics began by analyzing literary texts rather than philosophizing abstractly about language. Many reviewed the great works by male writers, embarking on a revisionist rereading of literary tradition. These critics examined the portrayals of women characters, exposing the patriarchal ideology implicit in such works and showing how clearly this tradition of systematic masculine dominance is inscribed in our literary tradition. Kate Millett, Carolyn Heilbrun, and Judith Fetterley, among many others, created this model for American feminist criticism, a model that Elaine Showalter came to call "the feminist critique" of "male-constructed literary history" ("Poetics" 25).

Meanwhile another group of critics including Sandra Gilbert, Susan Gubar, Patricia Meyer Spacks, and Showalter herself created a somewhat different model. Whereas feminists writing "feminist critique" have analyzed works by men, practitioners of what Showalter used to refer to as "gynocriticism" have studied the writings of those women who, against all odds, produced what she calls "a literature of their own." In *The Female Imagination* (1975), Spacks examines the female literary tradition to find out how great women writers across the ages have felt, perceived themselves, and imagined reality. Gilbert and Gubar, in *The Madwoman in the Attic* (1979), concern themselves with well-known women writers of the nineteenth century, but they too find that general concerns, images, and themes recur, because the authors that they treat wrote "in a culture whose fundamental definitions of literary authority are both overtly and covertly patriarchal" (45).

If one of the purposes of gynocriticism is to (re)study well-known women authors, another is to rediscover women's history and culture, particularly women's communities that have nurtured female creativity. Still another related purpose is to discover neglected or forgotten women writers and thus to forge an alternative literary tradition, a canon that better represents the female perspective by better representing the literary works that have been written by women. Showalter, in *A Literature of Their Own* (1977), admirably began to fulfill this purpose, providing a remarkably comprehensive overview of women's writing through three of its phases. She defines these as the "Feminine, Feminist, and Female" phases, phases during which women first imitated a masculine tradition (1840–80), then protested against its standards and values (1880–1920), and finally advocated their own autonomous, female perspective (1920 to the present).

With the recovery of a body of women's texts, attention has returned to a question raised a decade ago by Lillian Robinson: Doesn't American feminist criticism need to formulate a theory of its own practice? Won't reliance on theoretical assumptions, categories, and strategies developed by men and associated with nonfeminist schools of thought prevent feminism from being accepted as equivalent to these other critical discourses? Not all American feminists believe that a special or unifying theory of feminist practice is urgently needed; Showalter's historical approach to women's culture allows a feminist critic to use theories based on nonfeminist disciplines. Kolodny has advocated a "playful pluralism" that encompasses a variety of critical schools and methods. But Jane Marcus and others have responded that if feminists adopt too wide a range of approaches, they may relax the tensions between feminists and the educational establishment necessary for political activism.

The question of whether feminism weakens or fortifies itself by emphasizing its separateness—and by developing unity through separateness—is one of several areas of debate within American feminism. Another area of disagreement touched on earlier, between feminists who stress universal feminine attributes (the feminine imagination, feminine writing) and those who focus on the political conditions experienced by certain groups of women at certain times in history, parallels a larger distinction between American feminist critics and their British counterparts.

While it has been customary to refer to an Anglo-American tradition of feminist criticism, British feminists tend to distinguish themselves from what they see as an American overemphasis on texts linking women across boundaries and decades and an underemphasis on popular art and culture. They regard their own critical practice as more political than that of American feminists, whom they have often faulted for being uninterested in historical detail. They would join such American critics as Myra Jehlen to suggest that a continuing preoccupation with women writers might create the danger of placing women's texts outside the history that conditions them.

In the view of British feminists, the American opposition to male stereotypes that denigrate women has often led to counterstereotypes of feminine virtue that ignore real differences of race, class, and culture among women. In addition, they argue that American celebrations of individual heroines falsely suggest that powerful individuals may be immune to repressive conditions and may even imply that *any* individual can go through life unconditioned by the culture and ideology in which she or he lives.

Similarly, the American endeavor to recover women's history — for example, by emphasizing that women developed their own strategies to gain power within their sphere — is seen by British feminists like Judith Newton and Deborah Rosenfelt as an endeavor that "mystifies" male oppression, disguising it as something that has created for women a special world of opportunities. More important from the British standpoint, the universalizing and "essentializing" tendencies in both American practice and French theory disguise women's oppression by highlighting sexual difference, suggesting that a dominant system is impervious to political change. By contrast, British feminist theory emphasizes an engagement with historical process in order to promote social change.

In the essay that follows, Elaine Showalter reads *The Awakening* as "an account of Edna Pontellier's evolution from romantic fantasies of fusion with another person" to the acceptance of "solitude." She views *The Awakening*, moreover, as being *like* its heroine. Because, as Showalter puts it, "Chopin went boldly beyond the work of her precursors in writing about women's longing for sexual and personal emancipation," *The Awakening* "became a solitary book, one that dropped out of sight, and that remained unsung by literary historians and unread by several generations of American women writers."

Having introduced her argument, Showalter goes back to the beginning of Chopin's career, arguing that women novelists of the 1850–90 period tended to fall into one of two categories: sentimental novelists and local colorists. The sentimentalist group, which included Harriet Beecher Stowe, Susan Warner, and E. D. E. N. Southworth, published mainly during the 1850s and 1860s. Although they managed to offer what Showalter calls "a subversive critique of patriarchal power," they did so by writing about a compensating "women's culture," characterized by (nonerotic) friendships between women and the creativity of motherhood. Sentimentalists thought of themselves as moralists, not as artists; after all, they thought of art as a profession and of the professions as a masculine domain.

The local colorists, who became popular after the Civil War, included such writers as Sarah Orne Jewett and Mary E. Wilkins. Unlike their sentimentalist precursors, they were "attracted to the male worlds of art and prestige" and "asserted themselves as the daughters of literary fathers as well as literary mothers." Still, women local colorists (who were not without their influence on Chopin) wrote within fairly restrictive artistic boundaries, focusing on regional customs, sites, events, and "characters," representing local curiosities of all kinds in loving detail.

By the 1890s, however, a new generation of American women writers had appeared on the scene. For these women – whose forerunners included Louisa May Alcott and Elizabeth Stuart Phelps – depicting local color was not enough. Nor were they willing to restrict their subject matter to women's friendships and motherhood. Indeed they viewed motherhood as an obstacle to, not a metaphor for, women's creativity and artistic achievement. It was this group of women writers, which included Olive Schreiner, Ellen D'Arcy, Sarah Grand, and "George Egerton" (Mary Chavelita Dunne), that Chopin admired. But she was even more influenced by the unconventional male writer, Guy de Maupassant. (Her description of him as one who "looked out upon life with his own eyes" is mirrored almost perfectly in a description of Edna in chapter 32.)

Unconventional works by men like Maupassant, of course, had long been palatable to the public taste. In 1895, *The Woman Who Did* became a best-seller, in spite of – or perhaps because of – the fact that it and its author, Grant Allen, were openly advocating free love. By contrast, many of the best works by the new generation of women writers were either ignored or rejected because their authors' expressed or implied attitudes toward motherhood in particular and female sexuality in general were considered unacceptable attitudes for women to hold. The dismissive categorization of *The Awakening,* termed by Showalter the "first aesthetically successful novel" by an American woman, as a work belonging to "the overworked field of sex fiction" came despite the fact that "Chopin might have taken the plot from a notebook entry Henry James made in 1892."

Showalter's essay can easily be seen as growing out of "gynocriticism," a feminist approach to literature she named and helped to create. Returning to the long-neglected work of a woman writer, she sees it in light of other works by women writers. She discusses Edna Pontellier's awakening, furthermore, in terms of nineteenth-century women's culture – and one strong woman's dissatisfaction with it.

And yet Showalter's essay necessarily does more than that as well: necessarily because *The Awakening* is no longer a largely ignored, solitary work but, rather, part of America's literary canon. Responding to the text's altered cultural place, Showalter here breaks new ground in placing the text vis-à-vis not only other ignored or "solitary" works by women but also vis-à-vis the patriarchal tradition that would not embrace it in its own time. She places it, in other words, with respect to works that, regardless of their author's gender, dared to express fundamental desires for personal and sexual freedom.

Ross C Murfin

FEMINIST CRITICISM: A SELECTED BIBLIOGRAPHY

French Feminist Theories

Beauvoir, Simone de. *The Second Sex*. 1953. Trans. and ed. H. M. Parshley. New York: Bantam, 1961.

Cixous, Hélène. "The Laugh of the Medusa." Trans. Keith Cohen and Paula Cohen. *Signs* 1 (1976): 875–94.

Cixous, Hélène, and Catherine Clément. *The Newly Born Woman*. Trans. Betsy Wing. Minneapolis: U of Minnesota P, 1986.

French Feminist Theory. Special issue, *Signs* 7.1 (1981).

Irigaray, Luce. *This Sex Which Is Not One*. Trans. Catherine Porter. Ithaca: Cornell UP, 1985.

Jones, Ann Rosalind. "Writing the Body: Toward an Understanding of *L'Écriture féminine*." Showalter, *New Feminist Criticism* 361–77.

Kristeva, Julia. *Desire in Language: A Semiotic Approach to Literature and Art*. Ed. Leon S. Roudiez. Trans. Thomas Gora, Alice Jardine, and Roudiez. New York: Columbia UP, 1980.

Marks, Elaine, and Isabelle de Courtivron, eds. *New French Feminisms: An Anthology*. Amherst: U of Massachusetts P, 1980.

Moi, Toril, ed. *French Feminist Thought: A Reader*. Oxford: Basil Blackwell, 1987.

British and American Feminist Theories

Belsey, Catherine, and Jane Moore, eds. *The Feminist Reader: Essays in Gender and the Politics of Literary Criticism*. New York: Basil Blackwell, 1989.

Benhabib, Seyla, and Drucilla Cornell, eds. *Feminism as Critique: On the Politics of Gender*. Minneapolis: U of Minnesota P, 1987.

Collins, Patricia Hill. *Black Feminist Thought: Knowledge, Consciousness, and the Politics of Empowerment.* Boston: Unwin Hyman, 1990.

de Lauretis, Teresa, ed. *Feminist Studies/Critical Studies.* Bloomington: Indiana UP, 1986.

Feminist Readings: French Texts/American Contexts. Special issue, *Yale French Studies* 62 (1982). Essays by Jardine and Spivak.

hooks, bell. *Ain't I a Woman?: Black Women and Feminism.* Boston: South End, 1981.

Keohane, Nannerl O., Michelle Z. Rosaldo, and Barbara C. Gelpi, eds. *Feminist Theory: A Critique of Ideology.* Chicago: U of Chicago P, 1982.

Kolodny, Annette. "Dancing Through the Minefield: Some Observations on the Theory, Practice, and Politics of a Feminist Literary Criticism." Showalter, *New Feminist Criticism* 144–67.

The Lesbian Issue. Special issue, *Signs* 9 (Summer 1984).

Malson, Micheline, et al., eds. *Feminist Theory in Practice and Process.* Chicago: U of Chicago P, 1986.

Rich, Adrienne. *On Lies, Secrets, and Silence: Selected Prose, 1966–1979.* New York: Norton, 1979.

Showalter, Elaine. "Toward a Feminist Poetics." Showalter, *New Feminist Criticism* 125–43.

———, ed. *The New Feminist Criticism: Essays on Women, Literature, and Theory.* New York: Pantheon, 1985.

The Feminist Critique

Fetterley, Judith. *The Resisting Reader: A Feminist Approach to American Fiction.* Bloomington: Indiana UP, 1978.

Greer, Germaine. *The Female Eunuch.* New York: McGraw, 1971.

Millett, Kate. *Sexual Politics.* Garden City: Doubleday, 1970.

Robinson, Lillian S. *Sex, Class, and Culture.* 1978. New York: Methuen, 1986.

Wittig, Monique. *Les Guérillères.* 1969. Trans. David Le Vay. New York: Avon, 1973.

Woolf, Virginia. *A Room of One's Own.* New York: Harcourt, 1929.

Women's Writing and Creativity

Abel, Elizabeth, ed. *Writing and Sexual Difference.* Chicago: U of Chicago P, 1982.

Abel, Elizabeth, Marianne Hirsch, and Elizabeth Langland, eds. *The*

Voyage In: Fictions of Female Development. Hanover: UP of New England, 1983.

Auerbach, Nina. *Communities of Women: An Idea in Fiction*. Cambridge: Harvard UP, 1978.

Christian, Barbara. *Black Feminist Criticism: Perspectives on Black Women Writers*. New York: Pergamon, 1985.

Gilbert, Sandra M., and Susan Gubar. *The Madwoman in the Attic: The Woman Writer and the Nineteenth-Century Literary Imagination*. New Haven: Yale UP, 1979.

Jacobus, Mary, ed. *Women Writing and Writing about Women*. New York: Barnes, 1979.

Miller, Nancy K., ed. *The Poetics of Gender*. New York: Columbia UP, 1986.

Newton, Judith Lowder. *Women, Power and Subversion: Social Strategies in British Fiction, 1778–1860*. Athens: U of Georgia P, 1981.

Poovey, Mary. *The Proper Lady and the Woman Writer: Ideology as Style in the Works of Mary Wollstonecraft, Mary Shelley, and Jane Austen*. Chicago: U of Chicago P, 1984.

Showalter, Elaine. *A Literature of Their Own: British Women Novelists from Brontë to Lessing*. Princeton: Princeton UP, 1977.

Marxist and Class Analysis

Barrett, Michèle. *Women's Oppression Today: Problems in Marxist Feminist Analysis*. London: Verso, 1980.

Delphy, Christine. *Close to Home: A Materialist Analysis of Women's Oppression*. Trans. and ed. Diana Leonard. Amherst: U of Massachusetts P, 1984.

Hartsock, Nancy C. M. *Money, Sex, and Power: Toward a Feminist Historical Materialism*. Boston: Northeastern UP, 1985.

Kaplan, Cora. *Sea Changes: Culture and Feminism*. London: Verso, 1986.

Mitchell, Juliet. *Woman's Estate*. New York: Pantheon, 1971.

Newton, Judith, and Deborah Rosenfelt, eds. *Feminist Criticism and Social Change: Sex, Class and Race in Literature and Culture*. New York: Methuen, 1985.

Sargent, Lydia, ed. *Women and Revolution: A Discussion of the Unhappy Marriage of Marxism and Feminism*. Montreal: Black Rose, 1981.

Women's History / Women's Studies

Bridenthal, Renate, and Claudia Koonz, eds. *Becoming Visible: Women in European History*. Boston: Houghton, 1977.

Farnham, Christie, ed. *The Impact of Feminist Research in the Academy*. Bloomington: Indiana UP, 1987.

Kelly, Joan. *Women, History and Theory.* Chicago: U of Chicago P, 1984.

McConnell-Ginet, Sally, et al., eds. *Woman and Language in Literature and Society.* New York: Praeger, 1980.

Mitchell, Juliet, and Ann Oakley, eds. *The Rights and Wrongs of Women.* London: Penguin, 1976.

Newton, Judith L., et al., eds. *Sex and Class in Women's History.* London: Routledge, 1983.

Riley, Denise. *"Am I That Name?": Feminism and the Category of "Women" in History.* Minneapolis: U of Minnesota P, 1988.

Rowbotham, Sheila. *Woman's Consciousness, Man's World.* Harmondsworth: Penguin, 1973.

Schipper, Mineke, ed. *Unheard Words: Women and Literature in Africa, the Arab World, Asia, the Caribbean, and Latin America.* London: Allison, 1985.

Scott, Joan Wallach. *Gender and the Politics of History.* New York: Columbia UP, 1988.

Smith-Rosenberg, Carroll. *Disorderly Conduct: Visions of Gender in Victorian America.* New York: Knopf, 1985.

Feminism and Other Critical Approaches

Armstrong, Nancy, ed. *Literature as Women's History I.* A special issue of *Genre* 19–20 (1986–87).

Diamond, Irene, and Lee Quinby, eds. *Feminism and Foucault: Reflections on Resistance.* Boston: Northeastern UP, 1988.

Feminist Studies 14 (1988). Special issue on feminism and deconstruction.

Gallop, Jane. *The Daughter's Seduction: Feminism and Psychoanalysis.* Ithaca: Cornell UP, 1982.

Keller, Evelyn Fox. *Reflections on Gender and Science.* New Haven: Yale UP, 1985.

Meese, Elizabeth, and Alice Parker, eds. *The Difference Within: Feminism and Critical Theory.* Amsterdam / Philadelphia: John Benjamins, 1989.

Penley, Constance, ed. *Feminism and Film Theory.* New York: Routledge, 1988.

Feminist Criticism of *The Awakening*

Gilbert, Sandra M. "The Second Coming of Aphrodite." *Kate Chopin.* Ed. Harold Bloom. New York: Chelsea, 1987. 89–113.

Lant, Kathleen Margaret. "The Siren of Grand Isle: Adèle's Role in

The Awakening." *Kate Chopin*. Ed. Harold Bloom. New York: Chelsea, 1987. 115–24.

Urgo, Joseph R. "A Prologue to Rebellion: *The Awakening* and the Habit of Self-Expression." *The Southern Literary Journal* 20 (1987): 22–32.

A FEMINIST PERSPECTIVE

ELAINE SHOWALTER

Tradition and the Female Talent: *The Awakening* as a Solitary Book

"Whatever we may do or attempt, despite the embrace and transports of love, the hunger of the lips, we are always alone. I have dragged you out into the night in the vain hope of a moment's escape from the horrible solitude which overpowers me, and still each of us is alone; side by side but alone." In 1895, these words, from a story by Guy de Maupassant called "Solitude," which she had translated for a St. Louis magazine, expressed an urbane and melancholy wisdom that Kate Chopin found compelling. To a woman who had survived the illusions that friendship, romance, marriage, or even motherhood would provide lifelong companionship and identity and who had come to recognize the existential solitude of all human beings, Maupassant's declaration became a kind of credo. Indeed, *The Awakening*, which Chopin subtitled "A Solitary Soul," may be read as an account of Edna Pontellier's evolution from romantic fantasies of fusion with another person to self-definition and self-reliance. At the beginning of the novel, in the midst of the bustling social world of Grand Isle, caught in her domestic roles of wife and mother, Edna pictures solitude as alien, masculine, and frightening, a naked man standing beside a "desolate rock" by the sea in an attitude of "hopeless resignation" (44; ch. 9). By the end, she has claimed a solitude that is defiantly feminine, returning to the nearly empty island off-season, to stand naked and "absolutely alone" by the shore, and to elude "the soul's slavery" by plunging into the sea's embrace (136; ch. 39).

Yet Edna's triumphant embrace of solitude could not be the choice of Kate Chopin as an artist. A writer may work in solitude, but literature depends on a tradition, on shared forms and representations of experience; and literary genres, like biological species, evolve because of significant innovations by individuals that survive through imitation and revision. Thus it can be a very serious blow to a developing genre when a revolutionary work is taken out of circulation. Experimentation is retarded and repressed, and it may be several generations before the evolution of the literary genre catches up. The interruption of this evolutionary process is most destructive for the literature of a minority group, in which writers have to contend with cultural prejudices against their creative gifts. Yet radical departures from literary convention within a minority tradition are especially likely to be censured and suppressed by the dominant culture, because they violate social as well as aesthetic stereotypes and expectations.

The Awakening was just such a revolutionary book. Generally recognized today as the first aesthetically successful novel to have been written by an American woman, it marked a significant epoch in the evolution of an American female literary tradition. As an American woman novelist of the 1890s, Kate Chopin had inherited a rich and complex tradition, composed not only of her American female precursors but also of American transcendentalism, European realism, and fin-de-siècle feminism and aestheticism. In this context, *The Awakening* broke new thematic and stylistic ground. Chopin went boldly beyond the work of her precursors in writing about women's longing for sexual and personal emancipation.

Yet the novel represents a literary beginning as abruptly cut off as its heroine's awakening consciousness. Edna Pontellier's explicit violations of the modes and codes of nineteenth-century American women's behavior shocked contemporary critics, who described *The Awakening* as "morbid," "essentially vulgar," and "gilded dirt." Banned in Kate Chopin's own city of St. Louis and censured in the national press, *The Awakening* thus became a solitary book, one that dropped out of sight, and that remained unsung by literary historians and unread by several generations of American women writers.

In many respects, *The Awakening* seems to comment on its own history as a novel, to predict its own critical fate. The parallels between the experiences of Edna Pontellier as she breaks away from the conventional feminine roles of wife and mother, and Kate Chopin, as she breaks away from conventions of literary domesticity, suggest that Edna's story may also be read as a parable of Chopin's literary awakening. Both the author and the heroine seem to be oscillating between two worlds, caught between contradictory definitions of femininity and creativity, and seeking either to synthesize them or to go beyond them to an emancipated womanhood and an emancipated fiction. Edna Pontellier's "unfocused yearning" for an autonomous life is akin to Kate Chopin's yearning to write works that go beyond female plots and feminine endings.

In the early stages of her career, Chopin had tried to follow the literary advice and literary examples of others and had learned that such dutiful efforts led only to imaginative stagnation. By the late 1890s, when she wrote *The Awakening,* Chopin had come to believe that the true artist was one who defied tradition, who rejected both the "*convenances*" of respectable morality and the conventions and formulas of literary success. What impressed her most about Maupassant was that he had "escaped from tradition and authority . . . had entered into himself and looked out upon life through his own being and with his own eyes" (Seyersted, *Complete Works* 701). This is very close to what happens to Edna Pontellier as she frees herself from social obligations and received opinions and begins "to look with her own eyes; to see and to apprehend the deeper undercurrents of life" (115; ch. 32). Much as she admired Maupassant, and much as she learned from translating his work, Chopin felt no desire to imitate him. Her sense of the need for independence and individuality in writing is dramatically expressed in *The Awakening* by Mademoiselle Reisz, who tells Edna that the artist must possess "the courageous soul . . . that dares and defies" (83; ch. 21) and must have strong wings to soar "above the level plain of tradition and prejudice" (103; ch. 27).

Nonetheless, in order to understand *The Awakening* fully, we need to read it in the context of literary tradition. Even in its defiant solitude, *The Awakening* speaks for a transitional phase in American women's writing, and Chopin herself would never have written the books she did without a tradition to admire and oppose. When she wrote *The Awakening* in 1899, Chopin could look back to at least two generations of female literary precursors. The antebellum novelists, led by Harriet Beecher Stowe, Susan Warner, and E. D. E. N. Southworth, were the first members of these generations. Born in the early decades of the nineteenth century, they began to publish stories and novels in the 1850s and 1860s that reflected the dominant expressive and symbolic models of an American woman's culture. The historian Carroll Smith-Rosenberg has called this culture the "female world of love and ritual," and it was primarily defined by the veneration of motherhood, by intense mother-daughter bonds, and by intimate female friendships. As Smith-Rosenberg explains: "Uniquely female rituals drew women together during every stage of their lives, from adolescence through courtship, marriage, childbirth and child rearing, death and mourning. Women revealed their deepest feelings to one another, helped one another with the burdens of housewifery and motherhood, nursed one another's sick, and mourned for one another's dead" (28). Although premarital relationships between the sexes were subject to severe restrictions, romantic friendships between women were admired and encouraged. The nineteenth-century idea of female "passionlessness"—the belief that women did not have the same sexual desires as men—had advantages as well as disadvantages for women. It reinforced the notion that women were the purer and more spiritual sex, and thus were morally superior to men. Furthermore, as the historian Nancy F. Cott has argued, "acceptance of the idea of passionlessness created sexual solidarity among women; it allowed women to consider their love relationships with one another of higher character than heterosexual relationships because they excluded (male) carnal passion" (233). "I do not believe that men can ever feel so pure an enthusiasm for women as we can feel for one another," wrote the novelist Catherine Sedgewick. "Ours is nearest to the love of angels" (qtd. in Cott 233). The homosocial world of women's culture in fact allowed much leeway for physical intimacy and touch; "girls routinely slept together, kissed and hugged one another" (Smith-Rosenberg 69). But these caresses were not interpreted as erotic expressions.

The mid-nineteenth-century code of values growing out of women's culture, which Mary Ryan calls "the empire of the mother," was also sustained by sermons, child-rearing manuals, and sentimental fiction. Women writers advocated motherly influence—"gentle nurture," "sweet control," and "educating power"—as an effective solution to such social problems as alcoholism, crime, slavery, and war. As Harriet Beecher Stowe proclaimed, "The 'Woman Question' of the day is: Shall MOTHERHOOD ever be felt in the public administration of the affairs of state?" (qtd. in Kelley 327).

As writers, however, the sentimentalists looked to motherhood for their metaphors and justifications of literary creativity. "Creating a story is like bearing a child," wrote Stowe, "and it leaves me in as weak and helpless state as when my baby was born" (qtd. in Kelley 249). Thematically and stylistically, pre–Civil War women's fiction, variously described as "literary domesticity" or the "sentimental novel," celebrates matriarchal institutions and idealizes the period of blissful bonding between mother and child. It is permeated by the artifacts, spaces, and images of nineteenth-century American domestic culture: the kitchen, with its worn rocking chair; the Edenic mother's garden, with its fragrant female flowers and energetic male bees; the caged songbird, which represents the creative woman in her domestic sphere. Women's narratives were formally composed of brief sketches joined together like the pieces of a patchwork quilt; they frequently alluded to specific quilt patterns and followed quilt design conventions of repetition, variation, and contrast. Finally, their most intense representation of female sexual pleasure was not in the terms of heterosexual romance, but rather the holding or suckling of a baby; for, as Mary Ryan points out, "nursing an infant was one of the most hallowed and inviolate episodes in a woman's life. . . . Breast-feeding was sanctioned as 'one of the most important duties of female life,' 'one of peculiar, inexpressible felicity,' and 'the sole occupation and pleasure' of a new mother" (Ryan, *Womanhood* 144).

The cumulative effect of all these covert appeals to female solidarity in books written by, for, and about women could be a subversive critique of patriarchal power. Yet aesthetically the fiction of this generation was severely restricted. The sentimentalists did not identify with the figure of the "artist," the "genius," or the "poet" promulgated by patriarchal culture. As Nina Baym explains, "they conceptualized authorship as a profession rather than a calling. . . . Women authors tended not to think of themselves as artists or justify themselves in the language of art until the 1870s and after." In the writing of the sentimentalists, "the dimensions of formal self-consciousness, attachment to or quarrel with a grand tradition, aesthetic seriousness, are all missing. Often the women deliberately and even proudly disavowed membership in an artistic fraternity" (32). Insofar as art implied a male club or circle of brothers, women felt excluded from it. Instead they claimed affiliation with a literary sorority, a society of sisters whose motives were moral rather than aesthetic, whose ambitions were to teach and to influence rather than to create. Although their books sold by the millions, they were not taken seriously by male critics.

The next generation of American women writers, however, found themselves in a different culture situation. After the Civil War, the homosocial world of women's culture began to dissolve as women demanded entrance to higher education, the professions, and the political world. The female local colorists who began to publish stories about American regional life in the 1870s and 1880s were also attracted to the male worlds of art and prestige opening up to women, and they began to assert themselves as the daughters of literary fathers as well as literary mothers. Claiming both male and female aesthetic models, they felt free to present themselves as artists and to write confidently about the art of fiction in such essays as Elizabeth Stuart Phelps's "Art for Truth's Sake" (1897). Among the differences the local colorists saw between themselves and their predecessors was the question of "selfishness," the ability to put literary ambitions before domestic duties. Although she had been strongly influenced in her work by Harriet Beecher Stowe's *Pearl of Orr's Island* (1862), Sarah Orne Jewett came to believe that Stowe's work was "incomplete" because she was unable to "bring herself to that cold selfishness of the moment for one's work's sake" (qtd. in Donovan 124).

Writers of this generation chose to put their work first. The 1870s and 1880s were what Susan B. Anthony called "an epoch of single women," and many unmarried women writers of this generation lived alone; others were involved in "Boston marriages," or long-term relationships with another woman. But despite their individual lifestyles, many speculated in their writing on the conflicts between maternity and artistic creativity. Motherhood no longer seemed to be the motivating force of writing, but rather its opposite. Thus artistic fulfillment required the sacrifice of maternal drives, and maternal fulfillment meant giving up artistic ambitions.

The conflicts between love and work that Edna Pontellier faces in *The Awakening* were anticipated in such earlier novels as Louisa May Alcott's unfinished *Diana and Persis* (1879) and Elizabeth Stuart Phelps's *The Story of Avis* (1879). A gifted painter who has studied in Florence and Paris, Avis does not intend to marry. As she tells her suitor, "My ideals of art are those with which marriage is perfectly incompatible. Success—for a woman—means absolute surrender, in whatever direction. Whether she paints a picture, or loves a man, there is no division of labor possible in her economy. To the attainment of any end worth living for, a symmetrical sacrifice of her nature is compulsory upon her." But love persuades her to change her mind, and the novel records the inexorable destruction of her artistic genius as domestic responsibilities, maternal cares, and her husband's failures use up her energy. By the end of the novel, Avis has become resigned to the idea that her life is a sacrifice for the next generation of women. Thinking back to her mother, a talented actress who gave up her profession to marry and died young, and looking at her daughter, Wait, Avis takes heart in the hope that it may take three generations to create the woman who can unite "her supreme capacity of love" with the "sacred individuality of her life" (126, 246). As women's culture declined after the Civil War, moreover, the local colorists mourned its demise by investing its traditional images with mythic significance. In their stories, the mother's garden has become a paradisal sanctuary; the caged bird a wild white heron, or heroine of nature; the house an emblem of the female body, with the kitchen as its womb; and the artifacts of domesticity virtually totemic objects. In Jewett's *Country of the Pointed Firs* (1896), for example, the braided rag rug has become a kind of prayer mat of concentric circles from which the matriarchal priestess, Mrs. Todd, delivers her sybilline pronouncements. The woman artist in this fiction expresses her conflicting needs most fully in her quasi-religious dedication to these artifacts of a bygone age.

The New Women writers of the 1890s no longer grieved for the female bonds and sanctuaries of the past. Products of both Darwinian skepticism and aesthetic sophistication, they had an ambivalent or even hostile relationship to women's culture, which they often saw as boring and restrictive. Their attitudes toward female sexuality were also revolutionary. A few radical feminists had always maintained that women's sexual apathy was not an innately feminine attribute but rather the result of prudery and repression; some women's rights activists too had privately confessed that, as Elizabeth Cady Stanton wrote in her diary in 1883, "a healthy woman has as much passion as a man" (qtd. in Cott 236; n. 60). Not all New Women advocated female sexual emancipation; the most zealous advocates of free love were male novelists such as Grant Allen, whose best-seller, *The Woman Who Did* (1895), became a byword of the decade. But the heroine of New Woman fiction, as Linda Dowling has explained, "expressed her quarrel with Victorian culture chiefly through sexual means—by heightening sexual consciousness, candor, and expression" (441). No wonder, then, that reviewers saw *The Awakening* as part of the "overworked field of sex fiction" or noted that since "San Francisco and Paris, and London, and New York had furnished Women Who Did, why not New Orleans?"

In the form as well as the content of their work, New Women writers demanded freedom and innovation. They modified the realistic three-decker novels about courtship and marriage that had formed the bulk of midcentury "woman's fiction" to make room for interludes of fantasy and parable, especially episodes "in which a woman will cross-dress, experimenting with the freedom available to boys and men" (Vicinus xvi). Instead of the crisply plotted short stories that had been the primary genre of local colorists, writers such as Olive Schreiner, Ella D'Arcy, Sarah Grand, and "George Egerton" (Mary Chavelita Dunne) experimented with new fictional forms that they called "keynotes," "allegories," "fantasies," "monochromes," or "dreams." As Egerton explained, these impressionistic narratives were efforts to explore a hitherto unrecorded female consciousness: "I realized that in literature everything had been done better by man than woman could hope to emulate. There was only one small plot left for herself to tell: the *terra incognita* of herself, as she knew herself to be, not as man liked to imagine her—in a word to give herself away, as man had given himself away in his writings" (60).

Kate Chopin's literary evolution took her progressively through the three phases of nineteenth-century American women's culture and women's writing. Born in 1850, she grew up with the great best-sellers of the American and English sentimentalists. As a girl, she had wept over the works of Warner and Stowe and had copied pious passages from the English novelist Dinah Mulock Craik's *The Woman's Kingdom* (1868) into her diary. Throughout her adolescence, Chopin had also shared an intimate friendship with Kitty Garesché, a classmate at the Academy of the Sacred Heart. Together, Chopin recalled, the girls had read fiction and poetry, gone on excursions, and "exchanged our heart secrets" (Seyersted, *Kate Chopin* 18). Their friendship ended in 1870 when Kate Chopin married and Kitty Garesché entered a convent. Yet when Oscar Chopin died in 1883, his young widow went to visit her old friend and was shocked by her blind isolation from the world. When Chopin began to write, she took as her models such local colorists as Sarah Orne Jewett and Mary E. Wilkins, who had not only mastered technique and construction but had also devoted themselves to telling the stories of female loneliness, isolation, and frustration.

Sandra Gilbert has suggested that local color was a narrative strategy that Chopin employed to solve a specific problem: how to deal with extreme psychological states without the excesses of sentimental narrative and without critical recrimination. At first, Gilbert suggests, local color writing "offered both a mode and a manner that could mediate between the literary structures she had inherited and those she had begun." Like the anthropologist, the local colorist could observe vagaries of culture and character with "almost scientific detachment." Furthermore, "by reporting odd events and customs that were part of a region's 'local color' she could tell what would ordinarily be rather shocking or even melodramatic tales in an unmelodramatic way, and without fear of . . . moral outrage" (16).

But before long, Chopin looked beyond the oddities of the local colorists to more ambitious models. Her literary tastes were anything but parochial. She read widely in a variety of genres—Darwin, Spencer, and Huxley, as well as Aristophanes, Flaubert, Whitman, Swinburne, and Ibsen. In particular, she associated her own literary and psychological awakening with Maupassant. "Here was life, not fiction," she wrote of his influence on her, "for where were the plots, the old fashioned mechanism and stage trapping that in a vague, unthinking way I had fancied were essential to the art of story making" (Seyersted, *Complete Works* 700–01). In a review of a book by the local colorist Hamlin Garland, Chopin expressed her dissatisfaction with the restricted subjects of regional writing: "Social problems, social environments, local color, and the rest of it" could not "insure the survival of a writer who employs them" (Seyersted, *Complete Works* 693). She resented being compared to George Washington Cable or Grace King. Furthermore, she did not share the female local colorists' obsession with the past, their desperate nostalgia for a bygone idealized age. "How curiously the past effaces itself for me!" she wrote in her diary in 1894. "I cannot live through yesterday or tomorrow" (Seyersted, *Kate Chopin* 58). Unlike Jewett, Wilkins, King, or Woolson, she did not favor the old woman as narrator.

Despite her identification with the New Women, however, Chopin was not an activist. She never joined the women's suffrage movement or belonged to a female literary community. Indeed, her celebrated St. Louis literary salon attracted mostly male journalists, editors, and writers. Chopin resigned after only two years from a St. Louis women's literary and charitable society. When her children identified her close friends to be interviewed by her first biographer, Daniel Rankin, there were no women on the list.

Thus Chopin certainly did not wish to write a didactic feminist novel. In reviews published in the 1890s, she indicated her impatience with novelists such as Zola and Hardy, who tried to instruct their readers. She distrusted the rhetoric of such feminist best-sellers as Sarah Grand's *The Heavenly Twins* (1893). The eleventh commandment, she noted, is "Thou shalt not preach" (Seyersted, *Complete Works* 702). Instead she would try to record, in her own way and in her own voice, the *terra incognita* of a woman's "inward life" in all its "vague, tangled, chaotic" tumult.

Much of the shock effect of *The Awakening* to the readers of 1899 came from Chopin's rejection of the conventions of women's writing. Despite her name, which echoes two famous heroines of the domestic novel (Edna Earl in Augusta Evans's *St. Elmo* [1867] and Edna Kenderdine in Dinah Mulock Craik's *The Woman's Kingdom* [1868]), Edna Pontellier appears to reject the domestic empire of the mother and the sororal world of women's culture. Seemingly beyond the bonds of womanhood, she has neither mother nor daughter, and even refuses to go to her sister's wedding.

Moreover, whereas the sentimental heroine nurtures others and the abstemious local color heroine subsists upon meager vegetarian diets, Kate Chopin's heroine is a robust woman who does not deny her appetites. Wilkins's New England nun picks at her dainty lunch of lettuce leaves and currants, but Edna Pontellier eats hearty meals of paté, pompano, steak, and broiled chicken; bites off chunks of crusty bread; snacks on beer and Gruyère cheese; and sips brandy, wine, and champagne.

Formally, too, the novel has moved away from conventional techniques of realism to an impressionistic rhythm of epiphany and mood. Chopin abandoned the chapter titles she had used in her first novel, *At Fault* (1890), for thirty-nine numbered chapters of uneven length, ranging from the single paragraph of chapter 28 to the sustained narrative of the dinner party in chapter 30. The chapters are unified less by their style than by their focus on Edna's consciousness, and by the repetition of key motifs and images: music, the sea, shadows, swimming, eating, sleeping, gambling, the lovers, birth. Chapters of lyricism and fantasy, such as Edna's voyage to the *Chênière Caminada,* alternate with realistic, even satirical, scenes of Edna's marriage.

Most important, where previous works ignored sexuality or spiritualized it through maternity, *The Awakening* is insistently sexual, explicitly involved with the body and self-awareness through physical awareness. Although Edna's actual seduction by Arobin takes place in the narrative neverland between chapters 31 and 32, Chopin brilliantly evokes sexuality through images and details. In keeping with the novel's emphasis on the self, several scenes suggest Edna's initial autoeroticism. Edna's midnight swim, which awakens the "first-felt throbbings of desire," takes place in an atmosphere of erotic fragrance, "strange, rare odors . . . a tangle of the sea smell and of weeds and damp new-plowed earth, mingled with the heavy perfume of a field of white blossoms" (46; ch. 10). A similarly voluptuous scene is her nap at the *Chênière Caminada,* when she examines her flesh as she lies in a "strange, quaint bed, with its sweet country odor of laurel" (55; ch. 13).

Edna reminds Dr. Mandelet of "some beautiful animal waking up in the sun" (90; ch. 23), and we recall that among her fantasies in listening to music is the image of a lady stroking a cat. The image both conveys Edna's sensuality and hints at the self-contained, almost masturbatory, quality of her sexuality. Her rendezvous with Robert takes place in a sunny garden where both stroke a drowsy cat's silky fur, and Arobin first seduces her by smoothing her hair with his "soft, magnetic hand" (113; ch. 31).

Yet despite these departures from tradition, there are other respects in which the novel seems very much of its time. As its title suggests, *The Awakening* is a novel about a process rather than a program, about a passage rather than a destination. Like Edith Wharton's *The House of Mirth* (1905), it is a transitional female fiction of the fin-de-siècle, a narrative of and about the passage from the homosocial women's culture and literature of the nineteenth century to the heterosexual fiction of modernism. Chopin might have taken the plot from a notebook entry Henry James made in 1892 about "the growing divorce between the American woman (with her comparative leisure, culture, grace, social instincts, artistic ambition) and the male immersed in the ferocity of business, with no time for any but the most sordid interests, purely commercial, professional, democratic, and political. This divorce is rapidly becoming a gulf" (qtd. in Ziff 275). The Gulf where the opening chapters of *The Awakening* are set certainly suggests the "growing divorce" between Edna's interests and desires and Léonce's obsessions with the stock market, property, and his brokerage business.

Yet in turning away from her marriage, Edna initially looks back to women's culture rather than forward to another man. As Sandra Gilbert has pointed out, Grand Isle is an oasis of women's culture, or a "female colony": "Madam Lebrun's *pension* on Grand Isle is very much a woman's land not only because it is owned and run by a single woman and dominated by 'motherwomen' but also because (as in so many summer colonies today) its principal inhabitants are actually women and children whose husbands and fathers visit only on weekends . . . [and is situated,] like so many places that are significant for women, outside patriarchal culture, beyond the limits and limitations of the city where men make history, on a shore that marks the margin where nature intersects with culture" (25).

Edna's awakening, moreover, begins not with a man, but with Adèle Ratignolle, the empress of the "mother-women" of Grand Isle. A "self-contained" (35; ch. 7) woman, Edna has never had any close relationships with members of her own sex. Thus it is Adèle who belatedly initiates Edna into the world of female love and ritual on the first step of her sensual voyage to self-discovery. Edna's first attraction to Adèle is physical: "the excessive physical charm of the Creole had first attracted her, for Edna had a sensuous susceptibility to beauty" (32; ch. 7). At the beach, in the hot sun, she responds to Adèle's caresses, the first she has ever known from another woman, as Adèle clasps her hand "firmly and warmly" and strokes it fondly. The touch provokes Edna to an unaccustomed candor; leaning her head on Adèle's shoulder and confiding some of her secrets, she begins to feel "intoxicated" (37; ch. 7). The bond between them goes beyond sympathy, as Chopin notes, to what "we might as well call love" (32; ch. 7).

In some respects, the motherless Edna also seeks a mother surrogate in Adèle and looks to her for nurturance. Adèle provides maternal encouragement for Edna's painting and tells her that her "talent is immense" (75; ch. 18). Characteristically, Adèle has rationalized her own "art" as a maternal project: "she was keeping up her music on account of the children . . . a means of brightening the home and making it attractive" (43; ch. 9). Edna's responses to Adèle's music have been similarly tame and sentimental. Her revealing fantasies as she listens to Adèle play her easy pieces suggest the restriction and decorum of the female world: "a dainty young woman . . . taking mincing dancing steps as she came down a long avenue between tall hedges"; "children at play" (44; ch. 9). Women's art, as Adèle presents it, is social, pleasant, and undemanding. It does not conflict with her duties as wife and mother, and can even be seen to enhance them. Edna understands this well; as she retorts when her husband recommends Adèle as a model of an artist, "She isn't a musician, and I'm not a painter" (77; ch. 19).

Yet the relationship with the conventional Adèle educates the immature Edna to respond for the first time both to a different kind of sexuality and to the unconventional and difficult art of Mademoiselle Reisz. In responding to Adèle's interest, Edna begins to think about her own past and to analyze her own personality. In textual terms, it is through this relationship that she becomes "Edna" in the narrative rather than "Mrs. Pontellier."

We see the next stage of Edna's awakening in her relationship with Mademoiselle Reisz, who initiates her into the world of art. Significantly, this passage also takes place through a female rather than a male mentor, and, as with Adèle, there is something more intense than friendship between the two women. Whereas Adèle's fondness for Edna, however, is depicted as maternal and womanly, Mademoiselle Reisz's attraction to Edna suggests something more perverse. The pianist is obsessed with Edna's beauty, raves over her figure in a bathing suit, greets her as *"ma belle"* and *"ma reine,"* holds her hand, and describes herself as "a foolish old woman whom you have captivated" (84; ch. 21). If Adèle is a surrogate for Edna's dead mother and the intimate friend she never had as a girl, Mademoiselle Reisz, whose music reduces Edna to passionate sobs, seems to be a surrogate lover. And whereas Adèle is a "faultless Madonna" who speaks for the values and laws of the Creole community, Mademoiselle Reisz is a renegade, self-assertive and outspoken. She has no patience with petty social rules and violates the most basic expectations of femininity. To a rake like Arobin, she is so unattractive, unpleasant, and unwomanly as to seem "partially demented" (104; ch. 27). Even Edna occasionally perceives Mademoiselle Reisz's awkwardness as a kind of deformity and is sometimes offended by the old woman's candor and is not sure whether she likes her.

Yet despite her eccentricities, Mademoiselle Reisz seems "to reach Edna's spirit and set it free" (99; ch. 26). Her voice in the novel seems to speak for the author's view of art and for the artist. It is surely no accident, for example, that it is Chopin's music that Mademoiselle Reisz performs. At the *pension* on Grand Isle, the pianist first plays a Chopin prelude, to which Edna responds with surprising turbulence: "the very passions themselves were aroused within her soul, swaying it, lashing it, as the waves daily beat upon her splendid body. She trembled, she was choking, and the tears blinded her" (45; ch. 9). *Chopin* becomes the code word for a world of repressed passion between Edna and Robert that Mademoiselle Reisz controls. Later the pianist plays a Chopin impromptu for Edna that Robert has admired; this time the music is "strange and fantastic—turbulent, insistent, plaintive and soft with entreaty" (84; ch. 21). These references to Chopin in the text are on one level allusions to an intimate, romantic, and poignant musical *oeuvre* that reinforces the novel's sensual atmosphere. But on another level, they function as what Nancy K. Miller has called the "internal female signature" in women's writing, here a literary punning signature that alludes to Kate Chopin's ambitions as an artist and to the emotions she wished her book to arouse in its readers.

Chopin's career represented one important aesthetic model for his literary namesake. As a girl, Kate Chopin had been a talented musician, and her first published story, "Wiser than a God," was about a woman concert pianist who refused to marry. Moreover, Chopin's music both stylistically and thematically influences the language and form of *The Awakening*. The structure of the impromptu, in which there is an opening presentation of a theme, a contrasting middle section, and a modified return to the melodic and rhythmic materials of the opening section, parallels the narrative form of *The Awakening*. The composer's techniques of unifying his work through repetition of musical phrases, his experiments with harmony and dissonance, his use of folk motifs, his effects of frustration and delayed resolutions can also be compared to Kate Chopin's repetition of sentences, her juxtaposition of realism and impressionism, her incorporation of local color elements, and her rejection of conventional closure. Like that of the composer's impromptu, Chopin's style seems spontaneous and improvised, but it is in fact carefully designed and executed.

Madame Ratignolle and Mademoiselle Reisz not only represent important alterative roles and influences for Edna in the world of this novel, but as the proto-heroines of sentimental and local color fiction, they also suggest different plots and conclusions. Adèle's story suggests that Edna will give up her rebellion, return to her marriage, have another baby, and by degrees learn to appreciate, love, and even desire her husband. Such was the plot of many late nineteenth-century sentimental novels about erring young women married to older men, such as Susan Warner's *Diana* (1880) and Louisa May Alcott's *Moods* (1882). Mademoiselle Reisz's story suggests that Edna will lose her beauty, her youth, her husband, and children—everything, in short, but her art and her pride—and become a kind of New Orleans nun.

Chopin wished to reject both of these endings and to escape from the literary traditions they represented; but her own literary solitude, her resistance to allying herself with a specific ideological or aesthetic position, made it impossible for her to work out something different and new. Edna remains very much entangled in her own emotions and moods, rather than moving beyond them to real self-understanding and to an awareness of her relationship to society. She alternates between two moods of "intoxication" and "languor," expansive states of activity, optimism, and power and passive states of contemplation, despondency, and sexual thralldom. Edna feels intoxicated when she is assertive and in control. She first experiences such exultant feelings when she confides her history to Adèle Ratignolle and again when she learns how to swim: "intoxicated with her newly conquered power," she swims out too far (46; ch. 10). She is excited when she gambles successfully for high stakes at the race track, and finally she feels "an intoxication of expectancy" about awakening Robert with a seductive kiss and playing the dominant role with him (133; ch. 38). But these emotional peaks are countered by equally intense moods of depression, reverie, or stupor. At the worst, these are states of "indescribable oppression," "vague anguish," or "hopeless ennui." At best, they are moments of passive sensuality in which Edna feels drugged; Arobin's lips and hands, for example act "like a narcotic upon her" (98; ch. 25).

Edna welcomes both kinds of feelings because they are intense, and thus preserve her from the tedium of ordinary existence. They are in fact adolescent emotions, suitable to a heroine who is belatedly awakening; but Edna does not go beyond them to an adulthood that offers new experiences or responsibilities. In her relationships with men, she both longs for complete and romantic fusion with a fantasy lover and is unprepared to share her life with another person.

Chopin's account of the Pontellier marriage, for example, shows Edna's tacit collusion in a sexual bargain that allows her to keep to herself. Although she thinks of her marriage to a paternalistic man twelve years her senior as "purely an accident," the text makes it clear that Edna has married Léonce primarily to secure a fatherly protector who will not make too many domestic, emotional, or sexual demands on her. She is "fond of her husband," with "no trace of passion or excessive and fictitious warmth" (37; ch. 7). They do not have an interest in each other's activities or thoughts, and have agreed to a complete separation of their social spheres; Léonce is fully absorbed by the business, social, and sexual activities of the male sphere, the city, Carondelet Street, Klein's Hotel at Grand Isle, where he gambles, and especially the New Orleans world of the clubs and red-light district. Even Adèle Ratignolle warns Edna of the risks of Mr. Pontellier's club life and of the "diversion" he finds there. "'It's a pity Mr. Pontellier doesn't stay home more in the evenings,'" she tells Edna, "'I think you would be more—well, if you don't mind my saying it—more united, if he did.'" "'Oh! dear no!'" Edna responds, "with a blank look in her eyes. 'What should I do if he stayed home? We wouldn't have anything to say to each other'" (89; ch. 23). Edna gets this blank look in her eyes—eyes that are originally described as "quick and bright"—whenever she is confronted with something she does not want to see. When she joins the Ratignolles at home together, Edna does not envy them, although, as the author remarks, "if ever the fusion of two human beings into one has been accomplished on this sphere it was surely in their union" (75; ch. 18). Instead, she is moved by pity for Adèle's "colorless existence which never uplifted its possessor beyond the region of blind contentment" (76; ch. 18).

Nonetheless, Edna does not easily relinquish her fantasy of rhapsodic oneness with a perfect lover. She imagines that such a union will bring permanent ecstasy; it will lead not simply to "domestic harmony" like that of the Ratignolles, but to "life's delirium" (76; ch. 18). In her story of the woman who paddles away with her lover in a pirogue and is never heard of again, Edna elaborates on her vision as she describes the lovers, "close together, rapt in oblivious forgetfulness, drifting into the unknown'' (91; ch. 23). Although her affair with Arobin shocks her into an awareness of her own sexual passions, it leaves her illusions about love intact. Desire, she understands, can exist independently of love. But love retains its magical aura; indeed, her sexual awakening with Arobin generates an even ''fiercer, more overpowering love'' for Robert (104; ch. 28). And when Robert comes back, Edna has persuaded herself that the force of their love will overwhelm all obstacles: ''We shall be everything to each other. Nothing else in the world is of any consequence'' (130; ch. 36). Her intention seems to be that they will go off together into the unknown, like the lovers in her story. But Robert cannot accept such a role, and when he leaves her, Edna finally realizes ''that the day would come when he, too, and the thought of him would melt out of her existence, leaving her alone'' 136; ch. 39).

The other side of Edna's terror of solitude, however, is the bondage of class as well as gender that keeps her in a prison of the self. She goes blank too whenever she might be expected to notice the double standard of ladylike privilege and oppression of women in southern society. Floating along in her ''mazes of inward contemplation,'' Edna barely notices the silent quadroon nurse who takes care of her children, the little black girl who works the treadles of Madame Lebrun's sewing machine, the laundress who keeps her in frilly white, or the maid who picks up her broken glass. She never makes connections between her lot and theirs.

The scene in which Edna witnesses Adèle in childbirth (130–32; ch. 37) is the first time in the novel that she identifies with another woman's pain, and draws some halting conclusions about the female and the human condition, rather than simply about her own ennui. Edna's births have taken place in unconsciousness; when she goes to Adèle's childbed, ''her own like experiences seemed far away, unreal, and only half remembered. She recalled faintly an ecstasy of pain, the heavy odor of chloroform, a stupor which had deadened sensation'' (131; ch. 37). The stupor that deadens sensation is an apt metaphor for the real and imaginary narcotics supplied by fantasy, money, and patriarchy, which have protected Edna from pain for most of her life, but which have also kept her from becoming an adult.

But in thinking of nature's trap for women, Edna never moves from her own questioning to the larger social statement that is feminism. Her ineffectuality is partly a product of her time; as a heroine in transition between the homosocial and the heterosexual worlds, Edna has lost some of the sense of connectedness to other women that might help her plan her future. Though she has sojourned in the "female colony" of Grand Isle, it is far from being a feminist utopia, a real community of women, in terms of sisterhood. The novel suggests, in fact, something of the historical loss for women of transferring the sense of self to relationships with men.

Edna's solitude is one of the reasons that her emancipation does not take her very far. Despite her efforts to escape the rituals of femininity, Edna seems fated to reenact them, even though, as Chopin recounts these scenes, she satirizes and revises their conventions. Ironically, considering her determination to discard the trappings of her role as a society matron—her wedding ring, her "reception day," her "charming home"—the high point of Edna's awakening is the dinner party she gives for her twenty-ninth birthday. Edna's birthday party begins like a kind of drawing-room comedy. We are told the guest list, the seating plan, the menu, and the table setting; some of the guests are boring, and some do not like each other; Madame Ratignolle does not show up at the last minute, and Mademoiselle Reisz makes disagreeable remarks in French.

Yet as it proceeds to its bacchanalian climax, the dinner party also has a symbolic intensity and resonance that makes it, as Sandra Gilbert argues, Edna's "most authentic act of self-definition" (30). Not only is the twenty-ninth birthday a feminine threshold, the passage from youth to middle age, but Edna is literally on the threshold of a new life in her little house. The dinner, as Arobin remarks, is a coup d'état, an overthrow of her marriage, all the more an act of aggression because Léonce will pay the bills. Moreover, she has created an atmosphere of splendor and luxury that seems to exceed the requirements of the occasion. The table is set with gold satin, Sèvres china, crystal, silver, and gold; there is "champagne to swim in" (106; ch. 29), and Edna is magnificently dressed in a satin and lace gown, with a cluster of diamonds (a gift from Léonce) in her hair. Presiding at the head of the table, she seems powerful and autonomous: "There was something in her attitude . . . which suggested the regal woman, the one who rules, who looks on, who stands alone" (109; ch. 30). Edna's moment of mastery thus takes place in the context of a familiar ceremony of women's culture. Indeed, dinner parties are virtual set pieces of feminist aesthetics, suggesting that the hostess is a kind of artist in her own sphere, someone whose creativity is channeled into the production of social and domestic harmony. Like Virginia Woolf's Mrs. Ramsay in *To the Lighthouse*

(1927), Edna exhausts herself in creating a sense of fellowship at her table, although in the midst of her guests she still experiences an "acute longing" for "the unattainable" (109–10; ch. 30).

But there is a gap between the intensity of Edna's desire, a desire that by now has gone beyond sexual fulfillment to take in a much vaster range of metaphysical longings, and the means that she has to express herself. Edna may look like a queen, but she is still a housewife. The political and aesthetic weapons she has in her coup d'état are only forks and knives, glasses and dresses.

Can Edna, and Kate Chopin, then escape from confining traditions only in death? Some critics have seen Edna's much-debated suicide as a heroic embrace of independence and a symbolic resurrection into myth, a feminist counterpart of Melville's Bulkington: "Take heart, take heart, O Edna, up from the spray of thy ocean-perishing, up, straight up, leaps thy apotheosis!" but the ending too seems to return Edna to the nineteenth-century female literary traditions, even though Chopin redefines it for her own purpose. Readers of the 1890s were well accustomed to drowning as the fictional punishment for female transgression against morality, and most contemporary critics of *The Awakening* thus automatically interpreted Edna's suicide as the wages of sin.

Drowning itself brings to mind metaphorical analogies between femininity and liquidity. As the female body is prone to wetness, blood, milk, tears, and amniotic fluid, so in drowning the woman is immersed in the feminine organic element. Drowning thus becomes the traditionally feminine literary death. And Edna's last thoughts further recycle significant images of the feminine from her past. As exhaustion overpowers her,

> Edna heard her father's voice and her sister Margaret's. She heard the barking of an old dog that was chained to the sycamore tree. The spurs of the cavalry officer clanged as he walked across the porch. There was the hum of bees, and the musky odor of pinks filled the air. (137; ch. 39)

Edna's memories are those of awakening from the freedom of childhood to the limitations conferred by female sexuality.

The image of the bees and the flowers not only recalls early descriptions of Edna's sexuality as a "sensitive blossom," but also places *The Awakening* firmly within the traditions of American women's writing, where it is a standard trope for the unequal sexual relations between women and men. Margaret Fuller, for example, writes in her journal: "Woman is the flower, man the bee. She sighs out of melodious fragrance, and invites the winged laborer. He drains her cup, and carries off the honey. She dies on the stalk; he returns to the hive, well fed, and praised as an active member of the community'' (qtd. in Chevigny 349). In post–Civil War fiction, the image is a reminder of an elemental power that women's culture must confront. *The Awakening* seems particularly to echo the last lines of Mary E. Wilkins's ''A New England Nun'' (1891), in which the heroine, having broken her long-standing engagement, is free to continue her solitary life, and closes her door on ''the sounds of the busy harvest of men and birds and bees; there were halloos, metallic clatterings, sweet calls, long hummings.'' These are the images of nature that, Edna has learned, decoy women into slavery; yet even in drowning, she cannot escape from their seductiveness, for to ignore their claim is also to cut oneself off from culture, from the ''humming'' life of creation and achievement.

We can re-create the literary tradition in which Kate Chopin wrote *The Awakening,* but of course, we can never known how the tradition might have changed if her novel had not had to wait half a century to find its audience. Few of Chopin's literary contemporaries came into contact with the book. Chopin's biographer, Per Seyersted, notes that her work ''was apparently unknown to Dreiser, even though he began writing *Sister Carrie* just when the *The Awakening* was being loudly condemned. Also Ellen Glasgow, who was at this time beginning to describe unsatisfactory marriages, seems to have been unaware of the author's existence. Indeed, we can safely say that though she was so much of an innovator in American literature, she was virtually unknown by those who were now to shape it and that she had no influence on them'' (Seyersted, *Kate Chopin* 196). Ironically, even Willa Cather, the one woman writer of the fin-de-siècle who reviewed *The Awakening,* not only failed to recognize its importance but also dismissed its theme as ''trite.'' It would be decades before another American woman novelist combined Kate Chopin's artistic maturity with her sophisticated outlook on sexuality, and overcame both the sentimental codes of feminine ''artlessness'' and the sexual codes of feminine ''passionlessness.''

In terms of Chopin's own literary development, there were signs that *The Awakening* would have been a pivotal work. While it was in press, she wrote one of her finest and most daring short stories, ''The Storm,'' which surpasses *The Awakening* in terms of its expressive freedom. Chopin was also being drawn back to a rethinking of women's culture. Her last poem, written in 1900, was addressed to Kitty Garesché and spoke of the permanence of emotional bonds between women:

To the Friend of My Youth

It is not all of life
To cling together while the years glide past.
It is not all of love
To walk with clasped hands from the first to last.
The mystic garland which the spring did twine
Of scented lilac and the new-blown rose,
Faster than chains will hold my soul to thine
Thro' joy, and grief, thro' life—unto its close.
(Seyersted, *Complete Works* 735)

We have only these tantalizing fragments to hint at the directions Chopin's work might have taken if *The Awakening* had been a critical success or even a succès de scandale, and if her career had not been cut off by her early death. The fate of *The Awakening* shows only too well how a literary tradition may be enabling, even essential, as well as confining. Struggling to escape from tradition, Kate Chopin courageously risked social and literary ostracism. It is up to contemporary readers to restore her solitary book to its place in our literary heritage.

WORKS CITED

Baym, Nina. *Women's Fiction: A Guide to Novels by and about Women in America 1820–1870*. Ithaca: Cornell UP, 1978.

Chevigny, Bell G. *The Woman and the Myth*. Old Westbury, NY: Feminist, 1976.

Cott, Nancy F. "Passionlessness: An Interpretation of Victorian Sexual Ideology, 1790–1850." *Signs* 4 (1978): 219–36.

Egerton, George. "A Keynote to *Keynotes*." *Ten Contemporaries*. Ed. John Gawsworth. London: Benn, 1932.

Gilbert, Sandra. Introduction to *"The Awakening" and Selected Stories*. Harmondsworth: Penguin, 1984.

Kelley, Mary. *Private Woman, Public Stage: Literary Domesticity in Nineteenth-Century America*. New York: Oxford UP, 1984.

Phelps, Elizabeth Stuart. *The Story of Avis*. New Brunswick: Rutgers UP, 1985.

Ryan, Mary P. *The Empire of the Mother: American Writing about Domesticity*. New York: Haworth, 1982.

———. *Womanhood in America from Colonial Times to the Present*. New York: Watts, 1983.

Seyersted, Per, ed. *The Complete Works of Kate Chopin*. 2 vols. Baton Rouge: Louisiana State UP, 1969.

———. *Kate Chopin: A Critical Biography*. New York: Octagon, 1980.

Smith-Rosenberg, Carroll. *Disorderly Conduct: Visions of Gender in Victorian America*. New York: Knopf, 1985.

Vicinus, Martha. Introduction to George Egerton, *Keynotes and Discords*. London: Virago, 1983.

Ziff, Larzer. *The American 1890s*. New York: Viking, 1966.

The New Historicism and *The Awakening*

WHAT IS THE NEW HISTORICISM?

The new historicism is, first of all, *new:* one of the most recent developments in contemporary theory, it is still evolving. Enough of its contours have come into focus for us to realize that it exists and deserves a name, but any definition of the new historicism is bound to be somewhat fuzzy, like a partially developed photographic image. Some individual critics that we may label new historicist may also be deconstructors, or feminists, or Marxists. Some would deny that the others are even writing the new kind of historical criticism.

All of them, though, share the conviction that, somewhere along the way, something important was lost from literary studies: historical consciousness. Poems and novels came to be seen in isolation, as urnlike objects of precious beauty. The new historicists, whatever their differences and however defined, want us to see that even the most urnlike poems are caught in a web of historical conditions, relationships, and influences. In an essay on "The Historical Necessity for—and Difficulties with—New Historical Analysis in Introductory Literature Courses" (1987), Brook Thomas suggests that discussions of Keats's "Ode on a Grecian Urn" might begin with questions such as the following: Where would Keats have seen such an urn? How did a Grecian urn end up in a museum in England? Some very important historical and political realities, Thomas suggests, lie behind and inform Keats's definitions of art, truth, beauty, the past, and timelessness. They are realities that psychoanalytic and reader-response critics, formalists and feminists and deconstructors, might conceivably overlook.

Although a number of influential critics working between 1920 and 1950 wrote about literature from a psychoanalytic perspective, the majority of critics took what might generally be referred to as the historical approach. With the advent of the New Criticism, or formalism, however, historically oriented critics almost seemed to disappear from the face of the earth. Jerome McGann writes: "a text-only approach has been so vigorously promoted during the last thirty-five years that most historical critics have been driven from the field, and have raised the flag of their surrender by yielding the title 'critic' to the victor, and accepting the title 'scholar' for themselves" (*Inflections* 17). Of course, the title "victor" has been vied for by a new kind of psychoanalytic critic, by reader-response critics, by so-called deconstructors, and by feminists since the New Critics of the 1950s lost it during the following decade. But historical scholars have not been in the field, seriously competing to become a dominant critical influence.

At least they haven't until quite recently. In his essay "Toward a New History in Literary Study" (1984), Herbert Lindenberger writes: "It comes as something of a surprise to find that history is making a powerful comeback" (16). E. D. Hirsch, Jr., has also predicted a comeback. He suggested in 1984 that various avant-garde positions (such as deconstruction) have been overrated and that it is time to turn back to history and to historical criticism:

> We should not be disconcerted by its imposing claims, or made to think that we are being naive when we try to pursue historical study. Far from being naive, historically based criticism is the newest and most valuable kind . . . for our students (and our culture) at the present time. (Hirsch 197)

McGann obviously agrees. In *Historical Studies and Literary Criticism* (1985), he speaks approvingly of recent attempts to make sociohistorical subjects and methods central to literary studies once again.

As the word *sociohistorical* suggests, the new historicism is not the same as the historical criticism practiced forty years ago. For one thing, it is informed by recent critical theory: by psychoanalytic criticism, reader-response criticism, feminist criticism, and perhaps especially by deconstruction. The new historicist critics are less fact- and event-oriented than historical critics used to be, perhaps because they have come to wonder whether the truth about what really happened can ever be purely and objectively known. They are less likely to see history as linear and progressive, as something developing toward the present.

As the word *sociohistorical* also suggests, the new historicists view history as a social science and the social sciences as being properly historical. McGann most often alludes to sociology when discussing the future of literary studies. "A sociological poetics must be recognized not only as relevant to the analysis of poetry, but in fact as central to the analysis" (*Inflections* 62). Lindenberger cites anthropology as particularly useful in the new historical analysis of literature, especially anthropology as practiced by Victor Turner and Clifford Geertz. Geertz, who has related theatrical traditions in nineteenth-century Bali to forms of political organization that developed during the same period, has influenced some of the most important critics writing the new kind of historical criticism. Due in large part to Geertz's influence, new historicists such as Stephen Greenblatt have asserted that literature is not a sphere apart or distinct from the history that is relevant to it. That is what old historical criticism tended to do, to present history as information you needed to know before you could fully appreciate the separate world of art. Thus the new historicists have discarded old distinctions between literature, history, and the social sciences, while blurring other boundaries. They have erased the line dividing historical and literary materials, showing that the production of one of Shakespeare's plays was a political act and that the coronation of Elizabeth I was carried out with the same care for staging and symbol lavished on a work of dramatic art.

In addition to breaking down barriers that separate literature and history, history and the social sciences, new historicists have reminded us that it is treacherously difficult to reconstruct the past as it really was—rather than as we have been conditioned by our own place and time to believe that it was. And they know that the job is utterly impossible for anyone who is unaware of the difficulty and of the nature of his or her own historical vantage point. "Historical criticism can no longer make any part of [its] sweeping picture unselfconsciously, or treat any of its details in an untheorized way," McGann wrote in 1985 (*Historical Studies* 11). *Unselfconsciously* and *untheorized* are key words here; when the new historicist critics of literature describe a historical change, they are highly conscious of, and even likely to discuss, the *theory* of historical change that informs their account. They know that the changes they happen to see and describe are the ones that their theory of change allows or helps them to see and describe. And they know, too, that their theory of change is historically determined. They seek to minimize the distortion inherent in their perceptions and representations by admitting that they see through preconceived notions; in other words, they learn and reveal the color of the lenses in the glasses that they wear.

All three of the critics whose recent writings on the so-called back-to-history movement have been quoted thus far—Hirsch, Lindenberger, and McGann—mention the name of the late Michel Foucault. As much an archaeologist as a historian and as much a philosopher as either, Foucault in his writings brought together incidents and phenomena from areas of inquiry and orders of life that we normally regard as unconnected. As much as anyone, he encouraged the new historicist critic of literature outwardly to redefine the boundaries of historical inquiry.

Foucault's views of history were influenced by Friedrich Nietzsche's concept of a *wirkliche* ("real" or "true") history that is neither melioristic nor metaphysical. Foucault, like Nietzsche, didn't understand history as development, as a forward movement toward the present. Neither did he view history as an abstraction, idea, or ideal, as something that began "In the beginning" and that will come to THE END, a moment of definite closure, a Day of Judgment. In his own words, Foucault "abandoned [the old history's] attempts to understand events in terms of . . . some great evolutionary process" (*Discipline and Punish* 129). He warned new historians to be aware of the fact that investigators are themselves "situated." It is difficult, he reminded them, to see present cultural practices critically from within them, and on account of the same cultural practices, it is almost impossible to enter bygone ages. In *Discipline and Punish: The Birth of the Prison* (1975), Foucault admitted that his own interest in the past was fueled by a passion to write the history of the present.

Like Marx, Foucault saw history in terms of power, but his view of power owed more perhaps to Nietzsche than to Marx. Foucault seldom viewed power as a repressive force. Certainly, he did not view it as a tool of conspiracy used by one specific individual or institution against another. Rather, power represents a whole complex of forces; it is that which produces what happens. Thus, even a tyrannical aristocrat does not simply wield power, because he is formed and empowered by discourses and practices that constitute power. Viewed by Foucault, power is "positive and productive," not "repressive" and "prohibitive" (Smart 63). Furthermore, no historical event, according to Foucault, has a single cause; rather, it is intricately connected with a vast web of economic, social, and political factors.

A brief sketch of one of Foucault's major works may help clarify some of his ideas. *Discipline and Punish* begins with a shocking but accurate description of the public drawing and quartering of a Frenchman who had botched his attempt to assassinate King Louis XV. Foucault proceeds, then, by describing rules governing the daily life of modern Parisian felons. What happened to torture, to punishment as public spectacle? he asks. What complex network of forces made it disappear? In working toward a picture of this "power," Foucault turns up many interesting puzzle pieces, such as that in the early revolutionary years of the nineteenth century, crowds would sometimes identify with the prisoner and treat the executioner as if *he* were the guilty party. But Foucault sets forth a related reason for keeping prisoners alive, moving punishment indoors, and changing discipline from physical torture into mental rehabilitation: colonization. In this historical period, people were needed to establish colonies and trade, and prisoners could be used for that purpose. Also, because these were politically unsettled times, governments needed infiltrators and informers. Who better to fill those roles than prisoners pardoned or released early for showing a willingness to be rehabilitated? As for rehabilitation itself, Foucault compares it to the old form of punishment, which began with a torturer extracting a confession. In more modern, "reasonable" times, psychologists probe the minds of prisoners with a scientific rigor that Foucault sees as a different kind of torture, a kind that our modern perspective does not allow us to see as such.

Thus, a change took place, but perhaps not so great a change as we generally assume. It may have been for the better or for the worse; the point is that agents of power didn't make the change because mankind is evolving and, therefore, more prone to perform good-hearted deeds. Rather, different objectives arose, including those of a new class of doctors and scientists bent on studying aberrant examples of the human mind.

Foucault's type of analysis has recently been practiced by a number of literary critics as the vanguard of the back-to-history movement. One of these critics, Stephen Greenblatt, has written on Renaissance changes in the development of both literary characters and real people. Like Foucault, he is careful to point out that any one change is connected with a host of others, no one of which may simply be identified as the cause or the effect. Greenblatt, like Foucault, insists on interpreting literary devices as if they were continuous with other representational devices in a culture; he turns, therefore, to scholars in other fields in order to better understand the workings of literature. "We wall off literary symbolism from the symbolic structures operative elsewhere," he writes, "as if art alone were a human creation, as if humans themselves were not, in Clifford Geertz's phrase, cultural artifacts." Following Geertz, Greenblatt sets out to practice what he calls "anthropological or cultural criticism." Anthropological literary criticism, he continues, addresses itself "to the interpretive constructions the members of a society apply to their experience," since a work of literature is itself an interpretive construction, "part of the system of signs that constitutes a given culture." He suggests that criticism must never interpret the past without at least being "conscious of its own status as interpretation" (Greenblatt 4).

Not all of the critics trying to lead students of literature back to history are as "Foucauldian" as Greenblatt. Some of these new historicists owe more to Marx than to Foucault. Others, like Jerome McGann, have followed the lead of Soviet critic M. M. Bakhtin, who was less likely than Marx to emphasize social class as a determining factor. (Bakhtin was more interested in the way that one language or style is the parody of an older one.) Still other new historicists, like Brook Thomas, have clearly been more influenced by Walter Benjamin, best known for essays such as "Theses on the Philosophy of History" and "The Work of Art in the Age of Mechanical Reproduction."

Moreover, there are other reasons not to declare that Foucault has been the central influence on the new historicism. Some new historicist critics would argue that Foucault critiqued old-style historicism to such an extent that he ended up being antihistorical or, at least, nonhistorical. As for his commitment to a radical remapping of relations of power and influence, cause and effect, in the view of some critics, Foucault consequently adopted too cavalier an attitude toward chronology and facts. In the minds of other critics, identifying and labeling a single master or central influence goes against the very grain of the new historicism. Practitioners of the new historicism have sought to decenter the study of literature and move toward the point where literary studies overlap with anthropological and sociological studies. They have also struggled to see history from a decentered perspective, both by recognizing that their own cultural and historical position may not afford the best understanding of other cultures and times and by realizing that events seldom have any single or central cause. At this point, then, it is appropriate to pause and suggest that Foucault shouldn't be seen as *the* cause of the new historicism, but as one of several powerful, interactive influences.

It is equally useful to suggest that the debate over the sources of the movement, the differences of opinion about Foucault, and even my own need to assert his importance may be historically contingent; that is to say, they may all result from the very *newness* of the new historicism itself. New intellectual movements often cannot be summed up or represented by a key figure, any more than they can easily be summed up or represented by an introduction or a single essay. They respond to disparate influences and almost inevitably include thinkers who represent a wide range of backgrounds. Like movements that are disintegrating, new movements embrace a broad spectrum of opinions and positions.

But just as differences within a new school of criticism cannot be overlooked, neither should they be exaggerated, since it is the similarity among a number of different approaches that makes us aware of a new movement under way. Greenblatt, Hirsch, McGann, and Thomas all started with the assumption that works of literature are simultaneously influenced by and influencing reality, broadly defined. Thus, whatever their disagreements, they share a belief in referentiality—a belief that literature refers to and is referred to by things outside itself—that is fainter in the works of formalist, poststructuralist, and even reader-response critics. They believe with Greenblatt that the "central concerns" of criticism "should prevent it from permanently sealing off one type of discourse from another or decisively separating works of art from the minds and lives of their creators and their audiences" (5).

McGann, in his introduction to *Historical Studies and Literary Criticism,* turns referentiality into a rallying cry:

> What will not be found in these essays . . . is the assumption, so common in text-centered studies of every type, that literary works are self-enclosed verbal constructs, or looped intertextual fields of autonomous signifiers and signifieds. In these essays, the question of referentiality is once again brought to the fore. (3)

In "Keats and the Historical Method of Literary Criticism," he outlines a program for those who have rallied to the cry. These procedures, which he claims are "practical derivatives of the Bakhtin school," assume that historicist critics, who must be interested in a work's point of origin and in its point of reception, will understand the former by studying biography and bibliography. After mastering these details, the critic must then consider the expressed intentions of the author, because, if printed, these intentions have also modified the developing history of the work. Next, the new historicist must learn the history of the work's reception, as that body of opinion has become part of the platform on which we are situated when we study the book. Finally, McGann urges the new historicist critic to point toward the future, toward his or her *own* audience, defining for its members the aims and limits of the critical project and injecting the analysis with a degree of self-consciousness that alone can give it credibility (*Inflections* 62).

In the essay that follows, Margit Stange describes Edna Pontellier's story as a quest for "self-ownership." Stange relates this quest to the quest of nineteenth-century feminists for "female autonomy," which included the right of wives to refuse marital sex. That right was viewed as extremely important, for it meant that women, not men, would decide whether, when, and how often to have sex—and children.

Sex and childbirth were never far apart in the nineteenth-century mind, because even the feminists (and perhaps especially the feminists) of Chopin's day did not advocate the use of birth control devices. In an ideological climate in which a woman's "exchange" or "market" value was, to a great extent, her sexual or maternal value, a woman seeking self-ownership sought to "confirm" her "right" to "withhold" her "body," to make it her own property and to control its value.

Having quoted, very early in her essay, Elizabeth Cady Stanton's 1892 statement that to deny women "the right of property is like cutting off their hands," Stange goes on to show how Chopin uses hands to raise the issues of women, property, self-possession, and value. Women like Adèle Ratignolle, represented by their perfectly pale or gloved hands, are signs mainly of their husbands' wealth, and therefore of what Stange calls "surplus value." By insisting on supporting herself with her own hands (that is, through art) and having control of her own property (her inheritance), Edna seeks to come into ownership of a self that is more than mere ornament. Simply stated, she seeks to possess *herself.*

Stange connects Edna's efforts of self-revaluation with the passage of the Married Women's Property Acts. She also, however, continues to view those efforts in relation to the concepts of sexual rights and voluntary motherhood. Contrasting Edna with Adèle, who dutifully plays the social role of "mother-woman," Stange views Edna's extramarital activities, her "refusal to give herself for her children," and her move from the family home into her own little "pigeon house" in light of her ultimately frustrated desire *not* to live as a mother-woman, in light of her wish to "resituate her sexual exchange value in an economy of public circulation."

Stange's approach may be called new historicist because it blurs the boundary between literary criticism and historical scholarship, offering a thick description of Chopin's novel, not as a text to be analyzed in isolation, but rather as a form of representation that is part of a complex web of historical conditions and relationships. Stange's implicit definition of history, moreover, is broad enough to include the conditions of mothers at home and the political ideologies and discourses that kept them there.

Much as Stange views the drama of Edna Pontellier's life and death as being continuous with history, so she, like other new historicists, sees historical forces in terms of dramatic production and the behavior of actual people and literary characters in terms of public or cultural discourses. Thus, Stange refers to the role of the mother-woman as one "produced by deliberate public staging," and she argues that "Adèle produces her maternity through" a more "public discourse" than the one that advocates "voluntary motherhood."

Stange's interest in the "exchange value" of people and characters suggests a debt to Marxist criticism, and her essay also raises questions that would be pertinent to a feminist reading. It does not, however, tend to present Edna, first and foremost, as the victim of repressive ideology, nor does it imply that the feminism of today is necessarily better or more advanced than that of Chopin's day. Rather, it quietly and carefully builds bridges between our own historically determined views (that is, that the goal of self-ownership unfortunately still left women thinking of themselves in terms of property or chattel or that nineteenth-century feminists should have advocated contraception and free love) and historically determined ideologies rather different from our own.

Ross C Murfin

THE NEW HISTORICISM: A SELECTED BIBLIOGRAPHY

The New Historicism: Further Reading

American Literary History. A journal devoted to new historicist and cultural criticism; the first issue was Spring 1989. New York: Oxford UP.

Brown, Gillian. *Domestic Individualism: Imagining Self in Nineteenth-Century America.* Berkeley: U of California P, 1990.

Dollimore, Jonathan, and Alan Sinfield, eds. *Political Shakespeare: New Essays in Cultural Materialism.* Manchester, Eng.: Manchester

UP, 1985. See especially the essays by Dollimore, Greenblatt, and Tennenhouse.

———. *Radical Tragedy: Religion, Ideology and Power in the Drama of Shakespeare and His Contemporaries.* Brighton, Eng.: Harvester, 1984.

Goldberg, Jonathan. *James I and the Politics of Literature.* Baltimore: Johns Hopkins UP, 1983.

Graff, Gerald, and Reginald Gibbons, eds. *Criticism in the University.* Evanston: Northwestern UP, 1985. This volume includes sections devoted to the historical backgrounds of academic criticism; the influence of Marxism, feminism, and critical theory in general on the new historicism; changing pedagogies; and varieties of cultural criticism.

Greenblatt, Stephen. *Renaissance Self-Fashioning from More to Shakespeare.* Chicago: U of Chicago P, 1980. See chapter 1.

Hirsch, E. D., Jr. "Back to History." Graff 189–97.

History and . . . Special issue, *New Literary History* 21 (1990). See especially the essays by Carolyn Porter, Rena Fraden, Clifford Geertz, and Renato Rosaldo.

Lindenberger, Herbert. *The History in Literature: On Value, Genre, Institutions.* New York: Columbia UP, 1990.

———. "Toward a New History in Literary Study." *Profession: Selected Articles from the Bulletins of the Association of Departments of English and the Association of Departments of Foreign Languages.* New York: MLA, 1984. 16–23.

McGann, Jerome. *The Beauty of Inflections: Literary Investigations in Historical Method and Theory.* Oxford: Clarendon–Oxford UP, 1985. See especially the introduction and chapter 1, "Keats and the Historical Method in Literary Criticism."

———. *Historical Studies and Literary Criticism.* Madison: U of Wisconsin P, 1985. See especially the introduction and the essays in the following sections: "Historical Methods and Literary Interpretations" and "Biographical Contexts and the Critical Object."

Morris, Wesley. *Toward a New Historicism.* Princeton: Princeton UP, 1972.

Michaels, Walter Benn. *The Gold Standard and the Logic of Naturalism: American Literature at the Turn of the Century.* Berkeley: U of California P, 1987.

Thomas, Brook. "The Historical Necessity for—and Difficulties with—New Historical Analysis in Introductory Literature Courses." *College English* 49 (1987): 509–22.

Veeser, H. Aram, ed. *The New Historicism*. New York: Routledge, 1989.

Foucault and His Influence

As is pointed out in the introduction to the new historicism, some new historicists question the "privileging" of Foucault implicit in this section heading ("Foucault and His Influence") and the one following ("Other Writers and Works of Interest . . ."). They might argue for the greater importance of one of these other writers or point out that to cite a central influence or a definitive cause defies the very spirit of the movement.

Foucault, Michel. *Discipline and Punish: The Birth of the Prison*. 1975. Trans. Alan Sheridan. New York: Pantheon, 1978.

———. *The History of Sexuality*. Trans. Robert Hurley. Vol. I. New York: Pantheon, 1978. 2 vols.

———. *Language, Counter-Memory, Practice*. Ed. Donald F. Bouchard. Trans. Bouchard and Sherry Simon. Ithaca: Cornell UP, 1977. Consists of selected essays and interviews.

Dreyfus, Hubert L., and Paul Rabinow. *Michel Foucault: Beyond Structuralism and Hermeneutics*. Chicago: U of Chicago P, 1983.

Sheridan, Alan. *Michel Foucault: The Will to Truth*. New York: Tavistock, 1980.

Smart, Barry. *Michel Foucault*. New York: Horwood and Tavistock, 1985.

Other Writers and Works of Interest to New Historicist Critics

Bakhtin, M. M. *The Dialogic Imagination: Four Essays*. Ed. Michael Holquist. Trans. Caryl Emerson. Austin: U of Texas P, 1981. Bakhtin authored many influential studies of subjects as varied as Dostoyevsky, Rabelais, and formalist criticism. But this book, in part due to Holquist's helpful introduction, is probably the best place to begin reading Bakhtin.

Benjamin, Walter. "The Work of Art in the Age of Mechanical Reproduction." 1936. *Illuminations*. Trans. Harry Zohn. New York: Schocken, 1969.

Fried, Michael. *Absorption and Theatricality: Painting and Beholder in the Works of Diderot*. Berkeley: U of California P, 1980.

Geertz, Clifford. *The Interpretation of Cultures*. New York: Basic, 1973.

———. *Negara: The Theatre State in Nineteenth-Century Bali*, Princeton: Princeton UP, 1980.

Goffman, Erving. *Frame Analysis.* New York: Harper, 1974.
Jameson, Fredric. *The Political Unconscious.* Ithaca: Cornell UP, 1981.
Koselleck, Reinhart. *Futures Past.* Trans. Keith Tribe. Cambridge: MIT P, 1985.
Representations. Published by the University of California Press, this quarterly journal regularly contains new historicist studies and cultural criticism.

New Historicist Studies of *The Awakening*

Bauer, Dale Marie, and Andrew M. Lakritz. "*The Awakening* and the Woman Question." *Approaches to Teaching "The Awakening."* Ed. Bernard Koloski. New York: MLA, 1988. 47–52.
Dimmock, Wai-Chee. "Rightful Subjectivity." *Yale Journal of Criticism* 4 (1990): 25–51.
Gilmore, Michael T. "Revolt Against Nature: The Problematic Modernism of *The Awakening.*" *New Essays on "The Awakening."* Ed. Wendy Martin. New York: Cambridge UP, 1988. 59–87.
Rowe, John Carlos. "The Economics of the Body in Kate Chopin's *The Awakening. Perspectives on Kate Chopin: Proceedings of the Kate Chopin International Conference.* Natchitoches: Northwestern State UP, 1990. 1–24.

A NEW HISTORICIST PERSPECTIVE

MARGIT STANGE

Personal Property: Exchange Value and the Female Self in *The Awakening*

In the beginning of *The Awakening,* New Orleans stockbroker Léonce Pontellier, staying with his wife, Edna, at an exclusive Creole family resort, surveys Edna as she walks up from the beach in the company of her summer flirtation, Robert Lebrun. "'You are burnt beyond recognition' [Léonce says], looking at his wife as one looks at a valuable piece of personal property which has suffered some damage" (21). Léonce's comment is the reader's introduction to Edna, whose search for self is the novel's subject. To take Léonce's hyperbole—"you are burnt beyond recognition"—as literally as Léonce takes his role as Edna's "owner" is to be introduced to an Edna who exists as a recognizable individual in reference to her status as valuable property. This status appears to determine Edna's perception of herself: in response to Léonce's anxiety. Edna makes her first self-examination in this novel about a heroine who is "beginning to realize her position in the universe as a human being, and to recognize her relations as an individual to the world within and about her" (31–32). Edna, having been told "you are burnt beyond recognition,"

> held up her hands, strong, shapely hands, and surveyed them critically, drawing up her lawn sleeves above the wrists. Looking at them reminded her of her rings, which she had given to her husband before leaving for the beach. She silently reached out to him and he, understanding, took the rings from his vest pocket and dropped them into her open palm. She slipped them upon her fingers. (21)

In the context of the property system in which Edna exists as a sign of value, Edna's body is detachable and alienable from her own viewpoint: the hands and wrists are part of the body yet can be objectified, held out and examined as if they belonged to someone else—as indeed, in some sense that Léonce insists upon very literally, they do belong to someone else. Edna's perception of her own body is structured by the detachability of the hand and arm as signs of Léonce's ownership of her. Her hands also suggest the possibility of being an owner herself when they make the proprietary gesture of reaching out for the rings that Léonce obediently drops into the palm (this gesture of Edna's contrasts with a bride's conventional passive reception of the ring). The hands are the organs of appropriation; Elizabeth Cady Stanton, in a speech on female rights given in 1892, argued that "to deny [to woman] the rights of property is like cutting off the hands."[1] In having Edna put on the rings herself (a gesture Edna will again perform at a moment when she decisively turns away from her domestic role),

[1] "The Solitude of Self" (qtd. in DuBois 249). In this speech Stanton gave in 1892 on the occasion of her resignation from the presidency of the suffrage movement, Stanton argued for full civil rights for woman on the grounds of her aloneness and existential "self-sovereignty." In its argument and rhetoric, this speech of Stanton's is strikingly similar to Chopin's presentation of female selfhood (*The Awakening*'s original title was *A Solitary Soul*). Like the self Chopin's heroine discovers, Stanton's self is an absolute, possessive self whose metaphorical situation is that of a lone individual "on a solitary island" or "launched on the sea of life." In Stanton and in Chopin, female subjectivity and women's rights are grounded in absolute selfhood. For an account of early English feminists' commitment to absolute selfhood, see Catherine Gallagher, "Embracing the Absolute: The Politics of the Female Subject in Seventeenth-Century England," *Genders* 1 (Spring 1988): 24–39.

Chopin suggests that the chief item of property owned by the proprietary Edna is Edna herself. Thus the opening scene foreshadows the turning point of the plot at which Edna, deciding to leave Léonce's house, resolves "never again to belong to another than herself" (100).

"Self-ownership," in the second half of the nineteenth century, signified a wife's right to refuse marital sex—a right feminists were demanding as the key to female autonomy. First popularized by Lucinda Chandler in the 1840s and widely promoted by the feminists who followed her, the practice of self-ownership, as Chandler saw it, would mean that the woman "has control over her own person, independent of the desires of her husband" (2). "By the 1870s," writes historian William Leach, "self-ownership . . . had become the stock in trade of feminist thinking on birth control" (92) for it "meant that woman, not man, would decide when, where, and how the sexual act would be performed. It also meant that woman, not man, would determine when children would be conceived and how many" (89). "Voluntary motherhood"—woman's "right to choose when to be pregnant" (Gordon 109)—was usually evoked as the ground of self-ownership: "she should have pleasure or not allow access unless she wanted a child," explains advice writer Henry C. Wright (252). According to social historian Linda Gordon, by the mid-1870s, advocacy of voluntary motherhood was shared by "the whole feminist community" (109). Writing in 1881, reformer Dido Lewis demonstrates the central place of self-ownership/voluntary motherhood in the campaign for female autonomy when she evokes together the rights "of wife to be her own person, and her sacred right to deny her husband if need be; and to decide how often and when she should become a mother" (18).

While the feminist community promoted voluntary motherhood, it unanimously opposed the use of birth control devices. This opposition, which contradicts the advocacy of choice and control for women, was shared by suffragists, moral reformers, and free love advocates alike. Various kinds of contraceptive technology were accessible to middle-class women. However, as historian Gordon notes, nineteenth-century birth control practice was determined by ideology rather than the availability of technology. In the prevailing ideology of even the most radical feminist reformers, motherhood was an inextricable part of female sexuality. Why did feminists, whose goal was to win for women the civil and proprietary rights that would make them equal to men, choose to deny women the freedom to have sex without pregnancy? As Gordon points out, the linkage of self-ownership with reproduction certainly reflects the reality of many women's lives, which were dominated by multiple births and the attendant realities of risk, disease, and pain. Some of the resistance to birth control technology, Gordon suggests, was motivated by material conditions: birth control devices, by separating sex from reproduction, appeared to threaten the family structure that provided most middle-class women their only social standing and economic security. But even among those reformers who were not concerned with upholding the family (free love advocates and nonmarrying career women, for example), there was a strong resistance to contraception—a resistance that amounts to a refusal to separate motherhood from female sexuality.

To put voluntary motherhood practiced without birth control devices at the center of self-ownership is to make motherhood central to a woman's life and identity. The capacity to bear children is the sexual function that most dramatically distinguishes the sexual lives—and the day-to-day lives—of women from those of men. The ban on contraceptive technology enforces a lived distinction between male and female sexuality: without effective contraception, sex for a woman always means sex as a woman because it means a potential pregnancy. The opposition to contraceptive technology (as well as the idealization of motherhood of which it is a part) reflects a commitment to the sexualization of female identity. Through the practice of self-ownership, this differentiated sexuality with motherhood at its core becomes the possession that a woman makes available or withholds in order to demonstrate self-ownership. To ask why the feminist reformers opposed contraceptive technology is, then, to ask how motherhood functions in the construction of the self-owning female self. In making motherhood a central possession of the self, the feminists were defining that self as sexual and as female. The possession of this sexualized self through self-ownership amounts to the exercise of a right to alienate (confirmed by a right to withhold). This selfhood, then, consists of the alienation of female sexuality in a market. Charlotte Perkins Gilman, in her 1899 critique of this sexual market, attacked it as a market in which, "he is . . . the demand . . . she is the supply" (86). The feminists' opposition to birth control technology reflects a commitment to this market: underlying their constructions of female selfhood is the ideology of woman's sexual value in exchange.

Chopin's dramatization of female self-ownership demonstrates the central importance of the ideology of woman's value in exchange to contemporary notions of female selfhood. If, as Stanton declares in the speech on female selfhood quoted above, "in discussing the rights of woman, we are to consider, first, what belongs to her as an individual" (247), what Edna Pontellier considers as her property is, first, her body.

Her body is both what she owns and what she owns with. She begins to discover a self by uncovering her hands and "surveying them critically" with her eyes, thus making an appropriative visual assessment of herself as a proprietary being. Her hands and eyes will serve her in her "venture" into her "work" of sketching and painting (75). Thus her hands, by remaining attached (and not cut off like those of the woman who is denied the rights of property), serve her visual appropriation of the world and provide the first object of this appropriation: her own body.

Edna's hands appear in two states: naked and sunburned, and ringed. In the first state, they are conventionally "unrecognizable" as signs of her status as Léonce's wife. Sunburned hands, by indicating the performance of outdoor labor, would nullify Edna's "value" as a sign of Léonce's wealth. In the terminology of Thorstein Veblen's turn-of-the-century analysis of the ownership system, Edna is an item of "conspicuous consumption" that brings "reputability" (a degree of status) to Léonce. Such status-bearing wealth must be surplus wealth: useful articles do not serve to advertise the owner's luxurious freedom from need. Edna must, then, appear to be surplus—she must appear to perform no useful labor.[2] The rings—showy, luxurious, useless items of conspicuous consumption par excellence—restore her status as surplus. Yet this status is also constituted by the sight of her hands without the rings: the significance of the sunburned hands quickly collapses into the significance of the ringed hands when the sunburned, naked hands "remind" both Léonce and Edna of the ringed, value-bearing hands. And Edna's sunburn is directly constitutive of her "value," for it results from her conspicuous, vicarious consumption of leisure on Léonce's behalf (what Veblen calls "vicarious leisure"): she has been enjoying a

[2]Veblen argues that under the private property system, all personal property is a version of that original property whose "usefulness" was to serve as a trophy marking the personal "prepotence" of the trophy's Barbaric owner (23, 29). The first trophy to emerge from the economic "margin worth fighting for" is woman: the original form of ownership is the ownership of women by men. In Veblen's famous characterization of the contemporary bourgeois domestic ownership system, the wife advertises her status as surplus in her role as the chief item of household property as she earns "reputability" for her husband through vicarious consumption and vicarious leisure (65–67). Veblen suggests that, because the meaning of property—and thus the identity of its owner—is produced by the perceptions and positions of others, male selfhood is always mediated by property. Chopin, like Veblen, pokes fun at the figure of the male owner whose experiences of himself and the world are mediated by the arbitrary conventions and relations of ownership. In the opening pages of *The Awakening,* Léonce rather ridiculously governs himself according to his notions of property rights, granting, for example, the caged birds the right to sing because they are owned by Madame Lebrun, and himself the right to retreat to "his own cottage" (19).

holiday at the respectable, luxurious resort frequented by Léonce's Creole circle.

Thus Edna's hands appear in their naked and exposed state as a reminder of Léonce's property interests while they also, in this state, suggest an identity and proprietary interests of her own. The appropriative survey of the female body as a sign of mate ownership continues to engage Edna: her visual fascination fastens on the hands and body of her friend Adèle Ratignolle, whose "excessive physical charm" at first attracts Edna (32). Edna "like[s] to sit and gaze at her fair companion" (29). She watches Adèle at her domestic labors—"Never were hands more exquisite than [Adèle's], and it was joy to look at them when she threaded her needle or adjusted her gold thimble . . . as she sewed away on the little night-drawers" (27). Here, the hands are the organs of labor—but again, gender determines possessive status. Adèle's hands are perfectly white because she always wears dogskin gloves with gauntlets. The femininity of the laboring hands, their luxuriously aesthetic and spectacular quality, conspicuously signifies that the value of Adèle's labor does not stem from production for use: Edna "[can]not see the use" of Adèle's labor (27). Adèle's laboring hands signify her consecration to her "role" within the family, and they are marked with the gold of a thimble as Edna's are marked with the gold of a ring.

In their white, "exquisite" beauty, Adèle's hands are stably—organically—signs of her status as wealth. When Adèle jokes "with excessive naïveté" about the fear of making her husband jealous, "that made them all laugh. The right hand jealous of the left! . . . But for that matter, the Creole husband is never jealous; with him the gangrene passion is one which has become dwarfed by disuse" (29). (This ownership is not reciprocal: the question of jealousy pertains only to the husband; the wife's jealous, proprietary interest in her husband is not evoked.) Adèle's entire presence is a reminder of the property system in which woman is a form of surplus wealth whose value exists in relation to exchange. A woman of "excessive physical charm," Adèle is luxuriously draped in "pure white, with a fluffiness of ruffles that became her. The draperies and fluttering things which she wore suited her rich, luxuriant beauty" (33). Her body is as rich, white, and ornamental as her clothes; she appears "more beautiful than ever" in a negligee that leaves her arms "almost wholly bare" and "expose[s] the rich, melting curves of her white throat" (75).

In her rich and elaborate yet revealing clothing, Adèle is excessively covered while her body, already a sign of wealth, makes such coverings redundant. Adèle appears as a concretized *femme couverte*. Under the

Napoleonic Code which was still in force in Louisiana in the 1890s, wives were legally identical with their husbands; being in *couverture*, they had no separate legal or proprietary identity and could not own property in their own right. Adèle's beauty is her conspicuousness as a form of wealth: her looks are describable by "no words . . . save the old ones that have served so often to picture the bygone heroine of romance." These words—"gold," "sapphires," "cherries or some other delicious crimson fruit"—construct femininity as tangible property. The value of the woman is emphatically defined as social wealth that exists as an effect of the public circulation of the tropes—"the old [words] that have served so often"—that identify her as beautiful. Her beauty is the product and representation of its own circulation. Adèle's "excessive physical charm" is a kind of currency that makes her the "embodiment of every womanly grace and charm" (26).

It is in public display that Adèle's beauty manifests itself. The sight of woman as social wealth is the starting point of Edna's self-seeking. "Mrs. Pontellier liked to sit and gaze at her fair companion as she might look upon a faultless Madonna" (29). An amateur artist, Edna finds such "joy" in looking at Adèle that she wants to "try herself on Madame Ratignolle" (30). Adèle, "seated there like some sensuous Madonna, with the gleam of the fading day enriching her splendid color" (30), appears to Edna as a particularly "tempting subject" of a sketch. This sketch becomes the second sight that Edna "survey[s] critically" (the first being her hands); finding that it "[bears] no resemblance to Madame Ratignolle" (and despite the fact that it is "a fair enough piece of work, and in many respects satisfying"), Edna enforces her proprietary rights in regard to the sketch as she smudges it and "crumple[s] the paper between her hands" (30). Edna is inspired to make another try when she visits Adèle at home in New Orleans and finds her again at her ornamental domestic labor (Adèle is unnecessarily sorting her husband's laundry). "Madame Ratignolle looked more beautiful than ever there at home. . . . 'Perhaps I shall be able to paint your picture some day,' said Edna. . . . 'I believe I ought to work again'" (75). The sight of Adèle at home inspires Edna to do the work that will help her get out of the home. Later she will leave Léonce and support herself on the income from her art and from a legacy of her mother's.

In her insistence on owning her own property and supporting herself, Edna is a model of the legal opposite of the *femme couverte*—she is the *femme seule*. Thus Chopin connects her to the Married Women's Property Acts, property law reforms instituted in the latter part of the century that gave married women varying rights of ownership. Edna comes from "old Presbyterian Kentucky stock" (86). Kentucky belonged to the block of states with the most advanced separation of property in marriage. In fact, Kentucky had the most advanced Married Women's Property Act in the nation, granting married women not only the right to own separate property and make contracts, but the right to keep their earnings.

Thus Chopin connects Edna to the feminist drive for women's property rights. Elizabeth Cady Stanton, in her speech on female selfhood quoted above, makes possessive individualism the first consideration among women's rights: "In discussing the right of woman, we are to consider, first, what belongs to her as an individual." Chopin suggests that what a woman owns in owning herself is her sexual exchange value. The *femme couverte,* in being both property and the inspiration to own, allows Edna to be *femme seule.* The self she owns can be owned—is property—because it is recognizable as social wealth. Adèle, who concretizes the status of the woman and mother as domestic property, makes visible to Edna the female exchange value that constitutes a self to own. Thus Edna's possessive selfhood looks "back" to the chattel form of marriage, valorizing (in a literal sense) the woman as property. In Adèle, the "bygone heroine," Edna finds the capital which she invests to produce her market selfhood.

The way that Edna owns herself by owning her value in exchange is a form of voluntary motherhood: "Edna had once told Madame Ratignolle that she would never sacrifice herself for her children, or for any one. Then had followed a rather heated argument." In this argument Edna "explains" to Adèle, "I would give my life for my children; but I wouldn't give myself." Adèle's answer is, "a woman who would give her life for her children could do no more than that. . . . I'm sure I couldn't do more than that." Withholding nothing, Adèle cannot conceive of giving more than she already gives. Edna cannot at first identify what it is she has chosen to withhold: "I wouldn't give myself. I can't make it more clear; it's only something which . . . is revealing itself to me" (67).

The self at first exists in the presumption of the right to withhold oneself as a mother. But Edna, like the feminist advocates of selfownership, soon determines that voluntary motherhood means withholding herself sexually. After her first successful swim (during which she experiences a moment of self-support and the absolute solitariness of death), she stays on the porch, refusing Léonce's repeated orders and entreaties to come inside to bed (49–50). Later Edna stops sleeping with her husband altogether, so that Léonce complains to the family doctor, "she's making it devilishly uncomfortable for me. . . . She's got some sort of notion in her head concerning the eternal rights of women; and—you understand—we meet in the morning at the breakfast table" (85). It is by withholding herself sexually, then, that Edna exercises the "eternal rights of women" in insisting that she has a self and that she owns that self.

The freedom to withhold oneself has its complement in the freedom to give oneself. No longer sleeping with—or even living with—her husband, Edna declares herself free to have sex with whomever she chooses. She tells Robert, "I am no longer one of Mr. Pontellier's possessions to dispose of or not. I give myself where I choose" (129). Edna supposes that her self-giving is chosen because she has presumed the choice of not giving—she has made her motherhood voluntary. Adèle, in contrast, is the mother who never withholds and thus cannot choose but to give. Will and intention seem to be with Edna, whereas Adèle exercises no will (and has no self). Yet Adèle's giving is not an involuntary and therefore selfless reflex, but a consciously and intentionally developed identity. Adèle is Grand Isle's greatest exponent of the "rôle" of "mother-woman," a role that is produced through deliberate public staging (26). First presented to Edna as a beautiful vision of the "Madonna," Adèle produces her maternity through public discourse. Her children are "thoughts" brought out in speech: Adèle "thinks" (out loud) of "a fourth one" and, after giving birth to it, implores Edna, in a phrase that Edna will not be able to get out of her mind, to "think of the children . . . oh think of . . . them" (132).

"Madame Ratignolle had been married seven years. About every two years she had a baby. At that time she . . . was beginning to think of a fourth one. She was always talking about her 'condition.' Her 'condition' was in no way apparent, and no one would have known a thing about it but for her persistence in making it the subject of conversation" (27). Adèle produces her "role" of "mother-woman" by thinking and provoking thought, but it is impossible to determine whether Adèle thinks about getting pregnant—whether, that is, she practices self-ownership and voluntary motherhood by withholding herself from sex. The two-year intervals between her pregnancies might result from chance, or they might represent intentional spacing that keeps Adèle in or nearly in the "condition" that provides her identity. This ambiguity characterizes the "condition" of motherhood that Adèle is "always" producing for herself. Motherhood is a "role" and therefore consciously produced and paraded. Yet the intention and will that are used to stage the role conflict with its content, for the role of mother demands selflessness: the mother-women of Grand Isle "efface themselves as individuals" (26). Motherhood is never voluntary or involuntary. If motherhood is a social role that Adèle intentionally inhabits, it is also a condition that she can never actually choose, since intending to become pregnant cannot make her so. Thus, motherhood has a kind of built-in selflessness that is dramatically expressed in the scene when Adèle, who is usually in control of her presence, becomes pathetically hysterical and paranoic during labor and childbirth. Here, Adèle's intentional embrace of motherhood gets its force from the unwilled nature of the "torture" that it attempts to appropriate. Hardly able to speak after her ordeal in childbirth, Adèle whispers in an "exhausted" voice, "think of the children, Edna" (132).

Adèle's histrionics insist that nothing less than the self is at stake in the speculative risk-taking that is motherhood (which includes the absention from motherhood). The intention to become a mother is the kind of "weak" intention that Walter Benn Michaels connects with "acts that take place in the market, such as speculating in commodities" (237). Michaels places weak intention at the center of a market selfhood whose "self-possession" and "self-interest" are grounded in "the possibility of intention and action coming apart" (244, 241). Chopin's dramatization of the logic of voluntary motherhood—like Michaels's own example of Edith Wharton's self-speculating heroine Lily Bart (*The House of Mirth*)—emphasizes that self-speculation is gendered. For women, it is sexual; that is to say that sexuality is the content of the female self in the market. Contrary to Michaels's claim, Lily Bart is indeed "a victim of patriarchal capitalism" in a way that the male entrepreneurs in the novel are not (240), for the woman cannot choose whether to speculate or what to speculate in: by being a woman she is already sexually at risk. The "voluntariness" of female self-speculation is an effect of the commodity system which constructs female value along the polarities of accessibility and rarity. Lily Bart speculates in the marriage market by withholding sexual accessibility from that market—a risky behavior that results in her death (complete with hallucinated motherhood). "Voluntary motherhood" represents the inevitable risks of female self-speculation as the risk of pregnancy—which, in the nineteenth century, was the risk of life—and points to the enforced nature of female self-speculation by identifying all women as mothers.

Adèle and Edna embody the two poles of motherhood: Adèle is the "mother-woman" and Edna is "not a mother-woman." The axis of motherhood gives Edna her original sense of identity. What makes her "not a mother-woman" is her refusal to "give" herself for her children. Unlike Adèle, Edna does not embrace the role. Her motherhood seems arbitrary, externally imposed and unwilled, "a responsibility which she had blindly assumed." She is "fond of her children in an uneven, impulsive way. She [will] sometimes gather them passionately to her heart; she [will] sometimes forget them" (37). Her "half remembered" experience of childbirth is an "ecstasy" and a "stupor" (131). Edna's refusal to give herself as a mother, rather than making her the controller and proprietor of her life, entails the passivity of thoughtlessness. In refusing to be a mother-woman she absents herself from the motherhood that is thus all the more arbitrarily thrust upon her.

Indeed, Edna is inescapably a mother. Motherhood is what Edna withholds and thus she, too, is essentially a "mother-woman." Adèle's presence is a provocation and reminder of the self-constituting function of motherhood. Adèle's selflessness is an inducement to Edna to identify a self to give. For Edna, who "becom[es] herself" by "daily casting aside that fictitious self which we assume like a garment with which to appear before the world" (77), the friendship with Adèle is "the most obvious . . . influence" in the loosening of Edna's "mantle of reserve" (32). The Creole community recognizes no private sphere. Adèle's sexual and reproductive value is already located in the sphere of public exchange (or, the public is already like the private: the Creoles are like "one large family" [28]). In this Creole openness, Edna is inspired to resituate her sexual exchange value in an economy of public circulation.

"The candor of [Adèle's] whole existence, which every one might read," is part of a Creole lack of prudery that allows for the open circulation of stories about sex and childbirth. With "profound astonishment" Edna reads "in secret and solitude" a book that "had gone the rounds" and was openly discussed at table.

> Never would Edna Pontellier forget the shock with which she heard Madame Ratignolle relating to old Monsieur Farival the harrowing story of one of her *accouchements,* withholding no intimate detail. She was growing accustomed to like shocks, but she could not keep the mounting color back from her cheeks. (28)

The candor of Adèle's motherhood provokes blushes that simultaneously constitute Edna's reserve and "give her away" to the public. Her body, whether sunburned or blushing, is red from an exposure that privatizes and valorizes that body as her domestic, private attributes—sexuality, modesty, reproduction—are manifested as social value.

Adèle has nothing to hide because her body underneath her clothes is manifestly social wealth. Her bareness is as ornamentally "beautiful" as her ornamented, clothed self. The reserved, private, domestic self of Adèle reveals itself to Edna as the valuable product of circulation, and this revelation prompts Edna to explore her own possessive privacy. She becomes aware of having "thoughts and emotions which never voiced themselves. . . . They belonged to her and were her own" (67). Her erotic longings belong in this category. "Edna often wondered at one propensity which sometimes had inwardly disturbed her without causing any outward show or manifestation on her part" (36). This is a propensity to become silently infatuated with various men. These "silent" possessions of the self are owned in a way most clearly illustrated in the story of Edna's greatest infatuation, whose object was a "great tragedian."

> The picture of the tragedian stood enframed upon her desk. Anyone may possess the portrait of a tragedian without exciting suspicion or comment. (This was a sinister reflection which she cherished.) In the presence of others she expressed admiration for his exalted gifts, as she handed the photograph around and dwelt upon the fidelity of the likeness. When alone she sometimes picked it up and kissed the cold glass passionately. (36)

Edna's comment upon the fidelity of the likeness recapitulates the book's opening, in which Léonce's anxiety about Edna's lapse from recognizability, and his restoration of her recognizability via the wedding rings, consists of a discourse that constantly remembers and reinscribes her as a sign of him in his proprietary office. Her "fidelity" in this marital, possessive sense is her recognizability as such a sign. Edna's photograph is to Edna as Edna is to Léonce. It represents her possessive identity, her selfhood as an owner (thus there is a mirrorlike quality in the "cold glass" which shows her herself kissing herself). The photograph embodies and reflects Edna's erotic desire for the tragedian. It objectifies her sexuality in an image that is handed around, praised for its "fidelity," and kissed in private.

Like Adèle, the photograph concretizes erotic value that is both publicly produced and privately owned. The erotic availability and desirability of the actor whose photograph "anyone might possess" is a product of reproduction and circulation, as Edna's own kisses are incited by and followed by the circulation of the object. The mode of owning it is "handing it around" while she praises the "fidelity" of the likeness. That is, she assumes an individual possessive relationship to the photograph only in the context of its possession by any number of other owners, whose possession produces the "sinister reflection" of her own possessive, cherishing privacy. But Edna's position as an owner is not that of Adèle's husband—or of her own. Edna gives up possession in order to have this possessive relationship. In praising the "fidelity of the likeness" she does not praise its likeness to her but emphasizes that the photograph represents and thus "belongs to" its original—a man whose inaccessibility makes her infatuation "hopeless." Edna can see her photograph as property only by seeing it as male property—just as her own hands, in their function as signs of Léonce's ownership of her, appear detachable and therefore ownable. Yet the absence of Edna in what the photograph represents allows her to imagine a possessive self that is somehow hidden and concealed—and therefore her own. Alone with her photograph, she imagines it circulating. Circulating it, she is able to imagine being secretly alone with it. In her ownership of the photograph, Edna establishes her possessive relationship to her sexuality.

"I am no longer one of Mr. Pontellier's possessions to dispose of or not. I give myself where I choose," says Edna to Robert (129). She has withheld herself from her husband in order to give herself. Instead of being property "to dispose of or not," she intends to be property that is necessarily disposed of. The forms of value in which Edna exchanges herself are the duties and functions of the woman and wife—female sexual service, motherhood, and the performance of wifely domestic/social amenities. Edna reprivatizes and reserves this value by giving up her social and domestic duties as the lady of the house, by moving out of the impressive family home into a private domestic space, the "pigeon house," and by withholding sex from her husband. This reserved self is what she gives away at her "grand dinner," when she launches her sexual exchange value into wider circulation.

> Whatever came, she had resolved never again to belong to another than herself. "I shall give a grand dinner before I leave the old house!" Edna exclaimed. (100)

At the dinner, the "glittering circlet" of Edna's wedding ring (72) is now her crown.

> "Something new, Edna?" exclaimed Miss Mayblunt, with lorgnette directed toward a magnificent cluster of diamonds that sparkled, that almost sputtered, in Edna's hair. . . .
>
> " . . . A present from my husband. . . . I may as well admit that this is my birthday. . . . In good time I expect you to drink my health. Meanwhile, I shall ask you to begin with this cocktail,

composed . . . by my father in honor of Sister Janet's wedding." (108)

Her wedding rings had "sparkled," but the tiara (a conventional adornment of the "young matron") "sputters." This dinner marks the exploding of the intramarriage market, in which she repeatedly sells herself to the same man, into the public market, in which she circulates as the owner of her own sexual exchange value. In its very conception, the dinner collapses the private and public: "though Edna had spoken of the dinner as a very grand affair, it was in truth a very small affair and very select" (107). The absent beloved, Robert, is represented by Victor, his flirtatious younger brother. Flanking Edna are representatives of two modes of the market in sex value: Arobin, the gambler and playboy, represents adulterous and extramarital serial liaisons, while Monsieur Ratignolle enjoys the quasi-organic bond of Creole marriage.

The wealth of the Pontellier household is conspicuously displayed and offered to the guests. On the table "there were silver and gold . . . and crystal which glittered like the gems which the women wore" (107). The women, like the accoutrements, are presented as forms of wealth, and Edna is the queen among them. In her diamond crown, she both embodies and reigns over Léonce's riches. This dinner at which, like all women under exogamy, she leaves "the old house" is a version of the woman-giving potlatch, the marriage feast at which the father gives away the virgin daughter. The cocktail "composed" by the father for the daughter Janet's wedding is explicitly compared by Edna's lover Arobin to the gift of Edna herself: "it might not be amiss to start out by drinking the Colonel's health in the cocktail which he composed, on the birthday of the most charming of women—the daughter whom he invented" (108). Edna is thus the gift not just of Léonce, who makes her into a form of wealth by marking her as value, but of her father, too: that is, she is a bride. As a bride, she is an invention—man-made, brought into the world for, by, and on the occasion of the staging of ownership in the conspicuous consumption of a wedding/potlatch.

An "invention," Edna is thoroughly representational. As a sign of value she is hailed as a sign of her father's wealth of inventiveness in making signs/wealth. The dinner dramatizes the richness of her market-determined transformations: ceremonial drink, invention, queen, luxurious gift. To say that it is her "birthday" is to say that her self is born through exchange and consists of these multiple signs which circulate in the market. What Edna wears marks her as value:

> The golden shimmer of Edna's satin gown spread in rich folds on either side of her. There was a soft fall of lace encircling her shoulders. It was the color of her skin, without the glow, the myriad living tints that one may sometimes discover in vibrant flesh. There was something in her attitude, in her whole appearance . . . which suggested the regal woman, the one who rules, who looks on, who stands alone. (109)

The gold of her dress makes reference to the value in which she is robed. The lace "encircling" her shoulders refers to the skin which at the novel's opening effects Edna's transformation into "surplus." It is as if the lace is an extra skin—a conspicuously surplus skin—which in its decorative insubstantiality mirrors the meaning of Edna's skin. But the lace is not a true mirror. It points out the superior capacity of the "real" skin to change, to have "myriad tints" which allow it to be continually dissolved and recreated as a sign of value.

Edna as a sign of value is the referent of all the surrounding signs of value. She sits at the head of the table in her crown like "the regal woman, the one who rules, . . . who stands alone," as if she were the principle (and principal) of value that reigns over all its manifestations—the gold, silver, crystal, gems, and delicacies. Now Edna is like Adèle, the regal woman who has the "grace and majesty which queens are . . . supposed to possess" (31). And like Adèle, who is tortured and "exhausted" by childbirth, Edna experiences the complement of regal power in the exhausted passivity that overcomes her after the dinner, when the celebration of private wealth moves into the realization of value through the ceremonial enactment of breakage and loss.

Edna leaves the Pontellier house with Arobin, who pauses outside the door of the "old house" to break off a spray of jessamine, enacting this defloration. He offers it to Edna: "No; I don't want anything," she answers. Emptied, she says she feels as if "something inside of [her] had snapped." This metaphorical defloration empties Edna of the erotic desire whose ownership constitutes her selfhood. Edna's shoulders are bare of the encircling lace and Arobin caresses them. Edna is passive, but Arobin feels the "response of her flesh," which, in its consecration to value, embodies the sexuality that is created in circulation. Now, after Edna's ceremonial "self-giving," this eroticism no longer constitutes a sensation that Edna can appropriate as her own desire (112–13).

The loss of the self in maternal bloodshedding is enacted at the end of the dinner when the ceremony changes from a potlatch to a sacred, sacrificial rite. The desirous Mrs. Highcamp crowns Victor with a garland of yellow and red roses, effecting his magical transformation into a bacchanalian "vision of Oriental beauty." One of the transfixed guests mutters Swinburne under his breath: "There was a graven image of Desire / Painted with red blood on a ground of gold." This "graven image," like Edna's photograph, reflects her desire. Victor publicly sings the secret song that expresses the production of Edna's "private" desire as a suspicious reflection of circulation, *si tu savais ce que tes yeux me disent* ("if you knew what your eyes are saying to me") (110–11). She reacts with such consternation that she breaks her wineglass, and the contents—either red or gold, like the roses and the graven image—flow over Arobin and Mrs. Highcamp. Arobin has consecrated the evening's drinks as analogues of Edna, who has invited the guests to "drink her health"—that is, drink *her*—on her "birthday." In involuntarily shattering the glass, which, like the "cold glass" covering the photo, contains a possessive reflection of her value, Edna shatters the "mantle of reserve," symbolically releasing the maternal blood that constitutes her value.

The maternal quality of her self-giving—its involuntary and selfless aspects—overwhelms Edna again some time after the potlatch when, just as she is about to "give" herself to Robert, Edna is called away to witness Adèle enduring the agonies of childbirth. The sight of Adèle's "torture" overwhelms Edna (as does Adèle's exhausted plea to "think of the children"), leaving her "stunned and speechless" (132). When she returns to her little house, Robert is gone forever. Deprived of the chance to "give" herself to her desire, she spends the night thinking of her children. Later, she walks to the beach from which she will swim to her death "not thinking of these things" (136). Withholding herself from motherhood, insisting on her right to refuse to "sacrifice" herself for her children, Edna owns herself. In the logic of self-ownership and voluntary motherhood, motherhood is itself the ground on which woman claims ownership of her sexual value. Edna seizes the most extreme prerogatives of this self-ownership, withholding herself from motherhood by withholding herself from life and thus giving herself in a maternal dissolution.

Edna's death in the ocean dramatizes the self-ownership rhetoric of Elizabeth Cady Stanton. Stanton argues that "self-sovereignty" is the existential birthright of both women and men, for every human being "launched on the sea of life" is unique and "alone" (248). But women's self-sovereignty specifically denotes sexual self-determination. And Stanton insists that women—that is, mothers—earn a special presumptive self-sovereignty, for "alone [woman] goes to the gates of death to give life to every man that is born into the world; no one can share her fears, no one can mitigate her pangs; and if her sorrow is greater than she can bear, alone she passes beyond the gates into the vast unknown" (251). At the moment of extreme maternal giving, the moment when motherhood takes her life, the woman owns her self by withholding herself from motherhood.

Note: I would like to thank Catherine Gallagher and Walter Benn Michaels for their help with this essay at several stages of its composition. I am also grateful to David Lloyd, Tricia Moran, Lora Romero, and Lynn Wardley, who read this essay in draft and made helpful suggestions.

WORKS CITED

Chandler, Lucinda. "Motherhood." *Woodhull and Claflin's Weekly*, 13 May 1871: 1–2.

Gilman, Charlotte Perkins. *Women and Economics: The Economic Factor between Men and Women as a Factor in Social Evolution*. Ed. Carl Degler. New York: Harper, 1966.

Gordon, Linda. "Voluntary Motherhood: The Beginnings of the Birth Control Movement." *Women's Body, Woman's Right: Birth Control in America*. New York: Penguin, 1974.

Lewis, Dido. *Chastity, or Our Secret Sins*. New York: Canfield, 1881.

Michaels, Walter Benn. *The Gold Standard and the Logic of Naturalism: American Literature at the Turn of the Century*. Berkeley: U of California P, 1987.

Stanton, Elizabeth Cady. "The Solitude of Self." *Elizabeth Cady Stanton, Susan B. Anthony: Correspondence, Writings, Speeches*. Ed. Ellen Carol DuBois. New York: Schocken, 1981.

Veblen, Thorstein. *The Theory of the Leisure Class: An Economic Study in the Evolution of Institutions*. New York: Macmillan, 1899.

Wright, Henry C. *Marriage and Parentage*. Boston: Marsh, 1853.

Psychoanalytic Criticism and *The Awakening*

WHAT IS PSYCHOANALYTIC CRITICISM?

It seems natural to think about novels in terms of dreams. Like dreams, novels are fictions, inventions of the mind that, although based on reality, are by definition not literally true. Like a novel, a dream may have some truth to tell, but, like a novel, it may need to be interpreted before that truth can be grasped. Many novels describe dreams and reveal important aspects of character through dreams.

There are other reasons why it seems natural to make an analogy between dreams and novels. We can live vicariously through romantic fictions, much as we can through daydreams. Terrifying novels and nightmares affect us in much the same way, plunging us into an atmosphere that continues to cling, even after the last chapter has been read—or the alarm clock has sounded. Thus it is not surprising to hear someone say in class that Mary Shelley's *Frankenstein* is a nightmarish tale. Nor are we likely to be surprised by the claim of Frederick Karl, Joseph Conrad's biographer, that *Heart of Darkness* is characterized by the same kind of distortion, condensation, and displacement that Sigmund Freud described in his *Interpretation of Dreams* (1900).

Karl, who invokes Conrad's text and psychoanalytic theory in the same breath, is a Freudian literary critic. But what about the reader who simply compares *Frankenstein* to a nightmare, or Emily Brontë's

Wuthering Heights to a dream? Is such a reader a Freudian as well? Is he or she, too, a psychoanalytic critic?

To some extent, the answer to both questions has to be yes. We are all Freudians, really, whether or not we have read a single work by the famous Austrian psychoanalyst. At one time or another, most of us have referred to ego, libido, complexes, unconscious desires, and sexual repression. The premises of Freud's thought have changed the way the Western world thinks about itself. Psychoanalytic criticism has influenced the teachers our teachers studied with, the works of scholarship and criticism they read, and the critical and creative writers *we* read as well.

What Freud did was develop a language that described, a model that explained, a theory that encompassed human psychology. Many of the elements of psychology he sought to describe and explain are present in the literary works of various ages and cultures, from Sophocles' *Oedipus Rex* to Shakespeare's *Hamlet* to works being written in our own day. When the great novel of the twenty-first century is written, many of these same elements of psychology will probably inform its discourse as well. If, by understanding human psychology according to Freud, we can appreciate literature on a new level, then we should acquaint ourselves with his insights.

Freud's theories are either directly or indirectly concerned with the nature of the unconscious mind. Freud didn't invent the notion of the unconscious; others before him had suggested that even the supposedly "sane" human mind was conscious and rational only at times, and even then at possibly only one level. But Freud went further, suggesting that the powers motivating men and women are *mainly* and *normally* unconscious.

Freud, then, powerfully developed an old idea: that the human mind is essentially dual in nature. He called the predominantly passional, irrational, unknown, and unconscious part of the psyche the *id*, or "it." The *ego*, or "I," was his term for the predominantly rational, logical, orderly, conscious part. Another aspect of the psyche, which he called the *superego*, is really a projection of the ego. The superego almost seems to be outside of the self, making moral judgments, telling us to make sacrifices for good causes even though self-sacrifice may not be quite logical or rational. And, in a sense, the superego *is* "outside," since much of what it tells us to do or think we have learned from our parents, our schools, or our religious institutions.

What the ego and superego tell us *not* to do or think is repressed, forced into the unconscious mind. One of Freud's most important contributions to the study of the psyche, the theory of repression, goes something like this: much of what lies in the unconscious mind has been put there by consciousness, which acts as a censor, driving underground unconscious or conscious thoughts or instincts that it deems unacceptable. Censored materials often involve infantile sexual desires, Freud postulated. Repressed to an unconscious state, they emerge only in disguised forms: in dreams, in language (so-called Freudian slips), in creative activity that may produce art (including literature), and in neurotic behavior.

According to Freud, all of us have repressed wishes and fears; we all have dreams in which repressed feelings and memories emerge disguised, and thus we are all potential candidates for dream analysis. One of the unconscious desires most commonly repressed is the childhood wish to displace the parent of our own sex and take his or her place in the affections of the parent of the opposite sex. This desire really involves a number of different but related wishes and fears. (A boy—and it should be remarked in passing that Freud here concerns himself mainly with the male—may fear that his father will castrate him, and he may wish that his mother would return to nursing him.) Freud referred to the whole complex of feelings by the word "oedipal," naming the complex after the Greek tragic hero Oedipus, who unwittingly killed his father and married his mother.

Why are oedipal wishes and fears repressed by the conscious side of the mind? And what happens to them after they have been censored? As Roy P. Basler puts it in *Sex, Symbolism, and Psychology in Literature* (1975), "from the beginning of recorded history such wishes have been restrained by the most powerful religious and social taboos, and as a result have come to be regarded as 'unnatural,'" even though "Freud found that such wishes are more or less characteristic of normal human development":

> In dreams, particularly, Freud found ample evidence that such wishes persisted. . . . Hence he conceived that natural urges, when identified as "wrong," may be repressed but not obliterated. . . . In the unconscious, these urges take on symbolic garb, regarded as nonsense by the waking mind that does not recognize their significance. (14)

Freud's belief in the significance of dreams, of course, was no more original than his belief that there is an unconscious side to the psyche. Again, it was the extent to which he developed a theory of how dreams work—and the extent to which that theory helped him, by analogy, to understand far more than just dreams—that made him unusual, important, and influential beyond the perimeters of medical schools and psychiatrists' offices.

The psychoanalytic approach to literature not only rests on the theories of Freud; it may even be said to have *begun* with Freud, who was interested in writers, especially those who relied heavily on symbols. Such writers regularly cloak or mystify ideas in figures that make sense only when interpreted, much as the unconscious mind of a neurotic disguises secret thoughts in dream stories or bizarre actions that need to be interpreted by an analyst. Freud's interest in literary artists led him to make some unfortunate generalizations about creativity; for example, in the twenty-third lecture in *Introductory Lectures on Psycho-Analysis* (1922), he defined the artist as "one urged on by instinctive needs that are too clamorous" (314). But it also led him to write creative literary criticism of his own, including an influential essay on "The Relation of a Poet to Daydreaming" (1908) and "The Uncanny" (1919), a provocative psychoanalytic reading of E. T. A. Hoffmann's supernatural tale "The Sandman."

Freud's application of psychoanalytic theory to literature quickly caught on. In 1909, only a year after Freud had published "The Relation of a Poet to Daydreaming," the psychoanalyst Otto Rank published *The Myth of the Birth of the Hero*. In that work, Rank subscribes to the notion that the artist turns a powerful, secret wish into a literary fantasy, and he uses Freud's notion about the "oedipal" complex to explain why the popular stories of so many heroes in literature are so similar. A year after Rank had published his psychoanalytic account of heroic texts, Ernest Jones, Freud's student and eventual biographer, turned his attention to a tragic text: Shakespeare's *Hamlet*. In an essay first published in the *American Journal of Psychology*, Jones, like Rank, makes use of the oedipal concept: he suggests that Hamlet is a victim of strong feelings toward his mother, the queen.

Between 1909 and 1949 numerous other critics decided that psychological and psychoanalytic theory could assist in the understanding of literature. I. A. Richards, Kenneth Burke, and Edmund Wilson were among the most influential to become interested in the new approach. Not all of the early critics were committed to the approach; neither were all of them Freudians. Some followed Alfred Adler, who believed that writers wrote out of inferiority complexes, and others applied the ideas of Carl Gustav Jung, who had broken with Freud over Freud's emphasis on sex and who had developed a theory of the *collective* unconscious. According to Jungian theory, a great work of literature is not a disguised expression of its author's personal, repressed wishes; rather, it is a manifestation of desires once held by the whole human race but now repressed because of the advent of civilization.

It is important to point out that among those who relied on Freud's models were a number of critics who were poets and novelists as well. Conrad Aiken wrote a Freudian study of American literature, and poets such as Robert Graves and W. H. Auden applied Freudian insights when writing critical prose. William Faulkner, Henry James, James Joyce, D. H. Lawrence, Marcel Proust, and Toni Morrison are only a few of the novelists who have either written criticism influenced by Freud or who have written novels that conceive of character, conflict, and creative writing itself in Freudian terms. The poet H.D. (Hilda Doolittle) was actually a patient of Freud's and provided an account of her analysis in her book *Tribute to Freud*. By giving Freudian theory credibility among students of literature that only they could bestow, such writers helped to endow psychoanalytic criticism with the largely Freudian orientation that, one could argue, it still exhibits today.

The willingness, even eagerness, of writers to use Freudian models in producing literature and criticism of their own consummated a relationship that, to Freud and other pioneering psychoanalytic theorists, had seemed fated from the beginning; after all, therapy involves the close analysis of language. René Wellek and Austin Warren included "psychological" criticism as one of the five "extrinsic" approaches to literature described in their influential book, *Theory of Literature* (1942). Psychological criticism, they suggest, typically attempts to do at least one of the following: provide a psychological study of an individual writer; explore the nature of the creative process; generalize about "types and laws present within works of literature"; or theorize about the psychological "effects of literature upon its readers" (81). Entire books on psychoanalytic criticism even began to appear, such as Frederick J. Hoffman's *Freudianism and the Literary Mind* (1945).

Probably because of Freud's characterization of the creative mind as "clamorous" if not ill, psychoanalytic criticism written before 1950 tended to psychoanalyze the individual author. Poems were read as fantasies that allowed authors to indulge repressed wishes, to protect themselves from deep-seated anxieties, or both. A perfect example of author analysis would be Marie Bonaparte's 1933 study of Edgar Allan Poe. Bonaparte found Poe to be so fixated on his mother that his repressed longing emerges in his stories in images such as the white spot on a black cat's breast, said to represent mother's milk.

A later generation of psychoanalytic critics often paused to analyze the characters in novels and plays before proceeding to their authors. But not for long, since characters, both evil and good, tended to be seen by these critics as the author's potential selves, or projections of various repressed aspects of his or her psyche. For instance, in *A Psychoanalytic Study of the Double in Literature* (1970), Robert Rogers begins with the view that human beings are double or multiple in nature. Using this assumption, along with the psychoanalytic concept of "dissociation" (best known by its result, the dual or multiple personality), Rogers concludes that writers reveal instinctual or repressed selves in their books, often without realizing that they have done so.

In the view of critics attempting to arrive at more psychological insights into an author than biographical materials can provide, a work of literature is a fantasy or a dream—or at least so analogous to daydream or dream that Freudian analysis can help explain the nature of the mind that produced it. The author's purpose in writing is to gratify secretly some forbidden wish, in particular an infantile wish or desire that has been repressed into the unconscious mind. To discover what the wish is, the psychoanalytic critic employs many of the terms and procedures developed by Freud to analyze dreams.

The literal surface of a work is sometimes spoken of as its "manifest content" and treated as a "manifest dream" or "dream story" would be treated by a Freudian analyst. Just as the analyst tries to figure out the "dream thought" behind the dream story—that is, the latent or hidden content of the manifest dream—so the psychoanalytic literary critic tries to expose the latent, underlying content of a work. Freud used the words *condensation* and *displacement* to explain two of the mental processes whereby the mind disguises its wishes and fears in dream stories. In condensation several thoughts or persons may be condensed into a single manifestation or image in a dream story; in displacement, an anxiety, a wish, or a person may be displaced onto the image of another, with which or whom it is loosely connected through a string of associations that only an analyst can untangle. Psychoanalytic critics treat metaphors as if they were dream condensations; they treat metonyms—figures of speech based on extremely loose, arbi
tions—as if they were dream displacements. Thus figurativ
guage in general is treated as something that evolves as
conscious mind resists what the unconscious tells it to p

scribe. A symbol is, in Daniel Weiss's words, "a meaningful concealment of truth as the truth promises to emerge as some frightening or forbidden idea" (20).

In a 1970 article entitled "The 'Unconscious' of Literature," Norman Holland, a literary critic trained in psychoanalysis, succinctly sums up the attitudes held by critics who would psychoanalyze authors, but without quite saying that it is the *author* that is being analyzed by the psychoanalytic critic. "When one looks at a poem psychoanalytically," he writes, "one considers it as though it were a dream or as though some ideal patient [were speaking] from the couch in iambic pentameter." One "looks for the general level or levels of fantasy associated with the language. By level I mean the familiar stages of childhood development—oral [when desires for nourishment and infantile sexual desires overlap], anal [when infants receive their primary pleasure from defecation], urethral [when urinary functions are the locus of sexual pleasure], phallic [when the penis or, in girls, some penis substitute is of primary interest], oedipal." Holland continues by analyzing not Robert Frost but Frost's poem "Mending Wall" as a specifically oral fantasy that is not unique to its author. "Mending Wall" is "about breaking down the wall which marks the separated or individuated self so as to return to a state of closeness to some Other"—including and perhaps essentially the nursing mother ("Unconscious" 136, 139).

While not denying the idea that the unconscious plays a role in creativity, psychoanalytic critics such as Holland began to focus more on the ways in which authors create works that appeal to *our* repressed wishes and fancies. Consequently, they shifted their focus away from the psyche of the author and toward the psychology of the reader and the text. Holland's theories, which have concerned themselves more with the reader than with the text, have helped to establish another school of critical theory: reader-response criticism. Elizabeth Wright explains Holland's brand of psychoanalytic criticism in this way: "What draws us as readers to a text is the secret expression of what we desire to hear, much as we protest we do not. The disguise must be good enough to fool the censor into thinking that the text is respectable, but bad enough to allow the unconscious to glimpse the unrespectable" (117).

Whereas Holland came increasingly to focus on the reader rather than on the work being read, others who turned away from character and author diagnosis preferred to concentrate on texts; they remained skeptical that readers regularly fulfill wishes by reading. Following the theories of D. W. Winnicott, a psychoanalytic theorist who has argued that even babies have relationships as well as raw wishes, these textually oriented psychoanalytic critics contend that the relationship between reader and text depends greatly on the text. To be sure, some works fulfill the reader's secret wishes, but others—maybe most—do not. The texts created by some authors effectively resist the reader's involvement.

In determining the nature of the text, such critics may regard the text in terms of a dream. But no longer do they assume that dreams are meaningful in the way that works of literature are. Rather, they assume something more complex. "If we move outward" from one "scene to others in the [same] novel," Meredith Skura writes, "as Freud moves from the dream to its associations, we find that the paths of movement are really quite similar" (181). Dreams are viewed more as a language than as symptoms of repression. In fact, the French structuralist psychoanalyst Jacques Lacan treats the unconscious *as* a language, a form of discourse. Thus we may study dreams psychoanalytically in order to learn about literature, even as we may study literature in order to learn more about the unconscious. In Lacan's seminar on Poe's "The Purloined Letter," a pattern of repetition like that used by psychoanalysts in their analyses is used to arrive at a reading of the story. According to Wright, "the new psychoanalytic structural approach to literature" employs "analogies from psychoanalysis . . . to explain the workings of the text as distinct from the workings of a particular author's, character's, or even reader's mind" (125).

Lacan is but one of many psychoanalytic theorists who have resisted, revised, expanded, or developed Freud's theories. D. W. Winnicott has already been alluded to; R. D. Laing's controversial and often poetical writings about personality, repression, masks, and the double or "schizoid" self have (re)blurred the boundary between creative writing and psychoanalytic discourse. Lacan, however, is worth focusing on at greater length here because of the highly influential way in which he took Freud's whole theory of psyche and gender and added to it a crucial third term—that of language. In the process, he used but adapted Freud's ideas about the oedipal complex and oedipal stage, both of which Freud saw as crucial to the development of the child, and especially of male children.

Lacan points out that the pre-oedipal stage, in which the child at first does not even recognize its independence from its mother, is also a pre*verbal* stage, one in which the child communicates without the medium of language, or—if we insist upon calling the child's communications a language—in a language that can only be called *literal.*

("Coos," certainly, cannot be said to be figurative or symbolic!) Then, while still in the pre-oedipal stage, the child enters the *mirror* stage.

During the mirror period, the child comes to see itself and its mother, later other people as well, *as* independent selves. This is the stage in which the child is first able to fear the aggressions of another, desire what is recognizably beyond the self (initially the mother), and, finally, to want to compete with another for the same, desired object. This is also the stage at which the child first becomes able to feel sympathy with another being who is being hurt by a third—to cry, in other words, when another cries. All of these developments, of course, involve projecting beyond the self and, by extension, being able to envision one's own self (or "ego" or "I") as others view one—that is, as *another*. For these reasons, Lacan refers to the mirror stage as the *Imaginary* stage.

The Imaginary stage, however, is usually superseded. It normally ends with the onset of the oedipal stage, which it makes possible. (The Imaginary stage makes possible the oedipal stage insofar as it makes possible not only desire and fear of another but also the sense of another as a rival.)

The oedipal stage, as in Freud, begins when the child, having recognized the self *as* self and the father and mother as *separate* selves, recognizes gender and gender differences between its parents and between itself and one of its parents. For a boy, that recognition involves another, more powerful recognition, because the recognition of the phallus as the mark of difference from the mother involves, at the same time, the recognition that his older and more powerful father is also his rival. That realization, in turn, leads to the understanding that what once seemed wholly his and even undistinguishable from himself is in fact someone else's: something properly to be desired only at a greater distance and in the form of socially acceptable *substitutes*. (The old song "I Want a Girl Just Like the Girl Who Married Dear Old Dad" is a clear and straightforward restatement of the psychoanalytic theory that men's lives are searches for adequate and sufficient substitutes for the lost mother.)

The fact that the oedipal stage roughly coincides with the entry of the child into language is extremely important, even critical, for Lacan. For the linguistic order is essentially a figurative or "Symbolic order"; words are not the things they stand for but are, rather, stand-ins—substitutions—for those things. Hence boys, who in the most critical period of their development have had to submit to what Lacan calls the "Law of the Father"—a law that prohibits direct desire for and communicative intimacy with what has been the boy's whole world—enter more easily into the realm of language and the Symbolic order than do girls, who have never really had to renounce that which once seemed continuous with the self: the mother. The gap that has been opened up for boys, which includes the gap between signs and what they substitute for—the gap marked by the phallus and encoded with the boy's sense of his maleness—has not opened up for girls, or has not opened up in the same way, to the same degree.

Lacan, moreover, takes Freud a step further in the process of making Freud's gender-based psychoanalytic theory a theory of language as well. He suggests that the father does not even have to be present to trigger the oedipal crisis; nor, then, does his phallus have to be seen to catalyze the boy's (easier) transition into the Symbolic order. Rather, he argues, a child's recognition of his or her gender, gender that may be the same as or different from that of the now separate-seeming mother, is intricately tied up with a growing recognition of the system of names and naming. A child has little doubt about who its mother is, but who is its father—and how would one know? The father's claim rests on the mother's *word* that he is in fact the father; the father's relationship to the child is thus established through language and a system of marriage and kinship—names—that in turn is basic to rules of everything from property to law. Thus gender, for Lacan, is intimately connected in the mind of the developing child with names and language. Or, rather, the *male* gender is tied to that world in an association analogously as intimate as is the mother's early, physical (including umbilical) connection with the infant.

Lacan's development of Freud has had several important results. First, his sexist-seeming association of maleness with the Symbolic order, together with his claim that women cannot therefore enter easily into the order, has prompted feminists not to reject his theory out of hand but, rather, to look more closely at the relation between language and gender, language and women's inequality. Some feminists have gone so far as to suggest that the social and political relationships between male and female will not be fundamentally altered until language itself has been radically changed. (That change might begin dialectically, with the development of some kind of "feminine language" grounded in the presymbolic—the literal-to-imaginary—communication between mother and child.)

Second, Lacan's theory has proved of interest to deconstructors and other poststructuralists, in part because it holds that the ego (which in Freud's view is as necessary as it is natural) is a product or construct. The ego-artifact, produced during the mirror stage, *seems* at once unified, consistent, and organized around a determinate center. But the unified self, or ego, is a fiction, according to Lacan. The yoking together of fragments and destructively dissimilar elements takes its psychic toll, and it is the job of the Lacanian psychoanalyst to "deconstruct," as it were, the ego, to show its continuities to be contradictions as well.

In the essay that follows, Cynthia Griffin Wolff treats *The Awakening* as a novel describing, "with ruthless fidelity," one person's "psychic disintegration." Stating that "in some sense there are two Ednas," Wolff goes on to suggest that one of these is public and conventional: a social construct, for the most part. The other self, by contrast, is a passionate one, prone to fantasies and daydreams. According to Wolff's analysis, the actions of the public self keep the passionate, fantasizing self hidden. Thus, when Edna marries, her spouse is a man chosen by her outward, conventional self, a prosaic and unperceptive man who will never invade (because he will never suspect the existence of) Edna's hidden self and its fantasy life. The marriage to Léonce, then, is "a defensive maneuver," one ensuring "the secret safety" of Edna's increasingly powerful, hidden self.

Wolff uses R. D. Laing's term *schizoid* to describe a personality that would "cut itself off from direct relatedness with others," endeavoring to become, in the process, "its own object, . . . related directly only to itself." Such a personality, Wolff suggests, inevitably comes to find significant relationships terrifying. Freedom comes to be defined as inaccessibility, and even a husband or child's indifference can seem like smothering possessiveness to the schizoid personality. For Edna, possession symbolizes a "beckoning vision of replenishment which carries always with it the fear of annihilation," so she inevitably withdraws rather than risk exposure of her inner self.

Whereas other critics view the oppression Edna feels as being justified by the stultifying, patriarchal society she finds herself in, Wolff suggests that her "feelings of imprisonment" are "projections of her own fantasies and fears." Rather than viewing Léonce as a maddeningly repressive force, as other critics have done, Wolff points to evidence that he is surprisingly *un*proprietary for a husband of his day.

Edna, of course, takes lovers after marrying, a fact that might seem to contradict Wolff's reading of Edna as a personality trying to hide and protect a passionate, secret self. But with Robert Lebrun, Wolff contends, she is hoping to find another who will be the (secret) extension of her secret self. And with Alcée Arobin, a man for whom she has no feelings and who does not represent the threat of a more-than-physical relationship, she can explore her own sensual self while simultaneously keeping it safe and hidden. "The tragic paradox," Wolff writes, quoting Laing as her authority, "is that the more the [hidden] self is defended in this way, the more it is destroyed." The self-destruction of the passionate self that is completed by Edna's shocking suicide is, in Wolff's view, a long, slow process that *The Awakening* depicts chapter by chapter.

Wolff has fascinating things to say about almost every aspect of the novel. She suggests that the Creole society depicted by Chopin is one in which freedom of expression seems to minimize but not eliminate the need for destructive self-hiding, self-burial. She uses Freud's theory of developmental stages to explain why Edna's secret self, when it manifests itself, manages to be so destructive. (Her development arrested at the oral stage, Edna finds pleasure in that which is "delicious." Her appetite for sensuous pleasure tends to be just that—an appetite—and one tending toward the voracious.)

Wolff's treatment of Edna Pontellier as a dualistic personality, her description of that personality as one consisting of public and repressed selves, and her characterization of the hidden self as one in which fantasies are harbored, hidden, and expressed (either in daydreams or in destructive, "oral" behavior) proves her Freudian inheritance. And yet Wolff goes beyond Freud, not only in availing herself of R. D. Laing's theory and terminology but also in suggesting that the multiple nature of personalities may not be inevitable but, rather, the product of cultural contradictions (such as those that inhere in any double standard). Most important for us as readers, however, is not Wolff's place vis-à-vis Freud and his followers but, rather, the fact that by *using* psychoanalytic insights, Wolff comes up with a thoroughly compelling reading of *The Awakening* that is quite different in its attitudes and emphases from all the others in this volume.

Ross C Murfin

PSYCHOANALYTIC CRITICISM: A SELECTED BIBLIOGRAPHY

Some Short Introductions to Psychological and Psychoanalytic Criticism

Holland, Norman. "The 'Unconscious' of Literature." *Contemporary Criticism.* Ed. Norman Bradbury and David Palmer. Stratford-upon-Avon Series 12. New York: St. Martin's, 1970. 131–54.

Natoli, Joseph, and Frederik L. Rusch, comps. *Psychocriticism: An Annotated Bibliography.* Westport: Greenwood, 1984.

Scott, Wilbur. *Five Approaches to Literary Criticism.* London: Collier-Macmillan, 1962. See the essays by Burke and Gorer as well as Scott's introduction to the section "The Psychological Approach: Literature in the Light of Psychological Theory."

Wellek, René, and Austin Warren. *Theory of Literature.* New York: Harcourt, 1942. See the chapter "Literature and Psychology" in pt. 3, "The Extrinsic Approach to the Study of Literature."

Wright, Elizabeth. "Modern Psychoanalytic Criticism." *Modern Literary Theory: A Comparative Introduction.* Ed. Ann Jefferson and David Robey. Totowa: Barnes, 1982. 113–33.

Freud, Lacan, and Their Influence

Basler, Roy P. *Sex, Symbolism, and Psychology in Literature.* New York: Octagon, 1975. See especially 13–19.

Clément, Catherine. *The Lives and Legends of Jacques Lacan.* Trans. Arthur Goldhammer. New York: Columbia UP, 1983.

Freud, Sigmund. *Introductory Lectures on Psycho-Analysis.* Trans. Joan Riviere. London: Allen, 1922.

Gallop, Jane. *Reading Lacan.* Ithaca: Cornell UP, 1985.

Hoffman, Frederick J. *Freudianism and the Literary Mind.* Baton Rouge: Louisiana State UP, 1945.

Kazin, Alfred. "Freud and His Consequences." *Contemporaries.* Boston: Little, 1962. 351–93.

Lacan, Jacques. *Écrits: A Selection.* Trans. Alan Sheridan. New York: Norton, 1977.

———. *Feminine Sexuality: Lacan and the école freudienne.* Ed. Juliet Mitchell and Jacqueline Rose. Trans. Rose. New York: Norton, 1982.

———. *The Four Fundamental Concepts of Psychoanalysis.* Trans. Alan Sheridan. London: Penguin, 1980.

Meisel, Perry, ed. *Freud: A Collection of Critical Essays.* Englewood Cliffs: Prentice, 1981.

Muller, John P., and William J. Richardson. *Lacan and Language: A Reader's Guide to "Écrits."* New York: International, 1982.

Porter, Laurence M. *The Interpretation of Dreams: Freud's Theories Revisited.* Twayne's Masterwork Studies Series. Boston: Hall, 1986.

Reppen, Joseph, and Maurice Charney. *The Psychoanalytic Study of Literature.* Hillsdale: Analytic, 1985.

Schneiderman, Stuart. *Jacques Lacan: The Death of an Intellectual Hero.* Cambridge: Harvard UP, 1983.

Selden, Raman. *A Reader's Guide to Contemporary Literary Theory.* Lexington: U of Kentucky P, 1985. See "Jacques Lacan: Language and the Unconscious."

Trilling, Lionel. "Art and Neurosis." *The Liberal Imagination.* New York: Scribner's, 1950. 160–80.

Wilden, Anthony. "Lacan and the Discourse of the Other." In Lacan, *Speech and Language in Psychoanalysis.* Trans. Wilden. Baltimore: Johns Hopkins UP, 1981. (Published as *The Language of the Self* in 1968.) 159–311.

Psychoanalysis, Feminism, and Literature

Chodorow, Nancy. *The Reproduction of Mothering: Psychoanalysis and the Sociology of Gender.* Berkeley: U of California P, 1978.

Gallop, Jane. *The Daughter's Seduction: Feminism and Psychoanalysis.* Ithaca: Cornell UP, 1982.

Garner, Shirley Nelson, Claire Kahane, and Madelon Sprengnether. *The (M)other Tongue: Essays in Feminist Psychoanalytic Interpretation.* Ithaca: Cornell UP, 1985.

Irigaray, Luce. *This Sex Which Is Not One.* Trans. Catherine Porter. Ithaca: Cornell UP, 1985.

———. *The Speculum of the Other Woman.* Trans. Gillian C. Gill. Ithaca: Cornell UP, 1985.

Jacobus, Mary. "Is There a Woman in This Text?" *New Literary History* 14 (1982): 117–41.

Kristeva, Julia. *The Kristeva Reader.* Ed. Toril Moi. New York: Columbia UP, 1986. See especially the selection from *Revolution in Poetic Language,* 89–136.

Mitchell, Juliet. *Psychoanalysis and Feminism.* New York: Random, 1974.

Mitchell, Juliet, and Jacqueline Rose, "Introduction I" and "Introduction II." Lacan, *Feminine Sexuality: Jacques Lacan and the école freudienne.* 1–26, 27–57.

Sprengnether, Madelon. *The Spectral Mother: Freud, Feminism, and Psychoanalysis.* Ithaca: Cornell UP, 1990.

Psychological and Psychoanalytic Studies of Literature

Bettelheim, Bruno. *The Uses of Enchantment: The Meaning and Importance of Fairy Tales.* New York: Knopf, 1976. Although this book is about fairy tales instead of literary works written for publication, it offers model Freudian readings of well-known stories.

Crews, Frederick C. *Out of My System: Psychoanalysis, Ideology, and Critical Method.* New York: Oxford UP, 1975.

———. *Relations of Literary Study.* New York: MLA, 1967. See the chapter "Literature and Psychology."

Diehl, Joanne Feit. "Re-Reading *The Letter*: Hawthorne, the Fetish, and the (Family) Romance." *Nathaniel Hawthorne, The Scarlet Letter.* Ed. Ross C Murfin. Case Studies in Contemporary Criticism Series. Boston: Bedford–St. Martin's, 1991. 235–51.

Hallman, Ralph. *Psychology of Literature: A Study of Alienation and Tragedy.* New York: Philosophical Library, 1961.

Hartman, Geoffrey, ed. *Psychoanalysis and the Question of the Text.* Baltimore: Johns Hopkins UP, 1978. See especially the essays by Hartman, Johnson, Nelson, and Schwartz.

Hertz, Neil. *The End of the Line: Essays on Psychoanalysis and the Sublime.* New York: Columbia UP, 1985.

Holland, Norman N. *Dynamics of Literary Response.* New York: Oxford UP, 1968.

———. *Poems in Persons: An Introduction to the Psychoanalysis of Literature.* New York: Norton, 1973.

Kris, Ernest. *Psychoanalytic Explorations in Art.* New York: International, 1952.

Lucas, F. L. *Literature and Psychology.* London: Cassell, 1951.

Natoli, Joseph, ed. *Psychological Perspectives on Literature: Freudian Dissidents and Non-Freudians: A Casebook.* Hamden: Archon Books–Shoe String, 1984.

Phillips, William, ed. *Art and Psychoanalysis.* New York: Columbia UP, 1977.

Rogers, Robert. *A Psychoanalytic Study of the Double in Literature.* Detroit: Wayne State UP, 1970.

Skura, Meredith. *The Literary Use of the Psychoanalytic Process.* New Haven: Yale UP, 1981.

Strelka, Joseph P. *Literary Criticism and Psychology.* University Park: Pennsylvania State UP, 1976. See especially the essays by Lerner and Peckham.

Weiss, Daniel. *The Critic Agonistes: Psychology, Myth, and the Art of Fiction.* Ed. Eric Solomon and Stephen Arkin. Seattle: U of Washington P, 1985.

Lacanian Psychoanalytic Studies of Literature

Collings, David. "The Monster and the Imaginary Mother: A Lacanian Reading of *Frankenstein*." *Mary Shelley, "Frankenstein."* Ed. Johanna M. Smith. Case Studies in Contemporary Criticism Series. Ed. Ross C Murfin. Boston: Bedford–St. Martin's, 1992. 245–58.

Davis, Robert Con, ed. *The Fictional Father: Lacanian Readings of the Text.* Amherst: U of Massachusetts P, 1981.

———, ed. "Lacan and Narration." *Modern Language Notes* 5 (1983): 843–1063.

Felman, Shoshana, ed. *Literature and Psychoanalysis: The Question of Reading: Otherwise.* Baltimore: Johns Hopkins UP, 1982.

Froula, Christine. "When Eve Reads Milton: Undoing the Canonical Economy." *Canons.* Ed. Robert von Hallberg. Chicago: U of Chicago P, 1984. 149–75.

Homans, Margaret. *Bearing the Word: Language and Female Experience in Nineteenth-Century Women's Writing.* Chicago: U of Chicago P, 1986.

Muller, John P., and William J. Richardson, eds. *The Purloined Poe: Lacan, Derrida, and Psychoanalytic Reading.* Baltimore: Johns Hopkins UP, 1988. Includes Lacan's seminar on Poe's "The Purloined Letter."

Psychoanalytic Criticism of *The Awakening*

Batten, Wayne. "Illusion and Archetype: The Curious Story of Edna Pontellier." *The Southern Literary Journal* 18 (1985): 73–88.

Franklin, Rosemary F. "*The Awakening* and the Failure of Psyche." *American Literature* 56 (1984): 510–26.

A PSYCHOANALYTIC PERSPECTIVE

CYNTHIA GRIFFIN WOLFF

Thanatos and Eros: Kate Chopin's *The Awakening*

After its initially dramatic reception, *The Awakening* slipped into an undeserved state of neglect; now, partly as a result of the new feminist criticism, the pendulum has swung in quite the other direction, and Chopin has been hailed as an early advocate of women's rights. Edmund Wilson praised *The Awakening* as an anticipation of D. H. Lawrence in its treatment of infidelity (590). Kenneth Eble maintained that "the novel is an American *Madame Bovary* though such a designation is not precisely accurate. Its central character is similar: the married woman who seeks love outside a stuffy, middle-class marriage'' (vii–viii). Jules Chametzky was even more explicit: ''What does surprise one is the modernity . . . of Mrs. Chopin's insights into 'the woman question.' It is not so much that she advocates woman's libidinal freedom or celebrates the force of the body's prerogatives. . . . What Kate Chopin shows so beautifully are the pressures working against woman's true awakening to her condition, and what that condition is.''

There are differences, of course, among these evaluations, but the underlying similarity is unmistakable: all see the power of the novel as growing out of an existential confrontation between the heroine and some external, repressive force. Thus, one might say that it is the woman against stifling sexual standards or that it is the woman against the tedium of a provincial marriage. Chametzky offers, perhaps, the most detailed explanation: ''The struggle is for the woman to free herself from being an object or possession defined in her functions, or owned, by others.'' Certainly elements of the novel serve to confirm these interpretations especially if one takes seriously some of the accusations leveled by the heroine in moments of anger or distress. Edna is disillusioned by marriage; to her ''a wedding is one of the most lamentable spectacles on earth'' (86). Even so, the contemporary readings of the novel which stress Edna's position as a victim of society's standards do not capture its power; for although it is not a great novel—perhaps it is even a greatly flawed novel because of the elusiveness of its focus—reading it can be a devastating and unforgettable experience. And such an experience can simply not grow out of a work whose importance lies in the fact that it anticipates Lawrence or that it is a sort of American *Madame Bovary.* Such evaluations are diminishing. The importance of Chopin's work does not lie in its anticipation of ''the woman question'' or of any other question; it derives from its ruthless fidelity to the disintegration of Edna's character. Edna, in turn, interests us not because she is ''a woman,'' the implication being that her experience is principally important because it might stand for that of any other woman. Quite the contrary; she interests us because she is human—because she fails in ways which beckon seductively to all of us. Conrad might say that, woman *or* man, she is ''one of us.''

It is difficult to define Edna's character as it might have existed before we meet her in the novel, for even at its opening such stability as she may have had has already been disrupted. We do learn something of her background. She is the middle child of an ambiguously religious family. ''She comes of sound old Presbyterian Kentucky stock. The old gentleman, her father, I have heard, used to atone for his week-day sins with his Sunday devotions. I know for a fact, that his race horses literally ran away with the prettiest bit of Kentucky farming land I ever laid eyes upon" (86). The family has two faces, then: it "sins" (during the week) with its racing and land-grabbing; and it "atones" (on Sundays) with pious condemnations. The character of each of the daughters reflects this contradiction. So Margaret, the oldest "has all the Presbyterian undiluted" (86); she is "matronly and dignified, probably from having assumed matronly and housewifely responsibilities too early in life, their mother having died when they were quite young. Margaret was not effusive; she was practical" (35). She was also, quite possibly, in her remote and disapproving way, the principal mother-figure for Edna. Janet, on the other hand, "the youngest is something of a vixen" (86). Edna, caught between the two extremes, can live comfortably with neither portion of the family's double standard; instead she tries to evolve a habit or manner which will accommodate both.

The attempt to internalize this contradiction combines with other of Edna's psychic needs to produce an "identity" which is predicated on the conscious process of concealment. In some sense there are two Ednas: "At a very early period she had apprehended instinctively the dual life—that outward existence which conforms, the inward life which questions" (32). Therefore she is very little open to sustained emotional relationships because those elements of character which she might want to call her "real" self must remain hidden, revealed only to herself. "Edna had had an occasional girl friend, but whether accidentally or not, they seemed to have been all of one type—the self-contained. She never realized that the reserve of her own character had much, perhaps everything, to do with this" (35–36). Not that Edna *wants* to be so entirely alone. On the contrary, the cool distancing tone of her "visible" character conceals an ardent yearning for intensity, for passion. So Edna provides the passion she needs in the only manner which seems safely available to her—through daydreaming.

> Edna often wondered at one propensity which sometimes had inwardly disturbed her without causing any outward show or manifestation on her part. At a very early age—perhaps it was when she traversed the ocean of waving grass—she remembered that she had been passionately enamored of a dignified and sad-eyed cavalry officer who visited her father in Kentucky. She could not leave his presence when he was there, nor remove her eyes from his face, which was something like Napoleon's, with a lock of black hair falling across the forehead. But the cavalry officer melted imperceptibly out of her existence.

> At another time her affections were deeply engaged by a young gentleman who visited a lady on a neighboring plantation. It was after they went to Mississippi to live. The young man was engaged to be married to the young lady, and they sometimes called upon Margaret, driving over of afternoons in a buggy. Edna was a little miss, just merging into her teens; and the realization that she herself was nothing, nothing, nothing to the engaged young man was a bitter affliction to her. But he, too, went the way of dreams.
>
> She was a grown young woman when she was overtaken by what she supposed to be the climax of her fate. It was when the face and figure of a great tragedian began to haunt her imagination and stir her senses. *The persistence of the infatuation lent it an aspect of genuineness. The hopelessness of it colored it with the lofty tones of a great passion.*
>
> The picture of the tragedian stood enframed upon her desk. Any one may possess the portrait of a tragedian without exciting suspicion or comment. (36, italics added)

The emotional change here must be described as the development of an increasingly resistant barrier between the "real" external world and that world which was most authentic in Edna's experience—the inner world of her fantasies. Thus her libidinal energies are focused first on a real man who is in some ways genuinely available to her; he is apparently unmarried, unattached, and a frequent visitor to the family home. Still, he is a good deal older than she, and his chief attraction seems to be his resemblance to Napoleon (and perhaps the romantic aura attached to his having been a cavalry officer—one calls to mind the clanging spurs which echo in Edna's memory as she is drowning). The next object of Edna's affections is manifestly unavailable since he is engaged to her sister's friend, and although the realization that she was "nothing, nothing, nothing to the engaged man" may have made Edna consciously miserable, there is a form of safety, too, in nothingness. The passion is never expressed, always controlled, with only the substantial threat of "dreams" which melt away. Characteristically, she reserves her greatest passion for a figure of pure fantasy, the tragedian whose picture one can possess "without exciting suspicion or comment."

Given the apparent terror which genuine emotional involvement inspires in Edna, her marriage to a man like Léonce Pontellier is no accident. No one would call him remarkable; most readers might think him dull, insensitive, unperceptive, even callous. Certainly he is an essentially prosaic man. If one assumed that marriage was to be an intimate affair of deep understanding, all of these qualities would condemn Léonce. Yet for Edna they are the very qualities which recommend him. "The acme of bliss, which would have been a marriage with the tragedian, was not for her in this world" (37); such bliss, indeed, is not for anyone *in this world.* It is a romantic illusion, a dream—defined by its very inability to be consummated. What is more, the intensity of dreams such as these may have become disturbing to Edna. So she chooses to marry Léonce; after all "as the devoted wife of a man who worshiped her, she felt she would take her place with a certain dignity in the world of reality, closing the portals forever behind her upon the realm of romance and dreams" (37). The marriage to such a man as Léonce was, then, a defensive maneuver designed to maintain the integrity of the two "selves" that formed her character and to reinforce the distance between them. Her outer self was confirmed by the entirely conventional marriage while her inner self was safe—known only to Edna. An intuitive man, a sensitive husband, might threaten it; a husband who evoked passion from her might lure the hidden self into the open, tempting Edna to attach her emotions to flesh and blood rather than phantoms. Léonce is neither, and their union ensures the secret safety of Edna's "real" self.

> It was not long before the tragedian had gone to join the cavalry officer and the engaged young man and a few others; and Edna found herself face to face with the realities. She grew fond of her husband, realizing with some unaccountable satisfaction that no trace of passion or excessive and fictitious warmth colored her affection, *thereby threatening its dissolution.* (37, italics added)

If we try to assess the configuration of Edna's personality when she comes to Grand Isle at the novel's beginning, we might best do so by using R. D. Laing's description of the "schizoid" personality. As Laing would describe it, the schizoid personality consists of a set of defenses which have been established as an attempt to preserve some semblance of coherent identity.

> The self, in order to develop and sustain its identity and autonomy, and in order to be safe from the persistent threat and danger from the world, has cut itself off from direct relatedness with others, and has endeavored to become its own object; to become, in fact, related directly only to itself. Its cardinal functions become phantasy and observation. Now, in so far as this is successful, one necessary consequence is that the self has difficulty sustaining any *sentiment du réel* for the very reason that it is not "in touch" with reality, it never actually "meets" reality. (137)

Laing's insights provide at least a partial explanation for elements of the novel which might otherwise be unclear. For example, Edna's fragility or susceptibility to the atmosphere at Grade Isle (as compared, for example, with her robust friend Madame Ratignolle, or the grand aloofness of Mademoiselle Reisz) can be traced to the circular ineffectiveness of the schizoid mechanism for maintaining identity. To be specific, such a person must be simultaneously alert to and protected from any invitation to interact with the real world since all genuine interactions leave the hidden "real" self exposed to potential danger. Vigilance begets threat which in turn precipitates withdrawal and renewed vigilance.

More important, interpersonal relationships can be conceived of only in cataclysmic terms; "there is a constant dread and resentment at being turned into someone else's thing, of being penetrated by him, and a sense of being in someone else's power and control. Freedom then consists in being inaccessible" (Laing 113). Such habits of mind comport with Edna's outbursts concerning her own relationships. Certainly her rather dull husband seems not to notice her except as a part of the general inventory of his worldly goods: thus early in the novel he is described as "looking at his wife as one looks at a valuable piece of personal property which has suffered some damage" (21). Yet his attentions, such as they are, are rather more indicative of indifference than otherwise. Indeed, at every point within the narrative when he might, were he so inclined, assert his "rights," he declines to do so. After the evening swimming party, for example, when he clearly desires sexual intercourse and his wife does not wish to comply, he utters but a few sharp words and then, surprising for a man so supposedly interested in the proprietary relationship, slips on a robe and comes out to keep her company during her fitful vigil (see 49–51). After their return to New Orleans, he reacts to Edna's disruption of her "wifely functions" with but momentary impatience; he does not attempt coercion, and he goes to the lengths of consulting a physician out of concern for her well-being. Even when Edna has taken up residence in her diminutive "pigeon house" Léonce decides to leave her to her own ways. His only concern—a small-minded one, to be sure—is to save appearances.

It is hard to cast such an ultimately insignificant man in the role of villain—compared with a man like Soames Forsyte or with some of the more brutal husbands in Chopin's short stories, Léonce is a slender vehicle to carry the weight of society's repression of women. Yet Edna sees herself as his possession, even as she sees herself the prisoner of her children's demands. Her dying thoughts confirm this fixation: "She thought of Léonce and the children. They were a part of her life. But they need not have thought that they could possess her, body and soul" (137). Now if Léonce is not able to rise to the occasion of possessing her body and soul, the children as they are portrayed in the novel seem to exercise even less continuous claim upon her. They are always accompanied by a nurse whose presence frees Edna to pursue whatever interests she can sustain; what is more, they spend much of their time with their paternal grandmother, who seems to welcome them whenever Edna wishes to send them. Her emotional relationship with them is tenuous at best, certainly not demanding and by no stretch of the imagination stifling. "She was fond of her children in an uneven, impulsive way. She would sometimes gather them passionately to her heart; she would sometimes forget them" (37). Given the extraordinary latitude that Edna did in fact have, we might better interpret her feelings of imprisonment as projections of her own attitudes and fears. The end of the novel offers an ironic affirmation of such a view, for when she returns home from Madame Ratignolle's accouchement, even her apparently positive expectations with regard to Robert follow the same familiar definition: "She could picture at that moment no greater bliss on earth than possession of the beloved one" (133). The wording is somewhat ambiguous—she might possess him, he might possess her, the "possession" might be understood as a synonym for sexual union—still the key word here is *possession,* and it is Edna's word.

Possession, as descriptive of any intense emotional involvement, is both tempting and terrifying. To yield to possession is to become engulfed, to be nothing. The antiphonal emblematic figures that appear like phantoms while Edna is staying at Grand Isle reflect the dilemma. On the one hand there are the lovers, intimate, always together, seemingly happy, a beckoning vision of replenishment which carries always with it the fear of annihilation. And then there is the woman in black, the emblem of the self—destroyed in a bizarre act of self-preservation, withdrawn from all personal interaction—"safe" and "free."

One solution for the problem Edna faces would be to formulate a way to have her relationship with Robert without ever *really* having it. Temporarily she does effect such a solution, and she does so in two ways. First, while she is at Grand Isle, she systematically denies the possibility of an adult relationship with him; this denial takes the form of her engulfing him ("possessing" him, perhaps) by a kind of incorporation of his personality into her own. She accepts his attentions, his services, his affection; and in so far as these are important to her, she comes to regard them as extensions of her own will or desire. Robert is not conceived of as a separate, individuated being, and thus she repeatedly is surprised and dismayed when his actions unaccountably (to her) deviate from her wishes. We can see this aspect of their relationship very early in a trivial incident when Robert leaves her one evening and fails to return.

> She wondered why Robert had gone away and left her. It did not occur to her to think he might have grown tired of being with her the livelong day. She was not tired, and she felt that he was not. She regretted that he had gone. It was so much more natural to have him stay, when he was not absolutely required to leave her. (59)

This scene and Edna's reaction is a foreshadowing of the much more distressing separation when Robert leaves for Mexico.

> But can't you understand? I've grown used to seeing you, to having you with me all the time, and your action seems unfriendly, even unkind. You don't even offer an excuse for it. Why, I was planning to be together, thinking of how pleasant it would be to see you in the city next winter. (64)

She finds it difficult, if not impossible, to separate his will or his wishes from her own, to acknowledge his existence independent of hers. Only after he has left can she safely *feel* the intensity of passion that later comes to be associated with him; and she can do so because once physically absent, he can be made magically present as a phantom, an object in her own imagination, a figure which is now truly a part of herself. She has reawakened the cavalry officer, the young engaged man, the tragedian; "for the first time she recognized anew the symptoms of infatuation which she had felt incipiently as a child, as a girl in her earliest teens, and later as a young woman" (64). As a woman, however, Edna wants more.

Thus she evolves a second solution by which she can have a relationship with Robert without being forced to fuse the outer and the inner "selves" that comprise her identity. This stratagem is the affair with Arobin. She can respond sensually to the kiss which initiates their relationship precisely because she has no feeling for him. Her feelings are fixed safely on the *image* of Robert; "there was Robert's reproach making itself felt by a quicker, fiercer, more overpowering love, which had awakened within her toward him" (104). And this arrangement frees her from anxiety, leaving only a "dull pang of regret." When Robert does, in fact, return, the problem of fusing the outer world with the "real" world within returns with him; and, as before, the fantasy is easier to deal with.

> A hundred times Edna had pictured Robert's return, and imagined their first meeting. It was usually at her home, whither he had sought her out at once. She always fancied him expressing or betraying in some way his love for her. And here, the reality was that they sat ten feet apart, she at the window, crushing geranium leaves in her hand and smelling them, he twirling around on the piano stool. (119)

Robert's return and his sensuous awakening to her kiss precipitates the final crisis from which she must flee. She cannot, in the end, yield her "self" to the insistence of his passionate plea to stay; and his own subsequent flight destroys the fantasy lover as well. Both of Edna's selves are truly betrayed and barren, and she retrenches in the only manner familiar to her, that of a final and ultimate withdrawal. As Laing says:

> If the whole of the individual's being cannot be defended, the individual retracts his lines of defence until he withdraws within a central citadel. He is prepared to write off everything he is, except his "self." But the tragic paradox is that the more the self is defended in this way, the more it is destroyed. The apparent eventual destruction and dissolution of these in schizophrenic conditions is accomplished not by external attacks from the enemy (actual or supposed), from without, but by the devastation caused by the inner defensive manoeuvres themselves. (77)

This description of Edna's defensive patterns is an invaluable aid in understanding the novel; however, taken alone it does not lead to a complete explanation. We can understand, perhaps, why Edna's act of self-destruction seems the logical culmination of other apparently non-destructive behavior, but we cannot yet comprehend the manner of her dissolution, nor the significance to Edna (which must have been central) of Madame Ratignolle's accouchement or of Edna's own children, who seem to haunt her even though their *physical* presence scarcely enters the novel. More important, the tone of the novel—perhaps its most artistically compelling element—cannot yet be described or explained in any but the most general terms as a reflection of Edna's schizoid affinity for fantasy. Even the title of the work, *The Awakening*, suggests a positive quality with which Edna's systematic annihilation of self (albeit from the most "self-preserving" motives) seems oddly at variance. Thus though we might accept the psychic anatomy defined by Laing as schizoid, we must go beyond simple categorizing to understand the novel as a whole.

We might begin with the title itself. Surely one unavoidable meaning of the title has to do with Edna's secret "real" self. She had married a Creole and yet she

> was not thoroughly at home in the society of Creoles. . . . A characteristic which distinguished them and which impressed Mrs. Pontellier most forcibly was their entire absence of prudery. Their freedom of expression was at first incomprehensible to her, though she had no difficulty in reconciling it with a lofty chastity which in the Creole woman seems to be inborn and unmistakable. (27–28)

The unfamiliar mode of conduct which seems most puzzling to Edna is the ability to have affect—to show feeling, even passion—without going beyond certain socially approved limits; that is, it is not just the "freedom" of the Creole society but the coupling of that freedom with a confident sense of decorum, "lofty chastity," which confounds her.

> A book had gone the rounds of the *pension*. When it came her turn to read it, she did so with profound astonishment. She felt moved to read the book in secret and solitude, though none of the others had done so—to hide it from view at the sound of approaching footsteps. It was openly criticised and freely discussed at table. Mrs. Pontellier gave over being astonished, and concluded that wonders would never cease. (28)

As we have seen, "freedom" for Edna has always meant isolation and concealment, an increasingly sterile and barren existence; now suddenly she finds herself among people who have a different kind of freedom, the freedom to express feelings openly and without fear. What a temptation to that insistent inner being whose authenticity Edna so feverishly guards from attack! For this is a self which is starving—and Grand Isle offers nourishment in bounteous abundance.

However, danger lies in the possibility that this hidden self will emerge as voracious, omnivorous, and insatiable. Such a fear is probably always present in the schizoid personality; for these defense mechanisms

> can be understood as an attempt to preserve a being that is precariously structured. . . . The initial structuralization of being into its basic elements occurs in early infancy. In normal circumstances, this occurs in such a way as to be so conclusively stable in its basic elements (for instance, the continuity of time, the distinction be-

> tween the self and not-self, phantasy and reality), that it can henceforth be taken for granted: on this stable base, a considerable amount of plasticity can exist in what we call a person's "character." (Laing 77)

(It is precisely this plasticity which Edna observes among the Creoles and which she finds not shocking but deeply puzzling because it is absent in her own personality.) It is at this most elementary level that Edna's hidden self subsists. "The orientation of the schizoid personality is a primitive oral one, concerned with the dilemma of sustaining its aliveness, while being terrified to 'take in' anything. It becomes parched with thirst, and desolate" (Laing 161). And out of this desolation Edna's "self" ventures forward to seek resuscitation and confirmation.

The awakening is a sensuous one. It is important, however, not to accept this term as an exclusively or even primarily sexual one. To be sure, Edna's awakening involves a liaison with Arobin, and the novel leaves little doubt that this attachment includes sexual activity. Yet it would be naive and limiting to suppose that Edna's principal complaint ought to be described in terms of sexual repression (though she might find it reassuring to do so). Gratifying sexual experience cannot be isolated from sensuous experience in general, and entering into a sexual relationship is an act which necessarily "awakens" memories—echoes, if you will—of earlier sensuous needs and experiences. As Freud has observed, the mind is unique in its development, for "only in the mind is such a preservation of all the earlier stages alongside of the final form possible" (72). Now a reader of Chopin's novel might find himself more absorbed by the apparently genital aspects of Edna's sensuous life, the love affair with Robert and the attachment to Arobin; after all, this is in some sense the "appropriate" level for the expression of passion in an adult woman. The narrator, however, directs our attention in a different direction.

> That summer at Grand Isle she began to loosen a little the mantle of reserve that had always enveloped her. There may have been—there must have been—influences, both subtle and apparent, working in their several ways to induce her to do this; but the most obvious was the influence of Adèle Ratignolle. The excessive physical charm of the Creole had first attracted her, for Edna had a sensuous susceptibility to beauty. (32)

Why is Adèle and not Robert singled out as the primary force that rouses Edna from her slumber? Our introduction to Adèle gives some hints. "There are no words to describe her save the old ones that have served so often to picture the bygone heroine of romance and the fair lady of our dreams'' (26). If some portion of Edna's self has been arrested in dreams, perhaps Adèle is the embodiment of those dreams. And yet, despite the ''spun-gold hair'' and blue eyes, she is scarcely a conventional heroine. Her beauty derives its power from a sense of fullness, ripeness, and abundance. Her very essence might be described as a kind of plump succulence, and the narrator reverts to terms of nourishment as the only appropriate means of rendering her nature. She had ''two lips that pouted, that were so red one could only think of cherries or some other delicious crimson fruit in looking at them. She was growing a little stout, but it did not seem to detract an iota from the grace of every step, pose, gesture'' (26). Her hours are spent delightfully (to her) in mending and sorting children's clothes, and she is pregnant—a fact which pleases her and becomes her principal topic of conversation—when Edna meets her. She might have been painted by Renoir. She is, in Edna's terms, the quintessential ''mother-woman.''

Though Edna's own instincts for mothering are fitful, she is clearly attracted to the bounty of Adèle's nature, allowing herself to slip into caressing intimacy like a grateful child.

> Madame Ratignolle laid her hand over that of Mrs. Pontellier, which was near her. Seeing that the hand was not withdrawn, she clasped it firmly and warmly. She even stroked it a little, fondly, with the other hand, murmuring in an undertone, *''Pauvre chérie.''*
>
> The action was at first a little confusing to Edna, but she soon lent herself readily to the Creole's gentle caress. (35)

So far as one can tell, this is the first sensuous contact that Edna has had with anyone—perhaps in her conscious memory, certainly since adolescence. ''During one period of my life,'' she confides to Adèle, ''religion took a firm hold upon me; after I was twelve and until—until—why, I suppose until now, though I never thought much about it—just driven along by habit'' (35). This sensuous awakening loosens Edna's memory, and her mind drifts back through childhood, recalling the enveloping sea of grass, the succession of phantom lovers.

> Edna did not reveal so much as all this to Madame Ratignolle that summer day when they sat with faces turned to the sea. But a good part of it escaped her. She had put her head down on Madame Ratignolle's shoulder. She was flushed and felt intoxicated with the sound of her own voice and the unaccustomed taste of

> candor. It muddled her like wine, or like a first breath of freedom. (37)

The almost blinding intensity of this episode between Edna and Adèle contrasts vividly with the emotional paleness of Edna's real-world interactions with Robert (which must not be confused with her fantasies about him, especially after he leaves, nor with her increasingly narcissistic appreciation of her own body). Thus Edna's coming to rest upon Adèle's shoulder with trusting openness is preceded by an episode between Edna and Robert which is similar in action and yet altogether different in tone.

> During his oblivious attention he once quietly rested his head against Mrs. Pontellier's arm. As gently she repulsed him. Once again he repeated the offense. She could not but believe it to be thoughtlessness on his part; yet that was no reason she should submit to it. She did not remonstrate, except again to repulse him quietly but firmly. (30)

Several things must be noted here: Edna views Robert's action not as sensuously stimulating but as an imposition, even an affront; her resistance betrays no conflict (that is, the narrator does not suggest that she was tempted by the possible sexual content of his gesture or that she felt threatened or guilty), quite the contrary; her attitude is coolly distant. But then Robert is a man whose quasi-sexual flirtations are not to be taken seriously.

In many ways his patterns of behavior are similar to Edna's, and to some extent, this similarity makes him nonthreatening. He does not seek genuine emotional or sexual involvements, preferring to attach his affections to those women who are "safely" unattainable. "Since the age of fifteen, which was eleven years before, Robert each summer at Grand Isle had constituted himself the devoted attendant of some fair dame or damsel. Sometimes it was a young girl, again a widow; but as often as not it was some interesting married woman" (28–29). His psychic life is more firmly rooted in the world than Edna's; he does not pursue figures of pure fantasy. Still, his propensity for playing the role of hopeless, love-sick youth is so well known as to be able to be anticipated by those who know him. Thus "many had predicted that Robert would devote himself to Mrs. Pontellier when he arrived" (28). His attentions, gratefully received by a number of the ladies, more often than not take the form of ministering to their creature comforts: he fetches bouillon for Adèle, blankets and shawls for Edna.

Indeed, an astonishing proportion of that part of the novel which deals with Edna's sojourn at Grand Isle is paced by the rhythm of her basic needs, especially the most primitive ones of eating and sleeping. If one were to plot the course of Edna's life during this period, the most reliable indices to the passage of time would be her meals and her periods of sleep. The importance of these in Edna's more general "awakening" can be suggested if we examine the day-long boat trip which she makes with Robert.

There is an almost fairy-tale quality to the whole experience; the rules of time seem suspended, and the mèlange of brilliant sensory experiences—the sun, the water, the soft breeze, the old church with its lizards and whispered tales of pirate gold—melts into a dreamlike pattern. It is almost as if Edna's fantasy world had come into being. Indeed, there is even some suggestion that after the event, she incorporates the memory of it into her fantasy world in such a way that the reality and the illusion do, in fact, become confused. Later on in the novel when Edna is invited to tell a true anecdote at a dinner party, she speaks

> of a woman who paddled away with her lover one night in a pirogue and never came back. They were lost amid the Baratarian Islands, and no one ever heard of them or found trace of them from that day to this. It was pure invention. She said that Madame Antoine had related it to her. That, also, was an invention. Perhaps it was a dream she had had. But every glowing word seemed real to those who listened. (90–91)

Yet even this jewel-like adventure with Robert is dominated by the insistence of the infantile life-pattern—sleep and eat, sleep and eat. Edna's rest had been feverish the night prior to the expedition; "she slept but a few hours" (51), and their expedition begins with a hurried breakfast (52). Her taste for sight-seeing, even her willingness to remain with Robert, is so overwhelmed by her lassitude that she must find a place to rest and to be alone. Strikingly, however, once she is by herself, left to seek restful sleep, Edna seems somewhat to revive, and the tone shifts from one of exhaustion to one of sensuous, leisurely enjoyment of her own body.

> Left alone in the little side room, [she] loosened her clothes, removing the greater part of them. . . . How luxurious it felt to rest thus in a strange, quaint bed, with its sweet country odor of laurel lingering about the sheets and mattress! She stretched her strong limbs that ached a little. She ran her fingers through her loosened hair for a while. She looked at her round arms as she

> held them straight up and rubbed them one after the other, observing closely, as if it were something she saw for the first time, the fine, firm quality and texture of her flesh. (55–56)

Powerfully sensuous as this scene is, we would be hard put to find genital significance here. Reduced to its simplest form, the description is of a being discovering the limits and qualities of its own body—discovering, and taking joy in the process of discovery. And having engaged in this exploratory "play" for a while, Edna falls asleep.

The manner of her waking makes explicit reference to the myth of the sleeping beauty. "'How many years have I slept?' she inquired. 'The whole island seems changed. A new race of beings must have sprung up, leaving only you and me as past relics'" (57). Robert jokingly falls in with the fantasy: "'You have slept precisely one hundred years. I was left here to guard your slumbers; and for one hundred years I have been out under the shed reading a book'" (57). In the fairy tale, of course, the princess awakens with a kiss, conscious of love; but Edna's libidinal energies have been arrested at a pregenital level—so she awakens "very hungry" (56)—and her lover prepares her a meal! "He was childishly gratified to discover her appetite, and to see the relish with which she ate the food which he had procured for her" (57). Indeed, though the title of the novel suggests a reenactment of the traditional romantic myth, it never does offer a complete representation of it. The next invocation is Arobin's kiss, "the first kiss of her life to which her nature had really responded" (104); but as we have seen earlier, this response is facilitated, perhaps even made possible, by the fact that her emotional attachment is not to Arobin but to the Robert of her fantasy world. The final allusion to an awakening kiss is Edna's rousing of Robert (133); and yet this is a potentially genital awakening from which both flee.

Edna's central problem, once the hidden "self" begins to exert its inexorable power, is that her libidinal appetite has been fixated at the oral level. Edna herself has an insistent preoccupation with nourishment; on the simplest level, she is concerned with food. Her favorite adjective is "delicious": she sees many mother-women as "delicious" in their role (26); she carries echoes of her children's voices "like the memory of a delicious song" (116); when she imagines Robert she thinks "how delicious it would be to have him there with her" (124). And the notion of something's being good because it might be good to "eat" (or internalize in some way) is echoed in all of her relationships with other people. Those who care about her typically feed her; and the sleep-and-eat pattern which is most strikingly established at the beginning of the novel continues even to the very end. Not surprisingly, in the "grown-up world" she is a poor housekeeper, and though Léonce's responses are clearly petty and self-centered, Edna's behavior does betray incompetence, especially when we compare it (as the novel so often invites us to) with the nurturing capacities of Adèle. It is not surprising that the most dramatic gesture toward freedom that Edna makes is to move out of her husband's house; yet even this gesture toward "independence" can be comprehended as part of an equally powerful wish to regress. It is, after all, a "tiny house" that she moves to; she calls it her "pigeon house," and if she were still a little girl, we might call it a playhouse.

The decision to move from Léonce's house is virtually coincidental with the beginning of her affair with Arobin; yet even the initial stages of that affair are described in oral terms—Edna feels regret because "it was not love which had held this cup of life to her lips" (104). And though the relationship develops as she makes preparations for the move, it absorbs astonishingly little of Edna's libido. She is deliberately distant, treating Arobin with "affected carelessness" (105). As the narrator observes, "If he had expected to find her languishing, reproachful, or indulging in sentimental tears, he must have been greatly surprised" (105). She is "true" to the fantasy image of Robert. And in the real world her emotional energy has been committed in another direction. She is busy with elaborate plans—for a dinner party! And it is on this extravagant sumptuous oral repast that she lavishes her time and care (see 107–12). Here Edna as purveyor of food becomes not primarily a nourisher (as Adèle is) but a sensualist in the only terms that she can truly comprehend. One might argue that in this elaborate feast Edna's sensuous self comes closest to some form of expression which might be compatible with the real world. The dinner party itself is one of the longest sustained episodes in the novel; we are told in loving detail about the appearance of the table, the commodious chairs, the flowers, the candles, the food and wines, Edna's attire—no sensory pleasure is left unattended. Yet even this indulgence fails to satisfy.

> As she sat there amid her guests, she felt the old ennui overtaking her; the hopelessness which so often assailed her, which came upon her like an obsession, like something extraneous, independent of volition. It was something which announced itself; a chill breath that seemed to issue from some vast cavern wherein discords wailed. (109)

Edna, perhaps, connects this despair to the absence of Robert. "There came over her the acute longing which always summoned into her spiritual vision the presence of the beloved one, overpowering her at once with a sense of the unattainable" (109–10). However, the narrator's language here is interestingly ambiguous. It is not specifically *Robert* that Edna longs for; it is "the presence of the beloved one"—an indefinite perpetual image, existing "always" in "her spiritual vision." The longing, so described, is an immortal one and, as she acknowledges, "unattainable"; the vision might be of Robert, but it might equally be of the cavalry officer, the engaged young man, the tragedian—even of Adèle, whose mothering attentions first elicited a sensuous response from Edna and whose own imminent motherhood has kept her from the grand party. The indefinite quality of Edna's longing thus described has an ominous tone, a tone made even more ominous by the rising specter of those "vast caverns" waiting vainly to be filled.

Perhaps Edna's preoccupation with the incorporation of food is but one aspect of a more general concern with incorporating that which is external to her. Freud's hypotheses about the persistence in some people of essentially oral concerns makes Edna's particular problem even clearer.

> Originally the ego includes everything, later it separates off an external world from itself. Our present ego-feeling is, therefore, only a shrunken residue of a much more inclusive—indeed, an all-embracing—feeling which corresponded to a more intimate bond between the ego and the world about it. If we may assume that there are many people in whose mental life this primary ego-feeling has persisted to a greater or less degree, it would exist in them side by side with the narrower and more sharply demarcated ego-feeling of maturity, like a kind of counterpart to it. In that case, the ideational contents appropriate to it would be precisely those of limitlessness and of a bond with the universe . . . the "oceanic" feeling. (68)

A psychologically mature individual has to some extent satisfied these oral desires for limitless fusion with the external world; presumably his sense of oneness with a nurturing figure has given him sustenance sufficient to move onward to more complex satisfactions. Yet growth inevitably involves some loss. "The feeling of happiness derived from the satisfaction of a wild instinctual impulse untamed by the ego is incomparably more intense than that derived from sating an instinct that has been tamed" (79). To some extent all of us share Edna's fantasy of complete fulfillment through a bond with the infinite; that is what gives the novel its power. However for those few people in whom this primary ego-feeling has persisted with uncompromising force the temptation to seek total fulfillment may be both irresistible and annihilating.

Everywhere and always in the novel, Edna's fundamental longing is postulated in precisely these terms. And strangely enough, the narrator seems intuitively to understand the connection between this longing for suffusion, fulfillment, incorporation, and the very earliest attempts to define identity.

> But the beginning of things, of a world especially, is necessarily vague, tangled, chaotic, and exceedingly disturbing. How few of us ever emerge from such beginning! How many souls perish in its tumult!
>
> The voice of the sea is seductive; never ceasing, whispering, clamoring, murmuring, inviting the soul to wander for a spell in abysses of solitude; to lose itself in mazes of inward contemplation.
>
> The voice of the sea speaks to the soul. The touch of the sea is sensuous, enfolding the body in its soft, close embrace. (32)

Ultimately, the problem facing Edna has a nightmarish circularity. She has achieved some measure of personal identity only by hiding her "true self" within—repressing all desire for instinctual gratification. Yet she can see others in her environment—the Creoles generally and Adèle in particular—who seem comfortably able to indulge their various sensory appetites and to do so with easy moderation. Edna's hidden self longs for resuscitation and nourishment; and in the supportive presence of Grand Isle Edna begins to acknowledge and express the needs of that "self."

Yet once released, the inner being cannot be satisfied. It is an orally destructive self, a limitless void whose needs can be filled, finally, only by total fusion with the outside world, a totality of sensuous enfolding. And this totality means annihilation of the ego.

Thus all aspects of Edna's relationship with the outside world are unevenly defined. She is remarkably vulnerable to feelings of being invaded and overwhelmed; we have already seen that she views emotional intimacy as potentially shattering. She is equally unable to handle the phenomenal world with any degree of consistency or efficiency. She is very much at the mercy of her environment: the atmosphere of Mademoiselle Reisz's room is said to "invade" her with repose (117); Mademoiselle Reisz's music has the consistent effect of penetrating Edna's outer self and playing upon the responsive chords of her inner yearning;

even her way of looking at objects in the world about her becomes an act of incorporation; "she had a way of turning [her eyes] swiftly upon an object and holding them there as if lost in some inward maze of contemplation or thought" (21–22). Once she has given up the pattern of repression that served to control dangerous impulses, she becomes engaged in trying to maintain a precarious balance in each of her relationships. On the one hand she must resist invasion, for with invasion comes possession and total destruction. On the other hand she must resist the equally powerful impulse to destroy whatever separates her from the external world so that she can seek union, fusion, and (so her fantasies suggest) ecstatic fulfillment.

In seeking to deal with this apparently hopeless problem, Edna encounters several people whose behavior might serve as a pattern for her. Mademoiselle Reisz is one. Mademoiselle Reisz is an artist, and as such she has created that direct avenue between inner and outer worlds which Edna seeks in her own life. Surely Edna's own attempts at artistic enterprise grow out of her more general desire for sustained ecstasy. "While Edna worked she sometimes sang low the little air, '*Ah, si tu savais!*' " (77). Her work is insensibly linked with her memories of Robert, and these in turn melt into more generalized memories and desires. The little song she is humming

> moved her with recollections. She could hear again the ripple of the water, the flapping sail. She could see the glint of the moon upon the bay, and could feel the soft, gusty beating of the hot south wind. A subtle current of desire passed through her body, weakening her hold upon the brushes and making her eyes burn. (77)

In some ways, Edna's painting might offer her an excellent and viable mode for coming to terms with the insistent demands of cosmic yearning. For one thing, it utilizes in an effective way her habit of transforming the act of observing the external world into an act of incorporation: to some extent the artist must use the world in this way, incorporating it and transforming it in the act of artistic creation. Thus the period during which Edna is experimenting with her art offers her some of the most satisfying experiences she is capable of having.

> There were days when she was very happy without knowing why. She was happy to be alive and breathing when her whole being seemed to be one with the sunlight, the color, the odors, the luxuriant warmth of some perfect Southern day. . . . And she found it good to dream and to be alone and unmolested. (77–78)

Yet when Edna tells Mademoiselle Reisz about her efforts, she is greeted with skepticism: "'You have pretensions,'" Mademoiselle Reisz responds. "'To be an artist includes much; one must possess many gifts—absolute gifts—which have not been acquired by one's own effort. And moreover, to succeed, the artist must possess the courageous soul. . . . The brave soul. The soul that dares and defies'" (83). One implication of Mademoiselle Reisz's half-contemptuous comment may well be the traditional view that the artist must dare to be unconventional; and it is this interpretation which Edna reports later to Arobin, saying as she does, however, "'I only half comprehend her'" (103). The part of Mademoiselle Reisz's injunction that eludes Edna's understanding concerns the sense of purposiveness which is implied by the image of a courageous soul. Mademoiselle Reisz has her art, but she has sacrificed for it—perhaps too much. In any case, however, she has acknowledged limitations, accepted some, and grappled with others; she is an active agent who has defined her relationship to the world. Edna, by contrast, is passive.

The words which recur most frequently to describe her are words like melting, drifting, misty, dreaming, shadowy. She is not willing (perhaps not able) to define her position in the world because to do so would involve relinquishing the dream of total fulfillment. Thus while Mademoiselle Reisz can control and create, Edna is most comfortable as the receptive vessel—both for Mademoiselle Reisz's music and for the sense impressions which form the basis of her own artistic endeavor. Mademoiselle Reisz commands her work; Edna is at the mercy of hers. Thus just as there are moments of exhilaration, so

> there were days when she was unhappy, she did not know why,—when it did not seem worth while to be glad or sorry, to be alive or dead; when life appeared to her like a grotesque pandemonium and humanity like worms struggling blindly toward inevitable annihilation. She could not work on such a day, nor weave fancies to stir her pulses and warm her blood. (78)

Art, for Edna, ultimately becomes not a defense against inner turmoil, merely a reflection of it.

Another possible defense for Edna might be the establishment and sustaining of a genuine genital relationship. Her adolescent fantasies, her mechanical marriage, her liaison with Arobin, and her passionate attachment to the fantasy image of Robert all suggest imperfect efforts to do just that. A genital relationship, like all ego-relationships, necessarily involves limitation; to put the matter in Edna's terms, a significant attachment with a real man would involve relinquishing the fantasy of total fulfillment with some fantasy lover. In turn, it would offer genuine emotional nourishment—though perhaps never enough to satisfy the voracious clamoring of Edna's hidden self.

Ironically, Adèle, who seems such a fount of sustenance, gives indications of having some of the same oral needs that Edna does. Like Edna, she is preoccupied with eating, she pays extravagant care to the arrangement of her own physical comforts, and she uses her pregnancy as an excuse to demand a kind of mothering attention for herself. The difference between Edna and Adèle is that Adèle can deal with her nurturing needs by displacing them onto her children and becoming a "mother-woman." Having thus segregated and limited these desires, Adèle can find diverse ways of satisfying them; and having satisfied her own infantile oral needs, she can go on to have a rewarding adult relationship with her husband. Between Adèle and Monsieur Ratignolle there is mutual joining together: "The Ratignolles understood each other perfectly. If ever the fusion of two human beings into one has been accomplished on this sphere it was surely in their union" (75). The clearest outward sign of this happy union is that the Ratignolles converse eagerly and clearly with each other. Monsieur Ratignolle reports his experiences and thoughts to his wife, and she in turn "was keenly interested in everything he said, laying down her fork the better to listen, chiming in, taking the words out of his mouth" (76). Yet this picture of social and domestic accord is indescribably dismaying to Edna. She "felt depressed rather than soothed after leaving them. The little glimpse of domestic harmony which had been offered her, gave her no regret, no longing" (76).

Again, what has capitulated is the fantasy of complete and total suffusion; the Ratignolles have only a union which is as perfect as one can expect *"on this sphere"* (italics added). Yet the acme of bliss which Edna has always sought "was not for her in this world" (37). Edna wishes a kind of preverbal union, an understanding which consistently surpasses words. Léonce is scarcely a sensitive man (that is, as we have seen, why she chose to marry him). Yet Edna never exerts herself to even such efforts at communication with him as might encourage a supportive emotional response. She responds to his unperceptive clumsiness by turning inward, falling into silence. Over and over again their disagreements follow the pattern of a misunderstanding which Edna refuses to clarify. At the very beginning of the novel when Léonce selfishly strolls off for an evening of gambling, Edna's rage and sense of loneliness are resolutely hidden, even when he seeks to discover the cause of her unhappiness. "She said nothing, and refused to answer her husband when he questioned her" (24). Perhaps Léonce could not have understood the needs which Edna feels so achingly unfulfilled. And he is very clumsy. But he does make attempts at communication while she does not, and his interview with the family doctor (84–87) shows greater concern about Edna's problems than she manages to feel for his.

The attachment to Robert, which takes on significance only after he has left Grand Isle, monopolizes Edna's emotions because it does temporarily offer an illusion of fusion, of complete union. However, this love affair, such as it is, is a genuinely narcissistic one; the sense of fusion exists because Edna's lover is really a part of herself—a figment of her imagination, an image of Robert which she has incorporated into her consciousness. Not only is her meeting with Robert after his return a disappointment (as we have seen earlier); it moves the static, imaginary "love affair" into a new and crucial stage; it tests, once and for all, Edna's capacity to transform her world of dreams into viable reality. Not surprisingly, "some way he had seemed nearer to her off there in Mexico" (124).

Still she does try. She awakens him with a kiss even as Arobin had awakened her. Robert, too, is resistant to genuine involvement, and his initial reaction is to speak of the hopelessness of their relationship. Edna, however, is insistent (despite the interruption telling her of Adèle's accouchement). "'We shall be everything to each other. Nothing else in the world is of any consequence. I must go to my friend; but you will wait for me? No matter how late; you will wait for me, Robert?'" (130). And at this point, Edna seems finally to have won her victory. "'Don't go; don't go! Oh! Edna, stay with me,' he pleaded. . . . Her seductive voice, together with his great love for her, had enthralled his senses, had deprived him of every impulse but the longing to hold her and keep her" (130). And at this moment, so long and eagerly anticipated, Edna leaves Robert!

Robert's own resolve weakens during the interval, and it would be all too easy to blame Edna's failure on him. Certainly he is implicated. Yet his act does not explain *Edna's* behavior. "Nothing else in the world is of any consequence," she has said. If that is so, why then does she leave? No real duty calls her. Her presence at Adèle's delivery is of virtually no help. The doctor, sorry for the pain that the scene has caused Edna even remonstrates with her mildly for having come. "'You shouldn't have been there, Mrs. Pontellier. . . . There were a dozen women she might have had with her, unimpressionable women'" (132). To have stayed with Robert would have meant consummation, finally, the joining of her dreamlike passion to a flesh-and-blood lover; to leave was to risk losing that opportunity. Edna must realize the terms of this dilemma, and still she chooses to leave. We can only conclude that she is unconsciously ambivalent about achieving the goal which has sustained her fantasies for so long. The flesh-and-blood Robert may prove an imperfect, unsatisfactory substitute for the "beloved" of her dreams; what is more, a relationship with the real Robert would necessarily disenfranchise the more desirable phantom lover, whose presence is linked with her more general yearning for suffusion and indefinable ecstasy.

The totality of loss which follows Edna's decision forces a grim recognition upon her, the recognition that all her lovers have really been of but fleeting significance.

> To-day it is Arobin; tomorrow it will be some one else. . . . It makes no difference to me. . . . There was no one thing in the world that she desired. There was no human being whom she wanted near her except Robert; and she even realized that the day would come when he, too, and the thought of him would melt out of her existence, leaving her alone. (136)

Her devastation, thus described, is removed from the realm of romantic disappointment; and we must see Edna's final suicide as originating in a sense of inner emptiness, not in some finite failure of love. Her decision to go to Adèle is in part a reflection of Edna's unwillingness to compromise her dream of Robert (and in this sense it might be interpreted as a flight from reality). On the other hand, it might also be seen as a last desperate attempt to come to terms with the anguish created by her unfulfilled "Oceanic" longing. And for this last effort she must turn to Adèle, the human who first caused her to loosen the bonds of repression.

The preeminence of Adèle over Robert in Edna's emotional life, affirmed by Edna's crucial choice, is undeniably linked to her image as a nurturing figure and, especially here, as a mother-to-be. In this capacity she is also linked to Edna's own children—insistent specters in Edna's consciousness; and this link is made explicit by Adèle's repetition of the cryptic injunction to "think of the children" (132).

Now in every human's life there is a period of rhapsodic union or fusion with another, and this is the period of early infancy, before the time when a baby begins to differentiate himself from his mother. It is the haunting memory of this evanescent state which Freud defines as "Oceanic feeling," the longing to recapture that sense of oneness and sensuous pleasure—even, perhaps, the desire to be reincorpo- o the safety of preexistence. Men can never recreate this state union. Adult women can—when they are pregnant. Most pregnan omen identify intensely with their unborn children, and through that identification in some measure reexperience a state of complete and harmonious union.

> The biologic process has created a unity of mother and child, in which the bodily substance of one flows into the other, and thus one larger unit is formed out of two units. The same thing takes place on the psychic level. By tender identification, by perceiving the fruit of her body as part of herself, the pregnant woman is able to transform the 'parasite' into a beloved being. Thus, mankind's eternal yearning for identity between the ego and the nonego, that deeply buried original desire to reachieve the condition once experienced, to repeat the human dream that was once realized in the mother's womb, is fulfilled. (Freud 139)

Adèle is a dear friend, yes; she is a nurturing figure. But above all, she is the living embodiment of that state which Edna's deepest being longs to recapture. Trapped in the conflict between her desire for "freedom," as seen in her compulsive need to protect her precarious sense of self, and her equally insistent yearning for complete fulfillment through total suffusion, Edna is intensely involved with Adèle's pregnancy.

Edna's compulsion to be with Adèle at the moment of delivery is, in the sense which would have most significance for her, a need to view individuation at its origin. For if pregnancy offers a state of total union, then birth is the initial separation: for the child it is the archetypal separation trauma; for the mother, too, it is a significant psychic trauma. It is the ritual reenactment of her own birth and a brutal reawakening to the world of isolated ego:

> To make it the being that is outside her, the pregnant mother must deliver the child from the depths of herself. . . . She loses not only it, but herself with it. This, I think, is at the bottom of that fear and foreboding of death that every pregnant woman has, and this turns the giving of life into the losing of life. (Deutsch 160)

Edna cannot refuse to partake of this ceremony, for here, if anywhere, she will find the solution to her problem.

Yet the experience is horrendous; it gives no comfort, no reassuring answer to Edna's predicament. It offers only stark, uncompromising truth. Adèle's ordeal reminds Edna of her own accouchements.

> Edna began to feel uneasy. She was seized with a vague dread. Her own like experiences seemed far away, unreal, and only half remembered. She recalled faintly an ecstasy of pain, the heavy odor of chloroform, a stupor which had deadened sensation, and an awakening to find a little new life to which she had given being. (131)

This is Nature's cruel message. The fundamental significance to Edna of an awakening is an awakening to separation, to individual existence, to the hopelessness of ever satisfying the dream of total fusion. The rousing of her sensuous being had led Edna on a quest for ecstasy; but the ecstasy which beckoned has become in the end merely an "ecstasy of pain," first in her protracted struggle to retain identity and finally here in that relentless recognition of inevitable separation which has been affirmed in the delivery, "an awakening to find a little new life." Edna is urged to leave, but she refuses. "With an inward agony, with a flaming, outspoken revolt against the ways of Nature, she witnessed the scene of torture" (131–32).

In this world, in life, there can be no perfect union, and the children whom Adèle urges Edna to remember stand as living proof of the inevitability of separation. Edna's longing can never be satisfied. This is her final discovery, the inescapable disillusionment; and the narrator calls it to our attention again, lest its significance escape us. "'The years that are gone seem like dreams,'" Edna muses, "'If one might go on sleeping and dreaming—but to wake up and find—'" (133). Here she pauses, but the reader can complete her thought—"a little new life." "'Oh! well! perhaps it is better to wake up after all, even to suffer rather than to remain a dupe to illusions all one's life'" (133).

One wonders to what extent Edna's fate might have been different if Robert had remained. Momentarily, at least, he might have roused her from her despondency by offering not ecstasy but at least partial satisfaction. The fundamental problem would have remained, however. Life offers only partial pleasures, and individuated experience.

Thus Edna's final act of destruction has a quality of uncompromising sensuous fulfillment as well. It is her answer to the inadequacies of life, a literal denial and reversal of the birth trauma she has just witnessed, a stripping away of adulthood, of limitation, of consciousness itself. If life cannot offer fulfillment of her dream of fusion, then the ecstasy of death is preferable to the relinquishing of that dream. So Edna goes to the sea "and for the first time in her life she stood naked in the open air, at the mercy of the sun, the breeze that beat upon her, and the waves that invited her" (136). She is a child, an infant again. "How strange and awful it seemed to stand naked under the sky! how delicious! She felt like some new-born creature, opening its eyes in a familiar world that it had never known" (136). And with her final act Edna completes the regression, back beyond childhood, back into time eternal. "The touch of the sea is sensuous, enfolding the body in its soft, close embrace" (136).

WORKS CITED

Chametzky, Jules. "Our Decentralized Literature: A Consideration of Regional, Ethnic, Racial, and Sexual Factors." Paper delivered to the German American Studies Association, Heidelberg, June 5, 1971.

Deutsch, Helene. *The Psychology of Women.* New York: Grune, 1971. Vol. 2.

Eble, Kenneth. Introduction to *The Awakening.* New York: Capricorn, 1964.

Freud, Sigmund. "Civilization and Its Discontents." *The Standard Edition of the Complete Psychological Works.* Ed. James Strachey. London: Hogarth, 1971. Vol. 21.

Laing, Ronald D. *The Divided Self.* London: Penguin, 1965.

Wilson, Edmund. *Patriotic Gore.* New York: Oxford UP, 1966.

Deconstruction and *The Awakening*

WHAT IS DECONSTRUCTION?

Deconstruction has a reputation for being the most complex and forbidding of contemporary critical approaches to literature, but in fact almost all of us have, at one time, either deconstructed a text or badly wanted to deconstruct one. Sometimes when we hear a lecturer effectively marshal evidence to show that a book means primarily one thing, we long to interrupt and ask what he or she would make of other, conveniently overlooked passages, passages that seem to contradict the lecturer's thesis. Sometimes, after reading a provocative critical article that *almost* convinces us that a familiar work means the opposite of what we assumed it meant, we may wish to make an equally convincing case for our former reading of the text. We may not think that the poem or novel in question better supports our interpretation, but we may recognize that the text can be used to support *both* readings. And sometimes we simply want to make that point: texts can be used to support seemingly irreconcilable positions.

To reach this conclusion is to feel the deconstructive itch. J. Hillis Miller, the preeminent American deconstructor, puts it this way: "Deconstruction is not a dismantling of the structure of a text, but a demonstration that it has already dismantled itself. Its apparently solid ground is no rock but thin air" ("Stevens' Rock" 341). To deconstruct a text isn't to show that all the high old themes aren't there to be found in it. Rather, it is to show that a text—not unlike DNA with its double helix—can have intertwined, opposite "discourses"—strands of narrative, threads of meaning.

Ultimately, of course, deconstruction refers to a larger and more complex enterprise than the practice of demonstrating that a text means contradictory things. The term refers to a way of reading texts practiced by critics who have been influenced by the writings of the French philosopher Jacques Derrida. It is important to gain some understanding of Derrida's project and of the historical backgrounds of his work before reading the deconstruction that follows, let alone attempting to deconstruct a text. But it is important, too, to approach deconstruction with anything but a scholar's sober and almost worshipful respect for knowledge and truth. Deconstruction offers a playful alternative to traditional scholarship, a confidently adversarial alternative, and deserves to be approached in the spirit that animates it.

Derrida, a philosopher of language who coined the term "deconstruction," argues that we tend to think and express our thoughts in terms of opposites. Something is black but not white, masculine and therefore not feminine, a cause rather than an effect, and so forth. These mutually exclusive pairs or dichotomies are too numerous to list, but would include beginning/end, conscious/unconscious, presence/absence, speech/writing, and construction/destruction (the last being the opposition that Derrida's word deconstruction tries to contain and subvert). If we think hard about these dichotomies, Derrida suggests, we will realize that they are not simply oppositions; they are also hierarchies in miniature. In other words, they contain one term that our culture views as being superior and one term viewed as negative or inferior. Sometimes the superior term seems only subtly superior (*speech, masculine, cause*), whereas sometimes we know immediately which term is culturally preferable (*presence* and *beginning* and *consciousness* are easy choices). But the hierarchy always exists.

Of particular interest to Derrida, perhaps because it involves the language in which all the other dichotomies are expressed, is the hierarchical opposition speech/writing. Derrida argues that the "privileging" of speech, that is, the tendency to regard speech in positive terms and writing in negative terms, cannot be disentangled from the privileging of presence. (Postcards are written by absent friends; we read Plato because he cannot speak from beyond the grave.) Furthermore, according to Derrida, the tendency to privilege both speech and presence is part of the Western tradition of *logocentrism,* the belief that in some ideal beginning were creative *spoken* words, words such as "Let there be light,'' spoken by an ideal, *present* God. According to logocentric tradition, these words can now only be represented in unoriginal speech or writing (such as the written phrase in quotation marks above). Derrida doesn't seek to reverse the hierarchized opposition between speech and writing, or presence and absence, or early and late, for to do so would be to fall into a trap of perpetuating the same forms of thought and expression that he seeks to deconstruct. Rather, his goal is to erase the boundary between oppositions such as speech and writing, and to do so in such a way as to throw the order and values implied by the opposition into question.

Returning to the theories of Ferdinand de Saussure, who invented the modern science of linguistics, Derrida reminds us that the association of speech with present, obvious, and ideal meaning and writing with absent, merely pictured, and therefore less reliable meaning is suspect, to say the least. As Saussure demonstrated, words are *not* the things they name and, indeed, they are only arbitrarily associated with those things. Neither spoken nor written words have present, positive, identifiable attributes themselves; they have meaning only by virtue of their difference from other words (*red, read, reed*). In a sense, meanings emerge from the gaps or spaces between them. Take *read* as an example. To know whether it is the present or past tense of the verb—whether it rhymes with *red* or *reed*—we need to see it in relation to some other word (for example, *yesterday*).

Because the meanings of words lie in the differences between them and in the differences between them and the things they name, Derrida suggests that all language is constituted by *différance*, a word he has coined that puns on two French words meaning "to differ" and "to defer": words are the deferred presences of the things they "mean," and their meaning is grounded in difference. Derrida, by the way, changes the *e* in the French word *différence* to an *a* in his neologism *différance*; the change, which can be seen in writing but cannot be heard in spoken French, is itself a playful, witty challenge to the notion that writing is inferior or "fallen" speech.

In *De la grammatologie* [*Of Grammatology*] (1967) and *Dissemination* (1972), Derrida begins to redefine writing by deconstructing some old definitions. In *Dissemination,* he traces logocentrism back to Plato, who in the *Phaedrus* has Socrates condemn writing and who, in all the great dialogues, powerfully postulates that metaphysical longing for origins and ideals that permeates Western thought. "What Derrida does in his reading of Plato," Barbara Johnson points out, "is to unfold dimensions of Plato's *text* that work against the grain of (Plato's own)

Platonism'' (xxiv). Remember: that is what deconstruction does according to Miller; it shows a text dismantling itself.

In *Of Grammatology,* Derrida turns to the *Confessions* of Jean-Jacques Rousseau and exposes a grain running against the grain. Rousseau, another great Western idealist and believer in innocent, noble origins, on one hand condemned writing as mere representation, a corruption of the more natural, childlike, direct, and therefore undevious speech. On the other hand, Rousseau admitted his own tendency to lose self-presence and blurt out exactly the wrong thing in public. He confesses that, by writing at a distance from his audience, he often expressed himself better: ''If I were present, one would never know what I was worth,'' Rousseau admitted (Derrida, *Of Grammatology* 142). Thus, writing is a *supplement* to speech that is at the same time *necessary.* Barbara Johnson, sounding like Derrida, puts it this way: ''Recourse to writing . . . is necessary to recapture a presence whose lack has not been preceded by any fullness'' (Derrida, *Dissemination* xii). Thus, Derrida shows that one strand of Rousseau's discourse made writing seem a secondary, even treacherous supplement, while another made it seem necessary to communication.

Have Derrida's deconstructions of *Confessions* and the *Phaedrus* explained these texts, interpreted them, opened them up and shown us what they mean? Not in any traditional sense. Derrida would say that anyone attempting to find a single, correct meaning in a text is simply imprisoned by that structure of thought that would oppose two readings and declare one to be right and not wrong, correct rather than incorrect. In fact, any work of literature that we interpret defies the laws of Western logic, the laws of opposition and noncontradiction. In the views of poststructuralist critics, texts don't say ''A and not B.'' They say ''A and not-A,'' as do texts written by literary critics, who are also involved in producing creative writing.

Miller has written that the purpose of deconstruction is to show ''the existence in literature of structures of language which contradict the law of non-contradiction.'' Why find the grain that runs against the grain? To restore what Miller has called ''the strangeness of literature,'' to reveal the ''capacity of each work to surprise the reader,'' to demonstrate that ''literature continually exceeds any formula or theory with which the critic is prepared to encompass it'' (Miller, *Fiction* 5).

Although its ultimate aim may be to critique Western idealism and logic, deconstruction began as a response to structuralism and to formalism, another structure-oriented theory of reading. (Deconstruction, which is really only one kind of a poststructuralist criticism, is sometimes referred to as poststructuralist criticism, or even as poststructuralism.)

Structuralism, Robert Scholes tells us, may now be seen as a reaction to modernist alienation and despair (3). Using Saussure's theory as Derrida was to do later, European structuralists attempted to create a *semiology,* or science of signs, that would give humankind at once a scientific and a holistic way of studying the world and its human inhabitants. Roland Barthes, a structuralist who later shifted toward poststructuralism, hoped to recover literary language from the isolation in which it had been studied and to show that the laws that govern it govern all signs, from road signs to articles of clothing. Claude Lévi-Strauss, a structural anthropologist who studied everything from village structure to the structure of myths, found in myths what he called *mythemes,* or building blocks, such as basic plot elements. Recognizing that the same mythemes occur in similar myths from different cultures, he suggested that all myths may be elements of one great myth being written by the collective human mind.

Derrida could not accept the notion that structuralist thought might someday explain the laws governing human signification and thus provide the key to understanding the form and meaning of everything from an African village to a Greek myth to Rousseau's *Confessions.* In his view, the scientific search by structural anthropologists for what unifies humankind amounts to a new version of the old search for the lost ideal, whether that ideal be Plato's bright realm of the Idea or the Paradise of Genesis or Rousseau's unspoiled Nature. As for the structuralist belief that texts have "centers" of meaning, in Derrida's view that derives from the logocentric belief that there is a reading of the text that accords with "the book as seen by God." Jonathan Culler, who thus translates a difficult phrase from Derrida's *L'Écriture et la différence* [*Writing and Difference*] (1967) in his book *Structuralist Poetics* (1975), goes on to explain what Derrida objects to in structuralist literary criticism:

> [When] one speaks of the structure of a literary work, one does so from a certain vantage point: one starts with notions of the meaning or effects of a poem and tries to identify the structures responsible for those effects. Possible configurations or patterns that make no contribution are rejected as irrelevant. That is to say, an intuitive understanding of the poem functions as the "centre" . . . : it is both a starting point and a limiting principle. (244)

For these reasons, Derrida and his poststructuralist followers reject the very notion of "linguistic competence" introduced by Noam

Chomsky, a structural linguist. The idea that there is a competent reading "gives a privileged status to a particular set of rules of reading, . . . granting preeminence to certain conventions and excluding from the realm of language all the truly creative and productive violations of those rules" (Culler, *Structuralist Poetics* 241).

Poststructuralism calls into question assumptions made about literature by formalist, as well as by structuralist, critics. Formalism, or the New Criticism as it was once commonly called, assumes a work of literature to be a freestanding, self-contained object, its meanings found in the complex network of relations that constitute its parts (images, sounds, rhythms, allusions, and so on). To be sure, deconstruction is somewhat like formalism in several ways. Both the formalist and the deconstructor focus on the literary text; neither is likely to interpret a poem or a novel by relating it to events in the author's life, letters, historical period, or even culture. And formalists, long before deconstructors, discovered counterpatterns of meaning in the same text. Formalists find ambiguity and irony, deconstructors find contradiction and undecidability.

Here, though, the two groups part ways. Formalists believe a complete understanding of a literary work is possible, an understanding in which even the ambiguities will fulfill a definite, meaningful function. Poststructuralists celebrate the apparently limitless possibilities for the production of meaning that develop when the language of the critic enters the language of the text. Such a view is in direct opposition to the formalist view that a work of literary art has organic unity (therefore, structuralists would say, a "center"), if only we could find it.

Poststructuralists break with formalists, too, over an issue they have debated with structuralists. The issue involves metaphor and metonymy, two terms for different kinds of rhetorical *tropes,* or figures of speech. *Metonymy* refers to a figure that is chosen to stand for something that it is commonly associated with, or with which it happens to be contiguous or juxtaposed. When said to a waitress, "I'll have the cold plate today" is a metonymic figure of speech for "I'll eat the cold food you're serving today." We refer to the food we want as a plate simply because plates are what food happens to be served on and because everyone understands that by "plate" we mean food. A *metaphor,* on the other hand, is a figure of speech that involves a special, intrinsic, nonarbitrary relationship with what it represents. When you say you are blue, if you believe that there is an intrinsic, timeless likeness between that color and melancholy feeling — a likeness that just doesn't exist between sadness and yellow — then you are using the word blue metaphorically.

Although both formalists and structuralists make much of the difference between metaphor and metonymy, Derrida, Miller and Paul de Man have contended with the distinction deconstructively. They have questioned not only the distinction but also, and perhaps especially, the privilege we grant to metaphor, which we tend to view as the positive and superior figure of speech. De Man, in *Allegories of Reading* (1979), analyzes a passage from Proust's *Swann's Way,* arguing that it is about the nondistinction between metaphor and metonymy – and that it makes its claim metonymically. In *Fiction and Repetition: Seven English Novels* (1982), Miller connects the belief in metaphorical correspondences with other metaphysical beliefs, such as those in origins, endings, transcendence, and underlying truths. Isn't it likely, deconstructors keep implicitly asking, that every metaphor was once a metonym, but that we have simply forgotten what arbitrary juxtaposition or contiguity gave rise to the association that now seems mysteriously special?

The hypothesis that what we call metaphors are really old metonyms may perhaps be made clearer by the following example. We used the word *Watergate* as a metonym to refer to a political scandal that began in the Watergate building complex. Recently, we have used part of the building's name (*gate*) to refer to more recent scandals (*Irangate*). However, already there are people who use and "understand" these terms who are unaware that Watergate is the name of a building. In the future, isn't it possible that *gate,* which began as part of a simple metonym, will seem like the perfect metaphor for scandal – a word that suggests corruption and wrongdoing with a strange and inexplicable rightness?

This is how deconstruction works: by showing that what was prior and privileged in the old hierarchy (for instance, metaphor and speech) can just as easily seem secondary, the deconstructor causes the formerly privileged term to exchange properties with the formerly devalued one. Causes become effects and (d)evolutions become origins, but the result is neither the destruction of the old order or hierarchy nor the construction of a new one. It is, rather, *deconstruction*. In Robert Scholes's words, "If either cause or effect can occupy the position of an origin, then origin is no longer originary; it loses its metaphorical privilege" (88).

Once deconstructed, literal and figurative can exchange properties, so that the prioritizing between them is erased: all words, even dog and cat, are understood to be figures. It's just that we have used some of them so long that we have forgotten how arbitrary and metonymic they are. And, just as literal and figurative can exchange properties, criticism can exchange properties with literature, in the process coming to be seen not merely as a supplement — the second, negative, and inferior term in the binary opposition creative writing/literary criticism — but rather as an equally creative form of work. Would we write if there were not critics — intelligent readers motivated and able to make sense of what is written? Who, then, depends on whom?

"It is not difficult to see the attractions" of deconstructive reading, Jonathan Culler has commented. "Given that there is no ultimate or absolute justification for any system or for the interpretations from it," the critic is free to value "the activity of interpretation itself, . . . rather than any results which might be obtained" (*Structuralist Poetics* 248). Not everyone, however, has so readily seen the attractions of deconstruction. Two eminent critics, M. H. Abrams and Wayne Booth, have observed that a deconstructive reading "is plainly and simply parasitical" on what Abrams calls "the obvious or univocal meaning" (Abrams 457–58). In other words, there would be no deconstructors if critics did not already exist who can see and show central and definite meanings in texts. Miller responded in an essay entitled "The Critic as Host," in which he not only deconstructed the oppositional hierarchy (host/parasite), but also the two terms themselves, showing that each derives from two definitions meaning nearly opposite things. *Host* means "hospitable welcomer" and "military horde." *Parasite* originally had a positive connotation; in Greek, *parasitos* meant "beside the grain" and referred to a friendly guest. Finally, Miller suggests, the words *parasite* and *host* are inseparable, depending on one another for their meaning in a given work, much as do hosts and parasites, authors and critics, structuralists and poststructuralists.

In the essay that follows, Patricia S. Yaeger questions the views of critics who maintain that Edna Pontellier's adultery challenges the laws of patriarchy in a revolutionary way. Rather, Yaeger argues, "Edna Pontellier falls in love with Robert Lebrun precisely because this possiblility is inscribed within her, because adulterous desire is covertly regarded in her society as a path for woman's misconduct: such desire continues to involve an obsessional valorization of the masculine." Thus, according to Yaeger, *The Awakening* is *not* "subversive" and "emancipatory" in the way critics think of it as being.

Rather, Yaeger claims, the novel's real transgressive force lies in Chopin's "representation of a language Edna . . . seeks but does not possess." Offering an emancipatory alternative to the constrained, objectifying language of society that cuts off and shapes women's speech, this language beyond language is figured by the "amalgam of English and Creole" with which *The Awakening* begins and, more particularly, by the language of the parrot referred to in the novel's opening pages. For "the parrot mixes modes of speech at random; its polyvocal discourse directs our attention to a potential lack of meaning in words themselves – to a register of meaning beyond the reach of its language."

The parrot's language, Yaeger goes on to argue, is fundamentally *metonymic*. At once idiomatic and highly charged, it at the same time seems to be "empty speech"; grounded in associations that seem purely arbitrary, it is a "language which nobody understood." The parrot's language represents, in Yaeger's view, a possible alternative language for women, a language Edna Pontellier betrays in her last speech to her lover, a speech in which she "name[s] Lebrun as author of her growth, as source of her awakening. For what this last speech denies," Yaeger writes, "is the essential strangeness of Edna's initial self-consciousness, the tantalizing world of unvoiced dreams and ideas that Edna encounters at the novel's inception. By the end of the novel Edna has drifted into a system of self-explanation that – while it seems to account for her experience – also falsifies that experience by giving it the gloss of coherence, of a continuous narrative line."

Yaeger's essay is deconstructive insofar as it takes an accepted, binary opposition (fidelity/infidelity) and shows how both terms, in fact, describe culturally acceptable forms of behavior for women; insofar as it suggests that coherent accounts of ourselves and our experiences are, in fact, also incoherent falsification; and, perhaps, insofar as it posits the possibility of a language that contradicts our usual definitions of language. In imagining, via the text, the possibility of a language that does not pretend its literal terms are symbolic, that does not insist that its metonyms are Truth-telling metaphors – and that seems, from the point of view of the cultural norm, to be no more meaningful than a parrot's – Yaeger suggests the presence of an element in *The Awakening* far more subversive than that of Edna's adultery, namely, a threateningly contrapuntal "linguistic counterplot which glitters through the text with dis-articulate meaning."

Because Yaeger associates this un-language of "the unspoken, the unsayable," with women – women who often find themselves beyond the bounds of sayable literal or symbolic language – her essay could conceivably be identified as feminist. It does after all, seem to posit hope in the fact that women may ultimately have access to a liberating medium.

Furthermore, by referring to Theodor Adorno's criticism, Yaeger reveals a sympathetic familiarity with Marxist criticism that is somewhat uncommon among so-called deconstructors.

Finally, though, Yaeger's essay is more deconstructionist than feminist or Marxist because its focus tends to be more on the opposition between languages and discourses than on the reform of discourse by another. To put this another way: Yaeger's essay, which ends by analyzing Edna's final and uncomprehended address to Lebrun, is mainly about the not knowing, not understanding, that Western culture tends to hide. It views Chopin's novel as a text that "asks us to become aware of disjunctions between the disorder of words and the social order, between our usual perceptions and the world these perceptions are designed to organize." *The Awakening*, as viewed by Yaeger, "forces us to discover a universe that is anomalous, asynchronic, confusing," a world "outrageously unthinkable" in the language in which we usually think.

Ross C Murfin

DECONSTRUCTION: A SELECTED BIBLIOGRAPHY

Deconstruction, Poststructuralism, and Structuralism: Introductions, Guides, and Surveys

Arac, Jonathan, Wlad Godzich, and Wallace Martin, eds. *The Yale Critics: Deconstruction in America.* Minneapolis: U of Minnesota P, 1983. See especially the essays by Bové, Godzich, Pease, and Corngold.

Berman, Art. *From the New Criticism to Deconstruction: The Reception of Structuralism and Post-Structuralism.* Urbana: U of Illinos P, 1988.

Cain, William E. "Deconstruction in America: The Recent Literary Criticism of J. Hillis Miller." *College English* 41 (1979): 367–82.

Culler, Jonathan. *On Deconstruction: Theory and Criticism After Structuralism.* Ithaca: Cornell UP, 1982.

———. *Structuralist Poetics: Structuralism, Linguistics and the Study of Literature.* Ithaca: Cornell UP, 1975. See especially ch. 10.

Jefferson, Ann. "Structuralism and Post Structuralism." *Modern Literary Theory: A Comparative Introduction.* Totowa: Barnes, 1982. 84–112.

Leitch, Vincent B. *Deconstructive Criticism: An Advanced Introduction and Survey.* New York: Columbia UP, 1983.

Melville, Stephen W. *Philosophy Beside Itself: On Deconstruction and Modernism.* Theory and History of Literature 27. Minneapolis: U of Minnesota P, 1986.

Norris, Christopher. *Deconstruction and the Interests of Theory.* Oklahoma Project for Discourse and Theory 4. Norman: U of Oklahoma P, 1989.

———. *Deconstruction: Theory and Practice.* London: Methuen, 1982.

Raval, Suresh. *Metacriticism.* Athens: U of Georgia P, 1981.

Scholes, Robert. *Structuralism in Literature: An Introduction.* New Haven: Yale UP, 1974.

Selected Works by Jacques Derrida

Derrida, Jacques. *Dissemination.* 1972. Trans. Barbara Johnson. Chicago: U of Chicago P, 1981. See especially the concise, incisive "Translator's Introduction," which provides a useful point of entry into this work and others by Derrida.

———. *Of Grammatology.* Trans. Gayatri C. Spivak. Baltimore: Johns Hopkins UP, 1976. Trans. of *De la grammatologie.* 1967.

———. *Speech and Phenomena, and Other Essays on Husserl's Theory of Signs.* 1973. Trans. David B. Allison. Evanston: Northwestern UP, 1978.

———. *Writing and Difference.* 1967. Trans. Alan Bass. Chicago: U of Chicago P, 1978.

Poststructuralist Essays on Language and Literature

Barthes, Roland. *S/Z.* Trans. Richard Miller. New York: Hill, 1974. In this influential work, Barthes turns from a structuralist to a poststructuralist approach.

Bloom, Harold, et al., eds. *Deconstruction and Criticism.* New York: Seabury, 1979. Includes Miller's "The Critic as Host." Also see the essays by Bloom, de Man, Derrida, and Hartman.

de Man, Paul. *Allegories of Reading.* New Haven: Yale UP, 1979. See pt. I ("Rhetoric"), especially ch. 1 ("Semiology and Rhetoric").

———. *Blindness and Insight.* New York: Oxford UP, 1971. Minneapolis: U of Minnesota P, 1983. The 1983 edition contains essays not included in the original edition.

Johnson, Barbara. *The Critical Difference: Essays in the Contemporary Rhetoric of Reading.* Baltimore: Johns Hopkins UP, 1980.

Miller, J. Hillis. "Ariadne's Thread: Repetition and the Narrative Line." *Critical Inquiry* 3 (1976): 57–77.

———. Introduction. *Bleak House.* By Charles Dickens. Ed. Norman Page. Harmondsworth: Penguin, 1971. 11–34.

———. *Fiction and Repetition: Seven English Novels.* Cambridge: Harvard UP, 1982.

———. "*Heart of Darkness* Revisited." *Joseph Conrad, "Heart of Darkness."* Ed. Ross C Murfin. Case Studies in Contemporary Criticism Series. Boston: Bedford–St. Martin's, 1989. 209–24.

———. "Stevens' Rock and Criticism as Cure." *The Georgia Review* 30 (1976): 5–31, 330–48.

Deconstruction and *The Awakening*

Delbanco, Andrew. "The Half-Life of Edna Pontellier." *New Essays on "The Awakening."* Ed. Wendy Martin. New York: Cambridge UP, 1988. 89–107.

Other Work Referred to in "What Is Deconstruction?"

Abrams, M. H. "Rationality and the Imagination in Cultural History." *Critical Inquiry* 2 (1976): 447–64.

A DECONSTRUCTIONIST PERSPECTIVE

PATRICIA S. YAEGER

"A Language Which Nobody Understood": Emancipatory Strategies in *The Awakening*

Despite the academy's growing commitment to producing and publishing feminist interpretations of literary texts, insofar as feminist critics read Kate Chopin's *The Awakening* as a novel about sexual liberation, we read it with our patriarchal biases intact. Of course *The Awakening*'s final scene is breathtaking; Edna Pontellier transcends her circumscribed status as sensual entity—as the object of others' desires—and stands before us as her own subject, as a blissfully embodied being: ". . . she cast the unpleasant, pricking garments from her, and for the first time in her life she stood naked in the open air, at the mercy of the sun, the breeze that beat upon her, and the waves that invited her" (136). It is because of this new dignity and visibility Chopin gives to women's desires that *The Awakening* has been celebrated as one of the great subversive novels—a novel belonging to the tradition of transgressive narratives Tony Tanner describes in *Adultery in the Novel.* But in this essay I will suggest that Tanner's ideas are inadequate to account for the real transgressive force of Chopin's novel. Instead, I want to locate this force in Chopin's representation of a language Edna Pontellier seeks but does not possess, in her representation of "a language which nobody understood."

In *Adultery in the Novel* Tanner explains that eighteenth- and nineteenth-century novels derive a "narrative urgency" from their power to interrupt the status quo by representing characters or ideas which impinge on society's stability. While most bourgeois novels affirm marriage, the nuclear family, or genealogical continuity as the source of social stability, these same novels gather momentum by representing "an energy that threatens to contravene that stability of the family on which society depends": an energy frequently embodied in the adulterous woman (4). While prostitutes, orphans, adventurers, and other marginal characters dominate the early phases of the novel and disrupt its representations of family stability with a raw transgressive force, Tanner suggests that in the novel's later incarnations this same energy is embodied in the motive or act of adultery. "Marriage, to put it at its simplest . . . is a means by which society attempts to bring into harmonious alignment patterns of passion and patterns of property" (15).

According to Tanner, marriage and adultery are central to the bourgeois novel because marriage mediates between the opposed demands of private desire and public law.

> If society depends for its existence on certain rules governing what may be combined and what should be kept separate, then adultery, by bringing the wrong things together in the wrong places (or the wrong people in the wrong beds), offers an attack on those rules, revealing them to be arbitrary rather than absolute. (13)

This is a fine observation, and resembles the critique Edna Pontellier applies to her husband and children while contemplating suicide. But Edna's critique of her position within the nuclear family, her sense of herself as someone who should not be regarded as her husband's or children's property, is only a part of her story: her realization does not begin to explain the forces in her society that resist critique. While the adulterous impulses of the novelistic heroine challenge one form of patriarchy, I want to suggest that they enhance another: the power of woman's "extramarital" desire does not have the revolutionary power Tanner predicates.

Obsessed with the other, murdered, ostracized, or killed by her own hand, the adulterous woman is caught in an elaborate code that has already been negotiated by her society. Her actions may be defined as abnormal, but they are only mildly transgressive; adultery remains well within the arena of permissible social trespass. Edna Pontellier falls in love with Robert Lebrun precisely because this possibility is inscribed within her, because adulterous desire is covertly regarded in her society as a path for woman's misconduct: such desire continues to involve an obsessional valorization of the masculine.

> Edna often wondered at one propensity which sometimes had inwardly disturbed her. . . . At a very early age . . . she remembered that she had been passionately enamored of a dignified and sad-eyed cavalry officer who visited her father in Kentucky. She could not leave his presence when he was there, nor remove her eyes from his face, which was something like Napoleon's. (36)

Participating in the bourgeois family is one expression of the romantic obsession that shapes and destroys the bourgeois heroine. Participating in licentious desire for a man other than her husband is simply another. At the Pontelliers' dinner party early in the novel we can see how this desire remains within the schema of approved social narratives:

> The Colonel, with little sense of humor and of the fitness of things, related a somber episode of those dark and bitter days, in which he had acted a conspicuous part and always formed a central figure. Nor was the Doctor happier in his selection, when he told the old, ever new and curious story of the waning of a woman's love, seeking strange, new channels, only to return to its legitimate source after days of fierce unrest. It was one of the many little human documents which had been unfolded to him during his long career as a physician. The story did not seem especially to impress Edna. (90)

With his generous construction of what is and is not "legitimate," the doctor has told a story in Tanner's "New Testament tradition." According to Tanner, Christ is the ideal narrator, the narrator who, when "confronted with the woman taken in adultery," tries to make the "would-be lawgivers aware of her problematical reality, calling into question both the impersonal application of the law and the justification and rights of the would-be legislators. Effectively this implies the disintegration of society-as-constituted" (14). But what else might it imply? Christ, despite his distinct "femininity," and Mandelet, despite his generosity, still claim jural power by virtue of their gender; their acts and judgments do not imply "the disintegration of society as constituted," but rather its "fatherly" reformation, since these paternal figures define—if not society's center—then its gentlemanly margins. In their "generous" revisions of law we find the same plot transferred to another patriarchal economy. Neither Christ nor Dr. Mandelet suggests a revision of the traditional heterosexual plot which, while it may or may not involve marriage, always involves a hierarchical reading of woman's relation to man.

Tanner has more to say; he argues that even "without anything or anyone necessarily having changed place or roles (in social terms), the action of adultery portends the possible breakdown of all the mediations on which society itself depends, and demonstrates the latent impossibility of participating in the interrelated patterns that comprise its structure" (17). This apocalyptic view of transgression is appealing, but wrong. For Edna, the thought or practice of adultery seems revolutionary but is actually a conservative gesture within the larger scheme of things, another mode of social acquiescence. The most radical act of trespass Chopin's novel describes is not Edna's propensity to fall in love, or even the way she acts after falling, but the fact that she is disturbed by her own obsessions.

Before her romance with Lebrun intervenes, Chopin's novel holds Edna's awakening open for us as an extraordinary event that Chopin refuses to attach—except peripherally—to Lebrun until we have witnessed Edna's preliminary attempts at self-dialogue and self-knowledge. We should therefore take exception to Tanner's paradigm, his notion that adultery

> introduces an agonizing and irresolvable category—confusion—into the individual and thence into society itself. . . . If society depends for its existence on certain rules governing what may be combined and what should be kept separate, then adultery, by bringing the wrong things together in the wrong places (or the wrong people in the wrong beds), offers an attack on those rules, revealing them to be arbitrary rather than absolute. In this way, the adulterous woman becomes the "gap" in society that gradually

> extends through it. In attempting to ostracize her, society moves toward ostracizing itself. (12–13)

Society may read itself through the absence of the adulterous woman, but she, being absent, cannot read herself. It is the absence of such critique and not the absence of adultery that allows the maintenance of a sex/gender system that remains repressive and hierarchical and victimizes women by making them not only wives, but objects of romantic or domestic narratives. *The Awakening*'s most radical awareness is that Edna inhabits a world of limited linguistic possibilities, of limited possibilities for interpreting and reorganizing her feelings, and therefore of limited possibilities for action. In Edna's world, what sorts of things are open to question and what things are not? Although Edna initially attempts to move into an arena in which she can begin to explore feelings which lie outside the prescribed social code, finally she can only think about herself within that code, can only act within some permutation of the subject-object relations her society has ordained for her.

If this is so, can we still define *The Awakening* as one of the grand subversive novels, as a novel belonging to a great tradition of emancipatory fiction? We can make such claims for *The Awakening* only if Chopin has been successful in inventing a novelistic structure in which the heroine's very absence of speech works productively, in which Edna's silence offers a new dialogic ground from which we can measure the systematic distortions of her old ground of being and begin to construct a new, utopian image of the emergence of women's antithetical desires. Does Chopin's novel offer such utopian structures?

"She had put her head down on Madame Ratignolle's shoulder. She was flushed and felt intoxicated with the sound of her own voice and the unaccustomed taste of candor. It muddled her like wine, or like a first breath of freedom" (37). What are the conditions that permit Edna to feel intoxicated with the sound of her own voice, to experience this "unaccustomed taste of candor" in conversation with a friend? These feelings are customary, this rapture quite ordinary, in fictions by men. "The earth is all before me," Wordsworth insists in *The Prelude*. "With a heart / Joyous, nor scared at its own liberty, / I look about; and should the chosen guide / Be nothing better than a wandering cloud, / I cannot miss my way. I breathe again!" We know, of course, that Wordsworth has it wrong, that he has miles to go before he discovers anything remotely resembling liberty. Intoxicated by his own voice, thrilled at the prospect of articulate freedom, Wordsworth still claims prophetic powers; he permits his mind to wander and releases his voice to those "trances of thought and mountings of the mind" which hurry toward him. This makes gorgeous poetry, but for whom does it speak? Such moments are rarely recorded by women writers either on their own behalf or on behalf of their fictional heroines. In the scene in *The Awakening* where Edna returns to the beach from her unearthly swim, it is Robert Lebrun who speaks for her, who frames and articulates the meaning of her adventure, and the plot he invents involves a mystical, masculine sea-spirit responsible for Edna's sense of elation, as if romance were the only form of elation a heroine might feel. Edna repudiates Robert's story: "'Don't banter me,' she said, wounded at what appeared to be his flippancy" (48). And yet Robert's metaphors quickly become Edna's own:

> Sailing across the bay to the *Chênière Caminada*, Edna felt as if she were being borne away from some anchorage which had held her fast, whose chains had been loosening—had snapped the night before when the mystic spirit was abroad, leaving her free to drift whithersoever she chose to set her sails. Robert spoke to her incessantly. . . . (53)

The tension between Edna's imagined freedom and Robert's incessant speech is palpable, but unlike the speech of Edna's husband, Robert's words invite dialogue: "'I'll take you some night in the pirogue when the moon shines. Maybe your Gulf spirit will whisper to you in which of these islands and treasures are hidden—direct you to the very spot, perhaps,' 'And in a day we should be rich!' she laughed. 'I'd give it all to you, the pirate gold and every bit of treasure we could dig up'" (54). Not only is Robert's vision one that Edna can participate in and help create, but it is also like a fairy tale: romantic, enticing, utopian. As a "utopia," Robert's vision is not at all emancipatory; it offers only the flip side, the half-fulfilled wishes of an everyday ideology.

> "How many years have I slept?" she inquired. "The whole island seems changed. A new race of beings must have sprung up, leaving only you and me as past relics. . . ."
>
> He familiarly adjusted a ruffle upon her shoulder.
>
> "You have slept precisely one hundred years. I was left here to guard your slumbers; for one hundred years I have been out under the shed reading a book. The only evil I couldn't prevent was to keep a broiled fowl from drying up." (57)

This comic repartee is charming: as Michel Foucault explains in *The Order of Things*, utopias afford us special consolation.

> Although they have no real locality there is nevertheless a fantastic, untroubled region in which they are able to unfold; they open up . . . countries where life is easy, even though the road to them is chimerical. . . . This is why utopias permit fables and discourse: they run with the very grain of language and are part of the fundamental dimension of the *fabula*. (xviii)

What Robert Lebrun offers Edna is a continuing story, a mode of discourse which may be chimerical, but unlike Edna's talk with her husband is also potentially communal. This discourse mode cannot, however, invite its speakers to test the limits of their language; instead, it creates a pleasurable nexus of fancy through which Edna may dream. Freed from the repressive talk of her husband, Edna chooses another mode of oppression, a speech-world that offers space for flirtation that Edna finds liberating. But this liberation is also limiting, a form of stultification, and in exchanging the intoxicating sound of her own voice as she speaks on the beach for Robert's romantic voice, Edna Pontellier's growing sense of self is stabilized, frozen into a mode of feeling and consciousness which, for all its promise of sexual fulfillment, leaves her essentially without resources, without an opportunity for other internal dialogues. We may see *The Awakening* as a novel praising sexual discovery and critiquing the asymmetries of the marriage plot, but we must also recognize that this is a novel in which the heroine's capacities for thought are shut down, a novel in which Edna's temptations to think are repressed by the moody discourse of romance. In fact, the novel's explicitly utopian constructs partake of this romance framework; they do not function trangressively. Does Chopin offer her heroine—or her reader—any emancipatory alternative?

Let us begin to answer this question by considering a moment from Jacques Lacan's essay "From Love to the Libido"—a moment in which Lacan turns upon his audience and denies that we can ever define ourselves through another's language.

> What I, Lacan, . . . am telling you is that the subject as such is uncertain because he is divided by the effects of language. Through the effects of speech, the subject always realizes himself more in the Other, but he is already pursuing there more than half of himself. He will simply find his desire ever more divided, pulverized, in the circumscribable metonymy of speech. (188)

The hearing of a lecture, the writing of a psychoanalytic text, the reading of a novel: these are moments of self-divisiveness, of seeking what we are in that which we are not. It is this drive toward self-realization in the speech of the other that we have begun to discover in *The Awakening*. Chopin's novel focuses from its beginning on the difficulties we have maneuvering within the precincts of language. It opens with an exotic and showy image: "A green and yellow parrot, which hung in a cage outside the door, kept repeating over and over: '*Allez vous-en!! Allez vous-en! Sapristi!* That's all right!'" (19). The parrot's speech is nonsensical, and yet it illuminates its world in an intriguing way. An amalgam of English and Creole, this exotic speech alerts us to the fact that the parrot inhabits a multilingual culture and suggests the babble and lyricism bred by mixing world-views. But in addition to giving us a glimpse of the worlds we will encounter within the larger novel, these opening paragraphs make enigmatic statements about our relation to language itself; they open up an intriguing linguistic matrix.

> Mr. Pontellier, unable to read his newspaper with any degree of comfort, arose with an expression and an exclamation of disgust. He walked down the gallery and across the narrow "bridges" which connected the Lebrun cottages one with the other. . . .
>
> He stopped before the door of his own cottage, which was the fourth one from the main building and next to the last. Seating himself in a wicker rocker which was there, he once more applied himself to the task of reading the newspaper. The day was Sunday; the paper was a day old. (19–20)

In contrast to the giddy plurality of the parrot's speech, Mr. Pontellier's meditations are redundant and single-minded. Chopin asks us to associate his propriety with the backward tug of words which are "a day old" and already emptied of meaning. The parrot, on the other hand, speaks a language emptied of meaning but full of something else. "He could speak a little Spanish, and also a language which nobody understood, unless it was the mocking-bird that hung on the other side of the door, whistling his fluty notes out upon the breeze with maddening persistence" (19). Repetitive, discontinuous, incomprehensible: the speech of this parrot points to an immediate contrast between everyday speech and a more extraordinary speech world. The parrot mixes modes of speech at random; its polyvocal discourse directs our attention to a potential lack of meaning in words themselves—to a register of meaning beyond the reach of its language which is paradoxically articulated in *The Awakening* as "a language which nobody understood."

In reading the parrot's speech we are in the vicinity of what Lacan calls "metonymy":

> A lack is encountered by the subject in the Other, in the very intimation that the Other makes to him by his discourse. In the

> intervals of the discourse of the Other, there emerges in the experience of the child something that is radically mappable, namely, *He is saying this to me, but what does he want?*
>
> In this interval intersecting the signifiers . . . is the locus of what, in other registers of my exposition, I have called metonymy. It is there that what we call desire crawls, slips, escapes, like the ferret. The desire of the Other is apprehended by the subject in that which does not work, in the lacks of the discourse of the Other, and all the child's *whys* reveal not so much an avidity for the reason of things, as a testing of the adult, a *Why are you telling me this?* ever-resuscitated from its base, which is the enigma of the adult's desire. (214)

Reading Chopin's text we find ourselves, from our first overhearing of the parrot's empty speech, in the position of the child who asks "Why?" but unlike the child we can begin to formulate an answer. The register of desire—of something not described within language but premised and promised there—is provided for us in the "empty" referents of the parrot's speech and its highly charged iterations of the mockingbird's song. It is this enigmatic "language" Mr. Pontellier attempts to shun as he navigates his newspaper and the "bridges" connecting the coherent and well-mapped spaces between the cottages. But it is in the unmapped spaces, the spaces between words, the unspoken sites of desire that Edna Pontellier initially resides, and in order to understand how this transgressive impulse is structured into Chopin's novel we need to see that Chopin herself has divided the linguistic topography of *The Awakening* into an extra-linguistic zone of meaning imaged for us at the beginning of the novel in the speech of the parrot (a "language which nobody understood") and a countervailing region of linguistic constraints imaged for us in Mr. Pontellier's speech.

Although Lacan's reading of "metonymy" helps us to identify this linguistic topography, the novel's missing register of language should not be confused with the irrecoverable "lack" that Lacan defines at the heart of discourse, or the psychic dyslexia in which Julia Kristeva says "Woman" resides. Although "the feminine," in Kristeva's early essays, is said to be synonymous with the a-linguistic ("What I mean by 'woman' is that which is not represented, that which is unspoken, that which is left out of namings and ideologies" [166]), I want to suggest that Edna's absent language is not a manifestation of women's permanent expulsion from "masculine speech" but of what Jean-François Lyotard calls "le differend."

Lyotard explains that "in the *differend* something 'asks' to be put into sentences, and suffers the wrong of not being able to be at the moment. . . . It is the concern of a literature, of a philosophy, perhaps of a politics, to testify to these *differends* by finding an idiom for them" (30). Chopin testifies to these *"differends"* by using the metaphor of an absent or displaced vocality ("the voice of the sea," the multivoiced babble of the parrot) to emphasize Edna's need for a more passionate and intersubjective speech that would allow Edna to revise or rearticulate her relations to her own desire and to the social reality that thwarts this desire. This is to argue that *The Awakening* is a text that asks for another idiom to fill in the unspoken voices in Edna's story: an idiom that contemporary women writers and feminist critics have begun to provide. Thus Edna Pontellier speaks an unfinished discourse that reaches out to be completed by other speaking human beings: her "lost" speech—represented by her own speech fragments, by the sibilant voice of the sea and the chatter of the trilingual parrot—is not unfinished on an a-historical, metaphysical plane. Instead, Chopin's displaced metaphors of vocality help us to envision for her heroine a more radical speech situation, a linguistic practice that would reach out to the *"differend,"* to a politics that is not yet a politics, to a language that should be phrased but cannot yet (or could not then) be phrased. In this reading of Chopin's text the emancipatory moments in *The Awakening* do not consist of those instances of adulterous desire that drive Edna toward the transgressive side of the marriage plot. Instead, such emancipatory moments are contained in those unstable instances of self-questioning and dialogue with herself and with other women that the novel's romance plot helps to elide.

Before looking more closely at the way the *"differend"* operates in Chopin's novel, let us consider the moment of Edna's awakening in more detail. On the evening when Edna first begins, consciously, to recognize her powers and wants "to swim far out, where no woman had swum before" (46), her experience is one of multiple moods, of emotions which seem confused and inarticulate: "'A thousand emotions have swept through me to-night. I don't comprehend half of them. . . . I wonder if any night on earth will ever again be like this one. It is like a night in a dream. The people about me are like some uncanny, half-human beings. There must be spirits abroad to-night'" (47–48). Sensing the extraordinary reach of her feelings, Lebrun answers in kind:

> "There are," whispered Robert. "Didn't you know this was the twenty-eighth of August?"

> "The twenty-eighth of August?"
>
> "Yes. On the twenty-eighth of August, at the hour of midnight, and if the moon is shining—the moon must be shining—a spirit that has haunted these shores for ages rises up from the Gulf. With its own penetrating vision the spirit seeks some one mortal worthy to hold him company, worthy of being exalted for a few hours into realms of the semi-celestials. His search has always hitherto been fruitless, and he has sunk back, disheartened, into the sea. But to-night he found Mrs. Pontellier. Perhaps he will never wholly release her from the spell. Perhaps she will never again suffer a poor, unworthy earthling to walk in the shadow of her divine presence." (48)

While Robert Lebrun may have "penetrated her mood," he has also begun to alter its meaning. Edna's experience has been solitary and essentially mysterious; her swim has been a surpassing of limits, a mythic encounter with death—an experience suffused with metaphor, beyond comprehension. Robert's words do not begin to encompass its meaning, but he does attempt to communicate with her, to understand her mood. And since Edna lacks an alternative register of language to describe her tumultuous feelings, Robert's conceit soon becomes her own; his language comes to stand for the nameless feelings she has just begun to experience. Just as Edna's initial awakening, her continuing journey toward self-articulation and self-awareness is initially eccentric and complex, so this journey is finally diminished and divided, reduced in the romantic stories that she is told and the romantic stories she comes to tell herself, to a simplistic narrative that falsifies the diversity of her awakening consciousness. From this perspective, the pivotal event of Chopin's novel is not Edna's suicide, nor her break with her husband, but her openness to Robert Lebrun's stories, her vulnerability to the romantic speech of the other which has, by the end of the novel, become her speech as well:

> "I love you," she whispered, "only you; no one but you. It was you who awoke me last summer out of a life-long, stupid dream. Oh! you have made me so unhappy with your indifference. Oh! I have suffered, suffered! Now you are here we shall love each other, my Robert. We shall be everything to each other. Nothing else in the world is of any consequence. I must go to my friend; but you will wait for me? No matter how late; you will wait for me, Robert?" (130)

Edna's final retelling of her story is not an accurate self-portrait, but a radical betrayal of the "awakening" that emerges at the novel's beginning. This initial "awakening" does not involve the violent triangulation of adultery, romance, and erotic story-telling, but the exploration of a discontinuous series of images that are promisingly feminocentric. In fact, what is disturbing about Edna's last speech to Robert is its falsification of her story, its naming of Lebrun as author of her growth, as source of her awakening. For what this last speech denies is the essential strangeness of Edna's initial self-consciousness, the tantalizing world of unvoiced dreams and ideas that Edna encounters at the novel's inception. By the end of the novel Edna has drifted into a system of self-explanation that—while it seems to account for her experience—also falsifies that experience by giving it the gloss of coherence, of a continuous narrative line. Edna's thoughts at the beginning of the novel are much more confused—but they are also more heterogeneous and promising.

In the opening scenes of *The Awakening* this struggle among different social possibilities, among diverse points of view, fails to take place as explicitly realized dialogue. Even Edna's husband does not have the power to challenge the voices which annoy him, but only "the privilege of quitting their society when they ceased to be entertaining." "The parrot and the mocking-bird were the property of Madame Lebrun," Chopin tells us, "and they had the right to make all the noise they wished" (19). The detail seems trivial, but it is worth noting that just as Mr. Pontellier's reaction to the parrot's nonsensical speech is defined in terms of his relation to the parrot as someone else's possession, so his wife is defined in terms of property relations as well. "'What folly! to bathe at such an hour and in such heat! . . . You are burnt beyond recognition,' he added, looking at his wife as one looks at a valuable piece of personal property which has suffered some damage" (20–21). In Pontellier's linguistic world, the roles of speaker and listener are clearly defined in terms of social and material hierarchies. Edna Pontellier is someone her husband feels free to command and free to define, but she is not someone to whom Mr. Pontellier listens:

> "What is it?" asked Pontellier, looking lazily and amused from one to the other. It was some utter nonsense; some adventure out there in the water, and they both tried to relate it at once. It did not seem half so amusing when told. They realized this, and so did Mr. Pontellier. He yawned and stretched himself. Then he got up, saying he had half a mind to go over to Klein's hotel and play a game of billiards. (21)

When Pontellier—feeling "very talkative"—returns from Klein's hotel late at night, he blithely awakens his wife to converse.

> He talked to her while he undressed, telling her anecdotes and bits of news and gossip that he had gathered during the day. From his trousers pockets he took a fistful of crumpled bank notes and a good deal of silver coin, which he piled on the bureau indiscriminately with keys, knife, handkerchief, and whatever else happened to be in his pockets. (23)

Pontellier expects his words to have the same weight as his silver; the only difference is that he dispenses his language with greater abandon. But Edna Pontellier inhabits a speech-world very different from her husband's, a world oddly bereft of his cultural symbols. "Overcome with sleep," she continues dreaming as he speaks and answers him "with little half utterances." For her husband, Edna's separateness is maddening. Her words, like the words of the parrot Pontellier cannot abide, seem nonsensical; her "little half utterances" suggest a replay of the early morning scene on the beach. But this time the hierarchies are played out in earnest, and Pontellier reacts to his wife's inattention with a burgherlike furor. Nominally concerned for his children, he stalks to their rooms, only to find them inhabiting their own bizarre speech-worlds: "He turned and shifted the youngsters about in bed. One of them began to kick and talk about a basket full of crabs" (23).

While *The Awakening* traces the closure of its own intervals of desire and self-questioning, Chopin is also engaged in the radical mapping of those moments of speech in which our desires begin to address us. If the socio-symbolic world we inhabit encourages us to displace unspoken polyphanies with repetition, with customary stories, with narrative lines, the force of *The Awakening*'s subversive nocturnes, its metonymic intervals, belies the permanence of Pontellier's social forms and suggests a linguistic counterplot which glitters through the text with dis-articulate meaning. The child's response throws his father's patriarchal assumptions into even higher relief when Pontellier responds to his son's "utter nonsense" by chiding his wife: "Mr. Pontellier returned to his wife with the information that Raoul had a high fever and needed looking after. . . . He reproached his wife with her inattention, her habitual neglect of the children. If it was not a mother's place to look after children, whose on earth was it?" (24). When Pontellier uses his power of speech to awaken his wife and to define her, Edna answers with deliberate silence. But when Pontellier drifts off to sleep, this silence loses its power. "Turning, she thrust her face, steaming and wet, into the bend of her arm, and she went on crying there, not caring any longer to dry her face, her eyes, her arms. She could not have told why she was crying." What is remarkable about this episode is Chopin's emphasis on the unspoken, the unsayable:

> An indescribable oppression, which seemed to generate in some unfamiliar part of her consciousness, filled her whole being with a vague anguish. It was like a shadow, like a mist passing across her soul's summer day. It was strange and unfamiliar; it was a mood. She did not sit there inwardly upbraiding her husband, lamenting at Fate, which had directed her footsteps to the path which they had taken. She was just having a good cry all to herself. The mosquitoes made merry over her, biting her firm, round arms and nipping at her bare insteps. (24–25)

The oppression Edna feels is not merely "indescribable" and "vague," it also comes from an "unfamiliar" region of consciousness and can only be described through analogy. Edna's mood closes as swiftly as it has opened: "The little stinging, buzzing imps succeeded in dispelling a mood which might have held her there in the darkness half a night longer" (25). The biting mosquitoes add an ominous note and operate upon Edna like her husband's alien language; it is as if their determined orality forecloses on Edna's own right to speak.

In the morning the talk between wife and husband is amicably re-established through an economic transaction: "Mr. Pontellier gave his wife half the money which he had brought away from Klein's hotel the evening before" (25). When Mr. Pontellier responds with the appropriate cultural symbols, Edna is trapped as she was in her conversations with Robert; she can only voice gratitude. "'It will buy a handsome wedding present for Sister Janet!' she exclaimed, smoothing out the bills as she counted them one by one. 'Oh! we'll treat Sister Janet better than that, my dear,' he laughed, as he prepared to kiss her good-by" (25). This happiness continues when Mr. Pontellier returns to New Orleans. The medium of this continued harmony is something oral or edible, something, like language, that Edna can put in her mouth:

> A few days later a box arrived for Mrs. Pontellier from New Orleans. It was from her husband. It was filled with *friandises*, with luscious and toothsome bits—the finest of fruits, *patés*, a rare bottle or two, delicious syrups, and bonbons in abundance.
>
> Mrs. Pontellier was always very generous with the contents of such a box; she was quite used to receiving them when away from home. The *patés* and fruits were brought to the dining-room; the bonbons were passed around. And the ladies, selecting with dainty and discriminating fingers and a little greedily, all declared

> that Mr. Pontellier was the best husband in the world. Mrs. Pontellier was forced to admit that she knew of none better. (25–26)

Chopin's description of Edna's acquiescence, her praise of her husband, is edged with an undeclared violence; Edna is "forced to admit" what she does not feel. But what else could she say? "Mr. Pontellier was a great favorite, and ladies, men, and children, even nurses, were always on hand to say good-by to him. His wife stood smiling and waving, the boys shouting, as he disappeared in the old rockaway down the sandy road" (25). Edna has no words for describing her intricate feelings, and if she did, who would listen? She could only speak in a private "language which nobody understood, unless it was the mocking-bird that hung on the other side of the door, whistling his fluty notes out upon the breeze . . . (19).

In her essay on *The Awakening* [also reprinted in this volume], Cynthia Griffin Wolff argues that Edna's central problem is psychological, that once her "hidden self" has begun "to exert its inexorable power" we can see that Edna's "libidinal appetite has been fixated at the oral level" (208). I have begun, in contrast, to suggest that Edna's problem is linguistic and social, that her "orality" is frustrated, exacerbated by her social milieu. Wolff insists on the correspondence between Edna's "preoccupation with nourishment" and an infantile, "orally destructive self, a limitless void whose needs can be filled, finally, only by total fusion with the outside world, a totality of sensuous enfolding" (208, 211). She explains that this totality "means annihilation of the ego." But we have seen that Edna's need for fusion, her preoccupation with nourishment or oral surfeiting, does not arise from Edna's own infantility but from social prescription. Married to a Creole, Edna does not feel at home in his society, and she feels especially ill at ease with the Creole manner of speech. If the gap between Creole and Anglo-American cultures gives Edna a glimpse of the inadequacies of each, Edna's inability to deal fluently in the language her husband and lovers speak remains a sign of her disempowerment. As she sails across the bay with Robert to the *Chênière Caminada*, he flirts with a "young barefooted Spanish girl" named Mariequita. Mariequita is coy and flirtatious; she teases Lebrun and asks him sweet, ribald questions:

> Edna liked it all. She looked Mariequita up and down, from her ugly brown toes to her pretty black eyes, and back again.
>
> "Why does she look at me like that?" inquired the girl of Robert.
>
> "Maybe she thinks you are pretty. Shall I ask her?"

> "No. Is she your sweetheart?"
> "She's a married lady, and has two children."
> "Oh! well! Francisco ran away with Sylvano's wife, who had four children. They took all his money and one of the children and stole his boat."
> "Shut up!"
> "Does she understand?"
> "Oh, hush!" (52–53)

The scene is gay, but Mariequita's questions are filled with foreboding. Robert's knowledge of several languages, his power to control what others hear and speak, is a sign of his "right" to preside in a context where "no one present understood what they said" (52).

In a conversation with Alcée Arobin later in the novel we see how the paths for women's self-expression are continually limited. As Edna begins to explore her own deviance from social codes, Alcée Arobin usurps her role as story-teller; he begins to define her himself:

> "One of these days," she said, "I'm going to pull myself together for a while and think—try to determine what character of a woman I am; for, candidly, I don't know. By all the codes which I am acquainted with, I am a devilishly wicked specimen of the sex. But some way I can't convince myself that I am. I must think about it."
> "Don't. What's the use? Why should you bother thinking about it when I can tell you what manner of woman you are." His fingers strayed occasionally down to her warm, smooth cheeks and firm chin, which was growing a little full and double. (103)

The text moves from an emphasis on Edna's power of thought and speech to an emphasis on her erotic power, her flesh, as Arobin reasserts the old codes and "feeds" her with stories. Earlier in the novel Adèle Ratignolle is similarly primed. Counseling Robert Lebrun to leave Mrs. Pontellier alone, Madame Ratignolle is rebuked for her efforts to speak: "'It isn't pleasant to have a woman tell you—'" Robert Lebrun interrupts, "unheedingly, but breaking off suddenly: 'Now if I were like Arobin—you remember Alcée Arobin and that story of the consul's wife at Biloxi?'" Lebrun's speech operates not only as a form of entertainment, but as a form of repression. "And he related the story of Alcée Arobin and the consul's wife; and another about the tenor of the French Opera, who received letters which should never have been written; and still other stories, grave and gay, till Mrs. Pontellier and her possible propensity for taking young men seriously was apparently forgotten" (38–39). Lebrun dismisses Madame Ratignolle's concern for

Edna and reminds us that the women in Chopin's novel taste little if any verbal freedom. Visiting the Ratignolles, Edna observes that

> the Ratignolles understood each other perfectly. If ever the fusion of two human beings into one has been accomplished on this sphere it was surely in their union. . . .
>
> Monsieur Ratignolle . . . spoke with an animation and earnestness that gave an exaggerated importance to every syllable he uttered. His wife was keenly interested in everything he said, laying down her fork the better to listen, chiming in, taking the words out of his mouth. (75–76)

If Edna "is remarkably vulnerable to feelings of being invaded and overwhelmed," if, as Wolff insists, "she is very much at the mercy of her environment," this is because her environment is invasive and overwhelming, not only limiting her self-expression to acts of eating, but also rewarding women who, like Madame Ratignolle, are dutifully "delicious" in their roles, who put men's words in their mouths, who have "eaten" their husbands' language.

We have established that *The Awakening* revolves around the heroine's limiting life in the courts of romance and describes, as well, a frightening antagonism between a feminine subject and the objectifying world of discourse she inhabits. "The letter was on the bookshelf. It possessed the greatest interest and attraction for Edna; the envelope, its size and shape, the post-mark, the handwriting. She examined every detail of the outside before opening it" (66). What men say, what they write grows more and more portentous, and the cumulative weight of their saying is often the same: "There was no special message to Edna except a postscript saying that if Mrs. Pontellier desired to finish the book which he had been reading to her, his mother would find it in his room, among other books there on the table" (66). The world of alien discourse seems omnipresent in the novel, and when Edna tries to make her own mark, her efforts are fruitless. "Once she stopped, and taking off her wedding ring, flung it upon the carpet. When she saw it lying there, she stamped her heel upon it, striving to crush it. But her small boot heel did not make an indenture, not a mark upon the little glittering circlet" (72). In frustration Edna seizes a glass vase and flings it to the hearth. "She wanted to destroy something. The crash and clatter were what she wanted to hear" (72). If *The Awakening* can be defined as an emancipatory text, if it voices a conflict between men's speech and the speaking of women, this is a conflict articulated as a struggle between men's normative language and something unvoiced and enigmatic—a clatter, a "language which nobody understood." Edna's anger is speechless; her gesture all but impotent, for when a maid sidles into the room to clean up the glass she rediscovers her mistress's cast-off ring: "Edna held out her hand, and taking the ring, slipped it upon her finger" (72).

It is, in fact, only women of property like Madame Lebrun, the owner of the summer resort where the Pontelliers are staying, or artists like Mademoiselle Reisz who have the power of public expression. But Mademoiselle Reisz (who would seem, initially, to offer Edna another model for female selfhood) is surprisingly complicitous in limiting Edna's options. We find the strongest image of her complicity midway through the novel when she hands Edna the letter from Robert and asks Edna to read it while Mademoiselle Reisz plays heartrending music. "Edna did not know when the Impromptu began or ended. She sat on the sofa corner reading Robert's letter by the fading light." As Edna reads, Mademoiselle plays like a manic cupid, gliding "from the Chopin into the quivering lovenotes of Isolde's song, and back again to the Impromptu with its soulful and poignant longing" (84). The music grows fantastic; it fills the room, and Edna begins to sob "as she had wept one midnight at Grand Isle when strange, new voices awoke in her." Now she hears one voice only and this voice has an oppressive material weight. "Mademoiselle reëntered and lit a candle. Robert's letter was on the floor. She stopped and picked it up. It was crumpled and damp with tears. Mademoiselle smoothed the letter out, restored it to the envelope, and replaced it in the table drawer" (84). Like Mr. Pontieller's crumpled bank notes and small change, the letter has come to possess its own objectivity, its own material power. But if this is a letter that Mademoiselle Reisz can exchange for the pleasure of Edna's visit, it also represses her particular sonority. Mademoiselle Reisz's music is replaced by Robert's tune: "Robert's voice was not pretentious. It was musical and true. The voice, the notes, the whole refrain haunted her memory" (60).

The speech of the masculine "other" becomes for Edna Pontellier and the women of her society, an arena of self-loss and inner divisiveness. Madame Lebrun's expressions, like Edna's, remain vestigial, enigmatic. Her sewing machine echoes the "clatter" of Edna's broken vase.

> "I have a letter somewhere," looking in the machine drawer and finding the letter in the bottom of the work-basket. "He says to tell you he will be in Vera Cruz the beginning of next month"—clatter, clatter!—"and if you still have the intention of joining him"—bang! clatter, clatter, bang!

> "Why didn't you tell me so before, mother? You know I wanted—" Clatter, clatter, clatter! (41)

If Madame Lebrun does not possess Alcée Arobin's power of definition, she does possess his power of interruption, and the noise of her sewing machine half-prepares us for her jibe at her younger son: "Really, this table is getting to be more and more like Bedlam every day, with everybody talking at once. Sometimes—I hope God will forgive me—but positively, sometimes I wish Victor would lose the power of speech" (48).

Translated into the language of the other, Edna's own story fails to materialize. But what might it have looked like? What is the rhythm and content of Edna's speech when she is neither speaking like her father or lover nor to him? First, we have seen that Chopin plays with the hiatus between the stories Edna inherits and what, in Edna, is heterogeneous to these stories, but is not bound by them. In *The Awakening,* a story or framing device is frequently set against a "remainder" or supplement of meaning not encompassed within that frame. This remainder, this "excess" of meaning represents a *"differend"* which challenges the framing story's totalizing power, its explanatory validity. (Theodor Adorno puts this another way in his *Negative Dialectics:* "A matter of urgency to the concept would be what it fails to cover, what its abstractionist mechanism eliminates, what is not already a case of the concept" [8].) It is never a question of Edna's transcendence of local mythology, but rather of a negative and dialectical play between myth and that which resists mythic closure:

> "Of whom—of what are you thinking?" asked Adèle of her companion. . . .
>
> "Nothing," returned Mrs. Pontellier, with a start, adding at once: "How stupid! But it seems to me it is the reply we make instinctively to such a question. Let me see . . . I was really not conscious of thinking of anything; but perhaps I can retrace my thoughts."
>
> "Oh! never mind!" laughed Madame Ratignolle. "I am not quite so exacting. . . . It is really too hot to think, especially to think about thinking." (34)

Clearly Adèle Ratignolle's dislike of "thinking" is normative in Edna's society and acts as near-absolute rule. But Edna ventures into areas of the mind that are not well mapped, into memories excluded from Adèle Ratignolle's cultural typology. And in thinking of "Nothing," something old and familiar emerges:

> "But for the fun of it," persisted Edna. "First of all, the sight of the water stretching so far away, those motionless sails against the blue sky, made a delicious picture that I just wanted to sit and look at. The hot wind beating in my face made me think—without any connection that I can trace—of a summer day in Kentucky, of a meadow that seemed as big as the ocean to the very little girl walking through the grass. . . . She threw out her arms as if swimming when she walked, beating the tall grass as one strikes out in the water. Oh, I see the connection now!"
>
> "Where were you going that day in Kentucky, walking through the grass?" . . .
>
> "Likely as not it was Sunday," she laughed; "and I was running away from prayers, from the Presbyterian service, read in a spirit of gloom by my father that chills me yet to think of." (34–35)

As practitioners of free association and students of Freud we may see little that is remarkable in Edna's response. But this is to underestimate the radical quality of her awareness, to dismiss its acrobatic integrity. It is as if Chopin is aware, as Edna is only naively, that the mind wants to go beyond itself, to go toward extremes, to test the accuracy of its own boundaries. Even as the social order demands a closing of ranks—a synthesis or yoking together of disparate ideas in such a way that their disparity grows invisible—the individual has the capacity to challenge her own syntactic boundaries. Edna's talks with Madame Ratignolle present us with a radical example of thought as disconnection, or Edna's capacity to separate ideas from one context to pursue them in another. This is the precondition for dialectic, the capacity for critique that G. W. F. Hegel defines in his *Phenomenology:*

> The activity of dissolution is the power and work of the *Understanding,* the most astonishing and mightiest of powers, or rather the absolute power. The circle that remains self-enclosed and, like substance, holds its moments together, is an immediate relationship, one therefore which has nothing astonishing about it. But that an accident as such, detached from what circumscribes it, what is bound and is actual only in its context with others, should attain an existence of its own and a separate freedom—this is the tremendous power of the negative; it is the energy of thought, of the pure "I." (18–19)

What does this "power of the negative" mean for Edna, and what does it do for her? The images she conjures up seem aimless and accidental, beyond further synthesis, beyond dialectic. But this is precisely their virtue.

In escaping her father's old sermons, Edna strikes out into new physical space; she veers toward an arena of free feeling not designated by the paterfamilias. Similarly, in walking to the beach, Adèle Ratignolle and Edna have slipped momentarily outside the zone of paternal definition. "In some unaccountable way they had escaped from Robert," Chopin explains (32). The problem, of course, is that their escape is literally unaccountable, that outside the other's language they enter the arena of "Nothing," of a language which nobody speaks. And yet in talking with Adèle Ratignolle, Edna begins to see connections she has not seen before; her thoughts become unsystematic—they go forward before going astray. "Thought," as Maire Jaanus Kurrik suggests, "must admit that it is not only cogency but play, that it is random and can go astray, and can only go forward because it can go astray. Thought has an unshielded and open aspect, which is unsystematic, and which traditional philosophy has repressed for fear of chaos" (221). She adds that thought must "abdicate its idea of hegemony and autarky, and practice a disenchantment of the concept, its transcendence," if it is to challenge its own preconceptions (221). Edna is not so self-conscious about the nature of her thinking, but as her mind plays over the past in a random and heterodox fashion, we can recognize in her thoughts the potential disenchantment of the concept that most binds her, the concept of an obsessive attachment to men, of a romantic and excessive bondage to fatherlike figures. The image of the beloved cavalry officer that Edna remembers is followed by a series of images or memories of men who have "haunted" Edna's imagination and "stirred" her senses. These broken images come to her not as images of love, but as sources of puzzlement, disaffection, and wonder. Edna is open to thinking about the mystery of her affections; she notes in past amours an obsessive quality that demands perusal.

But something prevents Edna from thinking further, from becoming fully aware of the conditions which bind her. In this instance the conversation between Edna and Adèle is interrupted; as they converse on the beach their voices are blurred by "the sound of approaching voices. It was Robert, surrounded by a troop of children, searching for them" (37). Unable to continue their conversation, interrupted in the very moment when Edna had begun to feel "intoxicated with the sound of her own voice. . . . The women at once rose and began to shake out their draperies and relax their muscles," and Madame Ratignolle begins to lean "draggingly" on Robert's arm as they walk home (37–38).

Thought should, perhaps, be "unshielded" and "open"; if thinking is to occur at all the mind must open itself to what is playful, random and unsystematic. But thought can only go so far afield before it ceases to be thought at all; as Hegel suggests, mind or spirit possesses its power only "by looking the negative in the face, and tarrying with it. This tarrying with the negative is the magical power that converts it into being" (19). And this "tarrying with" is something that occurs over time and in a community of speakers; it is not the product of an instant. What prevents Edna's "tarrying with" the negative is not her own inadequacy or some incapacity inherent in speech as such, but Edna's lack of a speech community that will encourage these new speculations, her lack of a group of fellow speakers who will encourage the growth of her thought and its translation into praxis. Though Madame Ratignolle is sympathetic and offers Edna both physical solace and a sympathetic ear, open conversation between them is rare; they speak different languages. "Edna had once told Madame Ratignolle that she would never sacrifice herself for her children, or for any one. Then had followed a rather heated argument." Edna finds herself speaking a language as impenetrable to others as the parrot's babble: "The two women did not appear to understand each other or to be talking the same language" (67). The pull of the libidinal speech-world Edna shares with Robert, then, is immense. (Robert, Chopin explains, "talked a good deal about himself. He was very young, and did not know any better. Mrs. Pontellier talked a little about herself for the same reason. Each was interested in what the other said" [22].) What emerges from their conversation is not a critique of society, however, but gay, utopian play, a pattern of speech in which Edna is once again caught within the semiotic, the bodily residues of her social code, and is not permitted the range of meaning or the control over culturally established symbols that Robert Lebrun is able to command.

Given the power that Robert (and the romance plot itself) exerts over Edna's ordinary patterns of associative thinking, it is worth noting that Chopin's novel ends in a more heterogeneous zone, with Edna's attention turned neither toward Robert nor her husband and children, but toward her own past:

> She looked into the distance, and the old terror flamed up for an instant, then sank again. Edna heard her father's voice and her sister Margaret's. She heard the barking of an old dog that was chained to the sycamore tree. The spurs of the cavalry officer

> clanged as he walked across the porch. There was the hum of bees, and the musky odor of pinks filled the air. (137)

This lyrical ending is as enigmatic as the novel's beginning; it might be read as a regression toward oral passivity: toward an infantile repudiation of the validity claims, the social responsibilities adult speech requires. But I would suggest this extralinguistic memory comes to Edna at the end of her life because it is in such a sequence of images, and not the language of Robert Lebrun, that Edna can find the most accessible path to her story—that even in death Edna is seeking (as she sought on the beach) a path of emancipation; she is seeking a register of language more her own.

At the end of the novel as Edna swims out to sea and tries to address Robert once more, she fails again; she finds herself trying to speak a language no one understands. "'Good-by—because, I love you.' He did not know; he did not understand. He would never understand" (137). The story that Edna has told herself about her affection for Robert is inadequate. Close to death, she turns her mind toward the blurred edge of her womanhood, and the novel ends as it has begun, with a medley of distinct and disconnected voices. Here they represent a point of possible origin; they trace that moment in time when, still experiencing the world as a multitude of sounds, Edna's attention begins to shift from the plural voices of childhood toward the socially anticipated fulfillment of her sexual rhythms, toward the obsessive "clang" of the cavalryman's spurs. Just as the novel begins with the parrot's strange speech, with an order of speaking that satirizes and escapes from the epistemological confines of the heroine's world, so Edna's own awakening begins with and returns at her death to the rich and painful lure of desires that are still outside speech and beyond the social order. We must look again at this excluded order of meaning.

In *The Order of Things,* Michel Foucault describes the discontinuity and disjunction he feels in perusing a list of incommensurable words or objects encountered in a story by Jorge Luis Borges. Foucault experiences the variable terms of this list as "monstrous" and unnerving—Borges's reader is presented with an "order of things" which refuses orderly synthesis. This mode of disorder Foucault defines as a "heteroclite," a state in which "things are 'laid,' 'placed,' 'arranged' in sites so very different from one another that it is impossible . . . to define a common locus beneath them all" (xvii–xviii). In the opening sentences of *The Awakening,* the parrot's speech presents us with a similar confusion. Here different syntactic and semantic units from different language systems mingle but refuse to cohere, and we find ourselves contemplating a potential "heterotopia," a discontinuous linguistic space in which the communicative function of language itself is called into question. These discontinuous linguistic spaces, these "heterotopias," are disturbing "because they secretly undermine language . . . because they shatter or tangle common names, because they destroy 'syntax' in advance, and not only the syntax with which we construct sentences but also that less apparent syntax which causes words and things . . . to 'hold together'" (xviii). The opening sentences of Chopin's text have a similar effect upon their reader. In the discrepancies between different languages and the fractioned idioms these languages produce, we are presented with several categories of words and of things that cannot be held, simultaneously, in consciousness. The novel begins by challenging orthodoxy; it posits a world of saying in which ordinary ways of looking at things are called into question.

Chopin's novel pushes us from its beginning toward an area of speech which asks us to become aware of disjunctions between the disorder of words and the social order, between our usual perceptions and the world these perceptions are designed to organize. The potent, possible syntheses between the self and its world—the syntheses the symbolic order insists we believe in—are challenged and in their place we discover a universe that is anomalous, asynchronic, confusing: a world not so much out of joint as out of its inhabitants' thought, a world outrageously unthinkable. Chopin insists that Mr. Pontellier's manner of organizing himself within this world is to ignore its arch nonsense, to cling to its objects for fetishistic support. He reads his newspaper, fingers his vest pocket: "There was a ten-dollar bill there. He did not know; perhaps he would return for the early dinner and perhaps he would not" (21). Within the novel an extraordinary register of speech is always opening up and then quietly shutting down—a closure which returns us, inevitably, to the circumscribed world of other people's objects and other people's speech, to a linear world in which the intervals of desire are stabilized by cultural symbols that determine the perimeters of self-knowledge.

Chopin makes us aware that the world her novel is designed to represent is itself a heteroclite; her text points to a discrepancy between one kind of social order and its possible others. "It is here," as Foucault says in *The Order of Things,* in the region where the heteroclite becomes visible,

> that a culture, imperceptibly deviating from the empirical orders prescribed for it by its primary codes, instituting an initial separa-

> tion from them, causes them to lose their original transparency, relinquishes its immediate and invisible powers, frees itself sufficiently to discover that these orders are perhaps not the only possible ones or the best ones; this culture then finds itself faced with the stark fact that there exists, below the level of its spontaneous orders, things that are in themselves capable of being ordered, that belong to a certain unspoken order. . . . (xx)

To argue that Edna Pontellier commits suicide because she lacks a language, because of this "unspoken order," seems a cruel oversimplification of her character and of her material situation. And yet at the end of *The Awakening*, we are, like Edna, subjected to a multiplication of points of view and can see no way to contain this multiplicity within the novel's heterosexist milieu. To argue that Edna lacks a language, then, is not only to say that culture has invaded her consciousness, has mortgaged her right to original speech, but that Edna's language is inadequate to her vital needs, that it is singular when it should be plural, masculine when it should be feminine, phantasmic when it should be open and dialectical. And what becomes clear by the novel's end is that Robert Lebrun has served as an iconic replacement for that which Edna cannot say; his name functions as a hieroglyph condensing Edna's complex desires—both those she has named and those which remain unnameable.

In *Powers of Horror,* Julia Kristeva suggests that "phobia bears the marks of the frailty of the subject's signifying system," and Edna's love for Robert—although it is not phobic as such, reproduces this frailty as symptom; when Edna seeks nothing but the speech of her beloved, it makes her "signifying system" frail (35). Edna Pontellier has no language to help her integrate and interrogate the diversity of her feelings; she experiences neither world nor signifying system capacious enough to accommodate her desires. But by the end of the novel these contradictory desires become noisy, impossible to repress. As Edna helps Adèle Ratignolle through a difficult childbirth the romantic interlude that Edna has shared with Robert becomes faint; it seems "unreal, and only half-remembered" (131), and once again language fails her. When Dr. Mandelet asks if she will go abroad to relax, Edna finds herself stumbling for words:

> "Perhaps—no, I am not going. I'm not going to be forced into doing things. I don't want to go abroad. I want to be let alone. Nobody has any right—except children, perhaps—and even then, it seems to me—or it did seem—" She felt that her speech

> was voicing the incoherency of her thoughts, and stopped abruptly. (132)

After watching Adèle give birth and listening to her painful repetitions ("Think of the children; think of them"), Edna begins to reexperience the bodily sensations and feelings for her children that she has repressed; her extramarital desires grow more tumultuous. Once more her sentences split with the weight of this conflict, and as Mandelet tries to put them together, as he offers to "talk of things you never have dreamt of talking about before," Edna refuses his kind and magian powers, just as, in childhood, she refused her father's chill summons to prayer. She gives herself, instead, to the "voice" of the sea, to that sibilance in which every name drowns. And her mind returns to what she can claim of her childhood, to the story she told Adèle Ratignolle on the hot summer beach.

Kristeva has suggested that we consider "the phobic person as a subject in want of metaphoricalness" (37), and I have suggested that the same becomes true of a woman in love, a woman who becomes the subject of her culture's romantic fantasies. "Incapable of producing metaphors by means of signs alone," Kristeva argues,

> [this subject] produces them in the very material of drives—and it turns out that the only rhetoric of which he is capable is that of affect, and it is projected, as often as not, by means of *images*. It will then fall upon analysis to give back a memory, hence a language, to the unnameable and nameable states of fear, while emphasizing the former, which make up what is most unapproachable in the unconscious. (37)

I am not suggesting that Edna is in need of a Freudian or even a Kristevan analysis. I am suggesting instead that we can locate the power of the novel's final images in Edna's desire "to give back a memory, hence a language," to that within her which remains nameless. Lyotard proposes,

> There is a fact which our experience of speech does to permit us to deny, the fact that every discourse is cast in the direction of something which it seeks to seize hold of, that it is incomplete and open, somewhat as the visual field is partial, limited and extended by an horizon. How can we explain this almost visual property of speaking on the basis of this object closed in principle, shut up on itself in a self-sufficient totality, which is the system of *langue?* (32)

The "voice" of the sea Edna tries to embrace is more than a harbinger of death, more than a sign of dark and unfulfilled sexuality; the novel's final images frame and articulate Edna's incessant need for some other register of language, for a mode of speech that will express her unspoken, but not unspeakable needs.

WORKS CITED

Adorno, Theodor W. *Negative Dialectics*. Trans. E. B. Ashton. New York: Continuum, 1983.

Foucault, Michel. *The Order of Things: An Archaeology of the Human Sciences*. New York: Vintage, 1973.

Hegel, G. W. F. *Phenomenology of Spirit*. Trans. A. V. Miller. London: Oxford UP, 1977.

Kristeva, Julia. "Interview—1974." Trans. Claire Pajaczkowska. *m/f* 5/6 (1981): 164–67.

———. *Powers of Horror: An Essay in Abjection*. Trans. Leon S. Roudiez. New York: Columbia UP, 1982.

Kurrik, Maire Jaanus. *Literature and Negation*. New York: Columbia UP, 1979.

Lacan, Jacques. *The Four Fundamental Concepts of Psycho-Analysis*. Ed. Jacque-Alain Miller. Trans. Alan Sheridan. New York: Norton, 1978.

Lyotard, Jean-François. *Le Differend*. Paris: Minuit, 1983.

Tanner, Tony. *Adultery in the Novel: Contract and Transgression*. Baltimore: Johns Hopkins UP, 1979.

Wolff, Cynthia Griffin. "Thanatos and Eros." *The Awakening*. Ed. Margaret Culley. New York: Norton, 1976. 206–18. [Wolff's essay is also reprinted in this volume on pp. 233–58.]

Reader-Response Criticism and *The Awakening*

WHAT IS READER-RESPONSE CRITICISM?

Students are routinely asked in English courses for their reactions to texts they are reading. Sometimes there are so many different reactions that we may wonder whether everyone has read the same text. And some students respond so idiosyncratically to what they read that we say their responses are "totally off the wall."

Reader-response critics are interested in the variety of our responses. Reader-response criticism raises theoretical questions about whether our responses to a work are the same as its meanings, whether a work can have as many meanings as we have responses to it, and whether some responses are more valid than, or superior to, others. It asks us to pose the following questions: What have we internalized that helps us determine what is and what isn't "off the wall"? In other words, what is the wall, and what standards help us to define it?

Reader-response criticism also provides models that are useful in answering such questions. Adena Rosmarin has suggested that a work can be likened to an incomplete work of sculpture: to see it fully, we *must* complete it imaginatively, taking care to do so in a way that responsibly takes into account what is there. An introduction to several other models of reader-response theory will allow you to understand better the reader-oriented essay that follows as well as to see a variety of ways in which, as a reader-response critic, you might respond to literary works.

Reader-response criticism, which emerged during the 1970s, focuses on what texts do to, or in, the mind of the reader, rather than regarding a text as something with properties exclusively its own. A poem, Louise M. Rosenblatt wrote as early as 1969, "is what the reader lives through under the guidance of the text and experiences as relevant to the text." Rosenblatt knew her definition would be difficult for many to accept: "The idea that a *poem* presupposes a *reader* actively involved with a *text,*" she wrote, "is particularly shocking to those seeking to emphasize the objectivity of their interpretations" (127).

Rosenblatt is implicitly referring to the formalists, the old "New Critics," when she speaks of supposedly objective interpreters shocked by the notion that readers help make poems. Formalists preferred to discuss "the poem itself," the "concrete work of art," the "real poem." And they refused to describe what a work of literature makes a reader "live through." In fact, in *The Verbal Icon* (1954), William K. Wimsatt and Monroe C. Beardsley defined as fallacious the very notion that a reader's response is part of the meaning of a literary work:

> The Affective Fallacy is a confusion between the poem and its *results* (what it *is* and what it *does*). . . . It begins by trying to derive the standards of criticism from the psychological effects of a poem and ends in impressionism and relativism. The outcome . . . is that the poem itself, as an object of specifically critical judgment, tends to disappear. (21)

Reader-response critics take issue with their formalist predecessors. Stanley Fish, author of a highly influential article entitled "Literature in the Reader: Affective Stylistics" (1970), argues that any school of criticism that would see a work of literature as an object, that would claim to describe what it *is* and never what it *does,* is guilty of misconstruing what literature and reading really are. Literature exists when it is read, Fish suggests, and its force is an affective force. Furthermore, reading is a temporal process. Formalists assume it is a spatial one as they step back and survey the literary work as if it were an object spread out before them. They may find elegant patterns in the texts they examine and reexamine, but they fail to take into account that the work is quite different to a reader who is turning the pages and being moved, or affected, by lines that appear and disappear as the reader reads.

In a discussion of the effect that a sentence penned by the seventeenth-century physician Thomas Browne has on a reader reading, Fish pauses to say this about his analysis and also, by extension, about the overall critical strategy he has largely developed: "Whatever is persuasive and illuminating about [it] . . . is the result of my substituting for one question—what does this sentence mean?—another, more operational question—what does this sentence do?" He then quotes a line from John Milton's *Paradise Lost,* a line that refers to Satan and the other fallen angels: "Nor did they not perceive their evil plight." Whereas more traditional critics might say that the "meaning" of the line is "They did perceive their evil plight," Fish relates the uncertain movement of the reader's mind *to* that half-satisfying interpretation. Furthermore, he declares that "the reader's inability to tell whether or not 'they' do perceive and his involuntary question . . . are part of the line's *meaning,* even though they take place in the mind, not on the page" (*Text* 26).

This stress on what pages *do* to minds pervades the writings of most, if not all, reader-response critics. Wolfgang Iser, author of *The Implied Reader* (1974) and *The Act of Reading: A Theory of Aesthetic Response* (1976), finds texts to be full of "gaps," and these gaps, or "blanks," as he sometimes calls them, powerfully affect the reader. The reader is forced to explain them, to connect what the gaps separate, literally to create in his or her mind a poem or novel or play that isn't *in* the text but that the text incites. Stephen Booth, who greatly influenced Fish, equally emphasizes what words, sentences, and passages "do." He stresses in his analyses the "reading experience that results" from a "multiplicity of organizations" in, say, a Shakespeare sonnet (*Essay* ix). Sometimes these organizations don't make complete sense, and sometimes they even seem curiously contradictory. But that is precisely what interests reader-response critics, who, unlike formalists, are at least as interested in fragmentary, inconclusive, and even unfinished texts as in polished, unified works. For it is the reader's struggle to *make sense* of a challenging work that reader-response critics seek to describe.

In *Self-Consuming Artifacts: The Experience of Seventeenth-Century Literature* (1972), Fish reveals his preference for literature that makes readers work at making meaning. He contrasts two kinds of literary presentation. By the phrase "rhetorical presentation," he describes literature that reflects and reinforces opinions that readers already hold; by "dialectical presentation," he refers to works that prod and provoke. A dialectical text, rather than presenting an opinion as if it were truth, challenges readers to discover truths on their own. Such a text may not even have the kind of symmetry that formalist critics seek. Instead of offering a "single, sustained argument," a dialectical text, or self-consuming artifact, may be "so arranged that to enter into the spirit and assumptions of any one of [its] . . . units is implicitly to reject the spirit and assumptions of the unit immediately preceding'' (*Artifacts* 9). Such a text needs a reader-response critic to elucidate its workings. Another kind of critic is likely to try to explain why the units are unified and coherent, not why such units are contradicting and ''consuming'' their predecessors. The reader-response critic proceeds by describing the reader's way of dealing with the sudden twists and turns that characterize the dialectical text, making the reader return to earlier passages and see them in an entirely new light.

''The value of such a procedure,'' Fish has written, ''is predicated on the idea of meaning as *an event,*'' not as something ''located (presumed to be embedded) *in* the utterance'' or ''verbal object as a thing in itself'' (*Text* 28). By redefining meaning as an event, the reader-response critic once again locates meaning in time: the reader's time. A text exists and signifies while it is being read, and what it signifies or means will depend, to no small extent, on *when* it is read. (*Paradise Lost* had some meanings for a seventeenth-century Puritan that it would not have for a twentieth-century atheist.)

With the redefinition of literature as something that only exists meaningfully in the mind of the reader, with the redefinition of the literary work as a catalyst of mental events, comes a concurrent redefinition of the reader. No longer is the reader the passive recipient of those ideas that an author has planted in a text. ''The reader is *active,*'' Rosenblatt insists (123). Fish begins ''Literature in the Reader'' with a similar observation: ''If at this moment someone were to ask, 'what are you doing,' you might reply, 'I am reading,' and thereby acknowledge that reading is . . . something *you do*'' (*Text* 22). In ''How to Recognize a Poem When You See One,'' he is even more provocative: ''Interpreters do not decode poems: they make them'' (*Text* 327). Iser, in focusing critical interest on the gaps in texts, on what is not expressed, similarly redefines the reader as an active maker. In an essay entitled ''Interaction between Text and Reader,'' he argues that what is missing from a narrative causes the reader to fill in the blanks creatively.

Iser's title implies a cooperation between reader and text that is also implied by Rosenblatt's definition of a poem as ''what the reader lives through under the guidance of the text.'' Indeed, Rosenblatt borrowed the term ''transactional'' to describe the dynamics of the reading process, which in her view involves interdependent texts and readers interacting. The view that texts and readers make poems together, though, is not shared by *all* interpreters generally thought of as reader-response critics. Steven Mailloux has divided reader-response critics into several categories, one of which he labels "subjective." Subjective critics, like David Bleich (or Norman Holland after his conversion by Bleich), assume what Mailloux calls the "absolute priority of individual selves as creators of texts" (*Conventions* 31). In other words, these critics do not see the reader's response as one "guided" by the text but rather as one motivated by deep-seated, personal, psychological needs. What they find in texts is, in Holland's phrase, their own "identity theme." Holland has argued that as readers we use "the literary work to symbolize and finally to replicate ourselves. We work out through the text our own characteristic patterns of desire" ("UNITY" 816).

Subjective critics, as you may already have guessed, often find themselves confronted with the following question: If all interpretation is a function of private, psychological identity, then why have so many readers interpreted, say, Shakespeare's *Hamlet* in the same way? Different subjective critics have answered the question differently. Holland simply has said that common identity themes exist, such as that involving an oedipal fantasy. Fish, who went through a subjectivist stage, has provided a different answer. In "Interpreting the *Variorum*," he argues that the "stability of interpretation among readers" is a function of shared "interpretive strategies." These strategies, which "exist prior to the act of reading and therefore determine the shape of what is read," are held in common by "interpretive communities" such as the one comprised by American college students reading a novel as a class assignment (*Text* 167, 171).

As I have suggested in the paragraph above, reader-response criticism is not a monolithic school of thought, as is assumed by some detractors who like to talk about the "School of Fish." Several of the critics mentioned thus far have, over time, adopted different versions of reader-response criticism. I have hinted at Holland's growing subjectivism as well as the evolution of Fish's own thought. Fish, having at first viewed meaning as the cooperative production of readers and texts, went on to become a subjectivist, and very nearly a "deconstructor" ready to suggest that all criticism is imaginative creation, fiction about literature, or *metafiction*. In developing the notion of interpretive communities, however, Fish has become more of a social, structuralist, reader-response critic; currently, he is engaged in studying reading communities and their interpretive conventions in order to understand the conditions that give rise to a work's intelligibility.

In spite of the gaps between reader-response critics and even between the assumptions that they have held at various stages of their respective careers, all try to answer similar questions and to use similar strategies to describe the reader's response to a given text. One question these critics are commonly asked has already been discussed: Why do individual readers come up with such similar interpretations if meaning is not embedded *in* the work itself? Other recurring, troubling questions include the following interrelated ones: Just who *is* the reader? (or, to place the emphasis differently, Just who is *the* reader?) Aren't you reader-response critics just talking about your own idiosyncratic responses when you describe what a line from *Paradise Lost* "does" in and to "the reader's" mind? What about my responses? What if they're different? Will you be willing to say that all responses are equally valid?

Fish defines "the reader" in this way: "*the* reader is the *informed* reader." The informed reader is someone who is "sufficiently experienced as a reader to have internalized the properties of literary discourses, including everything from the most local of devices (figures of speech, etc.) to whole genres." And, of course, the informed reader is in full possession of the "semantic knowledge" (knowledge of idioms, for instance) assumed by the text (*Artifacts* 406).

Other reader-response critics use terms besides "the *informed* reader" to define "*the* reader," and these other terms mean slightly different things. Wayne Booth uses the phrase "the implied reader" to mean the reader "created by the work." (Only "by agreeing to play the role of this created audience," Susan Suleiman explains, "can an actual reader correctly understand and appreciate the work" [8].) Gerard Genette and Gerald Prince prefer to speak of "the narratee, . . . the necessary counterpart of a given narrator, that is, the person or figure who receives a narrative" (Suleiman 13). Like Booth, Iser employs the term "the implied reader," but he also uses "the educated reader" when he refers to what Fish calls the "informed" or "intended" reader. Thus, with different terms, each critic denies the claim that reader-response criticism might lead people to think that there are as many correct interpretations of a work as there are readers to read it.

As Mailloux has shown, reader-response critics share not only questions, answers, concepts, and terms for those concepts but also strategies of reading. Two of the basic "moves," as he calls them, are to show that a work gives readers something to do, and to describe what the reader does by way of response. And there are more complex moves as well. For instance, a reader-response critic might typically (1) cite direct references to reading in the text, in order to justify the focus on reading and show that the inside of the text is continuous with what the reader is doing; (2) show how other nonreading situations in the text nonetheless mirror the situation the reader is in ("Fish shows how in *Paradise Lost* Michael's teaching of Adam in Book XI resembles Milton's teaching of the reader throughout the poem"); and (3) show, therefore, that the reader's response is, or is perfectly analogous to, the topic of the story. For Stephen Booth, *Hamlet* is the tragic story of "an audience that cannot make up its mind." In the view of Roger Easson, Blake's *Jerusalem* "may be read as a poem about the experience of reading *Jerusalem*" (Mailloux, "Learning" 103).

In the essay that follows, Paula A. Treichler argues for a relationship between Edna Pontellier's struggle to be "an active subject" (as opposed to a passive object) and a gradually developing, textual tension between active and passive narrative voice, transitive and intransitive, verb structure, literal and figurative language. In the process, she shows how—and even why—*The Awakening* is a "complicated and intense reading experience," one requiring us constantly to struggle to resolve the manifold ambiguities created by tensions within the text.

At the beginning of the story, Chopin's narrative language reflects the fact that Edna is an object, a "passive receptacle." Reference is made, at one point, to "an indescribable oppression" that "seemed to generate some unfamiliar consciousness" and "fill her whole being"—as if Edna had not had the feelings herself but, rather, had been invaded by them. Our understanding of Edna's feelings of oppression is, in Treichler's view, inseparable from our readerly response to a formal, narrative sytle dense with "abstract nouns and adjectives," "latinate prefixes and suffixes," "chain[s] of prepositional phrases," and "the serviceable *it was* construction."

Then, just as we "grow used" to language that is as stiff and strangulating as the world in which Edna feels oppressed, that language gradually begins to change. Here and there it is more concretely descriptive, less figurative and metaphorical, more sensuously—and spiritually—evocative. There is a growing use of Edna's name or the pronoun *she* to serve as the "syntactic" and often "semantic" subject of otherwise passive constructions or sentences. The emerging complication of a once-formal discourse necessarily makes for a more difficult reading experience. But that difficulty becomes yet another means whereby we as readers may gain understanding, for it reflects the growing contradictions in—the "duality" of—an awakening Edna. Indeed, the bafflement we must increasingly contend with as readers becomes a means by which we perceive and come to understand Edna's bafflement with her own feelings and behavior. While discussing the linguistic complexity of the second part of the novel, Treichler suggests that walking comes to symbolize the "tentative . . . self-exploration" that must be undertaken if Edna is to attain the "freedom to move around." It is that freedom and the creation of an "I," of course, that ultimately allow her to move out of her husband's house and, more significantly, to commit adultery. Treichler then goes on to argue, however, that Edna's adultery is as much a part of her undoing as it is of her sensual awakening. Insofar as it involves "the masculine world that alienates her," acts of adultery end up inhibiting, rather than facilitating, the awakening of Edna's consciousness.

That Edna's freedom is not to be complete, Treichler submits, can be sensed by the reader well before Edna's suicide forces us to come to that conclusion. Verbal elements that had seemed to give way, earlier in the text, to an active, quickening language now reassert themselves—at first surprisingly—just when Edna seems to be "discovering personal freedom and overt sexuality." Calling "ominous" the recurrence of the novel's more formal, passive, latinate narrative language, Treichler suggests that the reader is well trained to read the omen. For by the time we reach the novel's concluding chapters, diction, verb forms, and modes of narrative presentation all "resonate with a verbal history internal to the text."

In outlining the manifold ambiguities of the text and the challenges faced by the reader, Treichler allows for differing interpretations of Chopin's novel. Unlike subjectivist reader-response critics, however, she stops short of suggesting that readers make the meaning of what they read. Rather, she argues that our changing experience of the text over time is inseparable from our reading of the story and its heroine. She also suggests, without quite stating it, that readers form an understanding of the text by dealing with what some reader-response critics would call "gaps." In the case of *The Awakening*, meaningful reading involves making sense of gaps or discrepancies between narrative modes and styles that would seem to belong to different books—books as different, in fact, as the world Edna struggles to be a part of and the one she would rather die than reenter.

Ross C Murfin

READER-RESPONSE CRITICISM: A SELECTED BIBLIOGRAPHY

Some Introductions to Reader-Response Criticism

Fish, Stanley E. "Literature in the Reader: Affective Stylistics." *New Literary History* 2 (1970): 123–61. Rpt. in Fish 21–67 and in Primeau 154–79.

Freund, Elizabeth. *The Return of the Reader: Reader-Response Criticism.* London: Methuen, 1987.

Holland, Norman N. "UNITY IDENTITY TEXT SELF." *PMLA* 90 (1975): 813–22.

Holub, Robert C. *Reception Theory: A Critical Introduction.* New York: Methuen, 1984.

Mailloux, Steven. "Learning to Read: Interpretation and Reader-Response Criticism." *Studies in the Literary Imagination* 12 (1979): 93–108.

———. "Reader-Response Criticism?" *Genre* 10 (1977): 413–31.

Rosenblatt, Louise M. "Towards a Transactional Theory of Reading." *Journal of Reading Behavior* 1 (1969): 31–47. Rpt. in Primeau 121–46.

Suleiman, Susan R. "Introduction: Varieties of Audience-Oriented Criticism." Suleiman and Crosman 3–45.

Tompkins, Jane P. "An Introduction to Reader-Response Criticism." Tompkins ix–xxiv.

Reader-Response Criticism in Anthologies and Collections

Fish, Stanley Eugene. *Is There a Text in This Class? The Authority of Interpretive Communities.* Cambridge: Harvard UP, 1980. In this volume are collected most of Fish's most influential essays, including "Literature in the Reader: Affective Stylistics," "What It's Like to Read *L'Allegro* and *Il Penseroso,*" "Interpreting the *Variorum,*" "Is There a Text in This Class?" "How to Recognize a Poem When You See One," and "What Makes an Interpretation Acceptable?"

Garvin, Harry R., ed. *Theories of Reading, Looking, and Listening.* Lewisburg: Bucknell UP, 1981. See the essays by Cain and Rosenblatt.

Leitch, Vincent B. *American Literary Criticism from the Thirties to the Eighties.* New York: Columbia UP, 1988.

Primeau, Ronald, ed. *Influx: Essays on Literary Influence*. Port Washington: Kennikat, 1977. See the essays by Fish, Holland, and Rosenblatt.

Suleiman, Susan R., and Inge Crosman, eds. *The Reader in the Text: Essays on Audience and Interpretation*. Princeton: Princeton UP, 1980. See especially the essays by Culler, Iser, and Todorov.

Tompkins, Jane P., ed. *Reader-Response Criticism: From Formalism to Post-Structuralism*. Baltimore: Johns Hopkins UP, 1980. See especially the essays by Bleich, Fish, Holland, Prince, and Tompkins.

Reader-Response Criticism: Some Major Works

Bleich, David. *Subjective Criticism*. Baltimore: Johns Hopkins UP, 1978.

Booth, Stephen. *An Essay on Shakespeare's Sonnets*. New Haven: Yale UP, 1969.

Eco, Umberto. *The Role of the Reader*. Bloomington: Indiana UP, 1979.

Fish, Stanley Eugene. *Self-Consuming Artifacts: The Experience of Seventeenth-Century Literature*. Berkeley: U of California P, 1972.

———. *Surprised by Sin: The Reader in Paradise Lost*. 2nd ed. Berkeley: U of California P, 1971.

Holland, Norman N. *5 Readers Reading*. New Haven: Yale UP, 1975.

Iser, Wolfgang. *The Act of Reading: A Theory of Aesthetic Response*. Baltimore: Johns Hopkins UP, 1978.

———. *The Implied Reader: Patterns of Communication in Prose Fiction from Bunyan to Beckett*. Baltimore: Johns Hopkins UP, 1974.

Jauss, Hans Robert. *Toward an Aesthetic of Reception*. Trans. Timothy Bahti. Intro. Paul de Man. Brighton, Eng.: Harvester, 1982.

Messent, Peter. *New Readings of the American Novel: Narrative Theory and Its Application*. New York: Macmillan, 1991.

Mailloux, Steven. *Interpretive Conventions: The Reader in the Study of American Fiction*. Ithaca: Cornell UP, 1982.

Prince, Gerald. *Narratology*. New York: Mouton, 1982.

Rabinowitz, Peter. *Before Reading: Narrative Conventions and the Politics of Interpretation*. Ithaca: Cornell, UP, 1987.

Steig, Michael. *Stories of Reading: Subjectivity and Literary Understanding*. Baltimore: John Hopkins UP, 1989.

Exemplary Short Readings of Major Texts

Anderson, Howard. "*Tristram Shandy* and the Reader's Imagination." *PMLA* 86 (1971): 966–73.

Berger, Carole. "The Rake and the Reader in Jane Austen's Novels." *Studies in English Literature, 1500–1900* 15 (1975): 531–44.

Booth, Stephen. "On the Value of *Hamlet.*" *Reinterpretations of English Drama: Selected Papers from the English Institute.* Ed. Norman Rabkin. New York: Columbia UP, 1969. 137–76.

Easson, Robert R. "William Blake and His Reader in *Jerusalem.*" *Blake's Sublime Allegory.* Ed. Stuart Curran and Joseph A. Wittreich. Madison: U of Wisconsin P, 1973. 309–28.

Kirk, Carey H. "*Moby-Dick:* The Challenge of Response." *Papers on Language and Literature* 13 (1977): 383–90.

Leverenz, David. "Mrs. Hawthorne's Headache: Reading *The Scarlet Letter.*" *Nathaniel Hawthorne, "The Scarlet Letter."* Case Studies in Contemporary Criticism Series. Ed. Ross C Murfin. Boston: Bedford–St. Martin's, 1991. 263–74.

Lowe-Evans, Mary. "Reading with a 'Nicer-Eye': Responding to *Frankenstein.*" *Mary Shelley, "Frankenstein."* Ed. Johanna M. Smith. Case Studies in Contemporary Criticism Series. Ed. Ross C Murfin. Boston: Bedford–St. Martin's, 1992. 215–29.

Rosmarin, Adena. "Darkening the Reader: Reader-Response Criticism and *Heart of Darkness.*" *Joseph Conrad, "Heart of Darkness."* Ed. Ross C Murfin. Case Studies in Contemporary Criticism Series. Boston: Bedford–St. Martin's, 1989. 148–69.

Reader-Response Criticism of *The Awakening*

Rankin, Elizabeth. "A Reader-Response Approach." *Approaches to Teaching "The Awakening."* Ed. Bernard Koloski. New York: MLA, 1988. 150–55.

Other Work Referred to in "What Is Reader-Response Criticism?"

Wimsatt, William K., and Monroe C. Beardsley. *The Verbal Icon.* Lexington: U of Kentucky P, 1954. See especially the discussion of "The Affective Fallacy," with which reader-response critics have so sharply disagreed.

A READER-RESPONSE PERSPECTIVE

PAULA A. TREICHLER

The Construction of Ambiguity in *The Awakening:* A Linguistic Analysis

The central narrative of Kate Chopin's novel *The Awakening* can be said to concern Edna Pontellier's struggle to define herself as an active subject and to cease to be merely the passive object of forces beyond her control. But the precise nature of this struggle, as well as its emotional and psychological dimensions, is less easily articulated. One textual counterpart to this complexity is the ongoing syntactic interplay between active and passive voice which parallels, and not infrequently undermines, the overt narrative. The relationship between formal grammatical patterns and obvious narrative meaning shapes our understanding of Edna's changing consciousness and serves as an index to its vicissitudes. The verb *awaken,* from which the novel's title and central metaphor derive, formally complicates in a similar way the active and passive elements of Edna's experience. Both transitive and intransitive, it can take a grammatical object but does not have to: someone can awaken, can be awakened, can awaken someone else. The title of the novel, a noun, is structurally unspecified and can draw on all these possibilities. Similarly, the novel's personal pronouns are revealing: one could argue that *The Awakening* charts Edna Pontellier's growing mastery of the first-person singular, and that when this "I" has been created, the book has successfully completed its mission and comes to an end.

The close analysis of verbal form remains a relatively uncommon approach to fiction in general, and to *The Awakening* in particular. Yet it permits us to study the crucial intersections between form and meaning which presumably are part of any literary experience. Thus we find that the book asserts from the outset the ambiguities of Edna's own role in her awakening and suggests, too, that our attempts as readers to delineate this role precisely may fail: that no unambiguous reading is possible. The form of the language, in other words, insists that the problems of Edna's situation are genuine and cannot be fully resolved; the meaning of the novel exists, in part, in its verbal form.

At the same time as the book progresses, the seemingly artless, even childlike, simplicity of Chopin's style gives way to a rather complicated and intense reading experience. In fact the language offers a verbal resolution to the novel's narrative problems which is nearly perfect, and which, in its craft, transcends the profound contradictions and ambiguities of the story.

I

Edna Pontellier first appears in *The Awakening* when her husband perceives her in the distance as "a white sunshade that was advancing at snail's pace from the beach"; as it moves closer, we learn that "beneath its pink-lined shelter were his wife, Mrs. Pontellier, and young Robert Lebrun." Thus the literal object we are first shown gives way to her official designation as "his wife" and at last to her proper name, at its most formal. (Only later is she regularly called "Edna Pontellier" or "Edna," a naming device that regulates our distance and sympathies.) This view of Edna as an object is made explicit when her husband looks at her "as one looks at a valuable piece of personal property which has suffered some damage" (20–21). The image is more than an ironic comment on the nature of the Pontelliers' conventional marriage, for Edna is to be an object in a much wider sense.

She is often, for example, a grammatical object. In an early scene she sits outside crying, angry and upset after her husband's complaints and trivial conversation have awakened her out of a sound sleep (the literal awakening here gives psychological plausibility to the metaphor). This passage offers the first overt signal of Edna's discontent—our first entry to her consciousness coincides with the beginnings of her awakening:

> An indescribable oppression, which seemed to generate in some unfamiliar part of her consciousness, filled her whole being with a vague anguish. It was like a shadow, like a mist passing across her soul's summer day. It was strange and unfamiliar; it was a mood. (25)

Though the narrative asserts that Edna is unusually moved, the language disguises her emotional involvement. She does not really participate in the sentence at all: Chopin does not even choose to say that Edna "feels oppressed," but rather presents the experience of oppression as something remote, existing without relationship to her. The syntactic subject of the sentence is "oppression," an abstraction whose concrete reality is further reduced by being "indescribable"; the formal and virtually content-free sequence of syllables offers little genuine information. The oppression has originated somewhere in "her consciousness" yet *she* has not generated it, and now it fills "her whole being with a vague anguish." No real causative agent is identified, though certainly the passage creates a sense of threat and dramatic opposition. Edna is the silent, baffled receptacle for feelings that fill her mindlessly, as though she were a hollow vessel. Both the content and formal elements of the passage sustain this picture. Further, the repeated indefinite pronoun *it* contributes to the sense of vague threat. The whole passage, in fact, is aggressively global and nonspecific, embodying a kind of verbal groping which duplicates Edna's dim, and at this point tentative, perception of the events that are coming to occupy her consciousness. As she tries to clarify her sense of oppression, she moves further from it: "It was like a shadow, like a mist passing across her soul's summer day" (another image of her as an object, a summer landscape that mist and shadows pass across). Though technically concrete, these nouns refer to the most insubstantial and transient of things; Edna, trying hard to view her oppression as temporary, is drawn by their impermanence. The construction *it was* somewhat weakens her attempt by asserting, more or less in the voice of an objective narrator, that the oppression indeed does exist—in contrast, for example, to the more equivocal verb phrase *seemed to generate* in the preceding sentence. Altogether, the words prepare us for the next turn of Edna's consciousness: "It was strange and unfamiliar; it was a mood." The words *strange* and *unfamiliar* commit Edna to the domain of her subjective consciousness where the threat can no longer be externalized. The suddenness with which we come to "it was a mood" suggests how she arrives, in panic, at a rationalization to reduce the threat: a mood is the most comforting and commonplace of all explanations for the inexplicable ways in which people, especially women, feel and behave, and thus serves, for the time being, to reassure her that her feelings are acceptable. Restored to relative normalcy, she becomes suddenly conscious of the mosquitoes and goes inside to sleep.

This introduction to Edna's consciousness is marked by language drawn from a world of formal abstraction. Its elements recur frequently in the novel—the abstract nouns and adjectives, dense with latinate prefixes and suffixes, the chain of prepositional phrases, the serviceable *it was* construction. We are given the sense that forces are at work, but they remain disguised, stubbornly unobservable, their point of origin and locus ambiguous and shadowy. Yet these abstract and "unreal" verbal elements acquire in the course of the book a convincing reality of their own. Indeed, they emerge as the dominant and unchanging reality behind the illusory visions that Edna experiences and become, in consequence, virtual protagonists in the novel's verbal drama. In the process we grow used to the language that at first distanced us from Edna's experience, and learn to recognize the grammar and vocabulary, the verbal territory, that mark the progress of her awakening. What appears to begin as needlessly abstract, awkward, and uninviting language comes to signal the complicated struggles of Edna's most essential self.

Just before the "indescribable oppression" passages I have been discussing, Edna is presented differently:

> The tears came so fast to Mrs. Pontellier's eyes that the damp sleeve of her *peignoir* no longer served to dry them. She was holding the back of her chair with one hand; her loose sleeve had slipped almost to the shoulder of her uplifted arm. Turning, she thrust her face, steaming and wet, into the bend of her arm, and she went on crying there, not caring any longer to dry her face, her eyes, her arms. (24)

Although this passage occurs in the same narrative context and also portrays Edna overcome by emotion, the mode of presentation establishes for Edna a strong and clear physical presence which in some ways challenges the notion of her passivity and helplessness. The nouns, pronouns, and verbs are concrete and visual, and describe not her "being" nor her "consciousness" but her sleeve, her arm, her face. Though *tear* and *sleeve* are the syntactic subjects in the first sentence, they do not crowd our sense of Edna herself; no more in control of the tears than she is of the oppression, she is nevertheless palpably *there* in the words and images of the narrative description. The passage does little more than catalogue Edna's clothes and the individual parts of her body, and does not particularly invoke the presence of a thinking self; yet the pronoun *she* anchors her physical self to the language (just as the pronoun *it* reinforced the vagueness of her oppression and further abstracted its reality).

Though Edna is behaving "passively," the repeated pronoun *she* and the concrete actions she performs inevitably help to create a portrait of her as forceful and independent, demonstrably capable of action. The passage illustrates another of the book's pervasive sentence structures, in which Edna's name or the pronoun *she* makes up the head noun phrase and serves as syntactic subject—and for the most part semantic subject, that is, performer of action, as well. (Compare the long paragraph that describes Edna's preparations for sleep at Madame Antoine's [55–56]; Edna is the nominal or pronominal subject of seven of the eight sentences in the passage and her name or *she* or *her* occurs twenty-two times.)

Per Seyersted has proposed that Chopin's ongoing exploration of behavioral alternatives for women led in her writing to "an interplay between her self-assertive and self-forgetting heroines" that amounted to "a running dialogue with herself on woman's lot" (111, 113). In *The Awakening,* these alternatives are explored simultaneously, not simply through the presentation of different kinds of women—Edna, Adèle Ratignolle, Mademoiselle Reisz, Madame Lebrun—but through the linguistic presentation of Edna herself. A key example is Edna's childhood memory "'of a summer day in Kentucky, of a meadow that seemed as big as the ocean to the very little girl walking through the grass'"; sharing this memory with Adèle Ratignolle, Edna at first speaks of herself as the little girl, someone else, removed in time and space; only then does she shift to the first person and identify the little girl with herself, at the present time: "'sometimes I feel this summer as if I were walking through the green meadow again: idly, aimlessly, unthinking and unguided'" (35). This is the emblematic image of Edna's duality: the body moves through the field as though swimming, without clear direction or purpose, without consciousness except, perhaps, as the body's silent witness. The image is striking, as though her body has always lived its life, but apart; now, it is beginning to be invaded with increasing aggression by consciousness, whose encroachment at first takes place in highly noncommittal language (marked, for example, by the repeated negating affixes *-less* and *un-*).

The first part of the book establishes contradictions and dualities, presumably to parallel what the narrative tells us about Edna—the "contradictory subtle play of features" (22), her "dual life" (32). She is continually baffled by her behavior and feelings, and fluctuates between apparent self-knowledge and apparent self-deception. Her perceptions are hedged in modals and conditional structures, negatives, and relative clauses. Any sense of guiding consciousness is undercut by verbal signals of doubt and hesitation. The caged birds that open the novel establish immediately the sense of constrained potential that marks these first chapters. When Edna does experience "a first breath of freedom" (37), it is compared to wine and intoxication, images of deceptive euphoria that suggest only an illusory loss of restraint. The first sentence of chapter VI, the short chapter that establishes the "voice of the sea" refrain, offers us similar complications: "Edna Pontellier could not have told why, wishing to go to the beach with Robert, she should in the first place have declined, and in the second place have followed in obedience to one of the two contradictory impulses which impelled her" (31). Not only are we *told* that Edna's own behavior baffles her, the sentence itself is a wordy puzzle through which we must work our way, in suspense to the heart—"one of the two contradictory impulses." The repeated modals and negatives, the mixture of active and passive voice, the almost clinical vocabulary, discourage Edna's too-close scrutiny of these "impulses"—and discourage us as well. This last point is important. For while the contradictory verbal signals underscore both Edna's own doubts and the contradictions we are told her character includes, they also thwart our own tendencies, as readers, to respond to the narrative from a single perspective.

But the verbal complications I have been describing fall away on the night Edna learns to swim, an event that integrates both modes of syntactic presentation and triumphantly celebrates a unity of emotions and will. The evening begins with the family entertainment at which Mademoiselle Reisz is asked to play the piano. Edna's unexpectedly passionate response to the music transcends the stolid domestic texture of the evening; to her own astonishment, the customary gentle, poetic images are absent, and in their place "the very passions themselves were aroused within her soul, swaying, lashing it, as the waves daily beat upon her splendid body. She trembled, she was choking, and the tears blinded her" (45). The response is an escalated version of her earlier crying, and again she is described as being at the mercy of forces beyond her control. But not only are these forces more concrete here, the figurative parallel between passions and waves (and soul and body) gives way at once to real waves as the guests walk down to the beach and Edna learns to swim.

She has been trying to learn to swim all summer, but "a certain ungovernable dread hung about her when in the water, unless there was a hand nearby that might reach out and reassure her" (46). Like the earlier oppression that filled her, "ungovernable dread" has "hung about her"—another globally vague picture which admits no guiding consciousness and shows Edna paralyzed and impotent, the passive recipient of instructions from others. Now there is a change:

> But that night she was like the little tottering, stumbling, clutching child, who of a sudden realizes its powers, and walks for the first time alone, boldly and with over-confidence. She could have shouted for joy. She did shout for joy, as with a sweeping stroke or two she lifted her body to the surface of the water. (46)

We find our way through the cluster of adjectives and commas to Edna's triumph: animated and active herself, engaged and roused, she can transform a figure of speech into a real shout of joy. The grammatical shift from "could have" to "did"—like the shift from the little child to Edna herself—signals real changes in her behavior and understanding. Her shout fuses body and consciousness.

Similarly, the passage fuses the contrasting verbal patterns I have described. It begins with *she* but the simile that follows deflects us momentarily from Edna herself with its explicit comparison of her to a child. Both the pronoun *that* and the definite article *the* give the images a still, emblematic quality that characterizes the entire scene. The participles—*stumbling, tottering, clutching*—are concrete and visual, and though they suggest faltering and vulnerability, they are intransitive, thus active, not passive. The digression has added suspense: the child "of a sudden realizes its powers" and walks "boldly and with over-confidence"; now Edna's action breaks through the mentalistic language of this symbolic picture, as though the "she" that began the sentence has gathered power that is now released. "She could have shouted for joy. She did shout for joy. . . ." This is one of the most unambivalent expressions of active force in the book: Edna passes from the metaphorical to the actual and offers a verbal model, in miniature, for what the story is about. The passage ends in the wholly immediate and concrete, "as with a sweeping stroke or two she lifted her body to the surface of the water."

Like the scene as a whole, the passage makes clear that swimming has both sensual and spiritual dimensions, and its risks are both sexual and political: "She wanted to swim far out, where no woman had swum before" (46). Edna's experience of the water is immediately, passionately sensuous, but its spiritual and political dimensions are continually affirmed: "A feeling of exultation overtook her, as if some power of significant import had been given her to control the working of her body and her soul" (46). We may dwell for a moment on this sentence, which not only relates the swimming experience to both body and soul explicitly but also formally fuses the passive and active elements of Edna's situation. *Exultation,* in the first clause, is the familiar abstract noun: as a replacement of *oppression,* only the nature of the emotion has changed; formally, Edna remains in the sentence the passive object of abstract forces beyond her control. But then the burden of responsibility shifts when the power is given to her: though still the recipient of this gift, the *her* which is the object of *given* is also the subject of the infinitive *to control.* The grammatical simultaneity of *her* as object and subject is equivalent to the fluctuating and sometimes paradoxical images that interlace subject and object, self and other, container and contained, inner and outer. For a moment at least, Chopin creates a perfect verbal merging between the forces that act on Edna from outside her and the imperatives of her own self, between the abstractions of consciousness and the concrete language of her physical world. Nowhere does the narrative voice achieve a fuller sense of integration than in this passage: "She turned her face seaward to gather in an impression of space and solitude, which the vast expanse of water, meeting and melting with the moonlit sky, conveyed to her excited fancy. As she swam she seemed to be reaching out for the unlimited in which to lose herself" (46–47).

The celebratory language and physical beauty of the scene, however, should not make us forget the threat, signaled first by the description of the little child who walks "with over-confidence" and echoed in words like *reckless, intoxicated,* and *overestimating her strength*. Though she may wish "to swim far out," she can in fact only manage a short distance; unaccustomed even to this exertion, she is overcome by exhaustion and a vision of death, and can barely swim back to shore. This experience, together with other features of the scene, deliberately invokes the earlier "voice of the sea" refrain and its sinister promises:

> The voice of the sea is seductive; never ceasing, whispering, clamoring, murmuring, inviting the soul to wander for a spell in abysses of solitude; to lose itself in mazes of inward contemplation.
> The voice of the sea speaks to the soul. The touch of the sea is sensuous, enfolding the body in its soft, close embrace. (32)

This passage conceals in poetic metaphor the threat which emerges suddenly when Edna, in the swimming scene, experiences both a vision of death and a real danger of drowning. Seduced by the sea's space and solitude, Edna seeks to lose herself in its mazes. The sea may speak to the soul, but its seduction of the body is a more literal and risky enfolding.

The swimming scene gives substance to what has only been metaphorical suggestion; it is the turning point in the novel which offers us, in a rush, a sudden access to Edna's possibilities and an expanded vision of her situation. (We did not know till this scene, for example, that Edna had even been trying to learn to swim.) This conversion of metaphor to experience gives the scene its power. The confusion and hesitance of Edna's earlier behavior fall away as she takes her life, literally, into her own hands. In the scene that follows, speaking to Robert and then to her husband, she uses the first-person pronoun with far greater authority than before, describing her feelings and her will. As a reading experience, the swimming scene is a triumph. For Edna, in perfect and dangerous solitude, an "I" has been created.

II

In her childhood Edna crossed "a meadow that seemed as big as the ocean," moving her arms "as if swimming when she walked" (34–35). The second section of the novel moves from ocean to city, where walking becomes, for Edna, something of an emotional and spiritual equivalent to swimming.

Her walking gives her some degree of physical freedom. "'I always feel so sorry for women who don't like to walk,'" she says later. "'They miss so much—so many rare little glimpses of life; and we women learn so little of life on the whole'" (127). But to her husband, this mobility is dangerous. "'She goes tramping about by herself,'" he tells Dr. Mandelet to indicate the seriousness of her mental condition, "'moping in street-cars, getting in after dark. I tell you she's peculiar'" (86). Their divergent points of view may remind us that the subtitle of *The Awakening,* originally its title, is *A Solitary Soul.* Solitude is a critical theme of the novel, closely related to the existence of the self and its responsibilities.

Edna's physical mobility parallels a tentative kind of self-exploration. When her husband and children leave, and she is alone at last, she experiences "a radiant peace" (92), a "genuine sigh of relief," "a feeling that was unfamiliar but very delicious" (92). "She walked all through the house, from one room to another, as if inspecting it for the first time" (92). The language recalls an earlier scene at Madame Antoine's when Edna inspected each part of her body, "observing closely, as if it were something she saw for the first time" (55). But Edna comes to realize that she will not find peace in her husband's house. Once she has "resolved never again to belong to another than herself" (100), she must seek a new space, and makes plans to move into the "pigeon house" around the corner. Edna's freedom to move around—to walk at random, to dine out, to visit the racetrack—mimics the mobility of the men in the novel, who are always off somewhere—the club, New York, Mexico. Yet it is merely the freedom that Edna wants, not the masculine world it represents—a world which all the male characters, to different degrees, belong to, and which Chopin seems repeatedly to question.

Cigars and newspapers are the props that Chopin sardonically furnishes for the male characters. When the novel opens, Robert is too young, poor, and inexperienced for cigars, and must make do with cigarettes, which he rolls himself. Mr. Pontellier, on the other hand, has earned the right to cigars and to the world of masculine economic and sexual power they stand for. Cigars may seem a rather obvious emblem of this power, but the men in the novel make few appearances without one, and this mildly subversive caricature of male privilege seems clearly intended. On the night Edna learns to swim, she sits outside in the moonlight—first with Robert, who smokes cigarettes, and then alone, in defiance of her husband. He counters her revolutionary mood with a show of power: he drinks wine, puts up his feet, and smokes a cigar while he waits. Finally outlasted, her mood broken, she goes in, pausing to ask him if he's coming. "'Yes, dear,'" he answers, "'Just as soon as I have finished my cigar'" (51). This is communication of a potent form, and when Robert later returns from Mexico, he too shifts to cigars: "'I suppose I'm getting reckless,'" he tells Edna, "'I bought a whole box'" (128). Leaving for Mexico neither Edna's provider nor her lover, he returns aspiring to be both: This almost cartoonlike assertion announces his acquisition of adult male status. Edna's statement that "I am no longer one of Mr. Pontellier's possessions to dispose of or not" violates the rules of this world of established masculine potency and shatters Robert's vision of a dignified transaction between gentlemen. It is to traditional roles and masculine codes, to men and cigars, that Robert's farewell note is loyal.

During Edna's periods of solitude, she achieves some measure of peacefulness and of control over her day-to-day activities. As Margaret Culley points out, Chopin permits us some glimpse of Edna alone by obligingly removing the men in her life from the novel for extended periods of time. Though it is not clear-cut, her solitary self-sufficiency does contrast with her dependence on men when they are around. I do not agree with Patricia Meyer Spacks that dependence is the chief issue in the novel, but certainly the masculine presence affects Edna's behavior as well as the language she uses, which is characterized by the familiar abstract nouns, stiff formal phrases, a sense of abstract passivity, and by the distancing *it was/there was* construction. With all her relationships to men unresolved—to Robert, to Arobin, and to her husband—she acknowledges at last that "she wanted something to happen—something, anything; she did not know what" (95). This is one of the first concrete admissions of Edna's active involvement, of her actively wanting something. The semantic uncertainty does not lessen the force of the verb. Her awakening consciousness, peaceful only in solitude, plays against her awakening sensuality, which depends for its fulfillment on the masculine world that alienates her.

Much of the narrative tension of the novel, as well as a host of images and metaphors, has seemed to be building toward the moment when Edna will at last commit adultery and experience an explicitly sexual awakening. For Seyersted, the scene in which Edna sleeps with Arobin is the novel's "single, crucial paragraph" where Chopin "explodes the myth of the noble, undivided passion" (171). As we might expect, the passage is powerful:

> Edna cried a little that night after Arobin left her. It was only one phase of the multitudinous emotions which had assailed her. There was an overwhelming feeling of irresponsibility. There was the shock of the unexpected and unaccustomed. There was her husband's reproach, looking at her from the external things around her which he had provided for her external existence. There was Robert's reproach, making itself felt by a quicker, fiercer, more overpowering love, which had awakened within her toward him. Above all, there was understanding. She felt as if a mist had been lifted from her eyes, enabling her to look upon and comprehend the significance of life, that monster made up of beauty and brutality. But among the conflicting sensations which assailed her, there was neither shame nor remorse. There was a dull pang of regret because it was not the kiss of love which had inflamed her, because it was not love which had held this cup of life to her lips. (104)

This passage asserts that sexual intercourse leaves Edna shocked and overwhelmed, that the "mist had been lifted" to reveal that sexual pleasure can occur without marriage or love—that it can, indeed, occur with a barely respectable man she does not even like. But the language of the passage is curious, and does not quite fulfill our expectations. Though Edna took the initiative in responding to Arobin's kiss ("she clasped his head" [104]), and thus implicitly was responsible, she is no longer in active control. Far from reinforcing her emotional commitment to the experience, as the swimming scene so clearly did (as when she achieved the "power . . . to control the working of her body and soul" [46]), this passage displaces her from the action almost entirely. Its syntactic construction is as extreme as any in the book. *There was* or *it was* occurs ten times, repetitively asserting the existence of feelings and responses, but denying Edna any connection to or responsibility for them. In part perhaps, Chopin's wariness led her to report her heroine's responses to sexual gratification without personally committing her to them, but this does not fully account for the stiffness and distance of the passage. At the moment when Edna should be wholly awakened, alive, and present, the language removes her. At the moment when her body should be fully engaged, abstractions absorb her experience.

Body is invaded by consciousness; the link cannot be undone. We may have believed that *The Awakening* has been building toward Edna's sexual fulfillment, but we are wrong. It cannot be, this language says; both body and spirit are awakening toward some final end, and this is not it. The book's verbal complications here thwart our temptation to read this passage as a release or a solution. As the pages that follow make clear, Edna's "problem" is never simply one of achieving the freedom to make sexuality possible or to forsake paternalistic conventions: it is rather a question of how a woman who has achieved a self—has become an "I"—can live in the world. The book builds toward a rather brutal exploration of the physiological consequences of women's choices. Here, as elsewhere, we see and hear connections which are not explicit. We carry the language of the novel along with us as we read.

This process is exemplified when Edna, in the midst of her elegant dinner party several nights later, suddenly experiences a total assault by the abstract forces, so familiar to us now, that have threatened her from the beginning:

> But as she sat there amid her guests, she felt the old ennui overtaking her; the hopelessness which so often assailed her, which came upon her like an obsession, like something extraneous, independent of volition. It was something which announced itself; a chill breath that seemed to issue from some vast cavern wherein discords wailed. There came over her the acute longing which always summoned into her spiritual vision the presence of the beloved one, overpowering her at once with a sense of the unattainable. (109–10)

That this language occurs at this point, when Edna is discovering personal freedom and overt sexuality, is ominous. Our recognition of the lexical and syntactic patterns duplicates, perhaps, Edna's acceptance of this turn of emotional events; the phrase *"the old ennui"* suggests how commonplace the oppression, once so "strange and unfamiliar" (25), has become. That oppression, introduced long ago, has solidified and thus become more genuinely threatening. It is now poignantly localized; unlike her first experience of oppression, "which seemed to generate in some unfamiliar part of her unconsciousness" (25), it here announces itself as "a chill breath that seemed to issue from some vast cavern wherein discords wailed." Again she is "overtaken," "come upon," "overpowered"—but now the earlier "mist" and "shadows" have given way to the permanence of a "vast cavern" of solid rock. To an extraordinary degree the passage compresses the verbal elements that have troubled Edna: the abstraction, vagueness, passivity that have characterized these moments of awakening consciousness.

Yet why should this language occur here? Why should it here threaten Edna's new life with a foreshadowing of despair and death? Using such language as evidence, Ruth Sullivan and Stewart Smith argue that Edna in the course of the book experiences "a series of depressions that become suicidal," that the facts of her life "paint a consistent portrait of the kind of woman who might commit suicide because she was denied love by a man important to her" (69). We might then read the dinner-party scene as a corruption of the innocence of the family entertainment at Grand Isle: when, for example, Robert's decadent brother Victor hums Robert's song, it is for Edna the transforming vision. Cynthia Griffin Wolff, similarly, describes Edna's "sense of inner emptiness" (for example, the "vast cavern" image), which she attributes to a "schizoid" personality, and an "infantile life-pattern" (469, 460, 461). Patricia Allen's analysis of male critics' responses to the novel notes their virtually uniform castigation of Edna for failing in her duties as a wife and mother; yet much of the same irritation and righteous outrage pervades these psychological studies, which seem to view Edna's depression as a result of her individual failures and personal maladjustments. But this analysis fails to account for our experience of the novel as a reading experience; and I would argue that the language, here and elsewhere, continually asserts the existence of an independent, impersonal state of affairs over which Edna has little control. Analysis of the central metaphor will clarify the argument.

III

Chopin achieves her effects by building up, over time, a network of images, words, verbal refrains, and grammatical textures, often through simple and quite artificial repetition, until the language we remember is continually energizing the language on the page. This growing resonance of language and imagery makes complex and sensuous what is essentially straightforward prose. In the closing chapters of *The Awakening*, this cumulative density is apparent, and contributes to the drama and sense of narrative completion that the reading experience creates.

Chopin's central metaphor of waking and sleeping, for example, depends on more than a hundred references to literal and metaphorical awakening, sleeping, and dreaming. At first the words themselves tempt us to make some fairly conventional equations: sleep means blindness, inertia, passivity, death; awakening means energy, activity, vision, life. Nothing in the prose denies us these meanings. But gradually, as they are linked to specific words, images, and narrative developments, the novel's unique associations supplant the personal and literary associations we have brought to it. By the time we reach the final scenes, most of the key words have occurred before and resonate with a verbal history internal to the text. This process of cumulative association—this intricate and increasingly paradoxical interweaving of meanings—radically changes their impact. Whatever we accept as the meaning of the novel must take into account this process of transformation.

The process can be briefly sketched. In an early scene, Edna is literally awakened by her husband. The night she learns to swim, her sleep is "troubled and feverish, disturbed with dreams" that leave fleeting impressions the next day upon "her half-awakened senses" (51). Her sensuality is later said to be awakened by Arobin (97), while Edna attributes her awakening to Robert (130). Elsewhere her awakening seems self-generated. The ambiguous structure of the word *awakening* encompasses these definitions, permitting Edna to be awakened, to awaken someone else as she awakens Robert [51]), or simply to awaken spontaneously (as she does on p. 56). Critics have noted that the act of awakening (like sleeping) figures both literally and symbolically in the novel (see Wheeler or Wolff, for example), and most of the key scenes, in fact, play upon these events. But the density and complexity of verbal reference are critical. Repeated references make clear Edna's "awakening sensuousness" (97); yet after Arobin kisses her hand, she feels like a woman who "realizes the significance of [unfaithfulness] without being wholly awakened from its glamour" (98). She is simultaneously, in other words, awakening *to* sensuality and awakening *from* it. Because in Chopin, the individual line or paragraph is inevitably subordinate to the cumulative verbal effect, such paradoxical usage thwarts any single perspective or definition.

When Edna meets Robert in the garden and returns with him for the final time to her little house, the imagery of sleeping, awakening and dreaming intensifies. "'Robert,'" Edna asks him as he sits in shadow, "as if in a reverie," "'Are you asleep?'" (128). This same question opened the intricate, political battle of wills between Edna and her husband the night she learned to swim (49ff). Here, it opens an exchange between Edna and Robert which parallels the earlier scene and clarifies Chopin's position in this novel on relationships between women and men. When Edna leans down and kisses Robert, she takes control of her life (as she did with Arobin) and shatters his evasive reticence; at first it seems that what she earlier characterized as a "delicious, grotesque, impossible dream" (50) is coming true, for Robert confesses his own "'wild dream of your some way becoming my wife'" (129). But in shock and surprise Edna replies, "'Your wife!'" and in this exclamation reveals the vast distance that separates her earlier consciousness from that which now tells Robert, "'You have been a very, very foolish boy, wasting your time dreaming of impossible things when you speak of Mr. Pontellier setting me free! I am no longer one of Mr. Pontellier's possessions to dispose of or not. I give myself where I choose'" (129).

Edna explicitly rejects her role as a possession and an object, and it is significant that she refers to her husband formally as "Mr. Pontellier"; for it was as "Mrs. Pontellier" that the novel introduced her and almost at once referred to her as both an object and a possession. Her statement at this point recalls her inward determination, earlier, "never to belong to another than herself"; but now she expresses herself aloud, and it is her new language, perhaps, that frightens Robert as much as what she says. It was in this language that she confronted him in an earlier scene and demonstrated the same mastery of the first-person singular pronoun: "'I suppose this is what you would call unwomanly; but I have got into a habit of expressing myself. It doesn't matter to me, and you may think me unwomanly if you like'" (127). In contrast to this language of the self are numerous references to literal and figurative voices in the novel which for Edna become increasingly unimportant as her own language emerges. By the time the doctor offers meaningful conversation—to "'talk of things you never have dreamt of talking about before'" (133)—it is a language Edna no longer speaks.

Robert turns pale during Edna's assertion of independence, but she does not yet recognize that they are at cross-purposes—that her insistence and initiative have at least shattered his vaguely self-congratulatory indecisiveness and, in fact, terrified him. "'It was you,'" she goes on, "'who awoke me last summer out of a life-long, stupid dream'" (130). Robert himself has been treated as a part of this dream until now, and so the sudden description of her whole life as a *stupid* dream (and of Robert's dream as a waste of time) confirms that, for Edna, the meaning of the word *dream* has changed: what was "delicious" fantasy is now rejected as delusion.

Chopin introduced the metaphor of sleeping and awakening by

rooting it in reality when Edna was awakened by her husband. Now Edna is called away to be with Adèle Ratignolle during childbirth, and as she sits at her bedside, the central metaphor is once more transformed into literal reality:

> Edna began to feel uneasy. She was seized with a vague dread. Her own life experiences seemed far away, unreal, and only half remembered. She recalled faintly an ecstasy of pain, the heavy odor of chloroform, a stupor which deadened sensation, and an awakening to find a little new life to which she had given being, added to the great unnumbered multitude of souls that come and go. (131)

This passage is of critical narrative importance, for together with Edna's response to the birth process itself and her exchange with Doctor Mandelet, it makes clear that for women the birth of children is a central and inescapable issue. It is a philosophical as well as physiological fact, for Edna having just declared her love for Robert, comprehends with vivid clarity the inescapable link between sexual fulfillment, childbirth, and responsibility for those "little lives." In the passage, multiple verb forms come together: for example, the phrase "heavy odor of chloroform" binds an earlier fragment "heavy with sleep" to Arobin's "narcotic" presence and to the "heavy odor of jessamine" (109) at Edna's dinner party; earlier, when Arobin and Robert have both left, Edna "stayed alone in a kind of reverie—a sort of stupor" (124); the stupor which deadens sensation recalls the Ratignolles' marriage of "blind contentment" (76). The drugged stupor of childbirth, its deadened sensations, resolves in women's terms the conventional paradox that out of death comes life. But the passage also gives specific reality to the sense of alien forces that has governed Edna's awakening consciousness: her original experience of "indescribable oppression" is in fact clearly described here. The "vague dread" that seizes her recalls her earlier "vague anguish," the "ungovernable dread" she experienced in the water, and the "vague dread" that had filled Adèle: in *The Awakening,* the source of this dread, the source of the oppression, lies in the reality of the female body. This reality is the source, in turn, of life's compelling illusions.

Edna's revelation leaves her "stunned and speechless with emotion," for its corollary is that her own sexual awakening is as deluded as her previous life has been; it is merely part of the "stupid life-long dream." Dazed, speaking as much to herself as to Doctor Mandelet, she completes the vision: "'The years that are gone seems like dreams—

if one might go on sleeping and dreaming—but to wake up and find—oh! well! perhaps it is better to wake up after all, even to suffer, rather than to remain a dupe to illusions all one's life'" (133). The deliciousness of the dream is at the root of its deceptive power. The "cup of life" that sexual passion holds out is nature's narcotic, which both intoxicates and drugs—"'a decoy,'" as the doctor says, "'to secure mothers for the race'" (132). Edna accepts responsibility for her vision. "'One has to think of the children some time or other,'" she says, speaking in the abstract but at once shifting to the first person: "'I don't want anything but my own way. . . . Still, I shouldn't want to trample upon the little lives'" (133). The change of the pronoun signals the self's recognition of responsibility, though not necessarily, as most readings have had it, for her own children; she is no more a "mother-woman" than she has ever been. Rather, she sees the inevitability of the connection, and the "unnumbered multitude" of young lives that result from the illusion of sexual fulfillment. These are "the realities" with which Edna has at last come "face to face"; this is the "alien force" that threatens to invade her.

Characteristically, Edna does not accept this vision without a struggle; her consciousness attempts one last evasion by reviving earlier dreams. "Numb with the intoxication of expectancy" (the language continues to link passion with pregnancy and death), she hopes Robert will have fallen asleep so that she can "awaken him with a kiss" and "arouse him with her caresses" (133). "She could picture at that moment no greater bliss on earth than possession of the beloved one" (133). But as the vocabulary itself should tell us, none of this is to be. Instead, we learn how dense the language has become when Edna finds the house empty and reads Robert's farewell note ("'I love you. Good-by—because I love you'" [134]):

> Edna grew faint when she read the words. She went and sat on the sofa. Then she stretched herself out there, never uttering a sound. She did not sleep. She did not go to bed. The lamp sputtered and went out. She was still awake in the morning, when Celestine unlocked the kitchen door and came in to light the fire. (134)

This "awakening," for Edna, is final. Her faintness momentarily invokes her customary tendency to dream and sleep, but not for long. Unlike the first awakening scene, here she does not cry nor succumb at last to sleep. In perfect solitude and silence, her mind is entirely occupied with itself. The threatening external forces have been internalized within her own body: the language of childbirth underlies the "vast cavern wherein discords wailed." Though the passage holds us fast to Edna's literal behavior, it is no longer purely concrete; its structures are invaded with meaning. In the terms that the book has created, to be alive is to sleep and to dream; out of the deathlike stupor of childbirth comes life, but conversely, to awaken, as Edna has done, is to die. When her consciousness fully awakens, it undoes itself. The passage doubles as a retrospective catalogue of her consciousness and a preparation for the decision she is making.

IV

Edna enters the final chapter through the eyes of Victor and Mariequita; she is again "Mrs. Pontellier," and her docile, conventional interaction with them informs us that the real Edna is elsewhere. Now as she moves "rather mechanically" toward the beach, we reenter her consciousness which we find has absorbed its external environment and is now "not noticing anything special except that the sun was hot." Edna's analysis of her situation is distanced verbally from her current consciousness by the past perfect tense ("she had done all the thinking which was necessary"), and is offered at this point, after the fact, to the reader. In her despondency, she has seen the inevitable connections between responsibility to one's self and to others, especially to one's children—those that already exist and those not yet born. Adèle's plea to "think of the children" does not mean to Edna what it means to her. To Edna, the body enters a duplicitous pact with nature to betray the self; the inevitability of this duplicity makes the children seem like alien antagonists who "overcome" and "overpower" her. As her body awakens and consciousness invades it, its fate becomes clear. To live as the creator and nurturer of new "little lives" perverts the self; to live alone and for herself alone, as Mademoiselle Reisz does, is for Edna impossible. The roots of the word *dream* include both "joy" and "deception"; Edna's vision of reality has robbed her of the possibility of either, and she must put aside all the fictions she has been offered. Maternal love, romantic love, sexual passion, economic independence, artistic achievement, physical comfort, civilized elegance: all, for Edna, are intensely duplicitous.

The paradox is this: Mrs. Pontellier has become an "I" and has mastered in her own speech the use of the pronoun. Her movement through space in the novel—swimming, walking—is important because she is the only female character capable of it: capable of change, capable of learning a new language. But at the point of her final movement, she speaks and embodies a language which cannot be spoken. Only in solitude can the true self speak and be heard.

This is what the last chapter is about. It is a stunning culmination of the novel's verbal patterns that gives them their final transformation. It condenses the processes that have been animating the reading experience and carries us along in a swift and yet often unexpected rush of words and images. The novel's metaphors become, in the last scene, its literal reality. Thus throughout the novel Edna has metaphorically removed her clothing: first she loosened "the mantle of reserve" (32); when Robert left for Mexico "her whole existence was dulled, like a faded garment which seems to be no longer worth wearing" (65); as she changes, "she was becoming herself and daily casting aside that fictitious self which we assume like a garment with which to appear before the world" (77); after the exhaustion of watching Adèle give birth, she lets "the tearing emotion" "fall away from her like a somber, uncomfortable garment, which she had but to loosen to be rid of" (133). Now, as she reaches the beach and changes into her bathing suit, she again transforms the metaphorical into the actual, stripping away her fictitious selves: "But when she was there beside the sea, absolutely alone, she cast the unpleasant, pricking garments from her, and for the first time in her life she stood naked in the open air, at the mercy of the sun, the breeze upon her, and the waves that invited her" (136).

It is thus no surprise that Edna walks literally into the sea. Life and death are inextricably linked, as the language has linked sleeping and awakening. "All along the white beach, up and down, there was no living thing in sight," Chopin writes, yet then at once adds to the scene "a bird with a broken wing," "beating the air above, reeling, fluttering, circling down, down to the water" (136). The bird's appearance here underscores the verbal processes of this final chapter, for it too has been a dual image throughout the novel; invoking both the "fluttering wings" of the mother-women and the bruised and exhausted artistic weaklings who, in Mademoiselle Reisz's words, come "'fluttering back to earth'" (103), the image links childbirth with death and confirms the novel's verbal movement. The obviousness, the expectedness of the image makes clear its participation not in a world of real things but in a visionary verbal structure. The language of Edna's experience supports this reading: "How strange and awful it seemed to stand naked under the sky! how delicious! She felt like some new-born creature, opening its eyes in a familiar world that it had never known" (136). This recalls the earlier comment that Edna had learned "to look with her own eyes;

to see and to apprehend the deeper undercurrents of life'' (115)—which links this clear-sightedness with the sea.

Edna's final movement into the sea makes literal, in the general way I have cited, the sea's metaphorical seductiveness; the link is explicit, because the ''voice of the sea'' refrain is repeated. But it forms a stricter parallel with the earlier swimming scene, both in its individual images and in its overall sense of personal will and spirit of victory. Learning to swim—awakening—made Edna's death inevitable. Her vision of death that night, of course, foreshadowed her final suicide. But what is more interesting is that the final scene restores to swimming its literal meaning. The earlier scene promised a metaphorical fulfillment; it promised that Edna's triumph was to be the beginning of a new life; it promised an awakening that was both sensual and spiritual. It *was* that, but its symbolic and metaphorical possibilities were always more appealing than any imaginable reality; similarly, no subsequent reality in Edna's experience ever moved her as much as her own power, while in the water, ''to control the working of her body and her soul'' (46). Thus she does not return to the sea because it is the ideal lover, or the unlimited she has sought, or a transcendent oneness ''in which to lose herself.'' Rather, she chooses the sea for itself. The joy of swimming is not what it promises or stands for; it is the ultimate end. What seemed metaphorical and symbolic is literal.

Similarly, Edna's suicide translates into narrative reality the verbal elements from which the novel has been built. It enacts the moment during the swimming scene when Edna was simultaneously both active subject and passive object. In the last paragraph, we see as well that the novel's language enacts this paradox, offering us a literal reality hallucinated by a consciousness which no longer exists:

> She looked into the distance, and the old terror flamed up for an instant, then sank again. Edna heard her father's voice and her sister Margaret's. She heard the barking of an old dog that was chained to the sycamore tree. The spurs of the cavalry officer clanged as he walked across the porch. There was the hum of bees, and the musky odor of pinks filled the air. (137)

At the beginning of the paragraph, Edna actively looks into the distance; she is the subject of the next two sentences, though now as a passive listener. Then the spurs clang across the porch, and she is no longer in the sentence at all. Sense impressions and memories float in space. The unique and individual consciousness, the ''I,'' has disintegrated; it is the reader, as much as Edna, who retains the meaning of the cavalry officer.

"There was the hum of bees, and the musky odor of pinks filled the air." Just as the novel opened with an image of two birds—an apparently literal image almost immediately undermined by the statement that one of them spoke "a language which nobody understood"—so here the apparently humdrum image of bees and pinks is undermined by the fact that they are as much a part of our reality as Edna's.

The self asserts itself and in doing so undoes itself. Suicide is perhaps the most profoundly ambivalent of all human acts, and one which here confirms the unresolvable ambiguities of Edna's own role in the novel. It represents active passivity, a decision no longer to decide. For Edna, this act translates many of the novel's metaphors into reality, and in turn parallels the critical fact about this story: that it is about a woman learning to perceive reality whose "I" supplants the language of illusion. In determining "never to belong to another than herself," and "to give up the unessential," she transcends the mythologies offered to her, and to us, and this is treated as a triumph, not a failure. No matter what specific interpretations one gives the story's ending, its language has been living its own life and preparing us for this resolution. The profoundly active and passive elements that animate the narrative, the struggles of the self to master a language, are given, in Edna's suicide, their perfect human emblem and perfect literal, and literary, resolution.

WORKS CITED

Allen, Patricia. "Old Critics and New: The Treatment of Chopin's *The Awakening.*" *The Authority of Experience: Essays in Feminist Criticism.* Ed. Arlyn Diamond and Lee R. Edwards. Amherst: U of Massachusetts P, 1977.

Culley, Margaret. "Edna Pontellier: 'A Solitary Soul.'" *The Awakening.* New York: Norton, 1976.

Seyersted, Per. *Kate Chopin: A Critical Biography.* Baton Rouge: Louisiana State UP, 1969.

Spacks, Patricia Meyer. *The Female Imagination.* New York: Knopf, 1972.

Sullivan, Ruth, and Stewart Smith. "Narrative Stance in Kate Chopin's *The Awakening.*" *Studies in American Fiction* 1 (Spring 1973): 62–75.

Wheeler, Otis B. "The Five Awakenings of Edna Pontellier." *The Southern Review* 11 (Winter 1975): 118–28.

Wolff, Cynthia Griffin. "Thanatos and Eros: Kate Chopin's *The Awakening.*" *American Quarterly* 25 (October 1973): 449–71. [Wolff's essay is also reprinted in this volume on pp. 233–58.]

Glossary of Critical and Theoretical Terms

Most terms have been glossed parenthetically where they first appear in the text. Mainly, the glossary lists terms that are too complex to define in a phrase or a sentence or two. A few of the terms listed are discussed at greater length elsewhere (feminist criticism, for instance); these terms are defined succinctly and a page reference to the longer discussion is provided.

AFFECTIVE FALLACY First used by William K. Wimsatt and Monroe C. Beardsley to refer to what they regarded as the erroneous practice of interpreting texts according to the psychological responses of readers. "The Affective Fallacy," they wrote in a 1946 essay later republished in the *Verbal Icon* (1954), "is a confusion between the poem and its *results* (what it *is* and what it *does*). . . . It begins by trying to derive the standards of criticism from the psychological effects of a poem and ends in impressionism and relativism." The affective fallacy, like the intentional fallacy (confusing the meaning of a work with the author's expressly intended meaning), was one of the main tenets of the New Criticism, or formalism. The affective fallacy has recently been contested by reader-response critics, who have deliberately dedicated their efforts to describing the way individual readers and "interpretive communities" go about "making sense" of texts.

See also: Authorial Intention, Formalism, Reader-Response Criticism.

AUTHORIAL INTENTION Defined narrowly, an author's intention in writing a work, as expressed in letters, diaries, interviews, and conversations. Defined more broadly, "intentionality" involves unexpressed motivations, designs, and purposes, some of which may have remained unconscious.

The debate over whether critics should try to discern an author's intentions (conscious or otherwise) is an old one. William K. Wimsatt and Monroe C. Beardsley, in an essay first published in the 1940s, coined the term "intentional fallacy'' to refer to the practice of basing interpretations on the expressed or implied intentions of authors, a practice they judged to be erroneous. As proponents of the New Criticism, or formalism, they argued that a work of literature is an object in itself and should be studied as such. They believed that it is sometimes helpful to learn what an author intended, but the critic's real purpose is to show what is actually in the text, not what an author intended to put there.

See also: Affective Fallacy, Formalism.

BASE *See* Marxist Criticism.

BINARY OPPOSITIONS *See* Oppositions.

BLANKS *See* Gaps.

CANON Since the fourth century, used to refer to those books of the Bible that the Christian church accepts as being Holy Scripture. The term has come to be applied more generally to those literary works given special status, or ''privileged,'' by a culture. Works we tend to think of as ''classics'' or the ''Great Books'' produced by Western culture — texts that are found in every anthology of American, British, and world literature — would be among those that constitute the canon.

Recently, Marxist, feminist, minority, and Third World critics have argued that, for political reasons, many excellent works never enter the canon. Canonized works, they claim, are those that reflect — and respect — the culture's dominant ideology and/or perform some socially acceptable or even necessary form of ''cultural work.'' Attempts have been made to broaden or redefine the canon by discovering valuable texts, or versions of texts, that were repressed or ignored for political reasons. These have been published both in traditional and in nontraditional anthologies. The more outspoken critics of the canon, especially radical critics practicing cultural criticism, have called into question the whole concept of canon or ''canonicity.'' Privileging no form of artistic expression that reflects and revises the culture, these critics treat cartoons, comics, and soap operas with the same cogency and respect they accord novels, poems, and plays.

See also: Cultural Criticism, Feminist Criticism, Ideology, Marxist Criticism.

CONFLICTS, CONTRADICTIONS *See* Gaps.

CULTURAL CRITICISM A critical approach that is sometimes referred to as ''cultural studies'' or ''cultural critique.'' Practitioners of cultural criticism oppose ''high'' definitions of culture and take seriously popular cultural forms. Grounded in a variety of continental European influences, cultural criticism nonetheless gained institutional force in England, in 1964, with the founding of the Centre for Contemporary Cultural Studies at Birmingham University. Broadly interdisciplinary in its scope and approach, cultural criticism views the text as the locus and catalyst of a complex network of political and economic discourses. Cultural critics share with Marxist critics an interest in the ideological contexts of cultural forms.

DECONSTRUCTION A poststructuralist approach to literature that is strongly influenced by the writings of the French philosopher Jacques Derrida. Deconstruction, partly in response to structuralism and formalism, posits the undecidability of meaning for all texts. In fact, as the deconstructionist critic J.

Hillis Miller points out, "deconstruction is not a dismantling of the structure of a text but a demonstration that it has already dismantled itself." See "What Is Deconstruction?" pages 259–70.

DIALECTIC Originally developed by Greek philosophers, mainly Socrates and Plato, as a form and method of logical argumentation; the term later came to denote a philosophical notion of evolution. The German philosopher G. W. F. Hegel described dialectic as a process whereby a thesis, when countered by an antithesis, leads to the synthesis of a new idea. Karl Marx and Friedrich Engels, adapting Hegel's idealist theory, used the phrase "dialectical materialism" to discuss the way in which a revolutionary class war might lead to the synthesis of a new social economic order. The American Marxist critic Fredric Jameson has coined the phrase "dialectical criticism" to refer to a Marxist critical approach that synthesizes structuralist and poststructuralist methodologies.

See also: Marxist Criticism, Structuralism, Poststructuralism.

DIALOGIC *See* Discourse.

DISCOURSE Used specifically, can refer to (1) spoken or written discussion of a subject or area of knowledge; (2) the words in, or text of, a narrative as opposed to its story line; or (3) a "strand" within a given narrative that argues a certain point or defends a given value system.

More generally, "discourse" refers to the language in which a subject or area of knowledge is discussed or a certain kind of business is transacted. Human knowledge is collected and structured in discourses. Theology and medicine are defined by their discourses, as are politics, sexuality, and literary criticism.

A society is generally made up of a number of different discourses or "discourse communities," one or more of which may be dominant or serve the dominant ideology. Each discourse has its own vocabulary, concepts, and rules, knowledge of which constitutes power. The psychoanalyst and psychoanalytic critic Jacques Lacan has treated the unconscious as a form of discourse, the patterns of which are repeated in literature. Cultural critics, following Mikhail Bakhtin, use the word "dialogic" to discuss the dialogue *between* discourses that takes place within language or, more specifically, a literary text.

See also: Cultural Criticism, Ideology, Narrative, Psychoanalytic Criticism.

FEMINIST CRITICISM An aspect of the feminist movement whose primary goals include critiquing masculine-dominated language and literature by showing how they reflect a masculine ideology; writing the history of unknown or undervalued women writers, thereby earning them their rightful place in the literary canon; and helping create a climate in which women's creativity may be fully realized and appreciated. See "What Is Feminist Criticism?" pages 158–69.

FIGURE *See* Metaphor, Metonymy, Symbol.

FORMALISM Also referred to as the New Criticism, formalism reached its height during the 1940s and 1950s but it is still practiced today. Formalists treat a work of literary art as if it were a self-contained, self-referential object. Rather than basing their interpretations of a text on the reader's response, the author's stated intentions, or parallels between the text and historical contexts (such as the author's life), formalists concentrate on the relationships *within* the text that give it its own distinctive character or form. Special attention is paid to repetition, particularly of images or symbols, but also of sound effects and rhythms in poetry.

Because of the importance placed on close analysis and the stress on the text as a carefully crafted, orderly object containing observable formal patterns, formalism has often been seen as an attack on Romanticism and impressionism, particularly impressionistic criticism. It has sometimes even been called an "objective" approach to literature. Formalists are more likely than certain other critics to believe and say that the meaning of a text can be known objectively. For instance, reader-response critics see meaning as a function either of each reader's experience or of the norms that govern a particular "interpretive community," and deconstructors argue that texts mean opposite things at the same time.

Formalism was originally based on essays written during the 1920s and 1930s by T. S. Eliot, I. A. Richards, and William Empson. It was significantly developed later by a group of American poets and critics, including R. P. Blackmur, Cleanth Brooks, John Crowe Ransom, Allen Tate, Robert Penn Warren, and William K. Wimsatt. Although we associate formalism with certain principles and terms (such as the "Affective Fallacy" and the "Intentional Fallacy" as defined by Wimsatt and Monroe C. Beardsley), formalists were trying to make a cultural statement rather than establish a critical dogma. Generally Southern, religious, and culturally conservative, they advocated the inherent value of literary works (particularly of literary works regarded as beautiful art objects) because they were sick of the growing ugliness of modern life and contemporary events. Some recent theorists even suggest that the rising popularity of formalism after World War II was a feature of American isolationism, the formalist tendency to isolate literature from biography and history being a manifestation of the American fatigue with wider involvements.

See also: Affective Fallacy, Authorial Intention, Deconstruction, Reader-Response Criticism, Symbol.

GAPS When used by reader-response critics familiar with the theories of Wolfgang Iser, refers to "blanks" in texts that must be filled in by readers. A gap may be said to exist whenever and wherever a reader perceives something to be missing between words, sentences, paragraphs, stanzas, or chapters. Readers respond to gaps actively and creatively, explaining apparent inconsistencies in point of view, accounting for jumps in chronology, speculatively supplying information missing from plots, and resolving problems or issues left ambiguous or "indeterminate" in the text.

Reader-response critics sometimes speak as if a gap actually exists in a text; a gap is, of course, to some extent a product of readers' perceptions. Different readers may find gaps in different texts, and different gaps in the same text. Furthermore, they may fill these gaps in in different ways, which is why, a reader-response critic might argue, works are interpreted in different ways.

Although the concept of the gap has been used mainly by reader-response critics, it has also been used by critics taking other theoretical approaches. Practitioners of deconstruction might use "gap" when speaking of the radical contradictoriness of a text. Marxists have used the term to speak of everything from the gap that opens up between economic base and cultural superstructure to the two kinds of conflicts or contradictions to be found in literary texts. The first of these, they would argue, results from the fact that texts reflect ideology, within which certain subjects cannot be covered, things that cannot be said, contradictory views that cannot be recognized as contradictory. The second kind of conflict, contradiction, or gap within a text results from the fact that works don't just reflect ideology: they are also fictions that, consciously or unconsciously, distance themselves from the same ideology.

See also: Deconstruction, Ideology, Marxist Criticism, Reader-Response Criticism.

GENRE A French word referring to a kind or type of literature. Individual works within a genre may exhibit a distinctive form, be governed by certain conventions, and/or represent characteristic subjects. Tragedy, epic, and romance are all genres.

Perhaps inevitably, the term "genre" is used loosely. Lyric poetry is a genre, but so are characteristic *types* of the lyric, such as the sonnet, the ode, and the elegy. Fiction is a genre, as are detective fiction and science fiction. The list of genres grows constantly as critics establish new lines of connection between individual works and discern new categories of works with common characteristics. Moreover, some writers form hybrid genres by combining the characteristics of several in a single work.

Knowledge of genres helps critics to understand and explain what is conventional and unconventional, borrowed and original, in a work.

HEGEMONY Given intellectual currency by the Italian communist Antonio Gramsci, the word (a translation of *egemonia*) refers to the pervasive system of assumptions, meanings, and values — the web of ideologies, in other words — that shapes the way things look, what they mean, and therefore what reality *is* for the majority of people within a given culture.

See also: Ideology, Marxist Criticism.

IDEOLOGY A set of beliefs underlying the customs, habits, and/or practices common to a given social group. To members of that group, the beliefs seem obviously true, natural, and even universally applicable. They may seem just as obviously arbitrary, idiosyncratic, and even false to outsiders or members of another group who adhere to another ideology. Within a society, several ideologies may coexist, or one or more may be dominant.

Ideologies may be forcefully imposed or willingly subscribed to. Their component beliefs may be held consciously or unconsciously. In either case, they come to form what Johanna M. Smith has called "the unexamined ground of our experience." Ideology governs our perceptions, judgments, and prejudices — our sense of what is acceptable, normal, and deviant. Ideology may cause a revolution; it may also allow discrimination and even exploitation.

Ideologies are of special interest to sociologically oriented critics of literature because of the way in which authors reflect or resist prevailing views in their texts. Some Marxist critics have argued that literary texts reflect and reproduce the ideologies that produced them; most, however, have shown how ideologies are riven with contradictions that works of literature manage to expose and widen. Still other Marxists have focused on the way in which texts themselves are characterized by gaps, conflicts, and contradictions between their ideological and anti-ideological functions.

Feminist critics have addressed the question of ideology by seeking to expose (and thereby call into question) the patriarchal ideology mirrored or inscribed in works written by men — even men who have sought to counter sexism and break down sexual stereotypes. New historicists have been interested in demonstrating the ideological underpinnings not only of literary representations but also of our interpretations of them. Fredric Jameson, an American Marxist critic, argues that all thought is ideological, but that ideological thought that knows itself as such stands the chance of seeing through and transcending ideology.

See also: Cultural Criticism, Feminist Criticism, Marxist Criticism, New Historicism.

IMAGINARY STAGE According to Lacanian psychoanalytic theory, the pre-oedipal, prelinguistic stage of child development that precedes the Symbolic stage. During the Imaginary stage, also called the mirror stage, the child conceives of the mother and indeed of the entire world as being indistinguishable from the self.

See also: Psychoanalytic Criticism, Symbolic Stage.

IMPLIED READER A phrase used by some reader-response critics in place of the phrase "the reader." Whereas "the reader" could refer to any idiosyncratic individual who happens to have read or to be reading the text, "the implied reader" is *the* reader intended, even created, by the text. Other reader-response critics seeking to describe this more generally conceived reader have spoken of the "informed reader" or the "narratee," who is "the necessary counterpart of a given narrator."

See Reader-Response Criticism.

INTENTIONAL FALLACY *See* Authorial Intention.

INTENTIONALITY *See* Authorial Intention.

INTERTEXTUALITY The condition of interconnectedness among texts. Every author has been influenced by others, and every work contains explicit and implicit references to other works. Writers may consciously or unconsciously echo a predecessor or precursor; they may also consciously or unconsciously disguise their indebtedness, making intertextual relationships difficult for the critic to trace.

Reacting against the formalist tendency to view each work as a free-standing object, some poststructuralist critics suggested that the meaning of a work only emerges intertextually, that is, within the context provided by other works. But there has been a reaction, too, against this type of intertextual criticism. Some new historicist critics suggest that literary history is itself too narrow a context and that works should be interpreted in light of a larger set of cultural contexts.

There is, however, a broader definition of intertextuality, one that refers to the relationship between works of literature and a wide range of narratives and discourses that we don't usually consider literary. Thus defined, intertextuality could be used by a new historicist to refer to the significant interconnectedness between a literary text and nonliterary discussions of or discourses about contemporary culture. Or it could be used by a poststructuralist to suggest that a work can only be recognized and read within a vast field of signs and tropes that is *like* a text and that makes any single text self-contradictory and "undecidable."

See also: Discourse, Formalism, Narrative, New Historicism, Poststructuralism, Trope.

MARXIST CRITICISM An approach that treats literary texts as material products, describing them in broadly historical terms. In Marxist criticism, the text is viewed in terms of its production and consumption, as a product *of* work that does identifiable cultural work of its own. Following Karl Marx, the founder of communism, Marxist critics have used the terms "base" to refer to economic reality and "superstructure" to refer to the corresponding or "homologous" infrastructure consisting of politics, law, philosophy, religion, and the arts. Also following Marx, they have used the word "ideology" to refer to that set of cultural beliefs that literary works at once reproduce, resist, and revise.

METAPHOR The representation of one thing by another related or similar thing. The image (or activity or concept) used to represent or "figure" something else is known as the "vehicle" of the metaphor; the thing represented is called the "tenor." In other words, the vehicle is what we substitute for the tenor. The relationship between vehicle and tenor can provide much additional meaning. Thus, instead of saying, "Last night I read a book," we might say, "Last night I plowed through a book." "Plowed through" (or the activity of plowing) is the vehicle of our metaphor; "read" (or the act of reading) is the tenor, the thing being figured. The increment in meaning through metaphor is fairly obvious. Our audience knows not only *that* we read but also *how* we read, because to read a book in the way that a plow rips through earth is surely to read in a relentless, unreflective way. Note that in the sentence above, a new metaphor — "rips through" — has been used to explain an old one. This serves (which is a metaphor) as an example of just how thick (another metaphor) language is with metaphors!

Metaphor is a kind of "trope" (literally, a "turning," i.e., a figure that alters or "turns" the meaning of a word or phrase). Other tropes include allegory, conceit, metonymy, personification, simile, symbol, and synecdoche. Traditionally, metaphor and symbol have been viewed as the principal tropes; minor tropes have been categorized as *types* of these two major ones. Similes, for instance, are usually defined as simple metaphors that usually employ "like" or "as" and state the tenor outright, as in "My love is like a red, red rose." Synecdoche involves a vehicle that is a *part* of the tenor, as in "I see a sail" meaning "I see a boat." Metonymy is viewed as a metaphor involving two terms commonly if arbitrarily associated with (but not fundamentally or intrinsically related to) each other. Recently, however, deconstructors such as Paul de Man and J. Hillis Miller have questioned the "privilege" granted to metaphor and the metaphor/metonymy distinction or "opposition." They have suggested that all metaphors are really metonyms and that all figuration is arbitrary.

See also: Deconstruction, Metonymy, Oppositions, Symbol.

METONYMY The representation of one thing by another that is commonly and often physically associated with it. To refer to a writer's handwriting as his or her "hand" is to use a metonymic "figure" or "trope." The image or thing used to represent something else is known as the "vehicle" of the metonym; the thing represented is called the "tenor."

Like other tropes (such as metaphor), metonymy involves the replacement of one word or phrase by another. Liquor may be referred to as "the bottle," a monarch as "the crown." Narrowly defined, the vehicle of a metonym is arbitrarily, not intrinsically, associated with the tenor. In other words, the bottle just happens to be what liquor is stored in and poured from in our culture. The hand may be involved in the production of handwriting, but so are the brain and the pen. There is no special, intrinsic likeness between a crown and a monarch; it's just that crowns traditionally sit on monarchs' heads and not on the heads of university professors. More broadly, "metonym" and "metonymy" have been used by recent critics to refer to a wide range of figures and tropes. Deconstructors have questioned the distinction between metaphor and metonymy.

See also: Deconstruction, Metaphor, Trope.

NARRATIVE A story or a telling of a story, or an account of a situation or of events. A novel and a biography of a novelist are both narratives, as are Freud's case histories.

Some critics use the word "narrative" even more generally; Brook Thomas, a new historicist, has critiqued "narratives of human history that neglect the role human labor has played."

NEW CRITICISM *See* Formalism.

NEW HISTORICISM One of the most recent developments in contemporary critical theory, its practitioners share certain convictions, the major ones being that literary critics need to develop a high degree of historical consciousness and that literature should not be viewed apart from other human creations, artistic or otherwise. See "What Is the New Historicism?" pages 190–201.

OPPOSITIONS A concept highly relevant to linguistics, since linguists maintain that words (such as *black* and *death*) have meaning not in themselves, but in relation to other words (*white* and *life*). Jacques Derrida, a poststructuralist philosopher of language, has suggested that in the West we think in terms of these "binary oppositions" or dichotomies, which on examination turn out to be evaluative hierarchies. In other words, each opposition — beginning/end, presence/absence, or consciousness/unconsciousness —contains one term that our culture views as superior and one term that we view as negative or inferior.

Derrida has "deconstructed" a number of these binary oppositions, including two — speech/writing and signifier/signified — that he believes to be central to linguistics in particular and Western culture in general. He has concurrently critiqued the "law" of noncontradiction, which is fundamental to Western logic. He and other deconstructors have argued that a text can contain opposed strands of discourse and, therefore, mean opposite things: reason *and* passion, life *and* death, hope *and* despair, black *and* white. Traditionally, criticism has involved choosing between opposed or contradictory meanings and arguing that one is present in the text and the other absent.

French feminists have adopted the ideas of Derrida and other deconstructors, showing not only that we think in terms of such binary oppositions as male/female, reason/emotion, and active/passive, but that we also associate reason and activity with masculinity and emotion and passivity with femininity. Because of this, they have concluded that language is "phallocentric," or masculine-dominated.

See also: Deconstruction, Discourse, Feminist Criticism, Poststructuralism.

POSTSTRUCTURALISM The general attempt to contest and subvert structuralism initiated by deconstructors and certain other critics associated with psychoanalytic, Marxist, and feminist theory. Structuralists, using linguistics as a model and employing semiotic (sign) theory, posit the possibility of knowing a text systematically and revealing the "grammar" behind its form and meaning. Poststructuralists argue against the possibility of such knowledge and description. They counter that texts can be shown to contradict not only structuralist accounts of them but also themselves. In making their adversarial claims, they rely on close readings of texts and on the work of theorists such as Jacques Derrida and Jacques Lacan.

Poststructuralists have suggested that structuralism rests on distinctions between "signifier" and "signified" (signs and the things they point toward), "self" and "language" (or "text"), texts and other texts, and text and world that are overly simplistic, if not patently inaccurate. Poststructuralists have shown how all signifieds are also signifiers, and they have treated texts as "intertexts." They have viewed the world as if it *were* a text (we desire a certain car because it *symbolizes* achievement) and the self as the subject, as well as the user, of language; for example, we may shape and speak through language, but it also shapes and speaks through us.

See also: Deconstruction, Feminist Criticism, Intertextuality, Psychoanalytic Criticism, Semiotics, Structuralism.

PSYCHOANALYTIC CRITICISM Grounded in the psychoanalytic theories of Sigmund Freud, it is one of the oldest critical methodologies still in use. Freud's view that works of literature, like dreams, express secret, unconscious desires led to criticism that interpreted literary works as manifestations of the authors' neuroses. More recently, psychoanalytic critics have come to see literary works as skillfully crafted artifacts that may appeal to *our* neuroses by tapping into our repressed wishes and fantasies. Other forms of psychological criticism that diverge from Freud, although they ultimately derive from his insights, include those based on the theories of Carl Jung and Jacques Lacan. See "What Is Psychoanalytic Criticism?" pages 218–33.

READER-RESPONSE CRITICISM An approach to literature that, as its name implies, considers the way readers respond to texts, as they read. Stanley Fish describes the method by saying that it substitutes for one question, "What does this sentence mean?" a more operational question, "What does this sentence do?" Reader-response criticism shares with deconstruction a strong textual orientation and a reluctance to define a single meaning for a work. Along with psychoanalytic criticism, it shares an interest in the dynamics of mental response to textual cues. See "What Is Reader-Response Criticism?" pages 297–307.

SEMIOLOGY, SEMIOTIC *See* Semiotics.

SEMIOTICS The study of signs and sign systems and the way meaning is derived from them. Structuralist anthropologists, psychoanalysts, and literary critics developed semiotics during the decades following 1950, but much of the pioneering work had been done at the turn of the century by the founder of modern linguistics, Ferdinand de Saussure, and the American philosopher Charles Sanders Peirce.

Semiotics is based on several important distinctions, including the distinction between "signifier" and "signified" (the sign and what it points toward) and the distinction between "langue" and "parole." *Langue* (French for "tongue," as in "native tongue," meaning language) refers to the entire system within which individual utterances or usages of language have meaning; *parole* (French for "word") refers to the particular utterances or usages. A principal tenet of semiotics is that signs, like words, are not significant in themselves, but instead have meaning only in relation to other signs and the entire system of signs, or langue.

The affinity between semiotics and structuralist literary criticism derives from this emphasis placed on langue, or system. Structuralist critics, after all, were reacting against formalists and their procedure of focusing on individual words as if meanings didn't depend on anything external to the text.

Poststructuralists have used semiotics but questioned some of its underlying assumptions, including the opposition between signifier and signified. The feminist poststructuralist Julia Kristeva, for instance, has used the word "semiotic" to describe feminine language, a highly figurative, fluid form of discourse that she sets in opposition to rigid, symbolic masculine language.

See also: Deconstruction, Feminist Criticism, Formalism, Poststructuralism, Oppositions, Structuralism, Symbol.

SIMILE *See* Metaphor.

SOCIOHISTORICAL CRITICISM *See* New Historicism.

STRUCTURALISM A science of humankind whose proponents attempted to show that all elements of human culture, including literature, may be understood as parts of a system of signs. Structuralism, according to Robert Scholes, was a reaction to "'modernist' alienation and despair."

Using Ferdinand de Saussure's linguistic theory, European structuralists such as Roman Jakobson, Claude Lévi-Strauss, and Roland Barthes (before his shift toward poststructuralism) attempted to develop a "semiology" or "semiotics" (science of signs). Barthes, among others, sought to recover literature and even language from the isolation in which they had been studied and to show that the laws that govern them govern all signs, from road signs to articles of clothing.

Particularly useful to structuralists were two of Saussure's concepts: the idea of "phoneme" in language and the idea that phonemes exist in two kinds of relationships: "synchronic" and "diachronic." A phoneme is the smallest consistently significant unit in language; thus, both "a" and "an" are phonemes, but "n" is not. A diachronic relationship is that which a phoneme has with those that have preceded it in time and those that will follow it. These "horizontal" relationships produce what we might call discourse or narrative and what Saussure called "parole." The synchronic relationship is the "vertical" one that a word has in a given instant with the entire system of language ("langue") in which it may generate meaning. "An" means what it means in English because those of us who speak the language are using it in the same way at a given time.

Following Saussure, Lévi-Strauss studied hundreds of myths, breaking them into their smallest meaningful units, which he called "mythemes." Removing each from its diachronic relations with other mythemes in a single myth (such as the myth of Oedipus and his mother), he vertically aligned those mythemes that he found to be homologous (structurally correspondent). He then studied the relationships within as well as between vertically aligned columns, in an attempt to understand scientifically, through ratios and proportions, those thoughts and processes that humankind has shared, both at one particular time and across time. One could say, then, that structuralists followed Saussure in preferring to think about the overriding langue or language of myth, in which each mytheme and mytheme-constituted myth fits meaningfully, rather than about isolated individual paroles or narratives. Structuralists followed Saussure's lead in believing what the poststructuralist Jacques Derrida later decided he could not subscribe to — that sign systems must be understood in terms of binary oppositions. In analyzing myths and texts to find basic structures, structuralists tended to find that opposite terms modulate until they are finally resolved or reconciled by some intermediary third term. Thus, a structuralist reading of *Paradise Lost* would show that the war between God and the bad angels becomes a rift between God and sinful, fallen man, the rift then being healed by the Son of God, the mediating third term.

See also: Deconstruction, Discourse, Narrative, Poststructuralism, Semiotics.

SUPERSTRUCTURE *See* Marxist Criticism.

SYMBOL A thing, image, or action that, although it is of interest in its own right, stands for or suggests something larger and more complex — often an idea or a range of interrelated ideas, attitudes, and practices.

Within a given culture, some things are understood to be symbols: the flag of the United States is an obvious example. More subtle cultural symbols might be the river as a symbol of time and the journey as a symbol of life and its manifold experiences.

Instead of appropriating symbols generally used and understood within their culture, writers often create symbols by setting up, in their works, a complex but identifiable web of associations. As a result, one object, image, or action suggests others, and often, ultimately, a range of ideas.

A symbol may thus be defined as a metaphor in which the "vehicle," the thing, image, or action used to represent something else, represents many related things (or "tenors") or is broadly suggestive. The urn in Keats's "Ode on a Grecian Urn" suggests many interrelated concepts, including art, truth, beauty, and timelessness.

Symbols have been of particular interest to formalists, who study how meanings emerge from the complex, patterned relationships between images in a work, and psychoanalytic critics, who are interested in how individual authors and the larger culture both disguise and reveal unconscious fears and desires through symbols. Recently, French feminists have also focused on the symbolic. They have suggested that, as wide-ranging as it seems, symbolic language is ultimately rigid and restrictive. They favor semiotic language and writing, which, they contend, is at once more rhythmic, unifying, and feminine.

See also: Feminist Criticism, Metaphor, Psychoanalytic Criticism, Trope.

SYMBOLIC STAGE According to Lacanian psychoanalytic theory, the stage in which the child (especially the male child) learns that what had seemed wholly his and even undistinguishable from himself (i.e., the mother) is in fact someone else's: something to be desired only in the form of socially acceptable substitutes. That recognition, according to Jacques Lacan, facilitates the child's entrance into language, for words themselves are not the things they stand for but, rather, are substitutes for those things. The Symbolic stage, which corresponds with what Freud called the oedipal stage, follows a pre-oedipal stage that Lacan termed the "Imaginary stage."

See also: Psychoanalytic Criticism.

SYNECDOCHE *See* Metaphor, Metonymy.

TENOR *See* Metaphor, Metonymy, Symbol.

TROPE A figure, as in "figure of speech." Literally a "turning," i.e., a turning or twisting of a word or phrase to make it mean something else. Principal tropes include metaphor, metonymy, simile, personification, and synecdoche.

See also: Metaphor, Metonymy.

VEHICLE *See* Metaphor, Metonymy, Symbol.

About the Contributors

THE VOLUME EDITOR

Nancy A. Walker is director of the Women's Studies program and professor of English at Vanderbilt University. She is the author of *A Very Serious Thing: Women's Humor and American Culture* (1988) and *Feminist Alternatives: Irony and Fantasy in the Contemporary Novel by Women* (1990). Her most recent book is *Fanny Fern* (1992).

THE CRITICS

Elaine Showalter is the Avalon Chair of the Humanities and professor of English at Princeton University. Her most recent book is *Sister's Choice: Tradition and Change in American Women's Writing* (1991).

Margit Stange is assistant professor of English at the University of California at Davis. She is working on a study of the discourse of women's value in exchange in turn-of-the-century American texts, including those of Kate Chopin, Charlotte Perkins Gilman, and Edith Wharton.

Paula A. Treichler is associate professor of Medical Humanities, Women's Studies, and Communications Research at the University of Illinois

College of Medicine. She is coeditor of *For Alma Mater: Theory and Practice in Feminist Scholarship* (1985).

Cynthia Griffin Wolff is the Class of 1922 Professor of Humanities at the Massachusetts Institute of Technology. Among her publications are *A Feast of Words: The Triumph of Edith Wharton* (1976) and *Emily Dickinson* (1986). She is currently at work on a biography of Harriet Beecher Stowe and on a study of multicultural elements in mid-nineteenth-century American narrative to be titled *The American Renaissance Rag*.

Patricia S. Yaeger is associate professor of English at the University of Michigan at Ann Arbor. She is the author of *Honey-Mad Women: Emancipatory Strategies in Women's Writing* (1988) and coeditor of *Nationalisms and Sexualities* (1992). She is working on two book-length studies to be titled *Dirt and Desire: The Grotesque in Southern Women's Writing* and *The Poetics of Birth*.

THE SERIES EDITOR

Ross C Murfin, general editor of *Case Studies in Contemporary Criticism*, is dean of the College of Arts and Sciences and professor of English at the University of Miami. He has taught at Yale University and the University of Virginia and has published scholarly studies of Joseph Conrad, Thomas Hardy, and D. H. Lawrence.

Pg 142/3 important!

144 ahead of her time

145 comparisons with realist writers.

(continued from page ii)

"Personal Property: Exchange Value and the Female Self in *The Awakening*" by Margit Stange. Reprinted from *Genders,* Vol. 5, 1989 by permission of the author and the University of Texas Press.

"Thanatos and Eros: Kate Chopin's *The Awakening*" by Cynthia Griffin Wolff. Reprinted from *American Quarterly,* Vol. 25, No. 4, October 1973, pp. 449–71. Reprinted with the permission of the American Studies Association. © Copyright 1973.

"'A Language Which Nobody Understood': Emancipatory Strategies in *The Awakening*" by Patricia S. Yaeger. From *NOVEL: A Forum on Fiction,* Vol. 20, No. 3, Spring 1987. Copyright NOVEL Corp. © 1987. Reprinted with permission.

"The Construction of Ambiguity in *The Awakening:* A Linguistic Analysis" by Paula A. Treichler. Reprinted by permission of Greenwood Publishing Group, Inc., Westport, CT, from *Women and Language in Literature and Society* edited by Sally McConnell-Ginet, Ruth Borker, and Nelly Furman. Copyright © by Praeger Publishers and published in 1980 by Praeger Publishers.